THE LINE BETWEEN LIES

A Novel

STEN SVEHN

HSJ Publishing

THE LINE BETWEEN LIES

First edition, 2026.

Published by HSJ Publishing, Rancho Santa Margarita, CA, USA

For permission requests, contact: stensvehn@gmail.com

ISBN Paperback: 979-8-9951667-7-1

ISBN eBook: 979-8-9951667-8-8

LCCN: 2026909990

This is a work of fiction. Names, characters, businesses, places, events, locales, and incidents are either the products of the author's imagination or used in a fictitious manner. Any resemblance to actual persons, living or dead, or actual events is coincidental, except where historical figures and events are explicitly referenced for context, as discussed in the Note on Sources at the end of this book.

THE ORDER

THE LINE BETWEEN LIES
1973–1990

THE LIST
1990–1993

THE NEW FIRE
1993–2000

AUSPEX
2008

'Outside of their duplicity, the only thing they had in common was a desire for absolute power.'

—James Jesus Angleton, Chief of Counterintelligence, CIA, 1954—1975

FIELD MANUAL

What follows is useful reference material. Four categories of Cold War intelligence: instruments, services, ground, and working vocabulary. Every entry names what exists, or once existed—a device with a serial number, a place on the map, an institution with an address, an operation within the historical record—and where the book draws on them, it says so. None of it is required to read this book, but it will give additional context.

INSTRUMENTS

Nagra SN. Swiss-made miniature reel-to-reel audio recorder, manufactured by Kudelski in the early 1960s—originally commissioned by President Kennedy for the US Secret Service and known within the factory as the *Série Noire*, the Black Series. Small enough to vanish inside a jacket pocket—the machine that sat in the room while no one knew it was listening. Elena's is a Soviet prototype, one of four, acquired off-book. It records onto its own small reels—what the Nagra records, only the Nagra can return. It carries a defect she tells no one about.

F-21 Ajax. Soviet subminiature still camera, custom manufactured at the Krasnogorsk Mechanical Plant for KGB use. Clockwork-driven, silent, no batteries required—a device that needed nothing from the world except a target. Often concealed inside everyday objects: Ronson lighters, cigarette cases, belt buckles, hollowed books. Elena's F-21 is concealed inside a Ronson lighter. Its film cassette is loaded with long-storage emulsion—fine-grain archival stock, silver-rich, sealed against time. She keeps it for sixteen years.

Makarov PB. Soviet suppressed pistol chambered in 9×18mm, developed in the mid-1960s for KGB and *Spetsnaz* close-range work. Unlike field-expedient suppressors that thread onto the barrel, the PB's silencer is integral to the weapon—part of the gun's body, not an afterthought. Designed for the distance at which you can see a man's eyes. The pistol Elena uses in Lillehammer.

Mercator K55K. German folding pocket knife made in Solingen since 1867, known to its users as the Black Cat for the leaping cat stamped into its black painted steel handle. Carried for more than a century by German soldiers, workmen, and anyone who needed a blade that would not fail them. Locks open with a back spring; closes flat into a coat pocket and weighs almost nothing. The knife Elena takes from East German engineer Voss in October 1977 and keeps in the drawer beside the stove.

Minox. Subminiature camera designed in the 1930s. No larger than a cigarette lighter. From the Second World War onward, the Minox was the instrument Western intelligence officers reached for when they had thirty seconds alone with a document. Calder carries one through his entire career.

Microdot. Photographic reduction of a document to a dot the size of a typewriter period. Hidden under postage stamps, behind watch dials, in the bindings of books—large information moved through small spaces. Elena learns the technique in a Stasi basement in 1975.

SERVICES

KGB. *Komitet Gosudarstvennoy Bezopasnosti.* The Soviet Committee for State Security, operational from 1954 until the dissolution of the USSR in 1991. Elena's service.

Mossad. *Ha-Mossad le-Modi'in ule-Tafkidim Meyuchadim*, the Institute for Intelligence and Special Operations. Israel's foreign intelligence service, founded in 1949, barely a year after the state itself.

Stasi (MfS). *Ministerium für Staatssicherheit*, the Ministry for State Security of East Germany, 1950 to 1990. At its peak it employed over ninety thousand officers and maintained files on roughly six million people—one-third of the population it claimed to protect. Headquartered in East Berlin. The service whose Zersetzung methodology the book draws on.

MI6 (SIS). The Secret Intelligence Service, the British foreign intelligence service. Calder's service. Headquartered at Century House on Westminster Bridge Road in Lambeth from 1964 until the move to Vauxhall Cross in 1994—decades spent in a building that looked like nothing so much as a provincial office block, which was rather the point.

BND. *Bundesnachrichtendienst*, West Germany's foreign intelligence service, founded in 1956 and built by the Americans after the Second World War. The fictional extraction of the engineer Voss in Chapter 9 is staged through this service.

CIA. Central Intelligence Agency, the United States foreign intelligence service. Founded in 1947 from the wartime Office of Strategic Services. The wealthiest and most technically resourced service of the Cold War. The MKULTRA program referenced in the author's note operated under this service in the 1950s and 1960s.

SDECE. *Service de Documentation Extérieure et de Contre-Espionnage*. France's foreign intelligence service from 1945 to 1982, when it was reorganized and renamed the DGSE.

GROUND

Lillehammer. Small town in south-central Norway, on the northern shore of Lake Mjøsa, about a hundred miles north of Oslo. In the early 1970s, a quiet place of around twenty thousand people—the kind of town where a stranger's face gets noticed. The book opens here on the night of 21 July

1973.

Kensington. Central London borough, west of Hyde Park and two miles from Westminster. White stucco mansion blocks and quiet plane-tree streets—the kind of neighborhood where a woman can live for nineteen years without being noticed. Alice Marsh's flat is here, a second-floor Victorian conversion in South Kensington.

Red Banner Institute. The KGB First Chief Directorate's training academy for foreign intelligence operatives, set in a compound outside Moscow where recruits learned languages, tradecraft, and how to become someone else entirely. Today incorporated into the Academy of Foreign Intelligence of the Russian Federation. Elena trains here from 1967 to 1970.

Berlin. Divided capital. Split into East and West by the Allied occupation after 1945, and physically walled from August 1961 until 9 November 1989. East Berlin was the capital of East Germany; West Berlin a Western enclave inside it. Most of the book's German scenes take place on the communist east side—Lichtenberg, Pankow, Friedrichshain, Checkpoint Charlie, Friedrichstraße station.

Normannenstraße. The street in the East Berlin district of Lichtenberg where the Stasi headquarters complex occupied an entire city block from 1950 until the dissolution of the East German state. Today the buildings house the Stasi Museum and the Stasi Records Archive—the paper remains of a surveillance state that kept meticulous records of its own cruelty. Pronounced 'nor-MAHN-nen-shtrah-suh.'

Lichtenberg. Working-class district of East Berlin, east of the city center. The streets around the Stasi headquarters were some of the most watched ground in Europe.

Friedrichshain. District of East Berlin south of Lichtenberg, between the city center and the eastern suburbs. Working-class housing built fast after the war on ground the British bombed flat in 1944. Rows of *Plattenbau* apartments, courtyards, basements deeper than the buildings above them suggested.

Bonn. Small city on the Rhine in western Germany, about 350 miles from Berlin. Capital of the Federal Republic (West Germany) from 1949 until reunification in 1990. Calder's first foreign posting.

Vienna. Capital of Austria. Neutral ground in a divided continent—the city Western and Eastern services chose when they needed to meet without choosing a side. The IAEA is headquartered here. The coffeehouses are old. Elena passes through repeatedly.

Hampstead Heath. Large hilly park in north London, nearly eight hundred acres of woodland and grassland rolling across some of the highest ground in the city.

Tel Aviv. Israel's largest metropolitan area, a Mediterranean coastal city founded in 1909 as the secular counterweight to Jerusalem. The book's Sara Lerner arc unfolds here from 1978 onward.

Bermondsey. Riverside district on the south bank of the Thames in central London, downstream from Tower Bridge. In 1990 it was still a working-class landscape of brick warehouses and empty dockyards, not yet touched by the money that would transform it. The book's climax takes place in a warehouse on the Bermondsey waterfront in January of that year.

WORKING VOCABULARY

Illegal. KGB term for an officer deployed to a foreign country under a fully fabricated identity, without diplomatic cover and without any traceable connection to the Soviet Union.

Wrath of God. Western shorthand for the Israeli targeted-killing program authorized after the 1972 Munich Olympics massacre and conducted by Mossad through the 1970s.

Gladio. NATO's stay-behind network—secret armies trained and equipped across Western Europe to conduct guerrilla warfare against a Soviet invasion that never came. Publicly acknowledged by the Italian prime minister in October 1990 after decades of denial.

Frank Olson. Biological weapons scientist at Fort Detrick. Dosed without his knowledge with LSD-25 by the CIA's MKULTRA program in 1953. Days later he fell to his death from a hotel window. The CIA called it suicide. KGB illegals were taught to recognize the compound. Elena did, in a Vienna coffeehouse in October 1985.

Diazepam. Benzodiazepine sedative marketed as Valium. By the early 1970s, the most widely prescribed drug in the West—handed out for anxiety, insomnia, marital distress, and any condition a general practitioner did not have time to ask further questions about. Margaret had a prescription.

Zersetzung. Literally 'decomposition.' The Stasi's methodology of dismantling opponents through psychological and social attrition rather than through arrest. Operatives entered targets' homes to move objects and alter small details. They planted rumors among colleagues, engineered the collapse of careers and marriages, and maintained surveillance calibrated to produce paranoia and isolation.

COINTELPRO. The Federal Bureau of Investigation's Counter Intelligence Program, active from 1956 to 1971. A domestic surveillance and disruption campaign that targeted American civil rights leaders, antiwar activists, and political organizations—proof that the methods of Zersetzung were not confined to the Eastern Bloc.

The story begins...

ACT I

COVER BUILDING

1973—1975

1

THIRTEEN SHOTS

Lillehammer, Norway—21 July 1973

The bartender had been watching her for an hour, long enough to know it wasn't beauty that held his attention. He'd seen beauty before. The Finnish cellist from last November—all cheekbones and sorrow—had ordered three glasses of Riesling and left without paying. But this one had something the cellist hadn't—a quality of attention. She tracked the room in small, economical glances. Once satisfied, she sat with the stillness of someone who knew exactly where her edges were.

He found himself itemizing the young woman.

Her dark hair was cut just above her shoulders. She had a jawline out of a Soviet recruitment poster, softened by a mouth that seemed perpetually deciding between a smile and something more dangerous. She was drinking gin and tonic—her second.

The next thing he noticed was the way she watched the door.

Not the way a woman waiting for a date watches a door, with hope and impatience. This woman watched the door the way a chess player watches the board between moves, with the calm certainty that whatever came next was something she had already planned for.

When she reached for her drink, her sleeve rode up and the bartender caught, for a half-second, a small mark on the inside of her left wrist—a compass rose, four directions, with a small inked dot at the center where the directions met. It was small enough to be hidden by a watch she wasn't wearing tonight. The sleeve fell back, and the mark was gone.

She felt him looking. She did not adjust her sleeve. The glass was cold against her palm. Outside, a car passed on the wet street and the headlights moved across the ceiling of the bar and were gone.

The bartender did not know about the other one.

No one in this bar would ever see the other one. An earlier mark. A line of Russian text along her ribcage, inked at seventeen by a dissident artist in a Leningrad apartment that no longer existed. He was arrested six months later. Elena never spoke his name again. The tattoo read: *I taught myself to live simply and wisely*. Anna Akhmatova. The poet who survived Stalin by outlasting him. It was the last true thing she put on her body.

Everything since—the accent, the passport, the name, the entire architecture of a life built on someone else's biography—was construction. Her name tonight was Alice Marsh. It had been Alice Marsh for two years. It would be Alice Marsh for seventeen more.

But tonight Elena was twenty-five years old. She was in Lillehammer, Norway. In fourteen minutes, a man named Rachid Hamidi would step into the wrong moment on the wrong street. Elena would watch. She would feel nothing and file everything. When it was done, she would kill someone else entirely.

Elena arrived in Norway three days ago with the New Zealand passport. The good one. The passport was a work of art, though not because of the forgery. Soviet document fabrication was standardized—and excellent. The inks came from the same suppliers legitimate governments used, the paper stock was identical, the lamination perfected by a Minsk laboratory that also produced forged pharmaceutical certificates.

The cover was not a mask she wore. It was a second skeleton grown inside her own body. One could not remove Alice Marsh from Elena Vasilieva without surgery. On the nights when she lay awake in hotel rooms that smelled like other people's cigarettes, she was not sure which skeleton would survive the operation.

But that was not tonight's problem.

Tonight's problem was in apartment 3B on Storgata, six blocks north. He was listening to the radio with a cup of tea, not yet aware that the last three years of his quiet Norwegian retirement were about to end.

His name was Grigor Petrov. Before that, he had been something else—a KGB signals intelligence officer at the Leningrad listening station. A man who spent his days intercepting NATO submarine communications and his evenings in communal apartment blocks that smelled like institutional resignation.

In 1970, he walked into the Norwegian embassy in Helsinki with a briefcase full of frequency tables and the names of four Soviet illegals operating in Western Europe. Two of those names belonged to people Elena had trained with and sat beside at the Red Banner Institute.

She'd practiced dead drops with them in parks around Moscow. One of them, a woman named Irina whose laugh could fill a hallway, was dead—killed in an operation that the official file attributed to bad luck and the unofficial file attributed to Western intelligence services that had been warned, by Petrov, about exactly what to look for.

Irina had been twenty-eight. She had a scar on her left hand from a training exercise and a habit of humming Shostakovich when she was concentrating. Elena thought about her infrequently.

She thought about her now, looking at the door of a bar in Lillehammer. She thought about the way Irina's laugh used to fill a hallway. She filed it.

Moscow had been patient with Petrov. Moscow was always patient. Patience was the only resource the Soviet system produced more reliably than paranoia. Elena simply had to wait for the right night—one when every police officer in Lillehammer would be very, very busy with something else.

The official term was economy of operation. Elena called it a good night.

Somewhere on the streets south of the bar, a team of Israeli operatives were moving into position. For months they had been tracking a man they believed was the architect of the Munich massacre. They had tracked him to Lillehammer. They had spent eleven days confirming his identity. They were certain. They were professional. They were about to fire thirteen rounds into Rachid Hamidi, a Moroccan waiter who had emigrated to Norway three years ago and worked at a restaurant on the town's main street. His only connection to the man they were hunting was that he was approximately the same height and had a similar complexion in a photograph that had been passed through too many hands.

His wife Marit was pregnant. She would be walking beside him when the shooting started. She would watch him die on the pavement outside a cinema where they'd just seen a movie.

Elena would learn all of this later, and file it.

Moscow had known about the assassination for eleven days, courtesy of a source inside Norwegian intelligence that Elena was not authorized to know about. She deduced the source's existence anyway, from the timing and specificity of her briefing. Someone inside the POT—the Norwegian Police Security Service—had been close enough to the channel to know both the date and the kill zone in advance. Not a peripheral contact. A senior duty officer, or someone with access to one.

The question she did not ask herself was why. A Norwegian officer handing Moscow the tactical details of an Israeli kill team on Norwegian soil served no interest she could map from where she stood. She placed the question beside the answer she didn't have yet, and kept both in the private archive she maintained for things that were useful and unauthorized. The archive was getting larger every year. She did not reflect on what that meant.

Elena was here to watch, to observe, to document, from a professional distance, exactly how Mossad operated in the field. Team size. Communication methods. Positioning. Timing between surveillance and execution. This was Step One of the long-term Moscow operation to map and ultimately co-opt the Israeli targeted killing program.

Step One had a bonus attached to it. Grigor Petrov. His apartment was eight minutes north. In twelve minutes, every officer in Lillehammer would be running south.

She had identified four of them before sundown.

Not because they were careless in any obvious way. The Israeli services had a reputation—one that Moscow's files confirmed without pleasure—for exactly this kind of work. Disciplined, patient, adaptive in the field. She had read the assessments. She believed them. They moved through

Lillehammer with the practiced spacing of a trained surveillance team, rotating through positions, never maintaining eye contact too long, never lingering without purpose. By most professional standards they were very good.

By Elena's they were legible. This surprised her. The surprise joined the assessment.

Lillehammer in July was a town of twenty thousand people, pale as birch bark, dressed in the worn practical clothes of a Norwegian summer. The faces on the main street were broad and fair, weathered by winters rather than sun. Against this the team stood out the way a new coin stands out in a handful of old ones—not dramatically, but enough. A civilian would register only a vague sense of displacement and move on.

Elena did not move on.

The man on the bench across from the cinema had purchased a newspaper an hour ago and had not read a word of it. He was perhaps thirty-five, olive-skinned, with close-cropped dark hair and the deep, even tan of a man who had spent time in a country with a genuine summer. His shoes gave him away—brown leather, clean-soled, the kind of shoe a man buys for a specific purpose in a specific city and wears once.

A couple who passed the bar twice in forty minutes had not spoken to each other the second time—not the silence of an argument, not the silence of comfort, but the specific held-breath of two people maintaining a role.

A second woman in her late twenties at the corner of the main street made herself clear when she touched her left ear twice in ten minutes. She was the most carefully assembled of the four—hair lightened, clothing chosen for the town rather than for herself, sensible flat shoes that actually showed some wear. Someone had prepared her with care. But the preparation addressed appearance, not posture.

Elena traced the direction of the woman's chin when she touched her ear. The receiver was on the opposite pavement: a man in a tan jacket who emerged from the same side street two minutes after each touch, adjusting his route each time.

Seven people over the course of the afternoon, by Elena's final count.

Certainty and accuracy were not the same thing. Elena had learned this early. It was the first mistake a good team could make.

She settled at a stool with the bar mirror behind her, framing the street.

She waited.

The night outside the bar was the pale gray of a Norwegian July that hadn't committed to dark. Past ten o'clock, and the sky still held onto residual northern light—just enough to see faces. The street lamps burned amber between stretches of wet cobblestone. The air carried pine from the hills above the town mixed with cold minerals from Lake Mjøsa.

The shots came without preamble.

Thirteen rounds. Elena counted them the way a musician counts beats—automatically, without deciding to, the pattern assembled before she'd consciously begun. Thirteen. At least three weapons. The reports overlapped at the beginning and the end, which told her the team had not been given a coordinated signal. Each shooter had pulled the trigger independently—as soon as the target was acquired, or as soon as the person beside them had already fired—and the result was the messy, compressive staccato of an execution whose timing had broken down at the moment it counted most.

She caught the variations in pitch and weight before the sound finished traveling through the bar's glass. Two heavier calibers and one lighter, firing four rounds at the end in a cluster too rapid for any of them to be accurate. The lighter weapon had been last and most panicked. Someone at the back of the formation who hadn't been certain of a clear line and had pulled the trigger anyway when the others stopped.

Amateur timing on a professional operation.

In the bar mirror, she watched the street.

The man in the tan jacket—the receiver, the one she'd tracked all afternoon—appeared at the far end of the block, moving east at a jog. Not a run, which was the mistake. A run communicated urgency. A jog communicated hesitation. His hands were in his jacket pockets, weapon already disposed of, which meant the weapon would be found by a competent investigator. She tracked the direction he'd come from.

The woman from the corner—the signaler—had broken cover immediately after the shots split the air. She looked back toward the cinema, stopped again. This was not exfiltration behavior. This was the physical transcript of a person who aborted protocol.

It was the third mistake.

Three distinct errors in thirty seconds. A team that had been disciplined for eleven days, precise for eleven days, had arrived at the moment and become human.

Then the car. A rental, half a block south. The engine caught, died, caught again—the mechanical panic of a driver who had been stationary too long and released the clutch too fast. It pulled away north. Through the bar's front window at an oblique angle, Elena caught the silhouette and the plate suffix before it turned. Not enough to read fully, but enough to know the plates were not Norwegian.

From the window of the bar she glanced back at the street, reflected, reversed, ghostly. A man was on the ground. A woman was standing over him. She was screaming and her hands were reaching for the man on the pavement, her pale coat was acquiring a dark red stain at the hem.

The sound arrived. Not the screaming—that came later, after the shock had metabolized into something more human. What arrived first was the aftermath: car doors slamming. Running feet. A voice shouting in Norwegian that Elena understood but did not react to, because Alice Marsh only spoke English and schoolgirl French.

Then the scream became a word. Rachid. And then Rachid again, and again, the name being shaped by a mouth that was learning, in real time, that the name would never again be answered.

Elena did not file the sound.

The name kept arriving.

The bartender dropped a glass. It shattered. Other patrons stood, moved toward the windows.

Elena remained on her stool. She took a sip of her gin and tonic. The ice had melted further and the drink was warm. She registered this the way she registered everything—as data, filed beside other data, waiting.

Marit Hamidi was on her knees in her husband's blood on a Norwegian street, and Elena was thinking about the ice in her drink.

She noted this without judgment. Judgment was a luxury. Elena felt things later, in hotel rooms, when the filing system powered down. Not now.

Now was the work.

She watched the reflection in the glass for another two minutes. The extraction had been sloppy.

The Norwegian police would round up six of the Israelis within forty-eight hours. It would cost Mossad years.

The bartender, now at the window like everyone else, did not see Elena go. While the others were watching the street, she walked out the door and turned left. Away from the chaos. Away from the flashing lights beginning to appear at the end of the street. Away from Marit Hamidi, still kneeling on the pavement in her husband's blood.

She turned north. Toward Storgata. Toward apartment 3B. Toward unfinished business.

The streets were emptying in the direction she was walking and filling up in the direction she'd come from, drawn by the magnetism of disaster, by the human compulsion to see the best and the worst. Elena moved north through the counter-current like a salmon heading upstream. Brisk but not hurried. Alert but not panicked. The body language of common sense.

She passed a couple running toward the cinema. The woman was asking the man what had happened. He said he didn't know.

Elena knew.

Storgata was quiet. The sky had begun to give up its northern light. A rain had come through while she was in the bar—briefly, the kind of Norwegian summer squall that arrived without announcement and left without apology. The stone still held the water. The pavement here was empty.

The building was unremarkable. Three stories of postwar Scandinavian facade, all right angles and muted colors. The front entrance had a buzzer system. The back entrance, which Elena mapped two days earlier during a walk that looked like tourism, was a service door used by delivery men and residents hauling groceries—left open during dinner hours. She would enter without drawing attention.

Every apartment in the building was silent—the residents

either asleep, out for the evening, or already drifting toward the commotion unfolding elsewhere in Lillehammer. She moved up the back stairwell. The third-floor landing smelled faintly of cabbage and furniture polish.

Apartment 3B had one lock. A standard Norwegian residential cylinder, manufactured by ASSA and sold in every hardware store in the country. She carried a compact pick set in the interior pocket of her coat, nested against her ribs beside the passport. Eleven seconds. The lock turned with a small, defeated click that sounded louder than it was, amplified by the empty hallway and her own expectations. Everything sounded louder at the frequency she ran on before a kill.

The building's heating system hummed through the walls like a mechanical pulse. A faucet dripped somewhere. A clock ticked. Elena opened the door and stepped inside.

The apartment swallowed her. A short hallway opened into a living room that doubled as a dining room; to the left, a half-kitchen was visible through a partly-open door.

The decor was the careful anonymity of a man taught by experience that possessions are liabilities. Nothing personal. Nothing that could not be abandoned in five minutes. Except a photograph of Lake Mjøsa on the wall above the sofa, taken from a trail Elena recognized.

Petrov had been a defector for three years, but he was still living like a man who expected to leave in a hurry. The only personal touch was a framed photograph on the bookshelf: a woman and a child, possibly his family, possibly someone else's.

Elena brushed by it. The photograph was not operationally relevant.

Beneath the window was a small writing table. On it lay a Western trade journal in English—*Nucleonics Week*, four months old, folded open to a column that had been circled in pencil. Elena catalogued the table the way she catalogued the photograph. She did not cross to it.

The radio was on. A Norwegian talk show. Voices discussing something agricultural—crop yields or subsidies, programming that existed in every country to fill airtime between things people wanted to hear.

Petrov was in the kitchen. Elena could see him through the half-open door, standing at the counter with his back partially turned. He was making tea, and a kettle was on the stove. The domestic mundanity of it—the tea, the radio, the worn slippers she could see on his feet—registered as confirmation. He wasn't expecting visitors. Wasn't expecting anything. He was set on living out the remainder of his life purchased with other people's names.

Elena crossed the living room in four steps. The carpet absorbed her footfalls. She reached into her coat as she moved, her fingers finding the grip of her favorite weapon, the Makarov PB—the suppressed variant, 9x18mm, standard KGB issue for close-range work. Effective to about fifteen meters. She would be using it at three.

Petrov turned. He was older than his file photograph. Thinner. Three years of Norwegian exile had sharpened his features in a way that could have been stress or might have been the diet—defectors never ate well.

The hair at his temples was gray, his skin old, and his eyes were the color of Baltic ice. When those eyes found Elena standing in his living room with a suppressed pistol in her hands, they did something she hadn't expected. They recognized the situation. Not her—he'd never met her, had no reason to know her face. But he recognized what she was. The weapon. The coat. The calm. He was a KGB man, even in retirement, and KGB men knew what the end of something looked like.

He started to ask a question. His tea was still steaming on the counter behind him. The first syllable was in Russian, which told Elena that his instincts had overridden his three years of pretending to be Norwegian. The body speaks the mother tongue when it panics. His mouth opened. The syllable was the beginning of a question he would not finish.

She fired twice.

The suppressor reduced the sound to something between a book being dropped and a heavy door closing.

The first round entered through the upper sternum slightly left of midline and went forward into the heart. The second followed a quarter-second later, higher, because his body was already beginning to fold forward and his head had shifted; it took him at the base of the throat. He staggered against the kitchen counter. His hand knocked the kettle, which rocked but did not fall. He went down onto the linoleum with the slow accuracy of a man whose legs had stopped receiving instructions. A thin dark line traced down the cupboard front where his shoulder had touched the wood on the way down. The radio continued. The faucet dripped.

Elena stood still for three seconds. She listened. The kitchen smelled now of bergamot and cordite at the same time. The building was quiet. No footsteps in the hallway. No doors opening.

She checked his pulse. There wasn't one. She looked at him for a moment longer than was necessary. His face had settled into an expression that wasn't quite surprise and wasn't quite resignation.

Elena remembered Irina's laugh. The hallway at the Red Banner Institute. The scar on her left hand.

She set it aside.

Her eye moved once. On the kitchen counter beside the kettle, a folded newspaper lay under a saltshaker. The visible page was creased at the fold from handling. The dateline at the head of the page was Rome, two years old. The headline fragment read *Incidente nelle miniere.* Petrov had not read Italian at the Red Banner Institute. Petrov had not read Italian when Moscow had first taken an interest in him. He had, on his own time and against what was left of his discipline, learned to read it, and had kept a two-year-old clipping under a saltshaker in an apartment he had furnished to be abandoned in five minutes.

She did not read the article. She did not take the page. She filed the observation in the same place she had filed the slippers.

Nothing was taken from the apartment. Nothing was left in it—Elena's gloves had been on since the stairwell, and the weapon she used would be at the bottom of the Mjøsa before morning.

She closed the door softly behind her.

Total time inside the apartment: ninety seconds.

The hallway was empty. The stairwell was empty. The street was empty.

Everyone was south, watching the aftermath of one killing, and they would not discover Petrov for another forty-eight hours. By then, Elena would be in London, making dinner plans with a man whose file she'd memorized but whose face she'd never seen—a man who worked for British intelligence under a Foreign Office title, and who did not yet know she existed.

She walked south. Counterintuitive and therefore correct. She walked toward the noise. Toward the police cars. Toward the growing crowd of Lillehammer residents.

They'd gathered at the edges of the Hamidi crime scene with the stunned, murmuring energy of people who'd never seen violence up close. Alice Marsh joined the crowd. She became part of it. A young woman in a dark coat, slightly distressed, slightly confused, quietly watching the police activity with the wide-eyed uncertainty of a tourist. She stood near the edge of the gathering for four minutes. Long enough to be unremarkable. Short enough to avoid being interviewed.

Her rented Volvo was close, reserved under Alice Marsh's name. It was parked five blocks from the bar in a residential area where the streetlights were spaced too far apart to completely illuminate the cars underneath them. She unlocked it and sat in the driver's seat. The Makarov PB went under the passenger seat, where it would remain until she reached the lake.

Petrov was not her first. He was her second, if you counted the training exercise in Crimea that her instructors maintained was simulated and that Elena, having seen the body afterward, knew was not. Her hands shook the way a surgeon's hands shake after a long procedure. Forty seconds. She counted them. The shaking stopped.

Engine started, she drove toward Oslo and the airport at Fornebu, taking the E6 through the invisible countryside. Pine forests in the headlights. Then darkness. Then pine again.

Within twenty minutes the first news reports arrived on the radio: a shooting in Lillehammer. One man dead. Police were on the scene. The announcer's voice had the controlled shock radio hosts have when they realize they're broadcasting something significant for the first time.

Elena listened. She noted the details that were correct and the details that were not. She composed the first draft of her operational report in her head, organizing the evening's intelligence into the clinical structure her handler Yuri would expect. When she delivered it in a Bloomsbury café three days from now it would include team composition, observed methodology, tactical failures, and forensic vulnerabilities of the Mossad assassination attempt.

The operation had been comprehensively botched. Elena's report would document exactly how and why, and Moscow would study it the way a medical school studies an autopsy —with professional attention to what had gone wrong inside the patient.

She did not include the image of Marit Hamidi in her pale coat. She did not include the sound. She did not include Petrov's face or the kettle that rocked but did not fall, or the radio discussing crop subsidies while a man died on a kitchen floor in his slippers. These were not relevant.

The road unwound beneath the Volvo's headlights. Tonight Elena was twenty-five years old. She'd just killed a man in his kitchen and watched another man die on the street. The news bulletin ended and the station returned to music —something Norwegian and soft. She did not recognize the song and did not turn it off.

She was driving through the Norwegian darkness toward her hotel room and an airport where the New Zealand passport would carry her through security without a second glance. She was very good at her job. Moscow had told her this. She believed them.

The machinery had built her. It was pleased with its work.

She drove.

The hotel in Hamar took forty minutes to reach. A roadside place with thin walls and a shower that took time to heat. Elena stood under the water for longer than needed. The practical reason was trace evidence. The real reason was that she was still running at the frequency she reached when she killed, and that frequency needed somewhere to go.

She stood under the water. The heat finding the muscles in her shoulders that had locked when the Makarov was raised. Her jaw loosened. She'd been clenching it since the stairwell without knowing it. The slow return of sensation to her hands, which had been working precisely but numb.

Elena looked down at herself. The water running along her ribcage, over the Akhmatova line, gathering at the curve of her hip and continuing down.

The body was twenty-five years old. It had done what it was asked to do and now it wanted to shake. But standing in the shower, in a hotel in Hamar at 3 AM, with the adrenaline fading and the filing system temporarily off, her body was also just a body. Skin and heat and water, being alive in a room where no one was watching.

The kettle. Petrov's hand had knocked it when the first round hit and the kettle rocked on the stove but did not fall. The image arrived without permission.

She turned off the water. She dried herself with a towel that was too thin and too rough. It reminded her of the towels at the training facility outside Moscow, which had been deliberately inadequate because your comfort was not the institution's concern.

She lay on the bed. The sheets were cold. Her skin was warm. The distance between these two temperatures closed slowly.

Before the drive to Fornebu the next morning, she would finalize the report. It would contain every relevant detail of the evening except one: a connection she had begun to see, wider than Lillehammer, wider than Petrov. She would cross the sentence out before delivering the report to Yuri. Her pen did not hesitate. That was what she noticed. A small omission. It was her first.

Somewhere in Europe, in a room she had not yet seen, a man with a gold ring on his right little finger was reading a cable from Lillehammer. He added a small pencil mark in the margin beside her name—*Elena Vasilieva.*

2

THE GALLERY

Back in London—October 1973

Elena saw him before he saw her.

He came through the door at seven-fourteen—fourteen minutes late, and therefore deliberate. On time at a gallery opening signaled eagerness. Too late signaled indifference. Exactly fourteen minutes late signaled a man who calculated the balance and had the self-discipline to execute it. It joined the weeks of observation that preceded it.

She was watching from the back of the room—the only genuine blind spot the Paxton Gallery offered, a corner where the lighting was slightly dimmer and where a structural column partially obscured the sightline from the entrance. This was not an accident. She walked the floor twice before the doors officially opened, and positioned herself the way she did in every room—the way a sniper positions a rifle.

His name was James Calder, and he was the reason she was here tonight wearing a dress she'd chosen with more care than the operation strictly required.

Moscow's file on him was thinner than Elena would have liked. It listed his cover as a junior analyst in the Foreign and Commonwealth Office's Research Department—a title that could mean anything and usually meant intelligence. Thirty-seven. Cambridge educated—History, rowed crew for his college, recruited in his final year by a man whose name Elena's file did not include.

Calder was currently assigned to the Counter-Proliferation desk at Century House—the division responsible for tracking missing nuclear materials and inventory discrepancies that governments preferred not to acknowledge. A small desk, with access to files that larger desks did not. Moscow wanted those files. Two prior postings before this one: Bonn, where he'd worked Soviet counter-intelligence, and Washington, where he'd listened in on NATO nuclear-sharing discussions. Since 1971 he'd been back in London, quietly promoted into the one desk that could read both postings as a single picture. Moscow's assessment: 'professionally promising, personally disciplined, and insufficiently senior to justify active targeting at this time.'

Elena had a different assessment. Four weeks of watching him from a distance told her he was significantly more capable than his file suggested. He moved through London's professional social circuits with the unhurried confidence of someone taught how to work a room by people who considered room-working a form of intelligence collection. He showed up at the right events, asked the right questions, and left the right impressions. He did it all with a naturalness that told Elena he'd either been doing this for much longer than his file indicated or he was one of those rare, infuriating people for whom social camouflage was a natural talent.

He was on a list of nine names Moscow had given her. She'd already assessed the other eight. Seven were unremarkable—men of moderate intelligence and predictable insecurities who could be cultivated through flattery over a period of months. The eighth was an alcoholic whose operational value was limited because his colleagues had already noticed. Calder was the ninth. He was also the only one she'd bothered to think about for four weeks straight.

Elena chose tonight's exhibition with him in mind. The Divided Lens: Photographs from Both Sides of the Wall—twenty-three images taken between 1961 and 1972, half from Western photographers looking east into Stasi territory, half from Eastern photographers looking west into the American sector. The guest list, which she obtained through a contact at the gallery who believed Alice Marsh was a fellow art historian, included two academics from King's College who consulted for the Foreign Office and a retired diplomat who served in Bonn, West Germany. And Calder. The exhibition was a niche, mildly intellectual event that would draw a man like him without making him feel as if he was being drawn anywhere.

Elena also chose it because she wanted to see the photographs. Several of the Eastern photographs captured something that Western coverage of the Wall almost never did. Tedium. The crushing boredom of living inside a system designed to contain you. Not the drama of escape attempts or protest marches, but the ordinary Tuesday afternoon of a woman hanging laundry on a balcony that overlooked the Wall and the death strip beside it, neither of which she'd noticed in years.

Elena understood that woman. She had been that woman, in a different way, in a different country. The laundry was real. The balcony was real. The death strip was also real. You lived with all of it simultaneously, and after enough time the simultaneity stopped feeling like a contradiction and started feeling like a fact.

She turned from the photograph she'd been studying and watched Calder remove his coat.

He was taller than she expected. His file listed five foot eleven, but files are written from photographs. In person, Calder had the rangy, slightly angular build of a man who'd been athletic in his twenties and was, at thirty-seven, maintaining it through discipline rather than enthusiasm. His jaw was sharp enough to be noticeable but not so sharp that it looked constructed. He was handsome in the way well-bred Englishmen sometimes are—not dramatically, but with a kind of structural integrity.

He was wearing a charcoal suit that fit him better than a Foreign Office salary could explain. Not extravagantly better. Subtly better—tailoring that only registered if you were looking for it, which Elena was. His shoes were leather, well-maintained, resoled at least once. His watch was the detail that confirmed everything else: a military-issue face on a civilian strap. The face was a CWC—standard British military, available only through service channels. The strap was brown leather, expensive, chosen to domesticate the watch into something that could pass as a fashion choice. It was a perfect small deception. Elena appreciated it the way she appreciated good forgery—with professional respect and the faint, involuntary pleasure of recognizing competence.

She adjusted her own watch. Hers was the opposite deception—civilian face, unremarkable strap, chosen not to reveal but to conceal. Beneath it, on the inside of her left wrist, the compass rose, four directions, the small inked dot at the center. His watch told you what he was if you knew how to read it. Hers told you nothing. The nothing was the point.

Inside Elena's clutch bag were the things Alice Marsh carried—lipstick, a compact, a silver pen, a card case—and one thing Alice Marsh would not. A Nagra, paperback-sized, Swiss-made: a reel-to-reel audio recorder, built for the specific professional problem of capturing a room's sound without the room knowing. Its microphone ran through a half-inch aperture cut into the bag's lining, the opening concealed behind the silk shirring at the seam—operationally invisible, audibly clean. The miniature reels it used were a proprietary format of its own. What the Nagra recorded, only a Nagra could play.

Elena had trained her thumb to the record button: exactly

the right pressure, too light and it wouldn't engage, too hard and the click was audible. She'd practiced until her thumb knew it the way her finger knew a trigger. A fresh reel threaded that afternoon. She had not yet decided whether to use it.

He scanned the room. Not obviously. He did it while removing his coat—the tradecraft equivalent of patting your head while rubbing your stomach—easy to describe, difficult to execute naturally. His eyes moved in a pattern Elena recognized because she used the same one. Clockwise sweep, starting from the door. Exits cataloged first. Then faces. Then relationships between faces—who was standing with whom, who arrived together, who was maintaining distance from whom. He completed the scan in under four seconds and emerged from his coat looking like a man who'd just arrived at a party and was wondering where the drinks were.

Elena watched Calder work the room. He greeted the gallery owner by name. He spoke briefly with one of the King's College academics—a heavyset man named Pemberton who consulted for the Ministry of Defence and who Elena had assessed six months ago as useful but not worth the investment. Calder's conversation with Pemberton lasted three minutes—long enough to be polite, short enough to be strategic. He laughed once, at something Pemberton said. The laugh was convincing. Elena wasn't sure it was genuine.

Then he moved to the photographs. He started on the Western side—the images taken from the free side of the Wall, looking east. He spent perhaps thirty seconds on each one. Standard gallery behavior. But when he crossed to the Eastern photographs, something changed. He slowed down. He stood in front of a particular image—a shot of the Wall taken from inside an East Berlin apartment, through a window, so that the Wall appeared framed by domestic curtains and a potted plant on the sill—and he studied it for nearly two minutes. His body language shifted in a way that most people in the room would not have noticed. His weight settled. His shoulders dropped. The professional scan was done. He was looking.

Elena, from her blind spot near the column, watched him look.

A man who slowed down for the Eastern photographs and not the Western ones had been on that side of the Wall, or had known someone who had, or had read enough files to know what the Wall had cost the people living next to it.

Before Elena left the blind spot behind the column, she slipped her hand into her clutch bag and pressed the Nagra's recording key through the lining. The reel started turning. Her thumb had found the exact pressure. No audible click.

She approached from his left side—the side away from the room's main traffic flow—and stopped beside him. She looked at the photograph he was studying: the Wall through the apartment window, the curtains, the potted plant. She said nothing for fifteen seconds. Silence, properly deployed, was louder than speech. It was the difference between interrupting someone's solitude and joining it.

Calder spoke first. Elena expected this and allowed it to happen.

'The curtains are the detail,' he said, still looking at the photograph. His voice was quieter than she expected. Not soft—quiet. The voice of a man who had learned that speaking at low volumes forced people to lean in, and that people who leaned in were people who were already listening. 'You look at the Wall and you see politics. You look at the curtains and you see a person who's been living next to politics for so long that they've decorated around it.'

It was a good observation. Better than good. It was an observation that revealed two things about Calder: that he understood the difference between ideology and experience, and that he understood it instinctively rather than intellectually.

She turned to look directly at him for the first time. He was already looking at her. His eyes were gray-green, the color of the Thames on an overcast day, and they were doing something she recognized—they were reading her. Not her face, not her body, but the architecture beneath both. The exact combination of signals that told a trained observer who they were talking to. He was assessing her the way she was assessing him: quickly, thoroughly, with the calm professional attention of someone for whom reading people was a survival mechanism, not a social skill.

Their eyes met. Three seconds. Four. Five. Elena did not break. Calder did not break. The moment extended into a sixth second and then Elena smiled—not a full smile, not the one she deployed when she wanted to disarm. The smaller version, the one that involved only the left side of her mouth and that she'd calibrated, through years of practice, to communicate one message: I see what you're doing, and I'm doing it too.

'The plant is the detail I noticed,' she said. Her accent was New Zealand by way of London, three years of careful vocal work that softened the Kiwi vowels into something transatlantic. 'It's a geranium. They're almost impossible to kill. You can neglect them for weeks and they just keep growing. I think that's the photograph's real subject. Not the Wall. That someone is still growing things next to it.'

He looked at her differently after that. The interest had been there since she arrived at his shoulder; what changed was the quality of his attention.

'I'm James,' he said.

'Alice,' she said. A beat too late, as if she'd had to choose which name to give.

Neither offered a last name. In the circles both of them operated in, this was either a sign of informality or a sign of caution. In this case, it was a sign of both.

They moved through the exhibition together without either of them suggesting it. It happened the way rain happens —one photograph leading to another and one observation building on the previous one, until they fell into a rhythm that felt too natural to have been arranged and too precise to have been accidental.

Calder was smart. Elena expected this. What she hadn't expected was the patience of his intelligence. He was the kind of smart that listens. That asks questions designed to reveal more about the asker than the answer. That holds silence comfortably and lets the other person fill it, because the other person's way of filling silence tells you more than anything they would say on purpose.

Elena recognized the technique because she used it herself. Watching him deploy it on her was like watching someone play chess with your own opening. Fascinating and slightly unnerving. She adjusted—stopped filling the silences and let them sit. Two people standing in front of a photograph of Checkpoint Charlie, saying nothing, both waiting for the other to speak, both aware that the waiting was itself the conversation.

Elena noticed his hands. She had noticed them when he arrived—the long fingers, the way he held his wine glass with the stem between the second and third finger, the economy of the gesture. She noticed the line of his jaw when he turned to look at a photograph. The breadth of his shoulders inside a jacket that pulled across his back when he reached across his body. She noticed she was noticing these things with a specificity that was not operational. A specificity that had warmth in it. Warmth had no place in the file.

He broke first. Not from weakness. From strategy. Breaking the silence was a gift. It signaled willingness to be vulnerable, to go first, to risk saying something that the other person could use. In negotiation, the first person to speak after a silence has ceded something. Calder ceded it deliberately, because he understood ceding a small advantage early created an obligation the other person would eventually feel compelled to repay.

'You know more about this than an art historian should,' he said.

They were standing in front of a photograph of East Berlin schoolchildren assembled in a yard for a state holiday, taken in 1969. They were holding small paper flags caught in mid-flutter. Their faces had the composed seriousness of children who had learned, by that age, what their faces were supposed to do.

'The way you talk about the Eastern perspective. It's not academic. It's specific.'

Calder was testing the edges of her cover, pressing gently on the joints to see where they flexed. A lesser operative would have deflected—changed the subject, turned the observation into a joke, redirected toward safer territory. Elena did something more dangerous. She leaned in.

'I read a lot,' she said. 'I've always been more interested in the people living inside systems than the systems themselves. The policy is in the textbook. The person is in the photograph.'

It was true. Not Alice Marsh true—Elena true. An accurate description of how she thought about the world: not in terms of ideology or institutional framework but as innocent individuals caught inside the machine, adapting to it, being shaped by it, and occasionally being destroyed by it. It was also, she realized as she said it, the first genuinely honest thing she'd told anyone in London since arriving two years ago.

The best lies are true. Elena just told Calder something she believed, and her cover was stronger for it.

The slip was small—a hairline crack on the surface of Alice Marsh, barely visible, something only someone paying very close attention would notice. Elena caught herself. She began the process of sealing the crack, of reassembling the character, of pulling Alice Marsh back over Elena Vasilieva like a coat over bare skin.

But Calder had noticed.

For half a second, they were both real people standing in a room looking at each other.

The masks went back on. Smoothly. Simultaneously. Like two musicians returning to the score after an improvised bar. The transition was so seamless that if anyone in the gallery had been watching—and no one was—they would have seen nothing remarkable.

The gallery was emptying, and the remaining guests were focused on the wine table and each other. Elena and Calder were just two people having a pleasant conversation about photography in the corner.

Elena felt something shift in her chest. It was not worth examining. Examining feelings in real time was a luxury she'd been trained out of at the Red Banner Institute. That data was only useful when it was processed later, at a distance, under controlled conditions. She set the shift aside and continued the conversation.

But she knew, with the certainty of someone who had spent years studying human behavior at the molecular level, that the half-second of honesty had changed the encounter. He'd seen something real. He would remember it. From this point forward, their foundation would be built on one genuine moment, buried beneath layers of professional performance, running quietly beneath every exchange that followed.

The gallery was nearly empty.

The wine was finished. The gallery owner was collecting glasses with the resigned efficiency of a man who'd done this two hundred times and knew exactly how many would be broken. Pemberton left with the other King's College academics. The retired diplomat from Bonn shook hands with Calder on his way out and gave Elena a polite nod—a courtesy. No tactical significance.

Elena and Calder were standing against the far wall of the gallery, near the column where she'd started the evening, surrounded by photographs of a divided city. They'd been talking for ninety minutes. The conversation covered the exhibition, Cold War photography, the aesthetics of surveillance, the question of whether documentation is itself a political act, the quality of light in Berlin in November, and the price of decent wine in London. It had not covered anything personal. Neither of them mentioned where they lived, what they did for work beyond the vaguest outlines, or whether they were seeing anyone.

The absence of personal information was itself information. Two people who talk for ninety minutes without exchanging biographical details are either very private or very practiced. Elena knew which she was. She was beginning to suspect which he was.

They were standing closer than the conversation required. Close enough that Elena could smell his cologne—something woody, understated, a scent chosen to be noticed subconsciously rather than consciously. She could see the individual threads in the weave of his lapel. She could see a small scar at the corner of his left eyebrow, old and faded, from something that required stitches. The scar was not in his file. Elena cataloged it. Wondered about its origin. Whether she would ever be close enough to ask.

She realized, with a suddenness that surprised her, that she wanted to be close enough to ask.

There was a moment—brief, uncataloged—when they both reached toward the same photograph. Not simultaneously. He extended his hand first, pointing at the bottom-left corner where the photographer's caption had been taped to the frame, and Elena did the same a half-second behind. Their hands existed in the same few inches of gallery air without touching, without quite touching, the gap between them the width of a decision neither of them made. She felt the warmth of his hand before she felt the photograph's frame. She withdrew first. He let her. Neither mentioned it. The conversation continued because it had been present in the air.

The photograph they had both reached for was the laundry image Elena had stopped in front of earlier—the woman on the balcony, the Wall past her shoulder, the line of sheets she was hanging as if the Wall behind them was a feature of the weather. Elena wouldn't know, for many years, why this image in particular had stayed with her, or why she would return to the woman on the balcony when she needed a shape that was not operational.

Calder was watching her the way Elena was watching him. With attention that started as professional and migrated, over the course of the evening, into territory that neither of them were going to name. His body was angled toward her. Not facing her directly—that would have been too explicit, too much like a declaration—but turned at an angle that communicated interest without committing to it. The physical equivalent of his fourteen-minute arrival: calculated, but designed to look natural.

The gallery owner was turning off the far lights. The signal was clear. The evening was over. Everything that was going to happen between Elena and Calder tonight had already happened. No touch. No kiss. No exchange of phone numbers. Not even a handshake. Both had nodded instead of extending a hand. The nod had been deliberate on Elena's part.

She suspected the nod had been deliberate on his part too.

'I should go,' she said as Alice Marsh would say it—with the slight reluctance of a woman who has enjoyed the evening and is not yet ready for it to end, but who has the social grace to recognize when a venue is closing around her. She gathered her coat from the rack by the door. It was a good coat. Camel-colored, wool-cashmere blend, a coat that said taste and modest means. Elena's actual preference—dark, functional, deep pockets for a passport and a weapon—was not appropriate for gallery openings.

'I hope I'll see you again,' Calder said. He said it simply. Without flourish. Without the upward inflection that would have turned it into a question. It was a statement of intent disguised as a social pleasantry, and both of them knew it, and neither of them acknowledged knowing it.

'I come to these things sometimes,' Elena said.

Sometimes now meant always. She would see him many times before Christmas. Many more before she left for Berlin. And then, after a long separation neither of them would speak about in the years that followed, she would see him again.

The October night was damp. Fitzrovia was quiet—the shops closed, the sodium lights throwing their yellow wash across brick and empty pavement, the hush of a London neighborhood after its working day. She turned toward high street, at the pace of a woman heading home after a pleasant evening, which was everything Alice Marsh was, and something else entirely.

The something else was running a rapid assessment that would have been impressive if anyone could have heard it. The conversation replayed in sequence—each of Calder's responses tagged for what it revealed about his training, his psychology, his posture, his vulnerabilities, his potential. Moments where his performance wavered: the two-minute pause at the Eastern photograph, the way his voice changed when he said 'the curtains are the detail,' the sharp focus in his eyes when she'd accidentally said something true. His physical tells: the way he distributed his weight when he was genuinely engaged versus when he was performing engagement, the tiny shift around his mouth when he was deciding whether to say something risky, the scar at his eyebrow that she wanted to know the story behind.

Elena was also doing something she did not include in assessments, because it wasn't operational and because she didn't yet have a category for it.

She was thinking about the half-second. The half-second when their masks dropped and they saw each other. Not Alice Marsh and the junior Foreign Office analyst. Each other. The actual people. For that instant, in a gallery in Fitzrovia, surrounded by photographs of a wall that separated people from each other by force, two people who separated themselves from everyone by choice had stopped separating.

She didn't know what to do with this. She had no protocol for it. The Red Banner Institute trained her for every social and psychological scenario in the field—seduction, interrogation, betrayal, isolation, the long slow erosion of identity that came with years of deep cover. Nobody trained her for the possibility that she might, at some point, meet someone who made the performance feel like a problem rather than a solution.

Elena walked through Kensington, her part of west London. The night air was cooling and carried the smell of the Thames, which was a mile south.

She thought about what the Red Banner Institute had taught her about loneliness: it was a signal, not a fact—a physiological state to be managed like cold or hunger. Data was for filing. Elena had filed loneliness dozens of times in two years and never once let the filing fail.

Tonight the filing failed.

James Calder. Not Target Nine. A man who, at this exact moment, was reading a glass of wine the way other men read newspapers—for information, for pattern, for the thing between the lines.

Elena would not debrief to her handler about the meeting. Not tonight. Tomorrow, in clinical language, she would describe the gallery opening, the guest list, the contacts she made, and the assessment of James Calder as a target of interest. She would note his intelligence, his training, his potential, and his vulnerabilities. She would recommend continued observation and eventual cultivation. Her report would be precise and comprehensive while containing every relevant detail of the evening except one.

She would not mention the half-second.

She did not yet know what it meant. Her handlers would have no use for the information. But some part of her—the part beneath Alice Marsh, where the Akhmatova tattoo marked the border—wanted to keep it. Just this one thing. Just this half-second.

She continued walking. Elena enjoyed the night. Alice was a morning person by necessity. She turned onto her street and let herself into her flat. The door locked behind her—one deadbolt, one chain, both installed by her, both unnecessary in a neighborhood this safe and both absolutely necessary in a life like hers. The coat went on its hook. A glass of water. She stood in her kitchen and closed her eyes, listening to the building settle around her.

Then Elena opened her clutch bag. The Nagra came out in her palm, still warm from her body. The miniature reel inside held ninety minutes of Calder. His voice about the photograph. His voice about the curtains. Everything Elena hadn't been able to write down because writing down would have meant looking away.

She rewound. The Nagra's earpiece went on. She pressed playback.

Elena had not known, until she heard the tape, that her own breath had been recorded. Not the breath of Alice Marsh. The small intake before she said *It's a geranium.* The pause after Calder said *the curtains are the detail.* Her breath. She rewound and listened again.

Then she noticed the other thing.

A ticking sound—small, sharp, metallic. Intermittent—once every four seconds, maybe five. Too regular for ambient room noise. Too irregular for a clock. Something inside the mechanism itself, something mechanical, something new. She listened to it four times to be sure. The tick was not on the microphone side. It was not in the room. It was inside the machine itself, scratching the tape as the machine recorded —a small mechanical wound the tape would carry.

Whatever was catching would continue to catch. Every reel she ran through it from now on—recording or playback—would carry another scratch from the same nick. The recorder was dying. Not this tape. Not the next one. But soon. She listened to the tick once more.

She would not report the tick. Reporting the tick would

mean surrendering the reel, and surrendering the reel would mean surrendering what was on it. The conversation about the photograph. The curtains. Calder's voice. Her own breath, which had been responding to him while Alice Marsh had been performing. She told herself the tick was within manufacturing tolerance. It was not within manufacturing tolerance. She knew this. She did not say so. The knowledge joined the private ledger in the part of her mind where the other unfiled things lived.

She unloaded the reel. She placed it in the kitchen drawer beside the stove. She returned the Nagra to its case on the top shelf of the wardrobe.

The reel was the recording—a hundred and eighty feet of tape on which the evening now existed as a pattern of particles. The tape was in the drawer. The drawer was hers.

She lay in the dark for a long time, listening to London breathe outside her window. Somewhere in this city, James Calder was also lying in the dark, probably beside his wife, probably replaying the evening the way Elena was replaying it—cataloging what he'd learned, assessing what he'd revealed, deciding what to do next. Both of them running the same calculation in parallel.

3

THE ARCHITECTURE OF ALICE MARSH

London—November 1973—January 1975

Elena met Yuri on a Thursday, at a café in Bloomsbury. They'd used the location four times before and would not use it again after today. The rotation of meeting places was standard protocol—no location used more than five times, no pattern in geography or timing, no overlap with any other aspect of Elena's working or personal schedule. Yuri called these meetings 'reviews.'

Yuri was fifty-three, heavyset, with the patient, slightly melancholic face of a man who'd spent thirty years in a profession that required him to trust no one and had succeeded. He was listed on the Soviet embassy's staff register as a cultural attaché—the diplomatic equivalent of a neon sign reading 'intelligence officer.'

He was already seated when she arrived. He'd ordered her a tea—Earl Grey, no milk, the way Alice Marsh took her tea, not the way Elena Vasilieva took it. But Yuri had never met Elena Vasilieva. He'd only met Alice Marsh, speaking English, in cafés and parks around London. If Yuri was ever compromised, he could describe a New Zealand art historian who spoke no Russian and whose real name he did not know. He had spent two years handling an agent he'd never met.

'How is work?' he asked.

The question had two possible answers. Anything about the weather meant she'd been compromised and the meeting should be aborted. Anything about the gallery where she worked in Mayfair meant all clear.

'Gerald is thinking about expanding into Impressionists,' she said. 'I told him it was a crowded market.'

Yuri nodded once.

They sat in the café for forty-five minutes. To anyone watching, they were a middle-aged man and a younger woman having a conversation that could have been professional, personal, or avuncular. The ambiguity was deliberate. Yuri drank coffee. Elena drank the Earl Grey she didn't like. They spoke in English throughout.

The business was straightforward. Lillehammer had been a success—the Mossad assessment was already circulating at Yasenevo, and Elena's report had been singled out for its precision. Moscow was pleased. Moscow was sufficiently pleased to expand her brief. Her assessments of the nine MI6-adjacent targets: seven had been categorized as cultivatable. One dismissed as an alcoholic liability. The ninth—James Calder—was flagged for continued observation.

Yuri conveyed this with the flat affect of a man reading from an internal memo, which he essentially was. Moscow's language had the institutional warmth of a tax assessment: 'Asset has demonstrated satisfactory operational performance in preliminary target identification. Recommend continued engagement with Target Nine with a view to long-term cultivation.'

Target Nine. A junior desk officer at Century House—two years into his posting, low on the institutional ladder, not yet trusted with the files that mattered. That was the shape of Calder's career. Bonn had given him Soviet counter-intelligence. Washington had given him NATO's nuclear-sharing architecture. The Counter-Proliferation desk in London was where those two educations met, and where his files contained information about missing NATO weapons that Moscow either wanted to know about or wanted to make sure nobody else knew about. The second possibility was a thought she filed without fully examining.

Moscow was not targeting Calder because he was vulnerable. Moscow was asking Elena to become the thing Calder's desk existed to find: the penetration that walked in through the front door wearing a good dress and an accent from the wrong hemisphere.

'He is junior now,' Yuri added. 'Moscow evaluates trajectories, not positions. His file suggests Deputy Section within five years. Possibly sooner. When he arrives there, we want you inside his life.'

Target Nine. Long-term cultivation. Calder had been reduced to a number and a bureaucratic recommendation. She understood why this was necessary. She understood all of it. She also understood that she'd spent weeks thinking about the way Target Nine's voice dropped when he was saying something he actually meant.

'There is a new assignment,' he said. He set down his coffee cup with the careful deliberation of a man who was about to say something important and wanted a physical gesture to signal the shift. 'He is a journalist. British. His name is Tom Hatch. He has been investigating NATO's stay-behind networks in Western Europe—the Gladio program. He is getting close to atomic material that Moscow considers sensitive.'

Elena knew about Gladio. Not extensively. The program was compartmentalized even within NATO. But she knew the shape: secret armies embedded in Western European countries, trained and equipped by NATO to conduct guerrilla warfare against the Soviet Union—and, the murmurs said, against anyone in Western Europe who looked like a sympathizer. They were built for the unthinkable. The murmurs suggested someone had decided it was time.

She also knew the byline. Tom Hatch. She'd read him before—two or three times, in cuttings that reached her desk through Moscow's European clipping service. A piece in the *Observer* about offshore shell companies that had the patient, forensic quality of a man who liked numbers. Another piece, she thought, about arms brokers in Cyprus. He did not write to shock. He wrote it like a man compiling an indictment, one paragraph at a time, with the understanding that the indictment would take years.

Elena noted the byline at the time because Hatch was the rare journalist who reported like an intelligence officer: with the assumption that every source was lying for their own reasons, and that the job was to triangulate until the truth fell out of the arithmetic. She'd found herself wondering, without quite meaning to, what he would make of her if she were a source. She hadn't wondered it long.

'What does Moscow want?' Elena asked.

The question was the first Elena had ever asked Yuri that she genuinely did not know the answer to. A British journalist was investigating NATO's nuclear weapons hidden on European soil. If Hatch succeeded, he would expose a secret Western military program that the Soviet Union had been trying to penetrate for decades. This was a gift. Moscow should be helping Hatch, not suppressing him. Moscow should be feeding him documents, not sending an illegal to neutralize his investigation.

Unless Moscow was not the one giving the order.

Elena added it to the archive. She suspected she was not going to like the explanation.

'Hatch needs to be *managed*. Not *eliminated—managed*. His investigation is approaching channels that cannot be exposed. If he follows the wrong thread, he arrives at doors that do not need to be opened.' Yuri paused. The pause was deliberate—the institutional silence that signaled classification boundaries. 'The management will require training. Extended training. You will need to be seconded to our colleagues in Berlin.'

Berlin. East Berlin. The Stasi.

Elena kept her face neutral. Alice Marsh would not know what the Stasi was. Alice Marsh would not feel anything about the word Berlin except perhaps a vague curiosity. Elena felt a great deal. Berlin meant the Wall. Berlin meant Normannenstraße and the Stasi's headquarters and an increasingly sophisticated psychological warfare apparatus. Berlin meant new handlers, new protocols, new risks. Berlin meant leaving London.

Berlin meant leaving Calder.

She did not say this. She did not consciously think it. But the thought existed somewhere beneath the professional surface, in the same place where she kept the half-second, next to the things she did not put in reports.

'When?' she asked.

'January,' Yuri said. 'You have two months.'

He reached into his coat pocket and placed something on the table between them. A cigarette lighter. A good one—Ronson, chrome, the kind of object a cultural attaché might give to an art historian as a professional courtesy, entirely unremarkable and entirely replaceable. Yuri did not smoke in Elena's presence. Elena did not smoke at all.

'From the Second Department,' Yuri said. 'It is not a lighter. There is a camera inside. One hundred and eighty frames on the current load. The shutter is driven by a clockwork mechanism and produces no sound.'

He glanced at the window. He waited for the street to clear before he continued.

'The lens is in the base. The cable release runs up your sleeve. They are proud of it.'

Elena picked up the lighter. It had the weight of something whose purpose was not lighting cigarettes. She turned it in her hand. The chrome was flawless. The hinged cap opened and closed with the small click of a real lighter. The shutter was nowhere visible. The lens was nowhere visible. Only a weight slightly heavier than a lighter should be, and the knowledge that the heaviness was every secret the device would ever help her steal.

'F-21?' she said.

'They did not call it that in the note. But yes.'

She slid it into her coat pocket. The lighter became one more object she had to keep close.

'Thank the Second Department,' she said.

'I already did,' Yuri said. 'They told me you were the only one in London they trusted with the prototype.'

Elena thought about two months. Time enough to establish the Calder relationship on a foundation solid enough to survive her absence. Time enough to build the channels she would need to maintain contact with him from Berlin. Time enough to do what Moscow was asking of her—turn a gallery acquaintance into an asset—and, she was beginning to suspect, time enough to do something else. Something more complicated and more dangerous and less easily filed.

'Understood,' she said.

Yuri finished his coffee. He left first. Elena sat alone with Alice Marsh's tea for another ten minutes, watching the lively Bloomsbury street through the window.

◆◆◆

She put on her coat and walked out into the city.

South through Russell Square, past the British Museum's long railed front, down through Holborn toward the river.

She was measuring things. Not distances. The weight of the Ronson in her coat pocket, which was noticeable. The shape of the phrase *managed,* not *eliminated,* which Yuri had deployed with professional neutrality. And the name. Tom Hatch. She said it to herself once at the corner of Great Russell Street.

Two months. She tested the number against the terrain. Two months of Colin's coffee. Two months of Helen's shortbread. Two months of the plane trees. Two months before the camel coat came off for the last time and the woman underneath it walked, in a different coat, into a city she had only ever seen in photographs.

Alice Marsh's face stayed on during her walk. Alice Marsh had no opinion about Berlin. Alice Marsh had never heard of Tom Hatch.

Beneath the camel coat and the face and the name, Elena Vasilieva carried the new assignment the way she carried everything—without permission, without inventory, in the part of herself no coat had ever reached.

That evening she sat at the kitchen table in her Kensington flat with the Ronson disassembled in front of her. Baseplate removed. Clockwork mechanism exposed. The screwdriver she used was a watchmaker's flat-head she'd bought at a tool shop on Portobello Road not long after she'd arrived in London. She kept it bundled in a felt roll in the cupboard under the sink—six screwdrivers, two pairs of needle-nose pliers, a jeweler's loupe, each one nested in its pocket like a surgical instrument. The roll cost her four pounds. It was the most valuable thing she owned that was entirely hers.

The Second Department's engineering was good. The tolerances were tight. But the cable release housing had a burr on the interior lip that would catch against the cable's braided sleeve and produce a drag of perhaps half a millimeter. Half a millimeter was nothing in a cigarette lighter. In a camera disguised as one, it was the width of a career. The device was operated through a coat sleeve; the drag would show as hesitation in Elena's hand; a trained watcher would notice.

Elena filed the burr down with a needle file she kept in the same felt roll. She tested the release. Smooth. She tested it again. Smooth. She reassembled the baseplate, tightening the four Phillips-head screws in a cross pattern the way you tightened the bolts on an engine block—opposing corners first, to distribute the compression evenly. The screwdriver turned in her fingers with the easy authority of an instrument that had been used for this kind of work many times before.

She held the reassembled lighter to the kitchen light. The chrome caught the bulb and threw a small bright line across the ceiling. It looked like a cigarette lighter. It would photograph documents at a distance of eighteen inches with a resolution sufficient for Moscow's analysts to read at a nine-point typeface. Elena had fixed the burr at her kitchen table with a four-pound tool kit—the particular patience of a woman who did not trust institutions to build things that worked the way she needed them to work.

She placed the lighter in the drawer beside the Nagra reel. The drawer was getting heavier.

Before bed she went through the week's Moscow cables at the same table. Routine traffic, no secrets, just the shape of what was moving. A line item—FLAMINGO, the entry had read; she would remember the word—had dropped out of a supply-chain index and reappeared a week later under a classification Moscow called archive-pending. Archive-pending was where things went when they were not being archived. She noted the discrepancy. She did not file the noting. That was the first thing she did not file.

Two months.

Elena walked back through a London that was already changing.

The plane trees had turned the rust-gold of London autumn three weeks ago and she hadn't really seen them until now. The scaffolding outside the dry cleaner she'd been meaning to use and would now never use. Two years she'd walked through this city, collecting it the way she collected everything—compulsively, without permission. And in two years she had not once let the collection feel like belonging, because Elena Vasilieva did not belong to cities; cities were terrain.

But the terrain had a deadline now, and the deadline was changing the way the terrain looked.

She did not let her face change. Alice Marsh's face was open and pleasant and mildly curious—a face she was wearing, and would keep wearing until she got home and locked the door. Underneath, the operational mind that had spent two years assembling Alice Marsh into something livable was running an inventory.

Two months to live as Alice Marsh.

Two months of mornings like the mornings she'd been having for two years.

She woke at six-fifteen every morning. Not because she was a morning person—Elena Vasilieva had been a night creature since adolescence, a girl who read Akhmatova under the covers in Leningrad with a penlight while her mother slept—but because Alice Marsh was a morning person. Alice Marsh jogged. Alice Marsh ate a sensible breakfast. Alice Marsh arrived at the gallery fifteen minutes early with a takeaway coffee and a competent expression.

The rituals were not normal. None of them were normal. But they looked normal, which in the intelligence business amounted to the same thing.

Her flat was on the second floor of a Victorian conversion in Kensington, on a street lined with more plane trees. She had chosen it for its exits and her neighbors' hours. The bathroom window, if you were slender enough and motivated enough, opened onto a drainpipe that reached the garden wall. Elena tested the drainpipe on her second night in the flat, at 2 AM, wearing dark clothes and soft shoes. It held her weight. She hadn't needed to use it since.

The main room faced east and received the morning sun through two tall windows that Elena dressed with sheer curtains.

She'd thought about that distinction recently. At a gallery. While looking at a photograph of an apartment window in East Berlin where someone had hung curtains next to a wall.

Two months and she would be on the other side of the window.

The jog was the first layer.

Alice Marsh jogged through Kensington Gardens three mornings a week. The route was consistent, and the consistency was the point. A woman who jogged the same route every Tuesday, Thursday, and Saturday became unremarkable. Unremarkable was the most valuable currency in the intelligence world.

But the jog was also countersurveillance. Seven observation points checked automatically, the way a pilot checks instruments. No one was watching her this morning. No one was ever watching her on these mornings. The absence of watchers was itself data.

Her favorite section came at the far end of the Serpentine, where the path curved into a wide stretch of grass. For ninety seconds on this stretch, the morning belonged to someone that did not need to be Alice Marsh.

She let herself feel it. The legs working. The breath coming easy now, past the first mile's resistance. The involuntary joy of the body moving at speed through open space—a joy that predated the training, predated the covers, predated everything except a girl running along the Neva embankment at fifteen with her coat unbuttoned, running for no reason.

That girl was still in there. Buried under the wrappings. Still running.

She finished the loop. She bought a coffee at the shop on the high street—the same shop, the same barista. Alice was pleasant and forgettable, which was the highest compliment the cover could pay itself.

Colin the barista would not know she was leaving. None of them would. That was the protocol. Alice Marsh would simply stop coming in one morning. The morning would become a week. The week would become a month. Colin would mention to a regular that this quiet New Zealander hadn't been in for a while. The regular would say that's a shame. That would be it. A life closing without ceremony, the way lives in this profession closed.

She took her coffee home. She showered and dressed in the clothes Alice Marsh would choose—professional, understated, the wardrobe of a woman with good taste and a modest income. Dark hair, cut in a style that was attractive without being memorable. Alice Marsh's expression was open, pleasant, interested without being forward. Elena had been wearing it.

She put on Alice's expression. She left the flat.

The gallery where Alice Marsh worked was called the Whitfield. It occupied the ground floor of a Georgian terrace in Mayfair and specialized in European art from the eighteenth and nineteenth centuries—Flemish portraits, Dutch interiors, the occasional Italian landscape. A gallery that survived on a small, loyal clientele of collectors who trusted the owner's eye and were willing to pay for it.

The owner was a man named Gerald Whitfield, sixty-three, with the mixture of knowledge and pretension that London's art world breeds in men surrounded by beauty they can appraise but not create. He'd hired her eighteen months ago on the strength of her thesis on Flemish portraiture.

He did not know that her competence was trained rather than natural. The best lies are true—Alice genuinely loved art, genuinely understood the market, genuinely cared about the gallery's future—and it was the principle on which every identity she now carried had been built.

The Whitfield served three purposes. The first was access—the client list included diplomats, civil servants, academics, and professionals who moved through London's institutional circles without thinking of themselves as part of any circle, and they brought their friends.

The second was cover. An art historian at a respected Mayfair gallery was a woman with a reason to be in London, a reason to know the people she knew, a reason to travel occasionally to Amsterdam or Vienna for a sale. Alice Marsh had a business card, a salary, a National Insurance number, an opinion on the provenance of Dutch interiors. The Whitfield made her real.

The third was the one Elena valued most. The gallery gave

her a place to think. Between clients, between phone calls, between the administrative tasks that filled the hours of a job that was important enough to be convincing and unimportant enough to leave her mind free, she sat at the desk in the back office and processed intelligence. Not on paper—never on paper. In her head. She organized, cross-referenced, analyzed. Built and maintained the mental database that was her primary tool. Gerald thought she was reading art journals. She was reading people.

Today, after Yuri's café meeting, after Berlin had been laid down in front of her like a new floor she was going to have to learn to walk on, Elena sat at the desk in the back office and thought about James Calder.

With previous targets, the process had been mechanical. She assembled data, identified patterns, designed approaches the way an engineer designs a bridge—with attention to stress points and failure modes.

With Calder, the process kept slipping. The analytical framework was there, and it was producing results—she had a clearer picture of his psychology now than Moscow's file had provided—though Moscow's file had been oddly specific in places. It contained a detail about Calder's performance review language that read less like an external intelligence assessment and more like an excerpt from an internal MI6 personnel evaluation. She did not understand it. It went into the archive.

Feelings are intelligence. Treat them as data. Process them at a distance. Never let them enter the working space in real time.

Elena followed this protocol. She'd seduced two targets in Moscow and one in Helsinki and felt nothing for any of them. They were operations. Operations end. Feelings generated during operations are operational feelings, and those feelings have a shelf life.

She was not sure about Calder. And now Calder had a shelf life of his own—sixty days, give or take, before she was on a train to a city where his name would be professionally inert and personally forbidden.

She turned to the art journals. She resolved nothing.

Alice Marsh had friends in London. Each one served a purpose. None of them knew this.

And there was Helen.

Helen was seventy-one. She lived alone in Chelsea. She'd been a nurse during the war. Her value was negligible. Elena visited her on Sunday afternoons because Alice Marsh would visit a lonely elderly friend on Sundays, and because Helen made very good shortbread, and because sitting in Helen's parlor was the closest thing to rest that Elena experienced in her secret life.

She had not told Moscow about Helen. It was a choice. She did not examine the choice too carefully.

The afternoon at the gallery passed without incident. Gerald sold a small Dutch painting he had been trying to move for weeks. Elena congratulated him. She meant it. A Soviet illegal two months from a Berlin secondment, carrying a cigarette lighter that photographed documents, she genuinely cared about the sale.

The day was ending. She went home.

This was when the card appeared on her kitchen table.

Not on the table exactly. It had been pushed through the mail slot at street level, and she collected it with the rest of her post on the way upstairs. But the rest of the post was bills and a clothing catalog, recognizable at a glance. The card was not.

It was a gallery invitation. Cream card stock, embossed

lettering, something London's art world produced in industrial quantities and distributed to mailing lists that overlapped so thoroughly that anyone on two of them received approximately three invitations per week. This one was for an exhibition of postwar German painting at the Paxton, the small Fitzrovia gallery where Alice Marsh had met James Calder. The exhibition opened next Thursday. Elena had not heard of most of the artists listed. None of this was unusual.

What was unusual was the handwriting on the back.

The photograph of the Wall was better from the Eastern side.—J

Elena stood in her kitchen holding the card. She stood there for a long time. The flat was quiet. The building was quiet. Mrs. Aldridge was presumably alive downstairs. David the solicitor was presumably at work. London was doing what London did in the late afternoon of a November Tuesday.

She was not alarmed. She was not afraid. Fear was a response she'd trained out of herself years ago. The assessment was already running.

Calder had found her address.

She'd given him only 'Alice' and a conversation about curtains and a half-second of accidental honesty, and from that he'd found her. Which meant he had resources. Which meant he had motivation. Which meant he'd used those resources and that motivation to locate a woman he met once at a gallery opening and to communicate, through the gesture of a handwritten note on the back of an invitation, that he was interested.

If the approach was operational, it was elegant—the card was deniable, unthreatening, and calibrated to create curiosity rather than suspicion. If it was personal, it was bold. Either way, it revealed something about Calder that his file hadn't included and that six weeks of observation had only hinted at: he was willing to make a move before he fully understood the board.

Elena turned the card over in her hands. The handwriting was confident. Small, precise, left-leaning. The pen was a fountain pen, not a ballpoint. The ink had the slight feathering on the card stock. A man who carried a fountain pen in 1973 had opinions about things most men didn't bother having opinions about. She cataloged this. She logged all of it.

Then she did something that surprised her.

Elena smiled.

Nothing like Alice Marsh's smile. None of the calibrated, quarter-turn, purpose-built version she deployed in social and operational situations. A different smile. The real one. The smile that happened to a face when the person behind it was genuinely pleased, genuinely surprised, and genuinely uncertain about what to do next. It lasted two seconds. It was the most honest expression Elena's face had produced since she arrived in London.

She looked at the card again, this time with the detachment the situation required.

He'd found her address. She should report it. She should inform Yuri that her cover had been penetrated to the level of residential identification by a probable MI6 officer. Yuri would assess the risk. Moscow would assess the risk. Protocols would be activated. The flat might need to be abandoned. The identity might need to be reinforced or replaced.

Or.

Or she could say nothing. She could treat the card as what it appeared to be—an invitation from a man who was interested in a woman. She could attend the exhibition next Thursday. She could see him again. She could continue the assessment of Target Nine that Moscow had already authorized, and she could do it from inside the relationship that Calder was clearly trying to build. That he'd found her address would become, in her report, a confirmation of his capability and his interest, not a breach.

She could do both things simultaneously—report the approach and continue the engagement. That was the professional answer. That was what the Red Banner Institute would have recommended. Report everything. Use everything. The personal and the operational are not in conflict because the personal does not exist.

Elena opened the drawer beside the stove. A small white candle. A pen. The diary she maintained in Alice's voice, in handwriting that was not her own. Yuri's welcome card, left on the table the day she moved in: *Welcome to your new home —Y.* The Ronson lighter from that morning. And at the back, beneath the diary, a single reel of audio tape she had placed there two weeks ago—because she did not want to listen to it again and did not want to destroy it either. The two decisions had canceled each other out.

She placed the card in the drawer beside the reel. The drawer closed with the soft wooden sound of a thing fitting into its place. Her hand stayed on the handle for a moment longer than it needed to.

Then the phone rang.

Alice Marsh's phone. The cream-colored rotary on the kitchen wall. Two rings. She answered it.

'How is work?' Yuri said. The code phrase. All clear.

'Gerald is still talking about the Impressionists,' she said. 'I told him the market is crowded.'

They moved through the usual items. The Hatch assessment. The gallery schedule she maintained for cover. His coffee. Her tea. The conversation had the practiced ease of two people who had been performing a professional friendship and had become competent at it.

'Anything else?' he said.

Her hand was still on the drawer handle.

The card was on the other side of the wood. Seven inches. The first card. The fountain-pen handwriting. The reference to the Wall from the Eastern side. The thing a man had gone to the trouble of finding her address for, which meant Calder had resources, which meant Calder had motivation, which meant she was standing in her kitchen with her hand on a drawer that Yuri could not see into and that she was about to not tell him about.

'No,' she said. 'Nothing else.'

She heard him replace his receiver. She set hers down.

She did not report the card from Calder to Yuri. Not that day. Not the next day. Not ever.

That night, she lay in bed in the dark.

Two months. Two months before Berlin. Two months before her morning coffee stopped being Colin's, and her favorite stretch of the Serpentine stopped being hers, and her Sunday afternoons stopped tasting like shortbread, and the woman she'd been pretending to be began the slow process of being filed away in a drawer somewhere in Moscow Center marked inactive.

Two months to build something with Calder. Two months to decide what the something was.

The ceiling was not visible. It was there, and she knew it was there, and she looked at it anyway. Somewhere above it were rooms where decisions got made by men she could name. Somewhere above those were rooms where decisions got made by men she could not. She had started, that autumn, to understand that the second kind of room was closer to her than the first.

She got up.

The flat was cold. She pulled a cardigan over the shoulders of her nightshirt and went into the sitting room and turned on the small television for the company of a voice that was not her own. It was a habit she had brought from Leningrad and a habit Alice Marsh had developed independently in her first London winter: the BBC late at night, the volume low, the light of the screen making the room feel smaller than it was. In two years of shared tenancy, Elena and Alice had not disagreed about it. Both found the Radio 4 voice soothing. Both went to sleep better with a correspondent's careful diction in the room. It was one of the few places the two women overlapped without friction.

She made tea. She carried the cup back to the sofa. She sat down with a quilt over her knees, as Alice Marsh would, and she was twelve seconds into the broadcast before she understood she was not going to sleep tonight.

The piece was *Panorama*. A half-hour investigation. The correspondent was walking through the empty square of a mountain village in northern Italy in the afternoon light of two weeks ago, and the voice-over was explaining that the village had, for thirty months, been a village no reporter had been permitted to enter. Elena set the cup down.

The cover had been mercury. A chemical leak from a storage facility serving a local mining operation. Twelve dead, the official bulletin said, in July 1971. The deaths had been absorbed into the smaller Italian news cycles of the summer and had fallen out of the papers with the quiet finality of a file being closed somewhere in Rome.

The BBC had not let it close.

The correspondent said—carefully, in the neutral register of a man whose editors had told him to be extremely careful—that the families of the dead had, across thirty months, done the thing the state had instructed them not to do. They kept the medical records. They requested autopsies; the autopsies were denied. They took the bodies, at their own expense, to laboratories in Switzerland. They pooled what came back. They wrote to newspapers, to hospitals, to a member of parliament. They formed a small committee. The committee hired a lawyer. The lawyer filed, in the spring of this year, a petition nobody in Rome had expected a petition to survive.

The petition alleged that the cause of death had been misattributed.

The BBC had obtained the Swiss laboratory reports.

The Swiss reports did not describe mercury exposure. They described a pattern of acute radiation syndrome consistent with proximity, at the moment of death, to a critical fission event of short duration.

Elena did not move.

The correspondent said that no known civilian source in the region could have produced such an event. He said the Italian authorities had declined to comment. He said the families were continuing their campaign. Then the correspondent said something else. He said the Swiss analysis had identified a characteristic isotopic fingerprint in the tissue samples, and that the fingerprint was consistent with a plutonium core of American manufacture, fabricated in the early 1960s, of a specific design used in a narrow category of portable devices that had never been officially deployed in civilian proximity anywhere in Europe.

She set her cup on the floor.

The BBC correspondent was reading from a summary a Swiss physicist had written. The summary was saying what Elena had been told eighteen months ago.

The briefing had been on a Thursday. Yasenevo. Spring 1972. Six men in a room, including the deputy director who had not previously appeared in any room Elena had been in. The deputy director had told them, in the dry institutional voice that meant the words were not to be repeated, that there were things in Western Europe whose existence had not been admitted to Moscow's allies, and that the things, if events arranged themselves badly, would have to be cleaned up by services not yet appointed for the cleaning.

He had not used the word *weapons*. He had used the word *inventory*.

Elena had filed the briefing in a category for which she had not previously had a use.

Tonight the BBC was using the word the deputy director had not used.

The BBC was saying it. On a Tuesday night. On Radio 4. At 22:48.

Someone had leaked the Swiss reports. The broadcast had the texture of something laid deliberately by a hand that knew where the load-bearing wall was.

The hand was already in the room with her.

The correspondent was sitting now with a woman in her sixties. The woman was wearing a black cardigan. She was holding a photograph of her daughter. The daughter had been twenty-four. The daughter had been two kilometers from the facility on the day the event occurred and had died four days later in a hospital in the north with her skin slipping from the back of her hands, and there had been a boy of eleven on the same ward whose mother had not been permitted in the room, and the state had written mercury on the death certificate, and the woman had refused the death certificate. In 1971. In 1972. Through every month of the thirty-six that followed. At some point during those months she began writing letters. The camera held on her face for the length of one sentence. The hand holding the photograph was steady; the other hand was not.

More than two hundred of them, the BBC said. To newspapers, to hospitals, to a member of parliament, to the Vatican, to the Red Cross, to three Swiss laboratories, to a physicist who had written back, to the World Health Organization, to a journalist in London whose name the correspondent chose not to mention.

Elena, hearing the omission, understood whose name it had been.

Her hand went to her ribcage without her deciding it. Under her palm her chest was not moving.

Six weeks ago in a Bloomsbury café, Yuri had set down his coffee and said the word *manage*. The journalist needed to be managed, not eliminated. His investigation was approaching channels that could not be exposed.

The journalist in London whose name the BBC would not say on air was the journalist Moscow had instructed her to manage before Christmas. The mother in the black cardigan, with two hundred letters in a kitchen in a village of seven hundred people, was the source.

Elena was the friction.

She was sitting under a quilt on a Kensington sofa watching the problem she had been designed to solve.

She thought about the word *maintenance*. It was the word the services used for the other word, the one no government was willing to put on paper. The bombs had been placed a dozen or fifteen years ago for a war that had not arrived. Plutonium aged whether the war did or not. Pits developed hot spots. Seals degraded. Somebody had to go into the cache sites and do the technical work, and somebody occasionally got it wrong.

The 1971 event had been a maintenance accident.

Elena's eye went, without permission, to the kitchen counter.

The Ronson was still there. Chrome. Unremarkable. Yuri had put it into her hand this afternoon at a Bloomsbury café, and she had brought it home and disassembled it at this table and filed down a burr on the cable release with a watchmaker's tool, and reassembled it, and set it on the counter. It had been a good afternoon's small work. One hundred and eighty frames of Second Department emulsion loaded and ready.

She looked at the lighter the way one looked at an object one had loved for a long time and just discovered had been, all along, something else.

Not a camera. An instrument.

Not hers. The hand's.

The report ended. The correspondent said the families' lawyer would file an expanded petition in the spring. He said the BBC would follow the story. He said good night. A weather map replaced him. Rain over the Midlands.

Elena did not turn the television off.

She thought of a document she had translated in September. Not the front page. A second page she had glanced at because her eye had caught a small mark in the margin, and the mark had been unusual enough to register before her training had time to file it. A pencil stroke. Faint. Left-leaning. The kind of mark a man with a fountain pen in his breast pocket made when he was not willing to uncap the pen for a single character. Beside the mark had been a notation she had not been cleared to understand. A site designation. Not the Italian village on the television. Somewhere else. A date, recent. An abbreviation that meant, she had later worked out, records denial—indefinite.

She had translated the appendix. She had signed the cover. She had passed the document back.

She had not thought about it again.

She was thinking about it now.

She understood, sitting in the soft blue light of a weather map, that the reason she had been given the September document, even for translation, was because the hand had known she could be trusted not to ask. Some mechanism somewhere had assessed her discipline and decided she was reliable. She had been reviewed. She had been approved. The not-asking had been noticed, and cataloged, and preferred.

The hand had been pleased with her.

That was the thing her body now registered as fear.

Not the village. Not the families. Not the hand. The pleasure. She had been a name on a page, and a pencil had marked her, and the pencil had been satisfied.

Elena got up slowly and turned the television off. The room went dark except for the streetlight through the kitchen curtains.

Somewhere in Europe, at this hour, a man in a room she had not seen was watching the same broadcast. His gold ring caught the light of a single lamp. He was not surprised by any of it. He took a pencil from his breast pocket, left-leaning, and made a small mark against a name in a margin. The name was not hers. He had already made the mark against hers.

In the drawer beside the stove, the card waited. The fountain-pen handwriting. The reference to the Eastern side of the Wall—a private joke, their private joke, built on a conversation that had happened once in a gallery now closed and dark and empty of everything except photographs of a divided city.

She thought about the woman on the balcony. The one who had hung curtains next to a death strip and stopped noticing the death strip years ago.

Elena had walked toward hers.

She had been walking toward it for two years and would walk toward it for seventeen more.

Sleep came eventually. Not gently. Not all at once.

The photograph of the Wall was better from the Eastern side.—J

She would go to the exhibition on Thursday. She already knew this. She'd known it the moment she read the card.

Two months. Then Berlin.

4

THE UNWRITTEN REPORT

London—October 1973—January 1975

London—October 1973. The morning after the gallery.

In the morning, Margaret Calder made breakfast. Eggs, toast, tea in the blue pot she bought at a market in Portobello the week after they were married. She was humming as she cracked the eggs—something tuneless, inherited from a mother she rarely spoke about. James sat at the kitchen table reading a newspaper and not seeing any of the words. He was thinking about a woman he met at a gallery opening. An art historian from New Zealand. Dark hair. She said something about a geranium that was not about a geranium.

Margaret asked if the exhibition had been interesting. He said it was. She asked if he'd met anyone memorable. He said he'd met a few people. Art historians. Academics. The usual crowd.

She set the eggs in front of him. She sat across from him. She watched him butter his toast with the care he gave to everything, and she noticed—because Margaret noticed things, had been noticing them since the morning he proposed and she said yes—that he was buttering it the way he buttered toast on the mornings after a difficult cable from a foreign station: with one hand on the cup of tea, anchoring himself against a thought he was not going to share. She had a Year Six register at school where children were marked present, absent, or late. Privately, when the staff room was empty, she had once added a fourth column called somewhere else. James was in the fourth column this morning. She did not say anything. She poured herself more tea.

He did not mention Alice Marsh by name. There was nothing yet to hide—only the dim sense that something might one day need hiding. The feeling he was carrying from last night —the unresolved awareness of having encountered someone who operated at his frequency—was still too new to have a shape. It was a signal without a classification. A frequency without a name.

He was walking toward it with the measured pace of a man who believed he was in control of the approach.

He wasn't. Neither was she.

A week passed before he moved. Then another handful of days. When he finally acted, the small gallery in Fitzrovia where he had met her was hosting an exhibition of post-war German painting, and the coincidence had the shape of permission. He bought an invitation card for fifty pence. He wrote four words on the back in fountain pen and addressed it to a woman whose home address he had spent an after-noon finding by methods his job did not authorize. He posted it on his way to a meeting he was already late for. He did not tell Margaret. He did not tell himself why.

She went to the exhibition on Thursday. He was already there.

This was how it began. November into December. Gallery cards appearing in her mailbox with the regularity of a tide schedule. Never the same gallery twice. Always a line on the back in fountain-pen handwriting—handwriting she was cataloging the way she read his vocal patterns and his posture and the small shift around his mouth when he was about to say something he hadn't planned. A reference to a prior conversation. A question she would need to see him to answer. Once, a single word: *Geraniums.* She stood in her kitchen reading that one and felt the real smile again—the uncontrolled one, the two-second one, the one that belonged to Elena rather than Alice. She was getting worse at stopping it.

November 1973. They saw each other at three exhibitions and one concert at Wigmore Hall. Brief encounters in public rooms. No phone numbers exchanged. No alone time. The slow build on both sides was deliberate. Elena because the approach required patience. Calder because he was married, and because he had not yet decided whether the approaching was a professional interest he could justify or a personal one he could not.

December 1973. The first dinner. A small restaurant in Kensington, candle-lit, tables far enough apart to prevent eavesdropping—a consideration both of them made without mentioning it. Two people professionally trained to read human behavior sitting across from each other and reading each other with the focused attention of scholars studying a text they suspected was a masterpiece but could not yet prove.

Elena learned his rhythms. The way he ordered wine—confidently, without consulting the list, always a red, never anything that cost more than the second-most-expensive bottle. The way he listened—with his whole body, his hands still, his eyes on hers with an intensity she found both flattering and diagnostic. His method of deflecting personal questions was redirection rather than evasion—pivoting back to her with a grace that felt like generosity. She was doing the same thing. They both knew it. Neither mentioned it.

She had not yet given Yuri a true account of him.

She would need to, soon. Moscow's authorization for continued observation of Target Nine was not the same as authorization for active cultivation, and what Elena was doing with Calder had moved well beyond observation. But each week she found a reason to delay the report. More data needed. Vulnerability profile incomplete. Status still under assessment. These were valid reasons. They were also lies. The real reason she delayed the report was that reporting it would turn Calder into an operation, and something in Elena was not ready for that. She was aware that the delay was itself a form of intelligence failure. She was aware of it and she was doing it anyway.

Saturday, 15 December 1973. Kensington Church Street.

Elena walked into the bookshop and found Calder standing at the history section with a woman in a blue scarf.

The woman was holding a stack of novels. She was looking at Calder with an expression Elena recognized immediately—because she'd spent her career studying the faces of people who did not know they were being studied. The expression was love. Uncomplicated, unguarded, domestic love.

Margaret Calder loved her husband the way geraniums grew: persistently, without drama, requiring very little and providing more than anyone bothered to notice.

Elena saw all of this in four seconds. Feeling something took longer.

Calder spotted her. His face did something complicated—a rapid sequence of recognition, pleasure, alarm, calculation, resolving in under a second into the warm neutral expression of a man encountering an acquaintance. He was very good.

'Alice,' he said. 'What a coincidence. This is my wife, Margaret. Margaret, this is Alice Marsh—we met at a gallery opening a few weeks ago. She's an art historian.'

Margaret turned to Elena with the open expression of a woman who had no reason to suspect anything. Her handshake was firm. Her eyes met Elena's without the faintest trace of territorial suspicion. 'How lovely to meet you,' she said. 'James never tells me about the people he meets at these things. I'm starting to think he goes just for the wine.' She touched his arm without looking. 'He keeps the interesting ones to himself.'

Elena laughed. Alice Marsh's laugh—warm, easy, slightly self-deprecating. 'The wine at gallery openings is usually terrible,' she said. 'I go for the arguments about brushwork.'

They talked for five minutes. Calder stood between them with the stillness of a man aware that two parts of his life had just met. Elena asked about the novels. Margaret asked about Flemish portraiture. Elena provided a three-minute summary of her thesis that was genuine, engaging, and designed to establish Alice Marsh as an intelligent but unthreatening presence in Margaret's social landscape.

'That's beautiful,' Margaret said. She was touching the silver cat on her bracelet without noticing. 'I always wondered why those Dutch painters kept painting the same rooms. I thought they ran out of ideas. You're telling me the rooms were the idea.' She laughed at herself, a low easy laugh. 'James, why don't you bring home things like this? I read a novel a week looking for the feeling Alice just gave me in thirty seconds.'

'You read novels, I read files,' Calder said lightly.

'And you wonder why I'm starving,' Margaret said—still light, still teasing—and there was a real hunger in it that Elena heard clearly.

Margaret filed something then. Not consciously. The filing was the kind Margaret did at school when a student answered a question too well, with a vocabulary a little too adult for the question asked. She logged Alice Marsh's kindness the way she filed those answers: as a thing that was pleasant and slightly elsewhere at the same time. The sensation passed in a second. Margaret's register had a fourth column for it, and the fourth column had never yet, in Margaret's adult life, been wrong. She did not know she was filing anything. She reached up and adjusted the blue scarf against a draft that was not there, which was what her hands did when her mind was processing at a depth her face was not advertising. Then she laughed at something Calder said, and the filing closed, and the moment was done.

By the time they parted, Margaret had invited Alice to a dinner party she and James were hosting in January.

Elena accepted. She said it would be lovely. She meant it in a way she could not justify, and the meaning joined the card and the smile and the shortbread.

The dinner party was for the second Saturday in January. Elena would be in Berlin by then. She would have to invent a reason to withdraw—a family emergency in New Zealand, a cousin's sudden illness, plausible fiction Alice Marsh could produce without strain. Margaret would be disappointed. Margaret would be gracious about it. Margaret would set out the extra place setting anyway, the way kind people did, and quietly clear it after the guests had forgotten Alice Marsh's name.

She thought about the bracelet. The four charms—the book, the silver cat, the heart, the letter M—and the small empty ring beside the M. The unfilled space had been there long enough for the clasp to have darkened at its edges. Margaret had been saving it for something. A fifth charm. A future. The kind of small specific future women like Margaret kept in the quiet corners of bracelets, in the expectation that the life they were already living would, in due course, mint its own next coin.

She walked home through Kensington with the weight of a woman who had just met the wife of the man she was about to seduce and found that the wife was kind. The weight was not guilt. Elena had been trained out of guilt. What she felt instead was something closer to geometry. The shape of the operation had changed. It now included Margaret. And Margaret had, in one fourth-column second at the bookshop, registered the outline of a thing she did not yet have a word for, and had chosen—because kind people chose this—to not look too carefully at it.

And the filing had not been the filing of a pleasant woman who had registered nothing. Margaret had registered something—a half-second long, meant to be invisible. Elena saw it because Elena had been trained, by other work, to see exactly that kind of seeing. Margaret's fourth column was not a passive shelf. It was a working drawer.

Elena did not enjoy complicated shapes. Complicated shapes were where operations went wrong.

The Stasi delayed the secondment twice. Yuri said it was bureaucratic. Elena did not ask whose bureau. Two months became six, then ten, then a year, and each extension was another month of Alice Marsh's life she was not supposed to have.

She met Yuri at rotating cafés. The conversations were the same conversations with different tablecloths. Target Nine remained cultivatable. His marriage was stable. Moscow was patient. Once, Yuri said *A kind wife extends the life of a cover* in the same tone he ordered coffee, and Elena understood he had been instructed to say it and that he knew she knew. The question inside the question was whether she was becoming reliable inside Alice Marsh or unreliable inside Elena. She gave the answer operations required. He did not sound convinced. He did not sound unconvinced. Yuri rarely sounded either.

She wrote twenty-two pages about what Target Nine did at his desk. She did not write that she had memorized his hands.

Hampstead Heath, London—November 1974. A Sunday.

He took her walking that morning. Margaret was visiting a sister in Kent. The air smelled of wet leaves and coal smoke. They walked the ponds in a silence that had begun, over the preceding year, to accommodate the things neither of them said. He had bought her a coffee from a kiosk at the edge of the park. She carried it with both hands through gloves she had not worn the previous year.

'I read something last week,' he said, 'that I wanted to ask you about.'

She waited.

'A small news item out of Italy. A magistrate in Palermo. Three weeks from a warrant about a shipping manifest. His car exploded outside his own house.'

Elena's hands did not move. Her pace did not change. Her breath did.

'The press attributed it to the Red Brigades,' Calder said. 'But I was reading a file last month—something else, something unrelated, I thought—and I came across a protocol number that shouldn't have been in a file about a magistrate in Palermo. It was a NATO protocol number. Small detail. Probably nothing.'

He was looking at a duck on the pond. He was not looking at her.

'I wondered,' he said, 'whether that kind of detail is the sort of thing an art historian ever thinks about. Whether, in your work, a number in the wrong place feels like the number in the wrong place.'

The moment took about four seconds and Elena used two of them to understand what was being offered. Calder was not asking her a question. He was telling her, in the only vocabulary available to him on a Sunday afternoon with his wife in Kent, that he had been looking at the same shape. He did not have the full shape. Neither did she. What they had was the recognition that the shape existed, and that each of them had seen it from a different side of a wall that was not in any atlas.

She could have said many things. She thought about the one Alice Marsh would say. She thought about the one Elena Vasilieva would say. She arrived at a third thing, which was neither.

'A number in the wrong place,' she said, 'is sometimes the number in the right place. It depends on whether you trust the file the number came from.'

Calder nodded once. Slowly. He did not ask her what she had meant. She did not ask him what he had meant.

They walked another hundred meters in silence. A dog ran past them with a stick in its mouth. His glove, inside his coat pocket, found her gloved hand. He did not look at her when he did this. She did not look at him.

She understood, walking beside him along a pond in a London park on a Sunday afternoon in November, that the thing between them had just acquired its second topic. The first topic had been themselves—the slow reading of each other's bodies and voices and rooms. The second topic was the shape. The shape was larger than either of them and neither of them had named it, and neither of them, she suspected, ever would.

She understood also that she was going to Berlin in eight weeks and that she was going to miss him in a way that operational vocabulary did not include.

She let him hold her hand.

A fortnight later he gave her a watch for a birthday she had invented. A gold Omega on a small leather strap. She put it on the inside of her left wrist, where the compass rose was, and she wore it every day after that.

By the time the new year arrived, the report was still unwritten, and Elena was still meeting Calder twice a week, and Berlin was twelve days away.

London—Tuesday, early January 1975. Six days before Berlin.

The day broke in two halves. The first half was operational. The second half was not.

The first half was a dead drop in Hampstead Heath.

She had used the same courier for fourteen months. Dmitri Volkov, Soviet trade delegation. They met every six weeks at rotating sites. They were never at the site at the same time. The packages looked, to anyone who might glance at them, like rubbish.

On the walk to the Heath that morning, Elena noticed a man.

He was sitting on a bench on South End Road, fifty meters from the entrance she planned to use. Gray coat, open newspaper, a takeaway coffee balanced on the armrest. He was reading the paper with the absorbed attention of someone who was either genuinely reading or performing absorption for the benefit of an observer. The distinction was invisible at fifty meters.

She walked past him. She did not change pace. She continued two hundred meters past the Heath entrance and turned left onto a residential street and stopped at a newsagent's window as if looking at the postcard display. In the glass she could see the street behind her. No one had followed. She walked a full rectangle—south on Downshire Hill, west on Keats Grove, north on Heath Street, east back to South End

Road. An eight-minute circuit that would surface any tail running a parallel route.

The man was still on the bench. Same newspaper. The coffee moved from the armrest to his left hand. He'd turned two pages. His shoes were wrong for surveillance—brown leather, thin-soled, the shoes of a man who hadn't expected to be outside for long. His posture was wrong too—slumped, with the heaviness of someone whose morning had become a problem he had not yet decided how to solve.

Elena logged him as civilian and entered the Heath through the south gate.

The drop site was a bench near the bathing ponds. Elena arrived at 14:15, seven minutes before her scheduled window. She walked the approach route at her standard pace—neither hurried nor leisurely, the pace of a woman taking an afternoon walk in a London park because London parks were what you walked in when the weather was decent and you had an hour to spare.

She saw the tail at 14:18.

He was good. Better than good—he was disciplined enough that a less experienced operative might have missed him entirely. He was walking approximately eighty meters behind Volkov, who was approaching the bench from the opposite direction. The tail was wearing a waxed jacket and carrying a folded newspaper and projecting the body language of a man on a casual walk, and all of this was executed with a competence that told Elena he was MI5.

Elena's heart rate increased by twelve beats per minute. The body's preparation for rapid decision-making under conditions where the margin for error was measured in seconds. She'd trained for this. She rehearsed this scenario dozens of times at the Red Banner Institute and once, memorably, in Helsinki, when a Finnish counter-intelligence team walked past a dead drop she was servicing and she kept walking without changing pace or direction and the Finns never looked at her twice.

She had thirty seconds to make a decision.

Option one: proceed. Twenty meters, one package, keep walking. If MI5 was tailing Volkov and not surveilling the site, the drop might go unnoticed. But might was not a word that survived contact with MI5's methodology. They would photograph the bench. They would recover the package. Elena would be a woman seen near a Soviet dead drop on the afternoon it was serviced—a coincidence MI5 did not believe in.

Option two: abort. Walk past the bench. Do not stop. Do not slow down. Give the abort signal and let Volkov see it and trust that he would respond correctly.

Twenty seconds.

Elena adjusted her scarf.

The gesture was small. A woman reaching up with her right hand to adjust the position of a wool scarf around her neck. The movement took less than two seconds. To the MI5 officer trailing Volkov—if he was even looking in her direction, which he probably was not, because his attention was on his target and not on a random woman walking in the opposite direction—it was nothing. A cold person adjusting her clothing.

To Volkov, it was an abort signal. Right hand, scarf, two-second contact. The signal had been established months earlier and had never been used. Today it was used.

Elena kept walking. She did not look at Volkov. She did not look at the bench. She did not look at the MI5 officer. She walked past all three of them at the same pace she'd been maintaining since she entered the park, with the same body language, the same facial expression, the same unremarkable Tuesday-afternoon-in-Hampstead-Heath energy she'd been projecting since she came through the gate.

She walked for another four hundred meters and exited through the south gate. A bus stop. A bus to Kensington. Home. The door locked behind her. She sat down on the edge of her bed.

Her hands were steady. They'd been steady throughout. They did not shake now. The assessment was clear: the abort was successful, the package was still in her coat pocket, Volkov received the signal and walked past the bench without stopping, and the MI5 tail continued following Volkov with no indication that the dead drop had been detected.

Elena sat on the edge of her bed for eleven minutes without moving. She was not processing the implications—those were already processed, already filed, already categorized as a near-miss requiring a change in courier protocols and drop-site rotation. She was processing something else. Something that surfaced during the thirty seconds of decision-making and that she'd suppressed in real time because real time did not accommodate the feeling she was having.

If the abort had failed—if MI5 had identified her today on a bench in Hampstead Heath—she would never have seen James Calder again. Not as Alice Marsh, not as Elena Vasilieva, not as anyone. The machinery would have consumed her. Moscow would have extracted her or abandoned her, and either way the result would have been the same. The half-second in the gallery. The card in the drawer. The geraniums. Gone. All of it. As if it had never happened.

Elena sat on the edge of her bed and she understood, with the clinical precision of a woman who'd been trained to recognize the symptoms of emotional compromise, that she was compromised.

She picked up the phone and called Calder. She told him she had a free evening. He said he would pick her up at seven.

She hung up. She pressed her palm against the cold surface of the phone's receiver and closed her eyes. She allowed herself, for exactly ten seconds, to feel the thing she'd been refusing to feel since October.

Then she opened her eyes. And she got ready for the second half of the day.

She wore a dress she hadn't worn before. Dark green, close-fitting, chosen not by Alice Marsh but by Elena Vasilieva, a distinction that would have alarmed her if she'd allowed herself to acknowledge it. She did not acknowledge it. She wore the dress.

He took her to a small restaurant in Marylebone that smelled of candle wax and white wine, the kind of place where the maître d' seated couples at tables with candles and did not rush them. The dinner was good. The wine was good. Calder was good—funny, attentive, alive in a way Elena hadn't seen in him before, as if some internal decision had been made and the energy that had been going into making the decision was now available for other purposes.

He talked about music. He talked about a concert he attended alone because Margaret didn't like jazz, and the aloneness had felt specific rather than general, and he'd sat in the audience thinking about a woman he met at a gallery who would have understood what the saxophone was doing in the second movement.

He was talking about Elena. He was telling her this without saying her name. She heard it.

The room was warm and the wine was in her blood and for a moment—a moment she would later identify as the precise instant her operational discipline began to fracture in ways that could not be repaired—she wanted to tell him the truth. Not the whole truth. Not the Leningrad truth or the KGB truth or the truth about the man she'd killed in a kitchen in Lillehammer while a waiter bled out six blocks south. Just one truth. Her real name. Two syllables. Elena. She wanted to hear him say it.

She did not tell him. She drank her wine. She smiled at him across the candle with Alice Marsh's face. The truth retreated to wherever truths go when they are not welcome, and the performance continued, and the evening progressed toward its obvious conclusion.

His flat. A different flat, not the one he shared with Margaret. A studio in Fitzrovia that he described, with the casual specificity of a prepared lie, as a space he used when he worked late. Elena understood what the flat was: an operational space, the kind of place intelligence officers kept for things that could not happen at home. She did not mention this understanding. She let him unlock the door. She let him offer her a drink.

The flat had the deliberate spareness of an operational space. A small desk in the corner held two folders and a locked drawer whose contents announced themselves the way an unplayed key announces itself to a pianist.

She had one hundred and seventy-eight frames left on the current load. She had forty seconds before Calder came back with the drinks. A trained illegal could photograph twelve pages in forty seconds. Two years of preparation in Leningrad, six months of refresher training in Moscow, and Yuri's quiet satisfaction when he placed the lighter on the café table —all of it was pointing at the top folder on the desk.

Her eye went to the folder beside the top one instead. Unmarked. Manila. The flap was not fully closed and the uppermost page was visible above the rim—not a page at all but a clipping from an Italian newspaper, glued onto backing paper, with a Rome dateline from July 1971. The headline read *Incidente nelle miniere* in the compressed typography of a third-of-the-way-down-page-four story. Mercury in an Apennine village. Twelve dead. The article was a few years old.

She had seen the headline before. Another kitchen, another night, a salt shaker and a question she had not let herself ask.

Calder had clipped it anyway. Calder was keeping it in a folder on his operational desk, in a flat kept for this kind of work, in a city that neither of them lived in the same way twice. Calder had been reading, for at least three and a half years, the same silences Elena had been reading.

She had always suspected this about him. She had suspected it since the half-second in the gallery. She had not, until now, had physical evidence. The physical evidence was in a manila envelope beside the folder she had been sent to photograph, and she was looking at it, and she was not photographing the folder either.

Elena turned away from the desk. The Fitzrovia street below was quiet. She could hear Calder in the kitchen. She had four minutes. She did not open the drawer. The not-opening was a decision she filed alongside the Apennine clipping and the thing in Calder's file that did not yet have a name she could write in any report Moscow would accept.

Her hand had moved toward the drawer before her mind had been consulted. The hand had stopped without her stopping it. She stood in the dark of a Fitzrovia studio with her hand at her side and understood, in the clean way that operational truths arrived, that she had just refused an order. The order had not been issued aloud. The order had been issued by every instructor she had ever had. The refusal was the first one. There would be more.

Calder came back with the drinks. She let the evening arrive at the place it had been heading since October.

He kissed her in the hallway. Not suddenly. Gradually, the way everything between them happened, with the patient, deliberate approach of two people who'd been circling each other for fifteen months and understood that the circling was part of the architecture. His hands found her waist. His mouth found hers. He kissed her the way he did everything: with attention, with focus, with the quality of presence that drew her to him in the first place. He was not performing. Or if he was, the performance was indistinguishable from the thing it imitated—the same problem Elena had been having with her own performance for weeks.

The hallway was dark. The flat smelled like clean laundry and old books and the faint, mineral scent of London tap water. Elena's back was against the wall. Her hands were in his hair—shorter than she expected, coarser, the texture of it a surprise. He was warm. The radiative warmth of a man's body against hers after fifteen months of proximity without contact. The warmth traveled through the fabric of her dress and into her skin and settled somewhere in her chest, in the place where she kept the things she didn't file. Behind her shoulder blade, a hairline crack in the plaster pressed against her spine. She would remember it, later, as the only part of the flat that had been honest with her.

His hands moved down her back and settled on her hips and pulled her against him. The pulling was not gentle. The not-gentle was the first honest thing his body had said in fifteen months. She felt the curve of his backside under her palms—hard, tensed, the body of a man bracing himself against a wall with a woman pressed against him—and the filing system tried to categorize the sensation and could not.

They moved to the bedroom. She let him lead. Not because she was passive—Elena was never passive—but because letting him lead was itself a choice, a strategic decision to allow him the illusion of control while she observed the way he exercised it. The way a man takes you to bed tells you everything his conversation conceals. These were not casual observations. They were intelligence.

Calder was present. Acutely, almost uncomfortably present. He undressed her with the deliberate care of a man who was aware that what he was removing was not just fabric but a layer of the barrier between them, and who wanted her to know that he understood this. His fingers found the zip at the back of the green dress. He paused. His mouth was on her neck and his fingers were on the zip and he paused, and the pause was a question, and she answered it by reaching behind herself and pulling the zip down the rest of the way.

The dress fell. She was standing in his bedroom in the dark in her underwear—a black bra, the underwear of a woman who had expected to go home alone and whose body was therefore unscripted, hers—and he was looking at her with an expression she'd never seen directed at Alice Marsh. The expression was hunger, but not the uncomplicated physical hunger she encountered in previous targets. This was hunger mixed with something else. Recognition. As if he were seeing, for the first time, something he'd suspected was there but hadn't been able to confirm until now.

She pulled his shirt over his head. His chest was lean—the body of a man who ran but did not lift. A scar on his left side, just above the hip—old, surgical, something he would explain years later in a story about a training exercise in Hereford that she would file and never forget. She ran her hand across his stomach. The skin was warm. The hair below his navel was dark and fine and her fingers followed it downward and she felt him inhale.

His fingers traced the tattoo along her ribcage. The Akhmatova line. He could not read it—the room was too dark and the script was Cyrillic and he did not speak Russian, or at least hadn't admitted to speaking Russian, which Elena noted even now, even here, even with his hand on her skin. He traced the letters without asking what they said. The restraint was either respect or strategy. In Calder, she was beginning to understand, these were the same thing.

What followed was slow. Specific. Elena always knew what she was doing.

But there was a moment, near the end, when his hand was in her hair and his breathing changed to the pattern she now recognized as the one he used when he was no longer thinking, and she realized that her own breathing had changed too.

The hand in her hair was the hand of a man who did not know what he was touching. Or: the hand of a man who'd decided not to ask. The woman beneath the hand was not entirely Alice Marsh.

Elena noted this the way a pilot notes the first vibration in an engine that has always been smooth. The filing system had gone quiet, and there was nothing in its place except sensation and the warm, dark, uncomplicated fact of another person's body against hers.

The moment lasted perhaps three seconds. Then the filing system came back on.

He whispered something against her throat. A name. Her name—Alice. She heard it the way you hear a word in a language you almost speak: with comprehension but without belief. He was saying the name of a woman who did not exist while lying in bed with a woman he'd never met. She kissed him again because kissing him was easier than thinking about the distance between those two things.

Afterward, she lay with her back against his chest. She could feel him softening against the curve of her lower back. His hand on her hip.

She had never let a target hold her from behind. She was permitting it. Between her thighs the warmth was still present—specific, unhurried, the body's own record, written in a language the filing system had no alphabet for. The fine hair on his wrist touching the fine hair on her belly, the touch so small and so involuntary that Elena felt it as pure sensation, arriving at a body that was, for this moment, just a body. She could feel his heartbeat through his wrist. The pulses were getting further apart. The trusting made her throat tight.

'What were you doing in Norway,' he said, against her hair. Not a question. A statement that had a question inside it.

'Walking,' she said. 'A lake. Rain that turned to snow. I was twenty-five and I thought I would never be that cold again.'

He was quiet for perhaps eight seconds. His thumb moved once against the bone of her hip. 'I was in Berlin,' he said. 'In the summer of that year. I understand the cold.'

She closed her eyes. They said nothing else.

Then the operational mind returned.

The performance had mostly held. She'd been Alice Marsh throughout—responsive, warm, present in the ways that Alice would be present. But the three seconds when the filing system had gone dark, and she'd been no one except a woman in a bed with a man she wanted to be in bed with—those had been real. And real things, in Elena's profession, were the most dangerous things of all.

She left at 4 AM—dressed in the dark, kissed his forehead, which was an Alice Marsh gesture and which also, to her considerable alarm, felt like an Elena gesture. She walked home through London in the early morning cold, and she composed her report to Yuri as she walked, and the report was clinical and precise and it described the successful initiation of a physical relationship with Target Nine. It did not mention the three seconds or the crack in the wall, or how, when he traced the Akhmatova tattoo without asking what it meant, she'd wanted him to ask.

By the time she reached her flat the sky was beginning to gray over Kensington. Six days. She had six days left in this city. Six days left in this name. Six days left in the small, contained, almost-livable life that Alice Marsh built and that Elena Vasilieva was about to leave behind in a drawer beside a card and a diary that wasn't hers.

She let herself in. She locked the door. She did not go to bed.

Elena sat at her kitchen table in the gray morning light and began the second draft of the report—the one she was going to send.

She wrote in English. She wrote in the handwriting that was not hers. She set the pen down and looked at what she had written, and what she had not.

Then she opened the drawer beside the stove. The card was there. The diary. The reel she could not bring herself to destroy. She took the card out and held it in her palm for a moment, the fountain-pen ink catching the gray morning light. She did not read it. She knew what it said.

She put it back. She closed the drawer.

The first draft, the true one, she kept in her head. She would carry it to Berlin. She would not write it down. It was not a report Moscow had asked for. It was not a report Moscow would read.

The first words were older than Alice Marsh. And the institution that would receive it, for the rest of her operational life, was herself.

ACT II

BERLIN APPRENTICESHIP

1975—1977

5

NORMANNENSTRASSE

East Berlin—January 1975

The cold in East Berlin was a different species from the cold in London.

Elena lived inside the design choice for two weeks.

She attended two embassy receptions, a film screening at the House of Soviet Culture, three cultural-liaison meetings at which she took notes about events nobody would ever read about. She bought bread. She walked along the Spree. The Red Banner Institute had trained her to dismantle journalists and recruit defectors; she was, in East Berlin, queuing for rolls behind women whose shoes had been resoled more than once.

The summons came on a Thursday in January, on Stasi letterhead, requesting her presence at Normannenstraße at 1 PM. No rank. No greeting. No signature beyond a stamped initial she could not identify. The preceding year had been waiting. They hadn't introduced her to the Hatch file. They hadn't introduced her to anyone who mattered. She had begun to suspect she was being assessed by absence—by who failed to speak to her—and had stopped asking herself when the assessment would end and the work would begin.

The letter told her the answer: today.

She thought about the day she crossed the border. It had been a Thursday in January then too—she had come by train from West Berlin, through the control at Friedrichstraße station that East Germans called the Palace of Tears because it was where they said goodbye to visiting relatives who could leave and they could not. The Western half of the city was the American sector. The Eastern half was the Stasi's. The Wall ran between them, and Friedrichstraße was one of the few seams the institutions had agreed to let civilians pass through. The name was accurate.

Elena had walked through the checkpoint under a Soviet diplomatic credential that identified her as Irina Sokolova, a cultural liaison attached to the Soviet embassy in East Berlin. The name was not an accident. She chose it herself, as operatives of her rank were permitted to do for short-term cover identities. Irina. The woman whose laugh could fill a hallway. The woman Petrov had killed by selling her name. Elena carried the name through Friedrichstraße like a stone in her pocket, small and heavy and private, and she had been carrying it without once putting it down.

That was a year ago. The letter was today.

At 12:30 she put on her coat—the dark wool she wore in Berlin, not the London camel—and walked to Bruhn's building. The guard at the entrance checked her pass with an expression that had settled into patience the way plaster settles into a mold.

Stasi headquarters occupied a complex of buildings in Lichtenberg with the aesthetic personality of a tax office designed by someone who disliked architecture. Concrete and glass, set back behind a fence and a guard post. It did not project power through grandeur. It projected power through its refusal to project anything.

Elena was escorted through three security checkpoints. Her Soviet credentials carried the institutional weight of a superpower. She passed each checkpoint without incident. The corridors were long and smelled like floor polish and cigarette smoke. She was led to an office on the fourth floor. The door was unmarked. The man behind the desk stood when she entered.

Major Werner Bruhn was not what she expected.

She suspected, from the two seconds his eyes took to complete their assessment of her, the reverse was also true. His gaze moved the way Stasi gazes moved—efficiently, without social performance. She could see him registering the data points: young, dark-haired, the jawline that every handler mentioned in their reports and that she'd stopped noticing. Bruhn held her gaze a half-second longer than the rest of the inventory required.

Bruhn was dangerous.

Elena knew this within ten seconds of entering his office. Not from anything he said—he had not yet spoken—but from the way he occupied space. He was a compact man with the build of someone who had been physical once and since traded muscle for stillness. His eyes were the detail that mattered. When he looked at Elena, she felt the uncomfortable sensation of being read by someone who was using the same operating system she used.

He did not extend his hand. He gestured to a chair across from his desk. The desk was clean. No papers, no files, no photographs. A single telephone. An ashtray that had been emptied recently. A cup of coffee that was still warm, which told Elena he'd been waiting for her and had timed his coffee accordingly.

One drawer of the desk was slightly warped. It did not close flush with the frame; the top edge projected perhaps a millimeter. Bruhn had positioned himself so that his left hand could rest on the desk in a way that concealed it. The drawer was the only imperfect object in the room. Elena noted it without commenting. A man whose desk was perfect except for one flaw he was hiding was a man who had made a decision about which flaws were permitted.

'Sit,' he said. His voice was quiet. Not soft—quiet, the way Calder's voice was quiet. He spoke Russian. His accent was precise—not native but trained, the product of years of study rather than immersion. He straightened a pen on his desk that did not need straightening—the small involuntary gesture of a man who preferred his surfaces aligned. 'We have a great deal to discuss and I prefer to do it efficiently.'

Elena sat. She matched his energy. She projected competence and receptivity without eagerness—the tone Moscow had instructed her to maintain with Stasi liaison officers. Her role was to learn from Bruhn while subtly communicating that she was not subordinate to him. It was a social maneuver she could have performed in her sleep.

While she performed it, she thought briefly about the man whose destruction she was here to design.

Tom Hatch had a face. She'd seen it once, in the small byline photograph that had run with his *Observer* piece on arms brokers in Cyprus—perhaps mid-thirties, narrow shoulders, the wry tilt at the corner of his mouth of a man who had been caught by the photographer in the middle of disagreeing with something. She liked the mouth. She had noted the byline because Hatch wrote the way a good analyst wrote: with the assumption that every source was lying for their own reasons and the job was to triangulate until the truth fell out of the arithmetic. A patient man. A man who did not mind taking years. The wrong kind of man, from Moscow's perspective, to be standing at the edge of a board they had thought was no longer in play.

Bruhn opened a drawer and removed a file. The file was thin —perhaps twenty pages. It was bound in a gray cover with no markings. He placed it on the desk between them with the care of a man placing something fragile.

'You have been told about the Hatch assignment,' he said. Not a question. 'Moscow believes you are ready for Operative Psychology. I have been asked to prepare you.' He paused. He looked at her with those reading eyes. 'Moscow's assessment is that you have natural aptitude. I will determine whether Moscow's assessment is accurate.'

She did not react to the challenge. She waited.

Bruhn pushed the file toward her.

'*Zersetzung*,' he said.

The word translated, roughly, as decomposition. In the context of the Stasi, it was engineered.

Bruhn did not lecture. He spoke the way a chess instructor speaks—describing positions, demonstrating consequences, asking questions designed not to test knowledge but to reveal the quality of the student's thinking. He opened the gray file and walked Elena through three case studies.

Case One. A university professor in Leipzig who wore the same brown corduroy jacket to every lecture and who had signed a petition criticizing government housing policy. Not a dissident—the petition was mild, the criticism was constructive, and the professor's record was otherwise impeccable. The Stasi did not arrest him. Arrest would have created a martyr, and martyrs were expensive. Instead, they ran a Zersetzung campaign that lasted fourteen months.

The campaign began with small things. His office was entered at night. Nothing was taken—things were moved. Papers rearranged. A drawer left open that he was certain he had closed. A book reversed so its spine faced inward. Each incident trivial. Each incident designed to produce the same specific psychological effect: doubt about his own memory, his own grip on physical reality.

Then it escalated. Anonymous letters to his colleagues questioning his competence, written in a voice close enough to the professor's own to be plausible. A rumor circulated through three independent channels that he had been seen drinking alone at unusual hours. His car developed problems that defied diagnosis. His wife received phone calls in which the caller breathed for thirty seconds and hung up. A photograph of his daughter at school arrived in the mail with no note.

After nine months, the professor requested a leave of absence for health reasons. After twelve months, he was seeing a psychiatrist. After fourteen months, he resigned his position. The petition was withdrawn. No arrest was made. No trial was conducted. No official action was taken. The professor's colleagues believed he had suffered a nervous breakdown brought on by overwork. His wife believed the same thing. The professor himself, in his darker moments, believed it too. The Stasi's file on the operation concluded with a single sentence that Bruhn read aloud: 'Target has been rendered operationally irrelevant through self-generated doubt.'

Elena listened with the cold admiration of a professional encountering excellence in a field she understood. The Red Banner Institute had not prepared her for this.

She did not say this. She asked a question instead.

'The letters to his colleagues,' she said. 'How did you replicate his academic voice without access to a substantial sample of his writing?'

Bruhn looked at her. The reading eyes sharpened. She'd asked the right question. Not the obvious question—the obvious question was about the ethics, or the legality, or the human cost. The right question was about the craft. About how the thing was done. About the mechanism.

'We didn't replicate it,' he said. 'We had access to years of his published papers, his internal university correspondence, and seven personal letters intercepted from his mail. The linguistic profile was constructed by a specialist in my department who had studied his syntax for two months before writing the first anonymous letter.'

Bruhn paused, watching to see whether Elena had followed the distinction. She had.

'The letters did not imitate his voice. They were written in a voice that was adjacent to his—close enough to be plausible, different enough to be deniable. The recipients were not linguists. They did not perform textual analysis. They read a letter that sounded like someone they knew and they formed an impression. That impression was the operation.'

Elena nodded. Zersetzung did not require the target to believe anything specific. It required the target's environment to become unreliable. The target would do the rest. The smarter the target, the more effectively they rationalized their own destruction.

She understood this because she had, without knowing the name for it, been doing a version of it to everyone she had ever operated against. The psychological profiling. The social network mapping. The calibrated manipulation of a target's information environment to produce a desired behavioral outcome. She'd learned these skills at the Red Banner Institute and refined them in the field. What Bruhn was giving her was the name.

Bruhn saw this. She could tell because his posture changed—a subtle shift, a quarter-inch of relaxation in his shoulders that communicated, in the body language of a man who did not relax casually, that his assessment of her had just been revised upward. He had expected to teach her. He was realizing that he was going to refine something that was already built.

'Moscow's assessment was accurate,' he said. He closed the gray file. He opened a second one.

Case Two was a pastor in Dresden. Nine months: social fracture from inside the congregation, ending in transfer to a smaller church. He never knew he had been targeted.

Case Three was different. Case Three was a woman.

Her name was Katarina. She was a schoolteacher in Rostock who had applied for an exit visa to join her sister in West Germany. The application was denied, which was standard. What was not standard was Katarina's response: she applied again. And again. And again. Seven times over two years, each application more detailed than the last, each one citing the human-rights framework the GDR had endorsed at the Conference on Security and Cooperation in Europe—provisions that, on paper, guaranteed freedom of movement. She was not a dissident. She was not political. She was a schoolteacher who wanted to live near her sister and who had the quiet stubbornness of a person who believed that rules meant what they said.

The Stasi's Zersetzung campaign against Katarina was the most personal of the three cases. They targeted her relationship with her students. Anonymous complaints were filed with the school's administration suggesting that her teaching methods were ideologically unreliable. The complaints came through *Inoffizielle Mitarbeiter*—the Stasi's vast network of civilian informants, neighbors and colleagues who reported on each other and rarely knew which of their reports fed which operations. Her lesson plans were subjected to review. Colleagues who had previously supported her distanced themselves. Her boyfriend received a visit from a man who identified himself as a concerned parent and who described, in terms that were specific enough to be alarming and vague enough to be deniable, certain aspects of Katarina's personal life that she had shared only with people she trusted.

The boyfriend left. The school transferred her. The exit visa applications stopped.

Bruhn presented this case with the same clinical detachment he had applied to the others. Elena listened with the same professional attention. But something was different with Case Three. Something registered in a part of Elena's mind that the training was supposed to have sealed off. Katarina was a schoolteacher. She wanted to see her sister. She'd done nothing except exercise a right that her government had formally agreed to recognize. And the machinery had consumed her. Not with violence. Not with arrest. With the patient, invisible cruelty of a system that understood people well enough to destroy them without leaving marks.

Elena thought about the woman on the balcony in the photograph. The curtains next to the death strip. The geranium that kept growing. She thought about Katarina in Rostock, going to school every morning to teach children whose parents had been told, through channels that could not be traced, that their teacher was not to be trusted.

She filed it carefully, in the place where she kept things that were too heavy to carry in the open. The shortbread. The card. The half-second. Katarina.

Bruhn was watching her. She did not know what he saw. She hoped he saw competence.

He closed the files. He placed them in the drawer. He lit a cigarette—the first he had smoked during the briefing. The briefing was doctrine. What came next was assessment.

'You have questions,' he said. Not asking. Stating. His cigarette smoke rose in a thin line toward the ceiling. The office had no windows. The ventilation was inadequate. This was almost certainly deliberate.

Elena did have questions. She had thirty, organized by priority, subcategorized by tactical relevance and personal interest. She chose the one that would tell Bruhn the most about what kind of operative she was.

'The professor in Leipzig,' she said. 'How long before he stopped trusting his own memory?'

Bruhn's mouth did something that was not quite a smile. It was the expression of a man who has received confirmation of something he suspected but needed to verify. She'd asked the right question again.

He did not answer immediately. The pause was not hesitation. It was the smaller pause of a man who had answered this particular question a hundred times and who, for reasons that had to do with the student in the chair across from him, was considering the answer rather than retrieving it. Half a second. No more. Elena noticed. She did not comment.

'Six weeks,' Bruhn said. 'The first six weeks are the most important. If the environmental changes are subtle enough and consistent enough, the target's mind begins to generate its own explanations. Stress. Overwork. Age. The mind will choose any explanation that preserves its sense of agency. The last explanation it will consider is the correct one—that someone is systematically dismantling the reliability of its own perception.'

He tapped the ash from his cigarette into the small brass ashtray at his right elbow. He did this with the same economy of motion he used for everything—no wasted gesture. Then he continued.

'By the time the target begins to suspect external interference, the self-doubt is already structural. It cannot be removed because it has been integrated into the target's self-model. They carry it the way they carry their own name.'

Elena absorbed this. She understood it not as abstract doctrine but as applicable knowledge. She could see Tom Hatch in a London flat at 2 AM, opening a drawer to find his files slightly rearranged, wondering if he'd left them that way, deciding that he must have, because the alternative was unthinkable. She could see the alternative becoming thinkable, gradually, over weeks and months, as the small changes accumulated into a pattern that his rational mind would refuse to acknowledge and his subconscious mind would refuse to ignore.

She could see herself designing this. And the part of her that recognized professional excellence in any field—the part that had admired the Makarov PB's suppression mechanism and the Alice Marsh passport's biographical depth and the way Calder scanned a room while removing his coat—that part admired Zersetzung. It was extraordinary. It was the most refined application of human psychological knowledge to the problem of human destruction that she had ever encountered.

She also understood, in the same moment and with the same clarity, that she was about to become someone who did this. Not as a hypothetical. Not as a training exercise. As a profession. She was going to walk out of this office and begin building a campaign to psychologically dismantle a British journalist whose only crime was asking questions the machinery did not want answered yet. She was going to do it because she was good at it. Because the institution had made 'good at it' the only identity she'd left that still fit.

The confirmation settled into her body the way the East Berlin cold had settled into the concrete outside—not arriving but revealing itself, as if it had always been there.

'I'm ready,' she said.

Bruhn studied her for a long moment. The cigarette had burned to the filter. He extinguished it in the ashtray with a single, precise motion.

'Yes,' he said. 'I believe you are.'

He walked her to the door. At the threshold the reading eyes softened—not the look of a teacher, but the look of a man who had recognized a traveling companion. He opened the door without naming the road either of them was walking.

She left the building at 4 PM. The January dark was already settling over East Berlin, turning the gray buildings grayer and the cold air colder. The driver was waiting with the Wartburg. Elena told him she would walk. He looked at her with the uncertain expression of a man who had not been briefed on this contingency. She told him again. He drove away.

She walked through Lichtenberg. The streets were quiet. Workers were heading home from factories and offices, moving through the dusk with the purposeful, unhurried pace of people who had nowhere to go except home. Elena walked among them, wearing Alice Marsh's camel coat—too Western for this city, too obviously foreign, but she hadn't yet acquired the local wardrobe and hadn't wanted to. For one more evening, she wanted to wear something that belonged to her London life.

She was leaving that life. Not permanently. She would return to London, Yuri had assured her. The secondment was temporary. Two years, perhaps three. Long enough to manage the Hatch operation and to learn everything Bruhn could teach her. Then back to London. Back to Alice Marsh. Back to

Calder.

But Elena knew, with the clarity that came with having just spent four hours being taught how to dismantle a person's life from the inside, that the woman who returned to London would not be the woman who had left. She would be something else. Something that Bruhn was building. Something that Moscow needed and Calder would never see and Alice Marsh would never contain and Elena Vasilieva had apparently always been, waiting inside herself like a capability that required only the right instruction set to activate.

She walked through East Berlin in the dark. She passed apartment buildings where families were eating dinner behind curtains. She passed a school where the lights were still on in one classroom—a teacher grading papers, visible through the window, head bent over a desk. Elena thought about Katarina in Rostock. She thought about the schoolteacher whose ecology had been shifted until she stopped applying for the visa that would have taken her to her sister.

What it meant to be good at this.

She thought about what Hatch was probably looking at, on the other side of the Wall, in a London office with a window and a stack of cuttings going back to 1965. He was looking at the same thing she had been turning over in her head since Yuri had said the word Gladio in the Bloomsbury café. Tactical nuclear charges. Cached along the old defensive lines. Placed by stay-behind operatives who had been trained for a war that had never arrived and were now, some of them, reporting to people whose names NATO had not authorized, whose loyalties Moscow could not verify, and whose true employer—Elena was now increasingly certain—was not any of the governments whose flags they nominally flew.

Bruhn knew. She was almost sure of it. He had not said so, and he would never say so in terms she could quote, but there had been a quality to his attention when he walked her through Case Three that suggested Bruhn understood the method beyond its application to journalists and pastors and schoolteachers. The method was scalable. The method had already been scaled. And the scaling, if Elena's autumn reading of the fragments had been correct, had been happening on both sides of the Wall, coordinated by men who spoke Russian to their superiors and German to their subordinates and English to each other in the hotels of neutral cities.

What Bruhn did not know was that he too was being operated. The desk above his was not a desk in the Stasi organization chart. Elena had been registering the same shape in Yuri's briefings. The hand had been shaping Bruhn's career the way it had been shaping hers.

If Hatch published what he was reconstructing, those men would have a problem. They would resolve it the way Palermo had been resolved: a methane story in a mountain village, the cover holding for another decade, the caches continuing their quiet migration into the custody of whoever they now belonged to. Elena could not prove the identity of that custody. Its appetite for a Europe with fewer cities in it was the only variable she had no reliable way to measure.

The question forming at the edge of her thinking was the question she could not yet ask.

She was not a spy anymore. She was a lever. And the hand on the lever was not hers.

She reached the guest quarters where she had been assigned a room. It was small, clean, functional—the Stasi's idea of hospitality, which was the same as the Stasi's idea of everything else: adequate, monitored, and slightly too cold. She sat on the narrow bed. She took off her London coat. She folded it carefully and placed it on the chair beside the bed, and for a moment, in the silence of a room that she was certain contained at least one listening device, she pressed her hand against the fabric and felt the weight of a life she was about to set down.

Then she unpacked. She arranged her things. She prepared for tomorrow, when the real work would begin—when Bruhn would open the Hatch file and show her the target and she would begin designing a campaign to take a man's life apart with the same meticulous care she had used to build Alice Marsh's life together.

The symmetry was not lost on her. She was, by nature and by training, a builder. She built identities. She built relationships. She built architectures of deception so complete that they could sustain human life for decades. And now she was going to learn how to reverse the process. How to take what was built and unbuild it. How to find the joints in a person's psychological structure and apply pressure until the structure collapsed under its own weight.

She lay down on the narrow bed. She stared at the ceiling. Somewhere in London, James Calder was probably doing the same thing—lying in the dark, thinking about a woman who was not beside him, wondering when she would return.

She'd told him she was visiting family in New Zealand. He hadn't asked where in New Zealand. Hadn't asked the name of the town or the family. He asked only when she would be back, and when she had been unable to answer with precision, he had taken her imprecision as affection rather than evasion—a careful choice. Calder was a man who understood what it meant to stay out of a room that was not his to enter. He had understood this about the Akhmatova tattoo he traced without asking what it meant. He was understanding it now about her absence. The waiting was his gift. She was about to repay it by learning how to make him distrust his own memory.

Elena closed her eyes. The professor in Leipzig, alone in his apartment, opening a drawer he was certain he had closed. The terrible loneliness of a man who cannot trust his own memory.

She thought about what it would feel like to create that loneliness in someone else.

She thought she would be very good at it.

Lichtenberg flat—third week.

On her third week—the ministry had moved her into a flat in Lichtenberg by then—Bruhn sent her to the basement.

Not the basement the files were kept in. A different basement, two floors further down, through a door that required a key Bruhn produced from his vest pocket and that he handed to her without explanation. The stairwell beyond the door was narrow, unlit, and smelled of something chemical—not lignite, not cleaning fluid, something sharper, more particular, the smell of a process that was being conducted in a space that had been designed for the conducting.

The room at the bottom was small. Concrete walls. A single workbench beneath a red safelight that turned everything the color of old blood. At the bench sat a woman Elena had not seen before—fifties, steel-gray hair pinned back, lab coat, the kind of glasses that magnified the eyes behind them into something amphibian. She did not introduce herself. She did not look up.

'Sit,' the woman said. 'Hands on the table.'

Elena sat. Hands on the table. On the workbench: a microscope with a modified stage, a rack of glass slides, three bottles of chemical solution labeled in handwriting Elena could not read at this distance, a single-lens reflex camera body without a lens, and a wooden box containing what appeared to be a set of watch lenses arranged by diameter in a velvet tray.

'You are going to learn to make microdots,' the woman said.

'A microdot is a photograph reduced to the size of a printed period. A single dot, properly made, contains an entire page of text readable under forty-times magnification. The dot can be concealed inside a letter, beneath a postage stamp, inside the binding of a book, in the period at the end of a sentence. The Americans found one during the war inside a period on a postcard. They have been looking for them ever since. They find approximately one in ten thousand.'

She unscrewed a lens from the velvet tray and held it to the red light. The lens was the size of Elena's smallest fingernail.

'The process has four stages. Photographing the original. Developing the negative. Re-photographing the negative through a reduction lens at a distance calibrated to produce a final image of 0.5 millimeters or less. Mounting the dot.' She set the lens down. 'The first three stages require patience. The fourth requires hands that do not shake. Show me your hands.'

Elena held them out. Flat. Still. The red light made her skin look like it belonged to someone who had been underwater for a long time.

The woman looked at Elena's hands for five seconds. Then she looked at Elena's face. Then she returned to the hands.

'Your hands are still,' she said. It was not a compliment. It was a measurement.

'I know,' Elena said.

They worked for four hours. The chemical smell was acetic acid and ammonium thiosulfate—fixer and stop bath, the same solutions Elena had encountered in a photography course the Red Banner Institute had required her to take years earlier and that she had remembered the way she remembered everything: precisely, permanently, without effort. The darkroom procedures were old muscle memory. The reduction photography was new.

The new part was the lens work. Selecting the correct reduction lens for the target size. Calculating the focal distance. Positioning the negative on a light stage and aligning the camera body—which was not a camera anymore, not in this configuration, but an optical reduction system that happened to use a camera's film gate—at the precise distance that would compress a full A4 page into a circle smaller than the head of a pin.

Elena asked about the lens geometry. The woman looked at her.

'Why,' the woman said.

'If the equipment is unavailable, I want to know if the process can be reproduced with commercial optics.'

The woman paused. She adjusted her amphibian glasses. She had been teaching this process for, Elena estimated, at least fifteen years. Elena suspected nobody asked that question before.

'It can,' the woman said. 'A reversed fifty-millimeter standard lens produces a reduction ratio of approximately nine to one. Two reversed lenses in series produce eighty to one. The depth of field at eighty-to-one is less than a tenth of a millimeter. Your negative must be perfectly flat. Your hands must be perfectly still. The exposure time at that reduction is between four and eight seconds depending on the emulsion. During those seconds, nothing in the system can move.'

'Nothing,' Elena said.

'Nothing.'

Elena made her first microdot on a January afternoon two floors beneath Stasi headquarters. The dot contained the full text of a decoded signal she had been given as a test document. Under the microscope, every letter was legible. The margins were clean. The focal plane was even across the entire image. The woman examined it for thirty seconds.

'Your first,' the woman said.

'Yes.'

The woman removed the slide from the microscope. She held it to the red light. The dot was invisible to the naked eye—a speck on a glass slide that could have been dust, or a flaw in the glass, or nothing at all.

'Most people require six attempts,' the woman said. 'Some require twenty. The hands are always the problem.' She set the slide down. 'Your hands are not the problem.'

Elena walked back up into the gray January light. She returned the key to Bruhn's office. He did not ask how it had gone. The woman in the basement would file a report, and the report would contain a number—the number of attempts required to produce a readable microdot—and the number would be one.

She thought about the dot on the walk back to her flat. Not about the tradecraft. About the physics. A full page of text—names, dates, locations, the entire architecture of a secret—compressed into a point so small the naked eye could not distinguish it from absence. The information was there. The information was also invisible. The dot existed in the space between presence and nothing, between evidence and dust, between the thing you were looking for and the thing you would never find unless you knew exactly where to look and had the right lens and the patience to hold still for eight seconds while the light did its work.

6
THE DEATH STRIP

Near Glienicker Bridge, East Berlin—February 1975

February in East Berlin arrived through the nose before anything else. The lignite smoke from every furnace in Lichtenberg—the soft brown coal the GDR burned for heat—sat in the back of the throat like a word you hadn't said yet, sweet and chemical and never entirely gone. The cold came off the Spree and settled into the concrete the way groundwater settles into old foundations—present all along, invisible until the season withdrew far enough to show what the walls had been holding.

The driver's name was Eckhard. He was furniture. He had been assigned to her for the duration of her secondment.

Tonight he was driving her to Potsdam. Bruhn had requested her presence at a debriefing—a West German academic who had been providing political intelligence for three years and who needed, in Bruhn's words, recalibration. Elena understood what recalibration meant. It meant the academic was becoming unreliable. It meant Bruhn wanted her to observe the techniques he used to restore an asset's compliance. It was a lesson disguised as a working task, which was how Bruhn conducted all his education.

She had been in East Berlin for five weeks. Nine briefings with Bruhn. Fourteen Zersetzung case files. The preliminary research on Tom Hatch that would form the foundation of the campaign she was designing. And—in the quiet hours between briefings—a clearer view of the thing she had first glimpsed from the wrong angle in October, when the BBC had carried a story about a village in northern Italy and the story underneath the story had been a signature she was only beginning to learn to read. The fingerprints had been wrong on one side of the Wall. The fingerprints were wrong on this side too. The fingerprints had been wrong the whole time.

Her understanding of the Stasi had moved, in those five weeks, from the abstract to the inhabited. Moscow's file on the organization had captured the statistics but not the shape. The Stasi did not watch East Germany. The Stasi was East Germany. Institution and population had grown into each other like roots growing through a foundation—you could not remove one without destroying the other. The KGB wanted to know what its citizens were doing. The Stasi wanted to know what they were thinking. The Stasi did not observe lives. It lived inside them.

The Stasi was only part of the shape. Elena had not been able to say this to herself until this week. Above the Stasi was Moscow. Above Moscow was a silence that neither service acknowledged, and the mutual silence was part of the instrument.

Eckhard turned off the main road. They were taking a route that passed through the western outskirts of Potsdam, near the Glienicker Bridge—the bridge where East and West exchanged captured spies. Stasi men in dark coats walked across in one direction. Americans in dark coats walked across in the other. Elena had never seen the bridge. She'd seen photographs.

The bridge was not impressive in itself—a steel truss structure over the Havel River, painted green, architecturally unremarkable. It was the point where the two systems touched. The only place where the Wall's logic was temporarily suspended, where a human being could cross from one world to the other not by tunneling or climbing or dying but by being traded.

Eckhard stopped the car. Not at the bridge. At a pull-off approximately four hundred meters south, in a wooded area where the road curved and the trees thinned enough to provide a partial view of a stretch of the Wall and the death strip that ran alongside it. He said he had to meet a contact and would return in twenty minutes.

He turned off the engine. He did not look at her. He opened the glove compartment and took out a small thermos and a pair of binoculars, which he placed on the passenger seat beside her. Behind the thermos, wedged against the vehicle registration papers, was a small photograph in a plastic sleeve—a girl of perhaps seven, school uniform, missing a front tooth, smiling into a camera Eckhard had apparently been holding. He did not touch the photograph. He did not need to. The photograph was there the way load-bearing walls were there: present, unacknowledged, structural. He poured coffee into the cap of the thermos without offering her any. Then he got out of the car and walked twenty meters up the road and stood with his back to the Wartburg, facing the trees. He was giving her the car.

Elena was alone.

Elena could see it through the windshield.

The *Todesstreifen*—the death strip—began approximately one hundred meters inside East German territory. The Wall itself was only the final obstacle. Before you reached it, you had to cross a band of open ground between fifty and several hundred meters wide, engineered with the purpose of making it impossible for a human being to traverse without being detected, wounded, or killed.

The strip was lit. Guard tower lights cast a flat, white illumination that eliminated shadows and made the space look like a surgical theater—everything visible, everything exposed, nothing left to ambiguity. The ground was raked sand. Not beach sand. A coarser grade, chosen because it showed footprints with the clarity of fresh snow.

The sand was raked daily by soldiers who dragged weighted wooden frames across it in the early morning, erasing the previous day's record and creating a clean surface on which every mark would be new and every new mark would be investigated. The daily raking was maintenance—the same word the Apennine bulletin had used, eighteen months earlier, for a crew in a pit at dawn. It was also a statement. We erase. We begin again. We are always watching.

The word had a family of applications. Sand at a border. A crew in a pit at dawn. A death certificate written in mercury. The differences were local. The principle was the same.

Beyond the sand were the obstacles. Vehicle ditches deep enough to stop a car. Signal wires connected to alarm systems at the guard towers. SM-70 directional mines mounted on metal posts, aimed horizontally at waist height, designed to fire a spray of metal fragments when a wire was disturbed. The mines were not designed to kill. They were designed to wound. A dead person in the death strip was a problem. A wounded person was a deterrent. The screaming carried further than the silence.

And the dogs. Belgian Malinois, trained by the *Grenztruppen*'s K-9 unit, maintained on thirty-meter wire leads that let them run a fixed perimeter without a handler. They were working animals that had been trained to bite and hold. To seize a limb and not release it until commanded or until the limb stopped moving. The dogs did not distinguish between a person attempting to cross the border and a person lying wounded in the sand. They were not trained to distinguish.

Elena sat in the cold car and looked at the death strip through the trees. The guard tower lights turned the space into something that looked almost clinical—a laboratory for the study of containment. She had spent five weeks learning how to dismantle people psychologically. The death strip dismantled them physically. The methods were different. The institutional logic was identical. You do not escape. Not because we will punish you but because we have engineered the conditions to make escape impossible. The Wall was not a threat. It was a fact. The death strip was the fact's grammar.

Behind both methods—behind the raked sand and the anonymous letter, behind the mine and the whisper—was the same principle. The institution that built the Wall and the institution that built Zersetzung were the same institution, and neither of them claimed to know what the larger thing they were part of was being used for.

Four flags. Four services. One hand beneath the table, moving all four. The flags had always been the cover. The hand had always been the work.

She looked at her notepad. She had brought it from the car's glove compartment intending to make notes during the drive—observations about the landscape, the route, the route between Berlin and Potsdam. The notepad was blank. She'd written nothing.

She raised the binoculars. Then she saw him.

He was in the strip.

Approximately one hundred meters from the Wall itself, which meant he was still deep inside the death strip, still surrounded by the full complement of the system's defenses. He was not running. He was moving slowly, with the careful, deliberate gait of someone testing weight on each step, as if the sand beneath his feet might give way or as if he believed that moving slowly would make him harder to see. It would not. The lights were designed to illuminate exactly this—a human figure in an open space. He was as visible as a moth on a white wall.

He was young. Early twenties. She could tell from the biomechanics—a body still growing into its own coordination. He moved with the combination of physical capability and psychological terror that young men produced when they were doing something they had planned for weeks and were now discovering was different from what they had imagined. Planning was abstract. The sand was not. The lights were not. The sound of his own breathing in the silence of the death strip was not.

He had a rope. She could see it coiled over his shoulder, a dark line against the lighter fabric of his jacket. The rope meant he had a plan for the Wall itself—a plan that involved reaching the concrete barrier and scaling it, which required approximately ninety seconds of exposed climbing on a surface that was deliberately smooth and slightly angled outward to prevent exactly this. The rope was preparation. The rope was hope made physical. The rope was the difference between a man who had decided to die in the strip and a man who believed he was going to live on the other side of it.

Elena watched. There was nothing to do. She was a Soviet intelligence officer in a Stasi vehicle on the Eastern side of the most fortified border in human history. She had no authority to intervene. She was watching because Eckhard had stopped the car where the trees were thin enough. Because a man had chosen this night, of all nights, to try.

He was perhaps sixty meters from the Wall when the SM-70 fired.

The sound was not what she expected.

She had read about the SM-70 in the technical briefings. The briefing had described the sound as comparable to a large firecracker. The sound was sharper than a firecracker and duller than a gunshot. It was the sound of metal and explosive doing something ugly at close range, and it arrived at Elena's car window with a flat, percussive finality that the word firecracker did not begin to describe.

The man went down.

Not immediately. There was a delay—perhaps a full second—between the mine's detonation and the man's fall. The body needed time to process what had happened to it. The shrapnel had struck his left leg below the knee. She could tell from the way he collapsed. Not straight down, which would have indicated a bilateral injury. Sideways and forward, favoring the right leg, the left leg folding beneath him the way a leg folds only when something has gone through it. He hit the sand on his left side. The rope slid off his shoulder and landed beside him in a loose coil that looked, in the flat white light of the guard tower, like something a sailor had dropped on a dock.

He did not scream immediately.

The detail she would remember most clearly was not the mine. Not the fall. The silence between the injury and the scream. The body's processing time. The gap between the event and the nervous system's acknowledgment of the event, during which the man lay in the raked sand of the *Todesstreifen* with his left leg bent at an angle that no leg should form. The world was quiet, and the guard tower lights hummed with the low electrical drone that all institutional lighting produced, and nothing moved.

Then the scream came.

It started low. A sound from deep in the chest, involuntary, the kind of sound that has no language in it because it comes from somewhere older than language. The sound rose. It found pitch. It became recognizably human. It became the sound of a young man in a strip of sand between two walls who had just discovered that the system he was trying to escape had been engineered to reach out and touch him even here, even now, even in the act of leaving.

Elena sat in the car. Her hands were on the notepad. Her pen was in her right hand. She had not written anything. The notepad was as blank as it had been when she opened it.

The dogs reached him before the guards.

He made a sound. A sound rather than a word.

She heard them first—the sharp, controlled barking of animals that had been trained to vocalize during pursuit, not from excitement but from training, because the sound of an approaching dog was itself a weapon and the K-9 trainers understood this. Two dogs. Belgian Malinois. They came from the northeast, running at the limit of their thirty-meter leads, which snapped taut as they reached the end of their range and then went slack as the wire system allowed them to pivot and approach from a different angle. The dogs were not running in a straight line. They were running the way trained animals ran—in calculated arcs designed to approach the target from multiple directions simultaneously.

The man on the ground saw them. He raised his right arm. The left arm was beneath him, possibly pinned, possibly damaged by the fall. He raised his right arm in a gesture that could have been defense or surrender or simply the involuntary motion of a body trying to make itself larger in the presence of a predator. The dogs did not distinguish between these possibilities. They had been trained to respond to a prone human body in the strip, and they responded.

The first dog reached him and took his raised arm. The bite

was instantaneous. The jaws closed on his forearm with a force Elena could not hear from this distance but could infer from the way the man's body jerked, a full-body spasm that told her the pain of the bite had registered on top of the pain of the shrapnel wound, the two sensations competing for dominance in a system that was already overloaded. The second dog circled, looking for an opening, and found one at his right leg—the good leg, the one he had been using to try to stand. The dog seized the calf. The man stopped trying to stand.

He was screaming steadily now. The screams had lost their pitch and become a continuous sound, the sound a body made when the pain had nowhere left to go.

The guards arrived.

Two of them. They came at a jog. Not a run. A jog. The pace of men responding to a situation the system's automated defenses had already resolved, whose role was administrative rather than combative. They carried Kalashnikov rifles, standard border-troop issue, held at port arms across their chests. They were young—not much older than the man in the sand. They had been conscripted into the border guard the way all young East German men were conscripted into something, and they'd been posted to this section of the Wall the way furniture was posted to a room.

One guard stood at the perimeter of the scene and shouted an order. Elena could not hear the words at this distance, but she could read the posture: the rigid, raised-chin stance of a man executing a procedure he had been drilled on but never performed. The second guard moved closer to the man on the ground. The dogs were still attached. The handler had not yet arrived to call them off.

The second guard looked at the man. The man's right arm was in the first dog's jaws. His right leg was in the second dog's jaws. His left leg was bent at the angle the mine had created. He was on his back in the raked sand, his face turned toward the guard tower light, and the light illuminated his features with the flat, shadowless clarity of a medical examination lamp.

He was young. Very young. Perhaps nineteen. His face was contorted in a way that pain produces and fear compounds, the muscles pulling in directions that faces are not designed to be pulled in. Fear and pain and the crushing realization that the thing you had planned for and hoped for and risked everything for had ended in raked sand with dogs on your limbs and guards standing over you deciding something.

The guards conferred. Elena watched them confer. They were deciding something. The doctrine was clear about attempts. It was less clear about the aftermath of a failed attempt, when the subject was immobilized but alive. The guards were young men standing in a gap in the doctrine, and the gap required a decision that their training had not fully prepared them to make.

One guard raised his weapon.

The man on the ground saw him. He did not close his eyes. Elena could see the angle of his face through the binoculars—the chin tilted up, seeking light rather than avoiding it. The guard did not close his eyes either. For perhaps a second and a half the two of them looked at each other across the raked sand the way men look at each other in weather neither of them chose to be out in. They were the same age. Elena could see that too. The recognition was one of the things the system had not anticipated and had not trained either of them to resist.

The sound reached Elena four seconds after the muzzle flash.

Elena saw the flash first. A brief, sharp flare at the weapon's muzzle that lasted less than a tenth of a second and that illuminated, in that fraction of a moment, the guard's face. He was not much older than the man he was shooting. Perhaps two years between them. Both born into a country that required one of them to be shot and the other to shoot him.

One shot.

The round took the boy at the base of the throat. The sand began to darken beneath his shoulder before his body had finished registering the impact. The man in the sand jerked. A single, involuntary spasm that traveled through his body from the point of impact outward, the way a stone dropped into still water produced concentric ripples. The scream stopped. The silence that replaced it was not the silence of the gap between the mine and the scream. It was a different silence. A completed silence. The silence of a system that had functioned as designed.

Then a second shot.

Because the first had not been sufficient. Elena could not determine from this distance whether the first shot had been poorly placed or whether the man's body had moved enough between impact and follow-up to require a second round. It did not matter. The second shot was the sound of certainty. The guard was making sure.

Elena lowered the binoculars. Her jaw was locked. She unclenched it deliberately. She did not need them for what came next.

The dogs were called off. A handler arrived—a third figure, visible in the guard tower light, moving with the unhurried pace of a man performing a routine function. He spoke to the dogs in a tone Elena could not hear. The dogs released. They moved to the handler's side. They sat. The discipline was precise. They had done what they were trained to do. They were done. They sat in the raked sand beside a man who was no longer moving and they waited for the next instruction with the patient, attentive stillness of animals that had no concept of what they'd just participated in.

The guards radioed. Elena could see one of them speaking into a handset, his free hand making a gesture she could not interpret at this distance. An official vehicle arrived from the Eastern side within twelve minutes. Two men in civilian clothing got out. They did not examine the body with urgency. They examined it the way you examined a piece of equipment that had malfunctioned and needed to be removed. They lifted the man onto a stretcher. They placed the stretcher in the vehicle. They drove away.

The guards remained. One of them—the one who had fired—stood at the edge of the area where the body had been. He stood there for approximately thirty seconds, looking at the sand. Elena could not see his face. She could see his posture. He was standing still, with the particular rigidity of a man who was processing something his body had done and that his mind had not yet caught up with. Then his partner said something to him. He turned. They walked back to the guard tower together. Their boots left prints in the raked sand. The prints would be erased in the morning.

Everything that followed was paperwork.

Elena looked at the notepad in her lap.

It was blank. She had been holding it for the entire duration of what she had just witnessed—from the moment she first saw the man in the strip to the moment the vehicle carried his body away. The pen was in her right hand. The cap was off. The nib had been resting against the paper long enough to leave a small dot of ink. It was the only mark she would make tonight.

Not because she had no thoughts. She always had thoughts. She had not written anything because there was nothing to file.

She could describe what she'd seen. She could describe it with the clinical precision that Bruhn was teaching her—the professional language, the institutional terminology, the vocabulary that intelligence services used to convert human experience into data. She could write: Witnessed border crossing attempt, sector 7, approximately 21:40. Subject male, early twenties, injured by SM-70 mine (left leg), restrained by K-9 units, terminated by border-troop personnel. Two rounds fired. Body removed by official vehicle at 21:58. No tactical significance.

She could write that. It would be accurate and complete and true in the way institutional language was always true: true to the facts, false to the meaning. It would not contain the boy or the rope or the wall that was six meters away and might as well have been the surface of the moon.

She put the cap back on the pen. She closed the notepad. She placed both in her coat pocket.

In her next report to Bruhn she did not mention this. She did not mention it because it was not operationally relevant. A man had attempted to cross the border and had been killed. This happened regularly. It was a function of the system. It was not intelligence. It was not actionable.

That Elena could not stop seeing the rope—that the image had lodged beside Helen's shortbread and Margaret's empty clasp and the twelve in the mountain village—was not the institution's concern. It was hers. The archive was no longer a filing system. It was a weight. And Elena was carrying it alone, because the institution did not recognize that such things had mass.

Eckhard returned. He got in the car. He started the engine. 'It's a machine,' he said, after a long silence. That was all.

'Who made the machine,' Elena said. It was not a question. She was looking at the road, not at him.

Eckhard drove for perhaps a kilometer before he answered. 'People who are no longer alive. And people who are. And the ones who have not been born yet will also have made it, once they are old enough.'

He did not mention what Elena had witnessed. He turned the heating up, though, which was the closest thing to acknowledgment his training permitted.

They drove to Potsdam. The road unwound in the Wartburg's headlights. Elena stared through the windshield at the darkness and the trees and the occasional light of a farmhouse that meant someone was awake at this hour for reasons that were probably ordinary—a child who could not sleep, a farmer checking livestock, a woman reading in bed because the book was good and the night was long. Ordinary reasons. Ordinary lives. Lived inside the same system that had just killed a man for trying to leave it.

The debrief took ninety minutes. Bruhn recalibrated the West German academic with the same patient clinical precision he brought to everything, and Elena watched, and took notes, and learned. The academic did not know he was being recalibrated. He believed he was having a professional conversation about source reliability in a safe room in Potsdam. Bruhn was moving the ground beneath him one quiet sentence at a time. The academic adjusted his posture to the movement without recognizing it as movement. By the end of the session he was grateful—the kind of grateful that meant he would report more usefully next month. No threat made. No pressure applied. No evidence that anything had changed except the color of the light in the room.

Elena watched Bruhn do this. She thought about the raked sand.

◆◆◆

Later that night, back in her room at the guest quarters, she lay in the narrow bed and stared at the ceiling. The building was quiet. The listening devices were listening to silence. She thought about the man in the death strip. She did not know his name. She would never learn it. He would appear in no report she would ever write and no file she would ever read. He existed only in the part of her memory that she could not reach with the institutional tools she'd been given, the part that stored things without categories, the part that was, increasingly, the only part of her that still recognized itself when the lights went out.

The professor in Leipzig. His opened drawers. His belief that it was his own fault. Zersetzung and the death strip were the same sentence written in two different languages, and Bruhn was teaching her the grammar of both.

She thought about Hatch. About what she was about to do to him. Hatch standing in a London kitchen at some hour that had not yet happened—cleaning his glasses, reading his own notes for the third time, trying to locate an anxiety he could not yet name. Both of them reaching for something better. Both stopped by a system engineered to stop them.

And she thought—because she couldn't stop thinking—about the voice above Bruhn, and the hand above that one, and the pattern that was emerging from the spaces between the things she had been told. The pattern suggested the weapons were not a residue of the Cold War but a working instrument of it. And if the instrument was ever used, the using would not look like a war. It would look like a series of separate accidents in separate cities on separate days, and the separateness would be the cover, and the cities would stop existing one at a time.

The boy in the strip was the first draft of that future. One body in raked sand. Multiply by however many cities the instrument was aimed at. The raking was the same. The cover was the same. Only the scale changed. Each accident would be written in mercury. Each city would forget itself.

The hand above Bruhn had not built the Wall. The hand above Bruhn had decided what the Wall would mean. The man who had fired the two shots tonight had been instructed on both.

She said the line to herself in Russian. Silently. The way she had said it to herself since she was seventeen in the Leningrad apartment.

Я научилась просто, мудро жить.

I taught myself to live simply and wisely.

She had not. She had taught herself the opposite—to live in the most complicated way a life could be lived, inside three names and four languages and the machinery of an institution that had stopped answering to the governments it had been built to serve. The line was a promise she had broken every day since she made it. She said it anyway. The saying was the thing.

Calder. She did not let herself think about him for long. He was in a flat in London, possibly asleep, certainly not aware that the woman he had loved for fifteen months was lying in a narrow bed in Lichtenberg carrying an image of a rope in the sand that she would not describe to him for another fifteen years.

She did not sleep. In the morning she would go to Normannenstraße and Bruhn would open the Tom Hatch file and the campaign would begin. Zersetzung left the components lying in the sand, and the target was left to reassemble them without knowing what had happened. The man in the strip did not have that option. The sand would be raked in the morning. The dogs would be fed. The guards would go home to apartments where their families would ask how their night was, and they would say it was fine, and they would mean it, because for them it was.

The machinery was running. It was always running.

Elena lay in the dark and did not sleep, did not write, did not file.

The notepad on the bedside table was blank. It would stay blank.

She would carry the night for the rest of her life.

7

THE 2 AM KITCHEN

East Berlin / London—1975—1976

Tom Hatch was a good journalist. That was the problem.

A mediocre journalist investigating the Gladio stay-behind networks would have been manageable. Mediocre journalists made mediocre mistakes, and the institutional response to their work was a few days of unfavorable headlines followed by the natural amnesia democratic societies applied to uncomfortable revelations. Hatch was not mediocre. He was thirty-four, Cambridge-educated, working for the *Guardian* with the patient methodology of a man who understood that the best investigative journalism was not about scandal but about apparatus. He did not chase headlines. He chased structures.

This made him valuable and dangerous in the same motion. Valuable because Gladio's eventual exposure would embarrass NATO. Dangerous because Hatch's investigation was proceeding in directions Moscow could not control—had not, Elena was beginning to suspect, ever truly controlled. Hatch needed to be managed. Not stopped. Not discredited. Managed. His investigation needed to be slowed, redirected, and shaped so that when he eventually published, the published version would tell a story the institution had decided could be told.

West Berlin—May 1975.

Elena sat in a café on the Kurfürstendamm in West Berlin, reading a newspaper that contained a lie she had planted three months ago. It was May 1975, three months after the death strip and a year before the press reception that would end with a man unconscious against a dumpster. The café was busy with the lunchtime crowd—office workers, tourists, students from the Free University who sat in clusters and argued about Marxism with the passionate ignorance of people who had never lived inside what they were advocating. Elena sat alone at a corner table with a cup of coffee and a notebook and the contained stillness of a woman who was working on something that required her full attention.

On the page opposite her own planted lie, the *Frankfurter Allgemeine* ran a photograph of a helicopter on the roof of an embassy in a city that had stopped being Saigon two weeks earlier. The image was small. It had not yet stopped being news.

She was building a map.

Not a physical map. A psychological one. She had been constructing it for three months, since Bruhn had handed her the Hatch file and she had begun the preliminary research that Zersetzung required. The map was entirely in her head. She'd never written it down and never would.

The map had four layers.

The first layer was Hatch's professional world. Who he worked with. Who he trusted. Which editors supported his investigation and which considered it a distraction. The journalists he competed with, the ones he admired, the ones whose work he dismissed. Elena had mapped this in three weeks by reading everything Hatch had published and everything published by his immediate professional circle, cross-referencing the bylines until she could identify, from a paragraph of unsigned text, which member of the *Guardian*'s foreign desk had written it.

The second layer was his personal life. Unmarried. A girlfriend in London named Claire who taught at a secondary school in Islington and who believed his extended stays in Berlin were entirely professional. Elena noted Claire with attention. Claire had a value. Margaret Calder also had a value. Elena kept both in the same ledger, three thousand kilometers apart and indistinguishable in kind.

The third layer was his intellectual scaffolding. Where his confidence outpaced his evidence, where his assumptions went untested because they aligned with his worldview. Elena discovered these the way she discovered everything: by listening to what Hatch did not say.

The fourth layer was the most important. Hatch's foundational belief about himself—the one that, if disturbed, would make everything else impossible.

Elena had found it. It had taken three months, but she'd found it. Hatch's foundational belief was that he was brave. Not physically brave—he was not a war correspondent and did not pretend to be. Intellectually brave. He believed that he had the courage to follow evidence wherever it led, regardless of consequences. This belief was the load-bearing wall of his professional identity. Remove it and the structure collapsed. Not because the belief was false—it was largely true, which made it more vulnerable. True beliefs, when they cracked, shattered completely.

Elena closed the notebook. She finished the coffee. She had everything she needed.

The campaign could begin.

What the eventual report would describe in three paragraphs took Elena eight weeks to execute.

The anonymous letter to the *Guardian* features editor was a single page, written on a typewriter purchased in Kreuzberg for this one letter. It was not threatening enough to warrant investigation nor specific enough to be traced. It was about resource allocation. It suggested that the paper's investment in a long-term investigation with uncertain commercial returns might be better directed elsewhere. It was written in the voice of a concerned colleague—not a competitor, not an enemy, but someone inside the institution who wanted what was best for the paper and who had doubts about the Gladio project.

She typed the letter in a sublet flat in Kreuzberg. When the letter was sealed and posted, she dismantled the typewriter and distributed the pieces across four locations.

The letter worked. Not at once, and not loudly. The features editor did not kill the investigation. He asked for a progress update, which was something he had not done before, and the request introduced a subtle pressure into Hatch's working environment that had not been there previously. The pressure was mild. It was designed to be mild. It registered not as opposition but as institutional friction—the kind every journalist experienced, and therefore invisible.

The academic source at King's College was handled through a cutout—a West German journalist Elena had cultivated for six months by presenting herself as a freelance researcher interested in NATO archival history. He passed a mild but pointed critique of one of the Hatch source's 1969 papers through a literary review neither of them had ever written for. The critique reached the academic within a week. His letter to Hatch arrived three days later, phrased with the careful distance of a man who had remembered that his reputation was not the same as Hatch's.

The housing-authority visit to Hatch's Berlin landlord was the simplest element. Elena filed an anonymous complaint about the building's fire escape. The inspection revealed a minor violation. The landlord had to vacate one fourth-floor apartment for repairs. Hatch's apartment was on the third. Three weeks of construction noise landed directly above his desk during the hours he was trying to write. Hatch did not blame the landlord. He blamed the city, and the noise, and the week, and slept badly.

This was Zersetzung. Not a single blow. A climate.

West Berlin—September 1975.

Elena met Hatch in September.

The meeting was engineered to look accidental. A journalism conference in West Berlin organized by the Free University, drawing foreign correspondents from across Western Europe and a small number of East German academics who had been permitted to attend as demonstration of the GDR's commitment to free intellectual exchange. Elena attended under the credentials of a Swedish academic, Ingrid Lindqvist—a cover identity Moscow maintained for this purpose. She had been Ingrid twice before. The identity would not catch Hatch's eye.

Hatch was easy to find. He was on a panel about investigative journalism in divided Germany, and he spoke with the intensity of a man who believed that what he was saying mattered. He was tall, thin, with wire-rim glasses he cleaned compulsively. When Hatch was thinking hard, his hands went to his glasses. When he arrived at a conclusion, the glasses went back on and stayed. Elena cataloged the tic within the first ninety seconds.

She approached him at the reception afterward.

She'd rehearsed nothing. A rehearsed approach would have been recognizable to Hatch at some layer beneath language—he had been interviewed enough times to know the difference between a real exchange and a performance. Elena approached him with genuine questions about his work, and the genuine-ness did what performance could not: it made him want to keep talking.

Hatch responded with the generous patience of a man whose obsession had rarely met a worthy audience. He cleaned his glasses once. He put them back on. He did not clean them again for forty minutes. This was the length of their first conversation.

At one point—she would find that she remembered this with unnatural specificity years later—Hatch said: 'The work I do requires me to assume I will disappear. If I do, the important thing is that the work does not disappear with me. That is what the drafts are for. That is what the people I trust are for.' He said it without drama, as if it were a mildly annoying condition of his profession, like travel. Elena smiled the way Ingrid Lindqvist would have smiled and said it must be lonely work. Hatch said it could be. Then he laughed and returned to Cyprus.

She was warm. She was curious. She was present in the conversation with the full attention of a woman who had been trained to produce the appearance of full attention and who had discovered, in the course of producing the appearance, that she was actually present. The distinction collapsed somewhere in the second ten minutes of the conversation. Ingrid Lindqvist's cover interest in Gladio was Elena's real interest in Gladio, because Elena had been reading the Italian fragments for six months by this point and had concluded that the fragments formed a pattern no cover story could convincingly mimic. She had to know what Hatch had found. Alice Marsh could have maintained a performance. Ingrid Lindqvist could not, because Ingrid Lindqvist was, in this particular conversation, mostly Elena.

Hatch was not a man who could be seduced into disclosure.

He was a man who could be accompanied into it.

They exchanged contact information. He called her the following week to ask about a document she had mentioned. She provided the document. It was genuine. The first piece of intelligence she gave him would always be genuine. This was Zersetzung's paradox: you built trust with truth to deploy lies through the trust you had built. The trust was the weapon.

Over the next eight months she met him four times.

Twice in West Berlin. Once in Amsterdam at a conference on archival access and post-war institutional memory. Once in Geneva in a café near the Gare Cornavin, one of the few places in Europe where Hatch did not feel watched.

At each meeting Hatch showed her a little more of his work. At each meeting Elena showed him a little less of hers. She made her questions slightly sharper, her observations slightly more informed, her silences slightly more generative. She was keeping two ledgers now. The operational one went to Bruhn. The private one stayed in her head—the shapes that did not fit, the rhythms, the small prose tells that marked a document as belonging to a particular institution.

She thought about Calder. Not operationally. She thought about his hands on the gallery invitation he'd given her in November, and the way he held a glass, and the way he looked at a painting as if the painting were a document that might contain something the painter hadn't intended to file.

She filed the thought. The distinction between filing and not filing had collapsed into a single motion that was neither.

Geneva—March 1976.

Geneva was where Hatch first said the word.

It was the third of their four meetings, March 1976. A café off the Place de Cornavin, late afternoon, a gray Swiss rain against the window that had been falling since noon and that was not going to stop before dinner. Hatch was tired. He had flown in from London that morning and had spent the previous three days in Rome on what he described, with the casual opacity of a journalist who had become fluent in telling the truth sideways, as a source conversation. He had brought a manila folder with him to Geneva and had placed the folder on the table between them with the air of a man who had decided something important during the flight.

'I want to show you something,' he said. 'And I want to tell you about the person it came from. But I need you to understand that I'm telling you because I trust you, and that the trust is doing the work my methodology usually does, and that if the trust turns out to be wrong I will have made the worst professional mistake of my life.'

Elena looked at him. She did not open the folder.

'Tell me what you want me to know, Tom.'

He exhaled. He cleaned his glasses. He put them back on.

'I have a source in Rome. A former colonel in Italian military intelligence. He left the service in 1972 in circumstances I haven't been able to fully reconstruct. Since then he's been running what I can only describe as a private investigation into elements of his former service he believes were—are—operating outside any legitimate chain of command. He contacted me after my last *Observer* piece. He reads English. He has been reading me for a long time. His motives are, as far as I can tell, clean. He wants the apparatus he served to be exposed because he believes the apparatus he served was, in his language, captured.'

Elena let the word sit. She did not fill the silence. A waiter passed behind her with three coffees on a tray; she did not look up. Hatch's hand was flat on the table, the fingers slightly spread. He was waiting to see what she would ask. She was deciding what Ingrid Lindqvist would ask.

'Those are the exact English words he used. Captured. He wouldn't elaborate on who he believed had done the capturing.'

'What's his name?'

'I'm not going to give you his name yet. I code-name him MONTECARLO in my notes. It's a stupid code name. I chose it after the second meeting because I was tired and because he had a coffee cup with a casino logo on it in his apartment. I want you to know that I'm going to give you the name eventually. I want you to know that I'm telling you there is a name. I need both of those things to be true before we look at what's in the folder.'

Elena nodded. The casino logo. She'd known already, in the minute before he opened the folder, that the name would be Sacco. She'd known it the way she knew the weather in a city before she'd been outside that morning—through the accumulation of small atmospheric readings that had been going on in her head for months.

Colonnello Amadeo Sacco had been a Moscow asset since 1968. Moscow believed this. The file Elena had been permitted to read in the Lichtenberg briefing room the previous April had listed Sacco as an active source, code name MERIDIAN. The file had contained a single photograph. Sacco at fifty-three, gray at the temples, a coffee cup on the desk in front of him with a casino logo on it.

Tom Hatch's source MONTECARLO was Moscow's source MERIDIAN.

One man. Three ledgers. Sacco on the file in Rome. MERIDIAN on the file in Moscow. MONTECARLO on the file in Hatch's coat pocket.

Moscow believed Sacco was Moscow's. Hatch believed Sacco was his. Neither of them was correct. The two of them had been brought to the same man by separate roads, and the roads had both been built.

Sacco was the thread.

Hatch opened the folder.

'I didn't type them,' he said. 'Before you look. I want you to know that. The pages came to me the way you are about to see them. The prose is not mine. It is not Sacco's either. Read the prose. Not only the words.'

He fell quiet. He did not fill the quiet.

Inside the folder were four photocopied pages. Italian military document, 1962. A logistics inventory. The classification stamp was a hybrid—neither NATO nor Warsaw Pact, as if produced by a hand with access to both systems. In the upper margin, in pencil, a small mark Elena had seen once before, on a folder in a Fitzrovia studio the January before Berlin. She filed the echo and did not name it. The cadence in the prose was neither Hatch's nor Sacco's, and she did not name that either. Weapons caches across northern Italy—small arms, explosives, radio equipment, and one line item she read and did not react to because reaction was a luxury she could not afford at the moment of reading.

She had been seeing marks like this one for some time. Always in the upper margin. Always in pencil. Always in the same hand. She was looking at one now in a Geneva café, on a document a British journalist had laid in front of her, and the mark was the same. The hand that had been writing in her margins had been writing in his too. The hand had brought them both to this table. The bringing was the operation. They were the instruments.

Sei unità di demolizione nucleare tattica. Custodia condivisa. Contatto di manutenzione: da definire.

Six tactical nuclear demolition units. Shared custody. Maintenance contact: to be determined.

Six. Each one a fissile core inside a steel shell, sixty pounds on a strong man's shoulders, manageable by a fit operator on foot in a single night. A second hand existed somewhere outside the formal chain. The first hand had stopped maintaining it.

Six was the number on Hatch's page. Six was the inventory Sacco had been permitted to see. Elena had read, across the preceding year, ledger fragments in other languages along other lines, and the arithmetic of their intersection was not six. It was a number she had refused to total in any notebook, because the total was not a number she wanted to carry in any form the institution could read back to her.

She looked at the page. She did not touch the page. She did not need to touch the page to know that the phrase *contatto di manutenzione: da definire* was the hand she'd been looking for, for fourteen months. Her fingertips had gone cold on the table. The rest of her was still warm. The cold was specific to the hands.

The café was not quiet. Behind her a man was ordering a second espresso, and a spoon had been set down on a saucer somewhere to her right, and the Swiss rain was audible against the window with the low percussive patience rain had in cities that knew how to wait out weather. She registered these sounds the way one registered sounds in a dream. They were outside the room. The room she was in had shrunk to the surface of the page, and the page had a sentence on it in Italian, and the sentence named a hand that had been moving behind every institution she had worked for since she was nineteen. Her breathing had slowed. She had not told it to. It had slowed because the body, without asking permission, had recognized that any motion now was evidence.

She was also looking at the reason Moscow had sent her to destroy Tom Hatch. Hatch had found this. Hatch had found the document that proved NATO's nuclear weapons were under shared custody—custody that did not belong to NATO. And Moscow had ordered Elena to prevent him from publishing it. The contradiction she'd carried since the Bloomsbury café was no longer a suspicion. It was a document on a table in a Geneva bistro, and the document said: the hand that hid the weapons and the hand that ordered Elena to protect the hiding were the same hand. Shared custody. Whose. The line did not say. The line had been deliberately left unsaid.

'Do you know what that phrase means,' she said. 'The shared custody.'

'No,' Hatch said. 'Sacco wouldn't elaborate. He told me the phrase was the reason he left the service. He told me that when a custody chain is listed as shared in an inventory like this and the maintenance contact is left unwritten, what it actually means is that someone outside the formal chain of command is holding the item and that the formal chain of command has been instructed, from somewhere above it, not to ask. He used an Italian phrase I didn't catch exactly. *Un anello non registrato*. An unregistered link.'

Hatch was watching her hands. He did not appear to be trying to. His eyes had the slightly unfocused attention of a man who was listening to himself think.

'Sacco gave me something else,' he said. 'Not a document. A list he wrote out from memory in my hotel room in Rome. Names of people who had been close to this inventory at one point or another in the last decade and who are no longer close to anything. I can't publish it. I can't corroborate it on my own. I'm telling you because I need to tell someone who isn't him.'

His hands were on the table beside the folder. He did not touch it.

'A magistrate in Sicily three weeks from signing a warrant about a Livorno shipping manifest. A minister on a road outside Rome whose surviving driver has no memory of the last half hour before the crash. A Soviet defector in Norway. Petrov. Killed in his flat the same night the Mossad team in Lillehammer were killing the wrong man six blocks away. Two rounds, close range. Small caliber. The Norwegians put it down to a burglary. Sacco did not.'

Elena kept her hands where they were.

'Sacco thinks Petrov had started to see the pattern in his Leningrad traffic before he defected. His defection was not about troop movements. It was about this.' Hatch gestured toward the folder without touching it. 'Which is why Sacco thinks the killing was never going to be solved in Norway. The jurisdiction that could have solved it was the jurisdiction that ordered it. I can't prove that. Sacco can't either. He told me anyway. He called Petrov the template. He said an unregistered link always has a cleaner.'

Hatch looked at her for a long moment.

'Does any of it sound familiar. You read the Scandinavian press. Anything like a Livorno manifest ever cross your desk.'

It was a reporter's question disguised as a conversational one. Elena heard the disguise. She also heard the faint edge beneath it—the edge of a man who had been alone with too much information for too long and who had just noticed that the woman across from him was processing it faster than a Swedish academic with an interest in NATO archives should.

'There was a reference in one of the Swedish quarterlies last year,' she said. 'Shipping out of Livorno. I took it for a customs matter. I can look for it when I am back in Stockholm.'

She said it the way Ingrid Lindqvist would say it. Academic. Helpful. Uncurious in the specific places that would have to remain uncurious. She was aware, while she was saying it, that another part of her mind was looking at Petrov's face in a Lillehammer kitchen and at the kettle he had knocked without toppling. The mind was allowed two processes. The face was allowed only one.

Elena closed the folder carefully. The care was for Hatch's benefit. Her hands needed to be doing something visible and steady. The part of her mind that was not visible was absorbing the realization that Hatch had been handed—by a man he and Moscow both believed they were running—the first written confirmation that the warheads were listed in a real document under a custody protocol that pointed away from any government she could name.

The thread had a name. The name was Sacco. The name was also not Sacco, because Sacco was an instrument. Whoever was running Sacco—whoever had pointed Sacco at Moscow and at Hatch and had arranged, through whatever subtlety, for both of them to be fed the same evidence—was not in this folder and was not in any file Elena had ever been permitted to read.

'Tom,' she said. 'I need a day with these pages before I can tell you what I think they mean. Can I keep the folder until tomorrow?'

'No,' Hatch said. 'I'm sorry. I'm keeping the folder with me. Sacco was clear about that. He said the pages go back to Rome with me when I leave Geneva. He said nothing about the pages leaving Geneva without me. I can let you look at them here, as long as you want, but I have to take them when I go.'

'How long do I have.'

'Twenty minutes. I'm sorry.'

Elena used the twenty minutes. She committed the four pages to memory with the discipline she'd been taught to apply to documents she would not be permitted to photograph. Layout. Phrasing. The specific wording of each line item. The handwritten annotations in the left margin of the second page, in what she recognized as two separate hands, one Italian and one—possibly—German. The date stamp at the bottom of the fourth page, smudged but legible. 4 Novembre 1962.

She gave the folder back. She did not tell Hatch that the shared-custody phrase was the first written evidence of the apparatus she'd been triangulating for a year. She did not tell him that Sacco was not the source but the valve, and that whoever was turning the valve had decided a certain amount of information needed to reach a certain arrangement of interests for the next move to be possible.

She did not tell him any of this.

She took her seat across from him an hour earlier as an operative designing his professional destruction. She stood up from the table as an operative who had been handed, by the man she was supposed to be destroying, the first confirmation of the thing she'd been half-looking for since the death strip.

She walked back to her hotel in the rain. She did not open an umbrella. The rain was in her hair and on her face and on her coat. She welcomed it because the rain was weather and the weather was the only thing in her current environment that was not performing a function.

She got to her hotel. She took the lift and stood against the back wall with her hands in her coat pockets, the small mirror opposite reflecting a woman whose face she did not need to look at tonight.

Her room was on the fourth floor. She did not turn on the overhead light. She crossed to the kitchenette by the window and filled the kettle.

Not the Italian document. Not the phrase *un anello non*

registrato. Not the six tactical nuclear demolition units maintained by a hand that had custody without a name. Those she had absorbed in the café with her face entirely still, and those were now carried in the second ledger she kept against the institution she worked for.

The kettle was smaller than all of that.

Petrov's hand had knocked a kettle in Lillehammer, and the kettle had rocked but not fallen. She had filed the image at the time the way she processed everything then—as scene noise, peripheral, the kind of detail an instructor would tell her to discard. It had come back in the months since, uninvited, at small hours, and she had kept filing it. Tonight it had a companion.

Sacco said Petrov was the template.

She let her eyes close. Petrov's face came back. She looked at it now the way she had not allowed herself to look at it at the time. His eyes finding her across his own living room. Not surprise. Not fear. The two expressions she had listed and dismissed on the drive to Hamar. What she had not listed, because she had not been willing to list it, was the third one.

Relief.

The face of a man who had been waiting a long time to find out who would be sent. Who had understood, in the half-second before the first round, that whatever cover story Moscow had been told about his dying, the reason for his dying was not in the cover story. Petrov had not been defecting about troop movements. He had been defecting about a hand. The same hand, she now understood, that had once used him to name Irina.

The hand had used Petrov to kill Irina—Irina with the laugh that could fill a hallway, twenty-eight years old, dead in an operation Moscow had attributed to bad luck. The hand had then used her to kill Petrov—because Petrov had begun, afterwards, to see the hand. Every motion in the sequence had been the hand's. The flags along the way had been camouflage. She had not taken a revenge Moscow had granted her. She had closed a loop the hand had opened.

She was an instrument that had been used against her own.

She did not cry. The training had removed crying as a response available to her body the way twenty years of surgery removes flinching. But her hand was on the handle of a cheap hotel kettle, and her forehead was against the cool tile above the counter, and for a minute her breath was not moving.

The kettle clicked off. Steam rose and was gone.

She stood for a long time. She did not make the tea.

Phase Three.

The operational report for Phase Three did not say what Hatch's kitchen looked like at 2 AM.

Elena knew what it looked like because she'd designed the conditions that produced it. She had not been in the kitchen. She'd never entered Hatch's London flat. The 2 AM kitchen was a constant. It was the place where the target ended up when the sleep stopped coming and the doubts started arriving, when the professional ground that had felt solid six months ago now felt uncertain in ways they could not articulate, and they stood in the half-light of their own home trying to remember whether the world had changed or they had.

Hatch's 2 AM kitchen had an ashtray full of cigarette butts. A half-empty bottle of whisky that had been full the day before. Notes spread across the table—printouts, photocopies, handwritten pages—that he was reviewing for the third time because the first two times had not produced the clarity he was looking for. He would be standing at the counter, or sitting at the table, or pacing between the two, and he would be thinking about the peer review comment that had come back and the features editor's latest request for a timeline and the landlord's new policy about noise after ten and that Claire had sounded different on the phone last night in a way he could not quite identify.

He would not know that any of these things were connected. He would not know that they'd been designed. He would attribute them to the ordinary friction of an ambitious investigation. He would blame himself for the anxiety. He would clean his glasses and put them back on and look at his notes again and wonder, in the corrosive way Zersetzung was designed to produce, whether he was as brave as he thought he was.

He cleaned his glasses three times in two minutes. Each time the notes looked the same. The pattern he was looking for was not in the notes. The pattern was in the spaces between the notes—in the things the four governments had chosen not to record. He could feel it. He could not see it. He put his glasses back on and tried again.

The 2 AM kitchen was the raked sand. Zersetzung was the death strip translated into the vocabulary of a writing life. The precision of the work was the rhythm of the raking. Elena had been taught the vocabulary by Bruhn and had seen the translation with her own eyes twelve months earlier, in the back of a car near Glienicker Bridge, while a boy who had been trying to get to a country with fewer bread queues died in a strip of sand that had been designed to kill him.

She was the precision now.

West Berlin—May 1976.

The press event was in May 1976.

A reception at a hotel in West Berlin for visiting foreign

correspondents. Elena was attending as Ingrid Lindqvist, the cover she had used several times by now. Hatch was there. He was standing near the bar, talking to a Swedish correspondent about something that required frequent glasses-cleaning, which meant it was substantive. Elena was seated at a table fifteen feet away, conducting the kind of oblique surveillance that looked, to anyone watching, like a woman eating canapés.

The operation was three months into Phase Three. Everything was running. The environmental pressures were producing the expected behavioral modifications. Hatch's sleep was disrupted. His publication timeline was slipping. His relationship with Claire was under strain. She was monitoring Hatch's responses with the patient attention of a gardener watching a plant respond to controlled changes in light and water.

Halfway through the second hour a Bavarian businessman left the bar and decided Elena was the night's project. The refusals took two minutes. The corridor took thirty seconds. The alley took eleven. He went down against a dumpster. She came back through the lobby with her blouse straightened and his wallet in a storm drain. Hatch never noticed.

Hatch looked up as she sat down.

'Everything all right?' he asked. He had finished his conversation with the Swedish correspondent and was holding a glass of wine with the distracted attention of a man who was thinking about something else. 'That fellow seemed rather persistent.'

'He wanted to tell me about his car,' Elena said. She picked up her glass. Her hands were steady. 'I told him I preferred trains.'

Hatch laughed. The laugh was genuine. It was also, from

Elena's perspective, confirmation that the situation had been contained. He had noticed the businessman. He had not noticed the exit. He had not noticed the four-minute absence. He had not noticed the slight elevation in her color that came from physical exertion performed at speed in a cold alley. He had noticed a boring man bothering a woman, and now the boring man was gone, and the woman was back, and the evening continued.

Elena sat with Hatch for another hour. They talked about Gladio. He had been thinking about the Geneva document—the 'unregistered link'—and was sketching out what a follow-up investigation might look like. He asked if she thought the phrase was worth pursuing. She told him it was the most important thing in the four pages. He nodded. He cleaned his glasses. He put them back on. He did not clean them again for the rest of the conversation.

She would not mention the alley in her report. A target had nearly been burned because a drunk could not read a room. She would also not mention her assessment of how close Hatch was to the Sacco thread. She would describe the Geneva meeting. She would describe the four pages. She would quote the shared-custody phrase. She would not describe what she had done with the phrase inside her own head in the twenty minutes she'd spent committing it to memory, or that for one of those minutes she had thought about Calder. The second ledger was the line she was beginning to hold between herself and the institution, and the line was thinner every month.

She said goodnight to Hatch. She walked back through the West Berlin night, through streets that were lit and free in a way the other side could not be. She passed bars and young people laughing about things that did not involve intelligence or the systematic destruction of a journalist's confidence. She passed them the way she passed through every environment—inside it and apart from it. Alone in the way only people who maintained a permanent performance were ever alone.

Her hands were steady. They had been steady throughout the evening. They had been steady when she kneed the businessman and steady when she put his head into the wall and steady when she sat back down across from Hatch and picked up her glass and made a joke about trains. Her hands were always steady. This was what the machine had built. This was what she was.

In the morning she would cross back into East Berlin and file her report. The report would be comprehensive. It would not contain the Geneva document. It would not contain the second ledger. The things she was keeping from Moscow were now, she understood, being kept against Moscow.

Elena lay in the hotel bed at four in the morning. She did not sleep. Hatch in his kitchen at two in the morning, cleaning his glasses, wondering whether he was as brave as he thought he was. The nineteen-year-old in the death strip two hundred kilometers east, who had tried to cross. The professor in Leipzig who had wondered which of his drawers he had truly closed. All three men, she understood, were instances of the same operation—variations on a single shape applied at different resolutions.

She was the precision now. Bruhn had taught her the doctrine. The institution had given her the tools. And she'd discovered, over the months in East Berlin, that the thing she was best at was the thing she could not write about. She thought about Calder. His hand on her cheek in the Fitzrovia flat. By the time she was in it again she would have done enough to him that the place would have changed. Some things could be written. Some could be filed. Some could only be carried.

And she was the only person in any of the three services

who was watching where the precision pointed. The watching had become a second job. The second job had no salary, no handler, no extraction plan. It had only the drawer in Kensington and the notebook in her handbag and the count, in her head, of cities that contained a basement she did not know the address of. The watching had not yet made her anything. By the time it would, the cities would have a name for what she had become.

Sacco was one of the carried ones. Hatch's kitchen was another. The rope in the sand was a third.

In the morning she crossed the border and went back to work. The Friedrichstraße guard stamped her papers without looking up. His breath in the cold air was the only thing about him she would remember.

8

THE ORCHID GROWER

East Berlin—1976

Bruhn handed her a second file while the Hatch campaign ran. The file on Ernst Kessler was thin. This was unusual.

Elena's files were never thin. Her files on operational targets were organisms. They grew. They branched. They developed internal structures of cross-reference and annotation that reflected months of patient accumulation. The file on Hatch had been forty-seven pages by the time she designed Phase One. The file on the Leipzig professor had been thirty-two. The file on Katarina had been twenty-eight, and Katarina had been a secondary target who barely warranted her own folder.

The file on Kessler was six pages. Four were institutional: his position at the Ministry of Chemical Industry, his security clearance level, the documents he had access to. Two were biographical: born Leipzig 1927, educated at the Technical University, widowed many years before (pneumonia, no children, no current attachments). He had been on the Stasi's passive-monitoring list for nineteen years without a single flag being raised. He was fifty, diabetic, overweight, and operationally transparent.

He was, from any professional angle, a closed system.

Elena read the file four times, because the absence of information was itself information. The shape was particular.

Kessler's file contained no women, no drinking companions, no professional rivals, no friendships that generated the kind of social traffic surveillance could intercept and interpret. The absence of women was the operationally significant gap. The honey trap required a vulnerability the file did not confirm.

Bruhn had been characteristically direct about the assignment. 'The ministry files on the Schwedt petrochemical complex,' he'd said, standing at his desk at Normannenstraße with the rigidity of a man who communicated urgency through posture rather than words. 'Kessler has access. He's the deputy director of industrial planning. The files contain specifications for the catalytic cracking units that Moscow wants compared against Western designs. You have eight weeks.'

'What's his vulnerability?' Elena had asked.

'Find one.'

Elena did not say so, because saying unhelpful things to Bruhn was its own vulnerability.

She accepted the file. She walked back to her Lichtenberg flat through a Berlin afternoon that had not yet committed to autumn or winter.

She would have to be careful with Kessler. Not because Kessler was dangerous. Because she was.

She began with surveillance.

Kessler's routine was the most boring thing Elena had ever observed, and Elena had once spent eleven days watching a dead drop site in Helsinki where nothing happened except weather.

He left his flat at the same hour each morning, took the S-Bahn south to his office on Mohrenstraße, worked, came home. Tuesdays and Fridays he stopped at a state grocery. On Fridays he added a small cake from the bakery counter—a practice his diabetes ought to have ended years ago—which he carried home with the careful attention of a man transporting something fragile.

The cake was the first interesting thing.

Not the cake itself. The way he carried it. Kessler was not a careful man in general. His coat was adequate but unattended, missing a button, the collar slightly bent. He moved through the world with the efficient inattention of a man who had decided that the world's surfaces were not worth polishing. But the cake he carried as if it were a document. Two hands. A small adjustment of his walking pace to minimize jostling. A small expression at the corner of his mouth that Elena, watching from forty meters through binoculars, identified as anticipation.

The cake mattered to Kessler. Very little else appeared to. She catalogued the cake the way she catalogued everything, and a small unprofessional part of her was pleased that the man had a thing he loved.

She followed him home one Friday. Through the kitchen window she saw him set the cake box on the counter with ceremonial care, put on a kettle, open the box, look at the cake. He did not cut it. Then he disappeared into the back room and did not come out for four hours.

This happened every evening. Home, kitchen, kettle, back room. On weekends the back-room hours lengthened. No guests. No outside appointments. Whatever Kessler was doing, he was doing it as a private devotion.

After five days of surveillance, the file remained thin. Kessler remained opaque. Bruhn's eight-week deadline had become seven.

Elena decided to try the standard approach.

◆◆◆

Elena chose a Wednesday. The state grocery on Breite Straße housed a canteen where ministry workers took lunch, and Elena observed that Kessler ate there on Wednesdays, alone, at a table by the window, with a book and a plate of whatever the canteen was offering, which was usually a variation on potatoes and moral austerity.

Elena prepared the way she always prepared. She understood the mechanics of male attention the way an engineer understood structural failure. It was a system.

She wore a fitted charcoal skirt that ended two inches above the knee. A cream silk blouse, top two buttons open. Not three. Three was a declaration. Two was an invitation that could be denied if necessary. She wore a thin gold chain she had owned for years because it caught the light in a way that drew the eye toward the throat. Her hair was down. She had used a perfume Moscow's Directorate S issued its female operatives for specifically this purpose—a scent engineered to register on male olfactory circuits as attractive rather than identifiable.

She looked at herself in the mirror of her Lichtenberg flat. The woman looking back was not Elena Vasilieva. She was not Alice Marsh. She was a weapon system that happened to be shaped like a woman.

She arrived at the canteen just after noon. Kessler was at his usual table, reading a book—Elena could see the spine from the doorway: Christa Wolf, *Nachdenken über Christa T.* He had a plate of potato soup and a bread roll. His glasses were slightly fogged from the soup. He did not look up when she entered.

Elena selected the table beside his. She sat at a three-quarter angle—not directly opposite, which would have been confrontational, and not side-on, which would have been dismissive. The angle placed her in his peripheral vision at the geometry most likely to trigger involuntary attention. She crossed her legs. The skirt shifted. She picked up a menu she did not need and studied it with the focused attention of a woman who was thinking about lunch and not about the man at the next table, which was the entire point of the performance.

Kessler turned a page.

Elena ordered the same potato soup he was eating—mirroring as rapport. She shifted in her chair, a natural adjustment that caused the silk blouse to move against her body.

Kessler finished his bread roll. He turned another page.

Elena recalibrated. The passive approach was not registering. She moved to active.

She dropped her napkin. Not dramatically. A natural fumble. The napkin landed on the floor between their tables. She leaned down to retrieve it. The lean was engineered. The angle of her torso brought the neckline of the blouse forward. The two unfastened buttons created an aperture that, from Kessler's seated position, would provide a view of the silk brassiere and the body it framed. The lean lasted three seconds. Long enough to be seen. Short enough to appear unintentional.

She straightened. She glanced at Kessler with the expression she reserved for moments when a target was supposed to have noticed something and she needed to gauge whether the noticing had occurred.

Kessler was looking at his book. He had not moved. He had not looked up. His soup was getting cold, and his attention was entirely, immovably, categorically fixed on Christa Wolf's exploration of memory and identity in the German Democratic Republic.

Elena ate her soup.

She was not accustomed to this. In every city where she'd deployed the standard approach, it had never failed to produce at least a first-order response—a glance, a shift in posture, the attentional recalibration that meant the approach had been registered. Kessler had not glanced. Not once.

Elena took the next step. She stood up from her own table, carried her tray and her unfinished coffee around to his side of the room, and asked, in her most pleasant German, whether she might join him because the canteen was crowded and she did not want to eat alone. The canteen was not particularly crowded. But the lie was the kind every German bureaucrat understood as a request rather than an accusation, and Kessler responded the way he responded to any request that did not involve flowers—with mild, pre-emptive accommodation.

'Of course,' he said. He moved his book six inches to the right. He did not actually invite her. He simply created the geometry that an invitation would have created. Elena sat down across from him. She set her coffee on the table. She said her name was Anna Krause and that she was a junior researcher from the horticultural section of the Academy of Sciences.

'Krause,' Kessler said, as if testing the syllable. 'I don't know any Krauses.'

'No reason you would,' Elena said, smiling.

Kessler did not return the smile. He returned to his book.

Elena began the trained approach in its second mode—direct conversation, three-second eye contact broken at the natural moment, a particular kind of lean forward that paired interest with availability. She asked him about the book. She confessed she'd read the Wolf novel twice and was not sure she understood the ending.

It was at this point that Kessler farted.

It was not a small fart. It was not the kind of fart that could be plausibly attributed to a chair creaking or a distant pipe in the wall. It was a particular acoustic event of approximately a second's duration, originating from the upholstery of the canteen chair, audible at a radius of at least three meters.

Then it bloomed in a different sense.

The smell arrived in Elena's nostrils approximately two seconds after the sound. Cabbage processed by a digestive system that had been managing too much of it. A top note her olfactory cortex cataloged, against her will, as sulfur. The combined effect was immediate and comprehensive.

Elena's body executed three involuntary motions in approximately two-tenths of a second. Her nostrils contracted. Her diaphragm canceled an inhalation mid-breath. Her eyes attempted a small panicked lateral motion toward the window. Each was suppressed within a further tenth of a second. Her training had been required to override olfactory revulsion. The override was harder than she would have anticipated.

Across the table, Kessler turned a page.

He had not, as far as Elena could detect, registered the event as a social occurrence. There was no flush above his collar. No micro-flicker at the corners of his eyes. No adjustment of posture that would have indicated mortification or even awareness. He had farted in front of an attractive woman in a public canteen and had returned to his book with the placid focus of a man who experienced his own body as background noise that the foreground of his attention had long since learned to filter out.

Elena maintained the performance. She continued her sentence about the Wolf novel as if no acoustic or olfactory event had occurred at the table at all. Professionally, she was a woman to whom such events did not occur. The performance was the operation. The cost of the performance was a piece of dignity she had not previously noticed she possessed and that she now recognized she'd been spending without inventory for months. The cost was higher than the operational return on the lunch.

Elena pressed on.

She uncrossed her legs and recrossed them in the opposite direction.

She leaned forward across the table. Not the engineered three-second lean of the napkin retrieval, which had been a peripheral move designed to operate on Kessler's peripheral vision. A direct lean. The kind that brought her face close enough to his to make conversation a thing requiring lowered voices, and that brought the silk blouse into the visual aperture of a man directly across from her.

She reached across the table and took his hand off his book. To anyone watching from any angle other than Kessler's, it would have read as a small emphatic touch—a woman illustrating a point. From Kessler's angle: her fingers had wrapped around the back of his hand, lifted it off the page, and were now moving it across the table toward her own body, the trajectory unhurried and unambiguous.

She brought his hand toward her. Her own free hand had unbuttoned, in a motion her training had built into reflex, the third button of the silk blouse. Three buttons were open now. She brought Kessler's hand to the inside curve of her collarbone, where the skin was warm and the geometry was no longer ambiguous on any frequency a heterosexual man had ever been known to receive. She held his hand there. She did not press it down. The four centimeters were the invitation. The four centimeters said: here is the door. Open it.

The fart was still in her nostrils. The sulfur top note had not yet dissipated. Elena was performing the most direct seduction her training had prepared her to perform while breathing through the residue of a gastric event in a public canteen at a Ministry of Chemical Industry. The two experiences were occurring in the same body in the same second. Elena did not know where to put either of them.

Kessler blinked. The canteen's fluorescent lights buzzed above them. A tray clattered two tables away. A man in a gray suit stood up and walked past without looking.

Elena had not been built to file the smell of cabbage processed by another human's intestines combined with the warmth of that human's hand against the inside curve of one's own collarbone. The combination was its own particular weather.

Kessler's hand did not move.

It did not pull away or press forward. It rested on Elena's collarbone with the precise weight of a hand placed there by an external force and having no internal opinion about whether it should stay. The hand of a man waiting for the conversation to return to orchids, neither resisting nor participating in the physical event his hand was currently part of.

Elena understood, with immediate clarity, that Kessler did not want sex. The hand on her collarbone was the hand of a man being polite about a gesture he did not understand. The lack of response was not refusal. Elena could have worked with refusal—refusal meant the man was on the same map as the operation. Kessler was not on the map.

Elena released his hand. She returned it to the page she took it from. The hand resumed its previous position with the same neutral inattention it had brought to the contact. Kessler turned a page.

She rebuttoned the third button of the blouse without looking down.

The fart, still faintly present, was now also part of the record.

It had been the background noise to the most direct invitation Elena had ever issued in the field, and the invitation had been received by a man who had not noticed the noise or the invitation or the warmth of his own hand on a stranger's collarbone.

Kessler closed his book. He put on his coat. He picked up his tray. He walked past Elena's table at a distance of approximately eighteen inches and out of the canteen without once, at any point, looking at her.

Elena sat at the empty table for a full minute. She was recalculating. The standard approach had produced nothing. The performance had been delivered to an empty theater. Kessler was an empty theater. Not gay. Gay men noticed and declined. Kessler was absent from the transaction entirely, the way a man reading a very good book was absent from the room.

She left the canteen and walked back to her flat. She changed out of the silk blouse and put on the wool trousers and sweater she wore for surveillance work.

In the evening, she poured herself a glass of cheap East German brandy and sat in her kitchen and laughed once, briefly, into the small empty room. The most precisely calibrated woman Moscow had produced in a decade had deployed the full apparatus of seduction against a chemist in a state canteen and the chemist had farted in her face and turned a page. Somewhere in Moscow her instructors would have been professionally devastated and personally delighted.

It was the most honest sound she had produced in some time.

Then she climbed the fire escape.

The building across from Kessler's flat in East Berlin was a residential block identical to his—five stories, concrete, the architectural style the GDR had perfected into a vocabulary of rectangles. The fire escape on its back side offered a line of sight directly into Kessler's back room. Elena climbed to the fourth floor after dark, when the fire escape was invisible from the street. She had binoculars, a small notebook, and a flask of coffee she'd made strong enough to last the night.

A cat was sitting on the fourth-floor landing.

It was not a house cat. It had the lean, angular shape of an animal that had never been fed by a hand it trusted. Gray, short-haired, with a torn left ear and eyes the color of polished steel. The ear had healed badly—old damage, untreated. The body had simply continued. That was what happened to the things that lived along the edges of buildings like this one: they either healed fast or they died, and the surviving ones carried their own history in their faces.

Elena lowered herself onto the landing slowly. She set down the binoculars. She extended her hand—not toward the cat, not close enough to touch, just far enough that the cat could register the offer. She had nothing to offer. Elena understood this. The gesture was for her own benefit. Some part of her wanted, for reasons she did not examine, to be the person who offered.

The cat looked at her hand. It did not move toward it. It did not move away. It held the position with the particular discipline of an animal that had learned, through repetition, that approaching and retreating were both more expensive than remaining still.

Elena withdrew her hand. When she looked back, the landing was empty. The cat had gone the way feral things went—without sound, without ceremony, into the dark geometry of the building's exterior.

She looked into the back room.

And she understood everything.

◆◆◆

Orchids.

The room was full of orchids. Not the kind people bought at florists and put on windowsills and forgot to water until they died. These were serious orchids. Research orchids. The room had been converted into a greenhouse. Even through binoculars at forty meters in November darkness, Elena could see that the windows had been fitted with supplemental lighting. Grow lights. Fluorescent tubes mounted at angles that told her Kessler had studied the light requirements of his specimens and had built an illumination system calibrated to their needs. Shelving lined three walls. On the shelves, in containers of various sizes, arranged with the meticulous organization of a man who maintained a filing system for living things, were orchids.

Dozens of them. The evidence of years—not months, years—of patient cultivation. She could see Kessler moving between the shelves with a misting bottle, attending to individual plants with a level of attention she had not seen him apply to any other activity in six days of surveillance. He examined leaves. He adjusted the position of pots. He knelt beside a specimen on a lower shelf and spent fifteen minutes doing something that involved small, very delicate movements of his hands.

He was happy. Elena could see it from forty meters away, through binoculars, in the dark. The man who moved through the world with efficient inattention was gone. In the greenhouse, Kessler was present. Kessler was attentive. Kessler was a man in the only room where he wanted to be.

Elena lowered the binoculars. She drank her coffee. She sat on the fire escape in the cold and thought about the canteen. The silk blouse. The napkin. The fart. The forty-five minutes of approach that had not produced a single glance. Now she understood. She had been broadcasting on a frequency Kessler's receiver was not tuned to.

Kessler's attention was not absent. It was allocated. He had given all of it—every circuit, every frequency, every gram of the attentiveness that other men distributed across women and ambition and social performance—to the things in his back room. The orchids had not left room for Elena. The orchids had not left room for anyone.

She revised her entire approach in ninety seconds.

The honey trap was dead. Not because it had been poorly executed. Dead because Kessler's wiring did not connect to the circuits she was transmitting on. The frequency she operated on did not reach Kessler. He was tuned to a different band. His band had petals.

She would have to invent the approach from scratch, in six weeks, for a man who could not be seduced because seduction required an audience and Kessler's audience was a roomful of orchids.

The new approach assembled itself in Elena's mind with the speed that came from having done this enough times to recognize the architecture before the blueprint was finished. She would become someone Kessler could talk to about orchids. She would acquire a real knowledge of orchids. Real enough to pass Kessler's scrutiny. The approach would take longer than the standard approach. Bruhn's eight-week deadline was already unrealistic. It had just become impossible.

This would require her to know about orchids.

Elena did not know about orchids. She knew they were plants. She knew they were popular. She knew the word derived from the Greek orchis, which meant testicle, a fact she'd learned at the Red Banner Institute from a linguistics instructor who had mentioned it as an example of etymology's occasional lack of dignity, and which she had retained because it was exactly the kind of information that was useless until it wasn't.

She needed to learn. Quickly. In a way that would survive scrutiny from a man who had spent decades studying the subject and who would detect a superficial education the way Elena detected a bad cover—instinctively, immediately, and with prejudice.

She had six weeks.

In the next three weeks she read eleven books on orchid cultivation.

She read them in German. She read about *Paphiopedilum rothschildianum*.

The species that changed the operation. *Paphiopedilum rothschildianum*—Rothschild's slipper orchid. One of the rarest on Earth, overcollected nearly to extinction, rediscovered after it had been presumed lost. A single plant took seven years to bloom from seed. Seven years of daily attention, of light and temperature and humidity, applied to a living thing that rewarded that patience with a flower that lasted three weeks and was gone.

Elena understood Kessler now. Not fully. Structurally. A man who spent seven years growing something that bloomed for three weeks was not motivated by results. He was motivated by process.

She recognized the principle. The network grew operatives the way Kessler grew *rothschildianum*: slowly, patiently, in completely controlled conditions, across years. Moscow called it cultivation. Kessler called it horticulture. The hand above Moscow, which had neither a name nor a department, did not call it anything. It simply waited for the bloom.

On the nineteenth day of her preparation, she walked into the only orchid nursery in East Berlin.

The nursery was in Treptow, in a greenhouse attached to the Botanical Garden that had survived the war, the division, and the state's conviction that ornamental horticulture was a bourgeois indulgence. The greenhouse had been there for generations. It was easier to maintain than to close.

The head of the nursery was a woman named Frau Lentz. She was sixty-seven, built like a fire hydrant, and she regarded Elena's arrival at her door with the suspicion of a person who had spent four decades defending a greenhouse from people who did not deserve access to it.

'I'm interested in orchid cultivation,' Elena said. 'Specifically *Paphiopedilum*.'

Frau Lentz looked at her for four seconds. Elena could see Frau Lentz's eyes moving from her face to her hands to her shoes to her posture, reading the physical text the way Elena read people at gallery openings and press receptions, extracting data from surfaces that most people did not know were transmitting.

'Why *Paphiopedilum*?' Frau Lentz asked.

Elena told her. She talked about the pollination mechanism—the way the pouch trapped insects and forced them past the reproductive structures in a sequence that was, from an engineering perspective, architecturally elegant. She talked about mycorrhizal dependency—that orchids grew in partnership with specific fungi and that severing the partnership killed the plant. She talked about *rothschildianum* specifically—the rediscovery, the conservation status, the seven-year bloom cycle. She talked with the authority of a woman who had read eleven books in the last three weeks and who had, without intending to, become interested.

She had not anticipated this. The orchids were interesting. Not operationally. Genuinely. Like a locksmith discovering that her own door was unlocked.

Frau Lentz listened. When Elena finished, the old woman's expression had not changed, but something behind it had shifted—the way a locked door looks the same from the outside whether the deadbolt has been thrown or withdrawn, but the person holding the key knows the difference.

'Come with me,' Frau Lentz said.

She led Elena through the greenhouse. Past the tropical section, where the humidity hit like a wall and the air smelled like wet soil and chlorophyll and the complex sweetness that large-scale plant respiration produced in enclosed spaces. Past the cacti and succulents, which sat in their dry section with the patience of organisms designed for waiting. Into a back room locked with a key Frau Lentz wore on a chain around her neck.

The room contained orchids Elena read about but never seen. A *Dracula vampira*, black-petalled and absurd. A *Bulbophyllum phalaenopsis* with leaves three feet long that smelled, according to Elena's reading, like rotting meat. And in the corner, on a low shelf under a dedicated grow light, a *Paphiopedilum rothschildianum*.

It was not in bloom. It would not bloom for another two years, Frau Lentz said. She said this the way other people said my daughter is at university—with pride, with patience, with the forward-looking tenderness of a person who was willing to wait because the waiting was part of the point.

'Who else in Berlin grows these?' Elena asked. The question was operational. The tone was not.

'One man,' Frau Lentz said. 'Kessler. At the ministry. He comes to me for supplies. I have been his source for growing medium and fertilizer for many years.' She paused. 'He has the only other *rothschildianum* in the country. His is further along than mine. He says it will bloom within the year.'

Elena heard the note in Frau Lentz's voice. Not jealousy. Something more interesting. Respect. The respect of one serious practitioner for another.

'I would very much like to meet him,' Elena said.

Frau Lentz looked at her again. The four-second evaluation. Then: 'I will see what I can do.'

The introduction happened on a Thursday.

Frau Lentz had arranged it at the greenhouse—neutral territory, orchid territory, the only kind of territory on which Kessler appeared to be comfortable. Elena arrived ten minutes early. She was wearing a green blouse she'd chosen because it was the color of *Paphiopedilum* leaves and because it was not the kind of blouse a woman wore when she was trying to attract a man. The message was: I am here for the orchids.

Kessler arrived precisely on time. He was shorter than she'd expected from the surveillance. He was wearing the same coat with the missing button. His glasses were thick-framed and sat slightly askew on a face that was weathered and unremarkable and belonged to a man who had stopped worrying about his appearance approximately two decades ago and had not regretted the decision.

He shook her hand. The handshake was brief, dry, and contained none of the signals that Elena's training had taught her to read in male-female handshakes—no extended grip, no thumb pressure, no angle adjustment. It was the handshake of a man who shook hands because social convention required it and who would have preferred to skip the convention and proceed directly to the orchids.

If he recognized her from the canteen six weeks earlier, he gave no sign. The woman who had sat beside him in a silk blouse had been a different organism in the same body. The current organism—green blouse, sensible shoes, here for the orchids—was registering as a new acquaintance.

They proceeded directly to the orchids.

Frau Lentz led them to the back room. Kessler entered the way a man entered a cathedral, not with reverence exactly but with the quality of attention that came from being in a place where the things that mattered to him most were kept. His eyes went to the *rothschildianum* immediately. He knelt beside it. He examined a leaf. He looked up at Frau Lentz.

'You've adjusted the nitrogen,' he said.

'Two weeks ago.'

'I can see it in the new growth. It's responding well.'

Frau Lentz made a sound Elena interpreted as satisfaction disguised as indifference.

Elena watched the exchange with the quiet concentration of a woman conducting an assessment. She was mapping Kessler the way she mapped everyone—language patterns, attention distribution, emotional registers. But Kessler's seams were not the kind she could exploit in any conventional way.

Kessler loved his orchids. This was a weakness—not the way loving a woman was a weakness, but the way caring about anything was. It gave the world a surface on which to grip you. But the grip had to be applied correctly. Orchids required you to enter the room and care about the same thing the target cared about, and you had to care genuinely, because people who had spent thirty years loving something could detect insincerity the way dogs detected fear—through channels that were not rational and could not be faked.

Elena decided to be genuine.

She was choosing to be honest about orchids to be dishonest about everything else. The honesty was the tool. The genuine interest she'd developed over three weeks of reading was the key that would open the door that seduction and coercion could not.

But the decision had a cost. The machinery of performance she maintained—the constant, exhausting machinery that kept Alice Marsh and every other cover identity running—did not have a setting for partial honesty. It was designed for total performance or total privacy. Introducing a genuine element into an operational context was like opening a window in a pressurized aircraft. The pressure differential wanted to equalize. The genuine wanted to spread.

She ignored this. She asked Kessler about his *rothschildianum.*

He talked for forty-five minutes.

Listening to Kessler talk about his *rothschildianum* was different from any forty-five-minute conversation Elena had previously listened to in an operational context. Every man Elena had ever targeted had, at some point in his monologue, exposed the small tell that meant the monologue was a performance—the pause where he checked whether she was still listening, the reach for the phrase he'd used before, the rhythm of a man who was watching himself talk. Kessler had no tell. He was not watching himself. He was inside the subject the way a swimmer was inside water.

He told her about the growing medium. He told her about the temperature cycles—the way a ten-degree drop at night triggered the hormonal cascade that eventually produced the bloom years later. He told her about humidity, about light, about the exact dust-particle count at which the orchid's fine aerial roots began to struggle. He told her he had lost two buds to blast the previous winter and the loss had taught him more about humidity than the two years of successful blooms that had preceded it.

He told her about patience.

'People think patience is passive,' he said. They were standing in Frau Lentz's greenhouse, and he was holding a leaf of the *rothschildianum* between his thumb and forefinger with a lightness that suggested he understood, at the level of muscle memory, exactly how much pressure a leaf could tolerate. 'It's not. Patience is the most active thing there is. Patience is paying attention every day and making small adjustments and trusting that the adjustments matter even when you can't see the results. Seven years. Seven years of daily attention. And then one morning you come in and the spike is there, and it's the most beautiful thing you've ever seen, and it lasts three weeks, and then it's over. And you start again.'

He looked at Elena. He was not performing sensitivity or depth or passion. He was a man standing in a greenhouse telling a woman about a flower, and the telling was the thing itself, not a vehicle for anything else.

'Why do you start again?' Elena asked. The question was genuine.

Kessler smiled. It was the first time Elena saw him smile, and the smile transformed his face the way sunrise transformed a landscape.

'Because the growing is the point,' he said. He was still looking at the plant, not at her. 'The flower is evidence. The growing is the relationship.'

Elena stood in the greenhouse and received this sentence the way she received intelligence—by taking it apart and examining its components. But the sentence did not want to be used. The sentence wanted to be heard. And Elena, standing in a greenhouse in Treptow in the winter of 1976, heard it.

She filed it anyway. Of course she did. But the place where she kept the things that were true and the place where she kept the things that were useful were getting harder to tell apart.

Kessler invited her to see his collection on their third meeting.

The invitation was not romantic. Elena was certain of this because she had spent two meetings refining her assessment and because the signals were unambiguous. Kessler's attention was allocated entirely to orchids, and the invitation was about orchids. He wanted to show her his collection. He wanted someone to be present for the things he cared about, because caring alone was not quite the same as caring. Elena understood this. She had been alone with her own caring for a long time.

It was restful. This surprised her. The constant ambient calculation—the awareness that every man in every room was running a subroutine assessing her as a sexual prospect—was something she carried as a weight until the weight was absent. The absence was like putting down a bag she had forgotten she was holding.

She went to his flat on a Saturday afternoon.

She did not bring the F-21. She left it on the kitchen table in Lichtenberg and looked at it for a long moment before closing the door. One hundred and seventy-eight frames—the same camera she had carried on previous operations. The F-21 was the standard tool. The standard tool produced standard outcomes. She was not going to use it today. She was going to walk into Kessler's flat carrying nothing, because what she needed from Kessler was not the thing a camera could take.

Kessler's front room was exactly what surveillance had predicted. Sparse, functional, the living space of a man who had allocated all his domestic attention to a single room. A desk. A lamp. A narrow bookshelf. A photograph, framed, of a woman in her forties with her hair up. His wife. Dead seven years.

Then he opened the door to the back room, and Elena stepped into his greenhouse.

It was more impressive than the binoculars had suggested. The shelving was hand-built. The grow lights demonstrated a sophisticated understanding of photosynthetic wavelengths. The humidity and temperature were calibrated with industrial-grade sensors repurposed for an amateur application at considerable effort. A butane torch on the workbench, its nozzle sooted. Beyond the window, a galvanized bucket on the balcony rail, surface still dimpled from the morning's rain. On the lower shelf, three pots wore small handwritten tags—*Dresden, Rostock, Leipzig*. Everything spoke of years.

And the orchids. A *Cattleya* with flowers the size of her hand. A *Dendrobium* in a cascade of yellow blooms hanging from a wire basket. A *Bulbophyllum* in active bloom, tiny maroon flowers arranged in a ring that looked like a diagram of something mathematical.

And in the corner, under its own light, the *rothschildianum.*

It was not in bloom. It would not bloom for three more months, Kessler said. He said this with the steadiness of a man who had been waiting for years and who had learned, through the discipline of orchid cultivation, that anticipation was not anxiety but attention. He knelt beside it. He showed her the new growth—a leaf emerging from the crown, pale green, the texture of something so new that it had not yet decided what it was going to be.

'Touch it,' he said.

Elena knelt beside him. She touched the leaf. It was cool and smooth and alive in the unmistakable way that living things were alive—with a temperature that was not the temperature of the room, with a presence that was not the presence of an object but of an organism.

'It's beautiful,' she said. She meant it.

Kessler looked at her. The look was not romantic, not evaluative, not operational. It was the look of a man who had found, after decades of solitary practice, someone who understood why it mattered. The look said: you see it. You actually see it.

They spent three hours in the greenhouse. He made tea afterward. They sat in his sparse living room and drank it and talked about orchids and about nothing else. At no point did Elena mention the Ministry of Chemical Industry. At no point did she mention Schwedt or petrochemical specifications.

She was not collecting intelligence. She was building trust. And the trust she was building was, for the first time in her career, built on a foundation that was not entirely a lie.

The files came on their seventh meeting.

He mentioned the files in passing. They were sitting in his living room after three hours in the greenhouse, drinking tea, and he was talking about the challenges of obtaining growing supplies in the GDR—the grinding frustration of a man whose passion required materials the socialist economy considered non-essential.

'The irony,' he said, 'is that my ministry processes ten thousand tonnes of organic chemical compounds annually. The Schwedt complex alone produces more polymers in a week than I would need in a lifetime for potting medium. But try requesting a kilogram of perlite through official channels and you'd think I was asking for weapons-grade uranium.'

He laughed. Elena laughed with him. The laugh was genuine.

'I have the specifications on my desk,' he continued. 'The entire Schwedt production matrix. Catalytic cracking outputs, polymer yields, everything. I could design the perfect growing medium from the ministry's own chemical outputs if anyone cared enough to let me try.'

Elena sipped her tea. She had been listening normally until he said Schwedt. After Schwedt she was listening in two languages. The rest of her was maintaining the conversation. The operational part was cataloging every word, estimating the density of intelligence the Schwedt specifications would contain, preparing questions designed to extract more without sounding like questions.

She noted, without permitting herself to dwell on it, that this was the second living room in three years where she had sat across from a man who poured her tea and talked to her about a thing he loved and trusted her with the telling. The first living room was in Kensington. The man in it had been drinking whisky instead of tea and had been talking about a painting instead of an orchid, but the rest of the shape had been identical. Elena did not know what to do with the pattern. She filed it in the place she kept the things she did not know what to do with, which was the most crowded file she maintained.

She did not ask to see the files. She talked about polymer substrates. She talked about pH requirements and bark-based media. The conversation moved, as conversations between enthusiasts always moved, from the general to the theoretical to the practical, from wouldn't it be nice to I could show you.

Kessler went to his briefcase. He returned with a folder. The folder contained the Schwedt petrochemical complex production specifications—catalytic cracking units, polymer yields, chemical outputs, thermal efficiency ratings. The documents Moscow wanted. The documents Bruhn had given her eight weeks to obtain.

Kessler handed her the folder the way he handed her a pot of orchids. With care, with trust.

'Have a look,' he said. 'Tell me if you see anything we could use for a substrate.'

Elena looked. She read every page with the speed of a woman who had been trained to photograph documents with her eyes and retain them with a precision that made microfilm redundant. She did not hurry. She read at the pace of a curious person encountering unfamiliar material, occasionally asking Kessler a question about a term she did not recognize, letting him define the vocabulary while she completed the reading.

She made two comments about polymer chain lengths that were relevant to both petrochemistry and horticulture.

She handed the folder back. She suggested two compounds that might work as substrate components. The suggestions were real. She'd done the research. Kessler wrote them down with the careful attention of a man receiving valuable information, which he was, although the valuable information he thought he was receiving and the valuable information Elena had actually extracted from the interaction were as different as the two sides of the Wall.

She left at six o'clock. He walked her to the door. He shook her hand—the same brief, dry, unfrightened handshake. He said he would try the polymer substrate and report on the results.

Elena walked to the S-Bahn. She had the documents. All of them. Every page retained with the photographic precision the Red Banner Institute had spent two years training into her. She would reproduce them from memory tonight. Bruhn would have them by noon. Moscow by the weekend. The operation was complete. Six weeks against an eight-week deadline.

A perfect operation.

It was the only operation in eighteen months in which no one had been harmed. The Kessler operation—designed by Moscow as routine industrial intelligence—had asked her to make something rather than break something. The making was indistinguishable from the breaking. The materials were different. The motion was the same.

OPERATIVE REPORT ABTEILUNG II

SUBJECT: KESSLER, ERNST

PERIOD: October—December 1976

CLASSIFICATION: RESTRICTED / HANDLER EYES ONLY

Subject's files on Schwedt petrochemical complex obtained in full. Access achieved through cultivation of personal relationship based on shared interest in botanical horticulture (orchid cultivation). No coercive measures employed. No sexual contact. No Zersetzung protocols initiated. Subject remains unaware of intelligence dimension of relationship.

Method: Standard approach (physical) attempted and abandoned after initial assessment indicated zero receptivity. Alternative approach designed around subject's primary psychological investment (orchid cultivation, specifically *Paphiopedilum rothschildianum*). Operative spent three weeks acquiring specialist botanical knowledge sufficient to establish credibility with subject. Introduction facilitated through subject's existing supply contact (Frau Lentz, Treptow Botanical Garden).

Access obtained through intellectual rather than physical approach.

Assessment: Subject may yield further intelligence on ministry operations if relationship is maintained. Recommend continued cultivation at current frequency.

Note: Subject's *rothschildianum* is expected to bloom in approximately three months. Operative requests permission to attend.

Bruhn read the report. He read it twice. The second reading took longer than the first. Elena attributed this to the final line, which was not standard operative language. She had included it knowing as much, and not caring. She had earned the right to one sentence that was hers rather than the institution's.

He looked up.

'You want to attend a flower blooming,' he said.

'I want to maintain the access channel,' Elena said. 'The relationship has ongoing intelligence value. The most natural way to maintain it is to continue engaging with the subject's primary interest.'

This was true. It was also a lie. Both at once. Bruhn could hear the operational frequency. He could not hear the other one. Nobody could. That was the frequency Elena kept for herself.

Bruhn approved the request. He made a note in the file. He did not smile, because Bruhn did not smile. Something at the corners of his mouth suggested the possibility.

'An orchid,' he said. 'You obtained classified ministry documents through an orchid.'

'Through patience,' Elena said. 'The orchid was the medium.'

She left Bruhn's office. She walked down the corridor at Normannenstraße, past the offices where men and women sat at desks and managed the systematic surveillance of sixteen million people. The work was vast and precise and patient.

The work was not entirely different from what Kessler did with his orchids, except in what the attention was allocated to.

She thought about Kessler's *rothschildianum*. Three months until it bloomed. Seven years of daily attention arriving at a single three-week flower. She thought about the leaf she'd touched in Frau Lentz's greenhouse. She thought about the canteen, the silk blouse, the fart. She thought about the file she had just delivered. Specifications for catalytic cracking units that would be compared against Western designs and would contribute, in some way, to the continuation of the thing she had been handed by Bruhn. A perfect operation. And its perfection was the problem. It was every kind of problem.

In her next report to Moscow, she would note that the Kessler operation had been completed ahead of schedule with no exposure risk. She would recommend ongoing cultivation of the source. She would describe the methodology in clinical terms that conveyed competence and efficiency and the bloodless register Moscow required.

She would not mention that she was looking forward to seeing the flower.

Outside, a tram went past. The rails in the pavement of Normannenstraße had been laid before the war. The wheels made the same sound they had made for fifty years. Elena listened until the sound was gone.

She thought about the photograph she would request from Kessler when the bloom came. A single image of the *rothschildianum* in flower, taken in his greenhouse, with the handbuilt shelving in the background and the grow light catching the cream-and-maroon pouch. She would keep the photograph in the drawer beside the stove in her Kensington flat, and it would be the only object in that flat that would not have to perform anything. The orchid would not know it had been photographed. The photograph would not know it was being kept. It would just be a flower in a drawer, and she would know what it meant.

Elena closed her eyes in the dark. The brandy was finished. The flat was quiet. Some things could be filed. Some things could be carried. The orchid was, in a category Elena had not yet found a word for, neither.

In the morning she went back to Normannenstraße. The orchid stayed.

In London, James Calder slept in a flat she had been performing the role of being away from. The work she had been refusing—mentioning him in any report, any cable, any conversation with Yuri—was the only refusal she was certain she would not undo. The refusal was the line she had drawn through her own usefulness. The line was small. The line was hers. The line was, she suspected without yet being able to say so, the only thing in any of the cities she lived in that the network did not yet own.

9

CHECKPOINT

Checkpoint Charlie—October 1977

Eleven seconds.

The corridor was a hundred meters of engineered disorientation—fenced walls, floodlights shadowless, footsteps returning off the barriers with a flatness that made a footfall behind sound like one beside. The Stasi checkpoint was behind them, on the East Berlin side of the Wall. Checkpoint Charlie—the American crossing—was ahead, on the West Berlin side. Voss was walking. Elena was walking. Neither of them had yet begun to run.

Then the two men stepped out from behind the scaffolding.

Voss understood in one second. The knife came into his hand from his coat pocket. He did not reach for it the way a startled man reaches for a tool. He reached for it the way a man reaches for a thing he has been carrying in that pocket for fourteen days.

He ran.

Elena followed.

The clock started the moment his feet left the concrete.

Four weeks earlier.

His name was Stefan Voss. Thirty-one. An engineer at the *Kombinat Mikroelektronik* in Erfurt who had spent four years designing integrated circuits for a state that would not let him attend the conferences where his designs were discussed, who had published three papers in journals he was not permitted to read once they left the country. Who had decided, in the slow corrosive way such decisions were made, that the Wall was not a border but a sentence, and that he had served enough of it.

He had approached a West German journalist at a trade fair in Leipzig. The journalist had passed the contact to the BND. Voss had been providing technical intelligence on East German semiconductor production for eleven months. The intelligence was good. The communication channel was not.

Moscow had intercepted the channel in March. The KGB had shared the intercept with the Stasi in April. Bruhn had opened the file in May.

By August, Bruhn had read the file twice and Elena had read it four times. The first reading was operational. The second looked for the shape beneath the content. The third tracked Voss's vocabulary—the *Fachsprache* of an engineer, the bureaucratic German of a Kombinat employee, and the silent English of someone who read Western journals after hours. The fourth reading she did not share with Bruhn.

What she found in the fourth reading was the design.

Not perfectly. Enough. Radiation-hardened logic chips. Compact form factors. Long shelf-life tolerances. Electronics designed to survive inside something that emitted and required isolation from its own output. The components Voss had been designing fit the shape Elena had been triangulating for a year.

He had been building brains for backpack-sized weapons missing from the NATO inventory since 1968. He had not known he was.

Or he had.

Elena did not yet know.

What she had also found in the fourth reading—and what she did not file in any report Bruhn was going to read—was a journal title three pages into the appendix, in a debrief footnote the BND case officer had not flagged. *Nucleonics Week*. The same English-language trade journal that had lain folded open on a writing table in apartment 3B on Storgata in July 1973. Petrov had read it. Voss had read it. The connection went into the small red notebook in pencil, in Russian.

If Voss was the network's—one of the unregistered maintenance contacts she was learning to name without naming—then walking him east was returning him to his employers. If Voss was the West's, then walking him east was sending him to Stasi cells he would not survive.

Bruhn would not be told. The desk above Bruhn would not tell Elena. The instrument did not require the answer to operate.

She closed the file. She would walk him east in either case.

Bruhn named the operation RETURN. He had a gift for names that sounded bureaucratic enough to survive a filing system and clinical enough to survive a conscience.

Elena's brief was four pages. She read it twice. She understood what Bruhn did not write on the second reading.

The operational shape was simple enough on paper. Voss was already in West Berlin on his authorized October colloquium. He had three days of permitted residence in the West and a return ticket he was not, in any meaningful sense, required to use. He could walk into a BND office on the Tiergartenstraße that afternoon and be a defector by evening. The plan had to give him a reason to go back.

Two reasons. The chips. The family.

Voss had given the BND eleven months of low-grade semiconductor intelligence and had held back the final designs—the radiation-hardened logic, the fabrication tolerances, the test data. Those lived in a small archival annex of the Kombinat that the ministry had relocated to East Berlin in 1975 for centralized records management. The annex was twenty minutes' walk from the colloquium hall.

And the family. Voss's wife and six-year-old son had traveled with him from Erfurt for the colloquium week and were staying with the wife's mother in Pankow, a quiet residential neighborhood in East Berlin. Voss could walk into Tiergartenstraße tonight; his wife and son could not. The geography of the colloquium had placed all three of them on the wrong side of the Wall at the same time, and Voss would not leave without them.

The plan used both as levers. Elena, playing Voss's BND extraction contact, would offer him the only deal he would take: cross east with him, get the family out by sea, walk with him to the annex for the documents, walk him back through the American checkpoint on West German papers. One operation. One Saturday. Family out, chips out, Voss out.

Four-fifths of the operation would be real. The sea extraction would be real. The wife and the son would reach Malmö. The documents would travel as far as Bruhn's filing system and no further.

The walk through the American checkpoint would end in the corridor.

She would wear Katrin Berger's face across the entire operation. Thirty years old, a freelance translator, a flat in West Berlin set up six months earlier for this work. The cover was good. The cover was real. The cover would be returning to West Berlin alone on Saturday evening.

Bruhn could have ordered Voss arrested in Pankow. He had

not. The arrest would have left a record at his mother-in-law's building, an absence in the colloquium hall, a noise the West would have heard within forty-eight hours. Bruhn wanted Voss with the documents in his hand, and he wanted the operation invisible. The corridor was the only place where invisibility and possession could be acquired in the same instant.

Bruhn wanted Voss back because the BND wanted him out. Elena wanted him because his file fit the shape in her head. Voss wanted Malmö.

Only one of them would get what they wanted.

Wednesday. Technische Universität Berlin.

The colloquium broke early. Voss signed out for the library to consult a journal the East did not receive. He walked the seven minutes through the late-October damp.

Elena was at the third-floor reading room when he arrived.

She had been there for forty minutes. Across the room, a student was asleep on her textbooks. Elena had been that student at Leningrad State once.

The volume Voss needed was beneath her hand.

He approached. He hesitated—a beat longer than the file predicted. His eye passed over her hand, her notebook, her coat on the back of the chair. A scan. Engineer's attention, reading a component before picking it up. He asked, quietly, for the volume.

She slid it a quarter-inch toward him. 'I've finished the article I was looking at. Please.'

Her German was West Berlin German. Clear, educated, rehearsed on a tape loop and corrected by an instructor who had grown up in the city.

He sat across from her. He opened the journal.

Eight minutes in, she slid her own notebook across the table. 'I am having difficulty with the calculation on this page. I wonder if you would look.'

The page held, in her hand, in the upper margin, in pencil, the four words she had carried in her head for four months.

Die Forelle schwimmt westlich.

It was the recognition phrase the BND had given Voss through a Rostock dead drop in June. He had repeated it to himself for sixteen weeks without writing it down.

His breathing did not change. His eye, however, rested on the phrase for a half-second longer than the phrase required. An engineer reading a line of code. Looking for the compiler error. Looking for the place where the syntax was too clean.

Elena did not miss it. She did not react either.

'The calculation is correct,' he said. 'The author has used an approximation that applies only to footnote seven.'

'I missed the footnote.'

'It is easy to miss.'

A pause. A second too long.

She closed her notebook. 'There is a café two streets from here. Would you permit me to buy you a coffee before the library closes?'

'Yes.'

He gathered his journal. He put on his coat. The top of a paperback showed from an inner pocket—a cloth spine worn to the color of old milk. A novel by Theodor Fontane, the nineteenth-century realist—a Western edition. He had been carrying it somewhere.

They left the library separately.

Elena walked two blocks east, two blocks south, and doubled back. Voss took a different route. He was not following tradecraft she had taught him. He was following tradecraft from somewhere else.

They arrived at the café within ninety seconds of each other and took the back table. The waiter was not listening.

Elena ordered coffee she would drink.

'My name,' she said, when the coffee arrived, 'is Katrin. I am the person the trout was going to meet.'

Voss's hands were around his cup. His eyes rested on the rim, as if the cup held the only safe surface in the café.

'I have been in the field fourteen years. I have extracted eleven people. Nine successfully. I am going to tell you how this is going to work, once, and you are going to listen without interrupting, because we have perhaps eight minutes before your minder notices the library has a back door.'

Voss listened.

'Your wife and your son first. Not through the American crossing, not through any checkpoint. A Swedish dockers' channel out of Rostock—a fishing boat that runs the Trelleborg route, a rented flat in Malmö, a Swedish address recorded in no file our ministry can reach. Saturday morning a courier will collect them from the Pankow flat and put them on the Rostock train. They will be at sea by Saturday afternoon. They will be in Malmö by Sunday morning.'

Voss's cup was very still.

'You attend the colloquium tomorrow and Friday. You behave. You return east on Friday evening with the delegation by the standard route. Friday night you tell your wife. The courier comes for her at six on Saturday morning.'

'You and I,' Voss said.

'I cross east with you Saturday morning. I am Katrin Berger, your BND escort, and I am with you for the duration of the operation. I will be at the Pankow flat when the courier arrives for your wife. After they leave, you and I walk to the annex. You retrieve the documents. We walk to the American checkpoint. Saturday afternoon we cross together on West German papers I will prepare. On the Western side a car. Hamburg. Stockholm. Malmö. Sunday afternoon you are with your son. Do you understand the schedule.'

'Yes.'

'One thing I require of you.'

'Yes.'

'On Saturday, as we approach the Stasi checkpoint, you walk at my pace. You do not speak. You do not look at me. You carry the papers where I tell you. If anything appears to deviate, you continue walking exactly as I continue walking. You do not stop. You do not run. The only instruction that matters in the corridor is the instruction to keep moving at the pace of an ordinary person returning from an ordinary afternoon. Do you understand.'

'Yes.'

Elena held his gaze for a moment—a hold she had made for years, that had, over those years, acquired the interior weight of a thing she believed while she performed it.

'I have done this before. You will be in Malmö by Sunday afternoon. Your wife will not have slept on Friday or Saturday. She will sleep on Sunday.'

Voss's eyes were wet. He did not cry. The wetness was the autonomic response of a man whose mind had not yet caught up with what he had just heard. He wiped his eye with the back of his wrist. He nodded.

'Thank you,' he said.

Then Voss did something the file had not predicted.

'The Trelleborg boat,' he said. 'Is it a regular service, or was it assembled for this.'

Elena did not answer for two seconds.

'It is a regular service. A crew who have moved cargo and occasionally people for a Swedish shipping family since nineteen fifty-two. The BND did not assemble it.'

'Good,' Voss said. 'If something breaks in Pankow and she cannot reach Rostock on Saturday, she will need a fallback. A regular service has other weeks. A built channel does not.'

Elena looked at him.

For one half-second—the same half-second she had spent with a man in a Fitzrovia gallery four years earlier—she looked at Stefan Voss the way a professional looks at a person she has miscategorized.

He was not a panicked engineer. He was an engineer who thought in contingencies. He had asked the question he would have asked a subordinate designing a backup power supply.

'If something breaks,' she said, 'send her to the address in Lübeck. There is a bakery. The owner's wife gives her tea. In the morning the owner drives her to the ferry. A different boat. The crew do not know her name.'

'Thank you.'

The second time.

This one she would carry.

'Fontane,' he said, touching the paperback through his coat. 'I have been carrying it for two years. I thought I would finish it in the new country.'

'You will.'

'A man has to take something with him. Or he arrives as nobody.'

Elena nodded. She did not look at the book again.

They parted at the café door.

Pankow, Friday evening.

Voss returned east with the colloquium delegation Friday afternoon and went to his mother-in-law's flat in Pankow where his wife and son had been staying for the colloquium week. He told his wife that night, after the boy was asleep. He told her in the small kitchen at the back of the flat. The radio was on—organ music from Leipzig, the Friday evening program. He had put water on for tea that nobody was going to drink.

A potato was in her hand, half-peeled. She put it down when he finished the sentence. The kettle was climbing toward its whistle; without looking at it she reached across and turned off the gas. Her hands went dry on the tea towel. Then she sat down at the kitchen table.

'Stefan.'

'Yes.'

'Tell me again.'

He told her again. He included the city. He included the address. He did not include the name of the boat, because he did not know it. He did not use the name Katrin. He said *the translator*.

She did not ask if it was safe. She did not ask why now. She did not ask where he would be while she was on the water.

'The boy will think it is a holiday.'

'Yes.'

'The blue suitcase is in the hall cupboard. I will pack tonight while he sleeps. The translator will see them before they leave?'

'Yes. She will come at six.'

Her face had rearranged itself around the new information. It was not a new skill.

'Stefan.'

'Yes.'

'When did you decide.'

He did not answer immediately.

'When did you begin to decide,' she said. 'Not when you made the contact. Before.'

'Three years,' he said.

'Before the Kaliningrad project.'

'Yes.'

'I thought so.'

'You did not say.'

'You did not say either. It was not a thing to say while you were still deciding. It was a thing to wait for.'

She looked at him for a long time.

'The book,' she said. 'You have been reading Fontane for two years. You do not read novels in the winter. You read mathematics in the winter. I thought you were reading it for you.'

'I was.'

'No. You were reading it for the person you were going to become.'

Voss did not answer.

'Are you coming.'

He had told her he was coming. He had said it twice. She was asking a different question and they both knew it.

'Yes.'

One nod. Then she was on her feet and gone—down the hallway to the small bedroom where the boy slept, back with the blue suitcase, which she placed on the kitchen table between them and did not yet open.

Pankow, Saturday 06:00.

Elena had crossed at Friedrichstraße at 05:14, on the Katrin Berger West German passport, in the dark before commuter traffic began. The border officer stamped the entry. He waved her through. He did not examine the passport for more than four seconds. Four seconds was correct.

She walked to Pankow through streets gray with the light before sunrise and reached the building at three minutes to six. The blue suitcase was already at the door. Voss let her in without speaking. The mother-in-law was at her sister's in Magdeburg for the weekend; she did not know any of this was happening in her flat.

The boy was awake but had not been told. He was eating bread at the kitchen table, half-asleep, the way six-year-olds eat at six in the morning. He looked up at Elena. She smiled the small unmemorable smile a translator smiles at a stranger's child.

The wife was in the bedroom finishing a small valise. Elena went to the doorway and waited until the wife looked up.

'The translator,' the wife said. The phrase Stefan had used in the kitchen.

'Yes.'

'The car?'

'Five minutes. The driver will say his name is Klaus. The boy will think you are taking the train to the sea.'

The wife nodded. She closed the valise. She straightened. She was forty years old and she was about to put a six-year-old on a fishing boat across the Baltic to a country she had never seen, on the word of a woman she had met two minutes earlier, while leaving her husband in a kitchen behind her with a man who had said he would follow.

She looked at Elena. Elena was the door she was being asked to walk through.

'If he does not come.'

'He will come.'

'If he does not. What do I tell him.'

The boy. The same question she had asked Stefan the night before. She was asking Elena now because Elena was the one who would know whether his answers had been true.

'Tell him his father was brave.'

'He is six. He does not know what brave means.'

'Tell him his father loved him.'

'He knows.'

The wife held Elena's eyes for a beat that was longer than the moment required. The eyes of a woman who had decided to walk through the door but had needed, first, to look at the person who was opening it.

'Tell him I tried.'

Elena nodded.

The wife picked up the valise. She picked up the boy. The blue suitcase was already at the door. The driver was downstairs. Voss kissed his son on the forehead and helped his wife into her coat in the hallway and did not say what they both knew he was about to say. The wife did not ask him to.

The door closed.

Voss stood with his back to the door for a count of seven. Then he turned. He looked at Elena.

'Where are the documents.'

'The annex.'

'Then we go.'

Central East Berlin. Saturday 11:40.

The Kombinat's Berlin annex was a four-story building on a quiet government-district street, fronted by a brass plate that read *Zentrales Archiv Mikroelektronik*. Voss had a key. He had been issued it during the 1976 records consolidation and never asked to return it. The Saturday duty officer was at lunch. They had thirty-five minutes.

Voss went directly to the third-floor microfiche storage. Fourteen cards were what the BND had asked for. He took fourteen. He sealed them in a flat tin and placed the tin in the inner pocket of his coat.

Then he turned to a drawer Elena had not been briefed on.

'What is that.'

'A duplicate set.' Voss did not look at her. 'A clerk made a parallel run in '75 because the fiche reader on the second floor had been miscalibrating. He kept the originals in this drawer for verification. They have never been logged out and never been logged in. The catalog does not know they exist.'

He removed a second tin. He held it open for Elena.

Eight microfiche cards. The brass plate of the cabinet was unmarked. The labels on the cards themselves were in a typeface Elena did not recognize—a Cyrillic-Latin hybrid she had seen exactly once before, on the Italian inventory document Tom Hatch had laid in front of her in Geneva in the spring of 1976. The same font. The same printer. The same hand-stamped institutional code in the upper left corner of each card.

FEUERWERK.

The fingerprint of a network Moscow did not run, in the cataloging of chips Voss had been told he was designing for the Soviet Union.

Elena's pulse did not change. Her face did not change. Her training closed over the recognition the way it closed over everything.

'Take them,' she said.

Voss took them. He sealed the second tin. He placed it beside the first.

While he was closing the drawer, Elena's left hand crossed the open file box on the bench beside her. Two index cards. She palmed them. Her hand went into her own coat. The motion took less than a second. It was not observed.

'The walk is forty-five minutes,' she said. 'We leave now.'

At the door of the annex she handed him the leather folder she had been carrying since West Berlin. A West German passport for Gerhard Mertens, forty-two, technical sales representative from Frankfurt, a face close enough to his to survive a four-second comparison. A driving license. A Bundesbahn rail pass. A Kempinski receipt dated that morning—she had checked in at seven and returned the key at nine without entering the room.

'Memorize the name. Memorize the Frankfurt address. Memorize the birthday. The rest will not be asked.'

He memorized. He repeated it back.

'You carry the tins. They are yours until Hamburg.'

He did not put them back in his coat immediately. He held them, the two flat tins catching the overcast light, and looked at her.

'Katrin.'

'Yes.'

'If I do not make Hamburg.'

'You will.'

'If I do not. There is a name in the lining of the novel. Behind the inside cover. A journalist in Leipzig. The one I first spoke to. He does not know I have given his name to anyone. He does not know the book exists. If something happens, the tins are for him.'

Elena met his eyes for the second time that morning.

'Yes,' she said.

She filed the instruction. The instruction was the first thing Voss had asked that the file had not predicted, and the first thing Elena had agreed to that Bruhn would not be told she had agreed to.

He put the tins in his coat.

'The American checkpoint is forty-five minutes' walk. Unhurried pace. Two West Germans returning from a Saturday in the East. Do not speak unless spoken to. If spoken to, remember Frankfurt. Remember you are tired because it is Saturday afternoon and you have spent a long day walking.'

'Yes.'

'Are you ready.'

'Yes.'

They stood. They walked out of the annex together, two West Germans on a Saturday afternoon, heading south toward the American checkpoint.

◆◆◆

The walk to the checkpoint was forty-five minutes.

Friedrichstraße was busy. Cars. Pedestrians. Tour buses. The air smelt of brown coal—the characteristic autumn smell of East Berlin heating.

Voss's hands were in his coat pockets. The trembling had not stopped. She could track it in his gait—a slight unevenness, the micro-hesitations of a body being told to walk toward something every instinct was telling it to walk away from.

At the corner of Charlottenstraße, without looking at her: 'The journals. In the West. They publish response pieces?'

'They do.'

'If I had written a response to the Hitachi paper from nineteen seventy-four, would they have published it.'

'They would have.'

'Interesting.'

The word arrived with the flat neutrality of a man filing a final observation about a system he had lived inside and would soon not live inside. He was already speaking in the past tense about a future he had not yet reached.

Elena heard the tense. She did not respond.

They walked another twenty minutes.

At the junction where Friedrichstraße met the approach to the checkpoint, Voss slowed. Elena did not. He caught her pace in two strides.

'Katrin.'

'Yes.'

'The trout. In the song.'

'Yes.'

'What does it mean. *Die Forelle.*'

The reference was Schubert.

'It is a warning,' Elena said. 'The trout sees the fisherman too late. The poet is watching the trout. The poet knows the trout is going to die. The poet is singing about the knowing.'

Voss nodded once.

'I thought it might be that.'

They reached the Stasi checkpoint.

Elena showed her Katrin Berger documentation. The Stasi officer examined it with the careful attention his service required for Western papers leaving the country. Thirty seconds. Forty. He stamped the exit.

He turned to Voss. He examined the Gerhard Mertens papers.

He examined them for one and a half seconds.

He stamped the exit. He waved them through.

Elena's pulse went cold at the base of her throat.

One and a half seconds. East German guards did not examine a Western passport for one and a half seconds. They examined it for thirty, sometimes sixty. The speed was not a kindness. The speed was a coordination.

She kept walking. Voss kept walking.

Voss had seen the speed. He had not said anything. His hand in his coat pocket was no longer trembling.

They entered the corridor.

A hundred meters between two checkpoints. Behind them, the Stasi checkpoint on the East Berlin side. Ahead of them, the American checkpoint—Checkpoint Charlie—on the West Berlin side. The Wall ran on either side of the lane: the inner wall behind, the outer wall ahead, the death strip between the two walls condensed into a single fenced corridor between the two checkpoints. Floodlights flat and shadowless, too bright for the overcast. Footsteps returned off the barriers without direction, so that a step behind sounded like a step beside. It was the most enclosed space in Berlin, and the walls were not physical.

They walked. Twenty meters. Thirty.

Voss did not speak.

Elena did not either.

At forty-seven meters the two men stepped out from behind the scaffolding on the northern side of the construction zone.

They were dressed as workmen. They were not workmen. The body language was operators who had been waiting for an interval and had been told the interval was ending.

Voss understood in one second.

He understood the architecture of the four weeks—the library, the café, the trout, the Malmö address, his wife sleeping in a country she had never been told she would see. He understood that Malmö was real, because a woman named Katrin had given it to his wife as the one thing she would not take back, and that his wife and his son would spend the rest of their lives in Sweden waiting for a husband and a father who was never going to arrive. He understood this in the same second the Mercator knife came into his hand from his coat pocket.

He had been carrying the knife for fourteen days.

He looked at Elena. It was not surprise. It was the look of an engineer tracing a fault through a schematic and finding that the fault was the circuit itself.

'The boat was real,' he said. Quietly. Only to her.

'Yes.'

'Thank you.'

The fourth time.

He ran.

He ran to the left. Toward scaffolding and temporary barriers—checkpoint infrastructure being renovated, raw concrete where a wall had been partially demolished and not yet rebuilt. Bruhn's plan had assumed a clear corridor. This was a gap.

The gap would cost her eleven seconds she would never forget.

Voss was fast. Faster than his file. The file said he was an engineer whose physical fitness was average. The file had not accounted for a man who had been running this moment in his head for fourteen days.

Elena pursued. The decision was made at the level where training lived—the pre-verbal layer installed by two years of repetition. The training said: the asset is running. Pursue.

She was faster. Five kilometers every morning, close-quarters combat twice a week—the weapon the Red Banner Institute had built was closing the distance at a rate Voss's adrenaline could not match.

He vaulted a waist-high sawhorse. He stumbled on loose gravel and kept running.

He was heading for the scaffolding. Cover logic. Or—the deliberate logic of a man not trying to escape, only making the capture expensive.

She vaulted the barrier. Four strides closed the distance.

Voss turned.

The knife was already in his hand.

A Mercator K55K. The Katzenmesser. Nine centimetres of carbon steel, a leaping cat stamped into the handle. An engineer's working knife. A tool he owned already. He had carried it for fourteen days because he had understood this moment was possible.

He held it wrong. Overhand—blade pointing downward from a fist. The grip of a man who had chosen visibility over effectiveness.

The overhand grip sacrificed reach.

Elena understood the geometry. She was willing to step inside.

Voss swung the knife down. Fast. Fixed trajectory.

Elena moved left. Not back. Left and forward, inside the arc.

Her left hand caught his wrist at the top of the descending arc, where the arm's momentum was at its lowest and the leverage highest. Not to stop the arm—to redirect it, using his own downward force to rotate the wrist inward.

The joint gave. Not broke. Yielded.

The knife dropped from a hand whose grip signals had been overridden by pain signals from the wrist. It landed on the gravel.

Elena did not pick it up. She maintained the lock and pulled him three steps from the fallen weapon.

Voss tried to pull away. Elena stepped behind him. Her right arm came across his throat. Not a choke. A restraint. Enough pressure to communicate the possibility of more.

Voss drove his elbow into her ribs. Panic producing force without technique. Elena absorbed the impact and increased the pressure.

Voss stopped. His body made the choice for him. Two counted seconds. Compliance stabilized. She released the trachea and walked him back through the gravel, over the barrier, into the corridor.

Eleven seconds.

The knife behind them.

Bruhn's people had closed on them in the construction site. Two men in workmen's clothes. They did not wear uniforms because the crossing was designed to be invisible—a bureaucratic event, a quiet absorption of a human being into a category. A category labeled RETURN.

Elena handed Voss to the two men. She transferred the wrist lock to the taller, who took it with the practiced ease of a man who had received many such transfers. The second man produced a syringe.

Elena looked away.

Her left hand, free now, crossed Voss's coat pocket in the same motion that released him. The novel came out. Her hand went into her own coat before the second man had positioned the syringe. The motion took a second and a half. It was not observed.

She looked at Voss. She looked at him the way she had looked at Petrov in Lillehammer—directly, without flinching. This was the small respect owed to people you had turned into outcomes. You did not pretend the turning had happened without you.

Voss looked back. His eyes were wet—not crying, the involuntary leak of a man accepting a reality he could not change.

He said nothing.

His eyes said: *I saw you.*

Her eyes said: *I know.*

The syringe went in.

The two men led him through the gap, past the barrier, into a black Wartburg waiting on Friedrichstraße.

Elena did not look back.

She had known, in the fourth reading of his file, that the chips had not been built for the circuits he thought they were built for. She had known he had not known. She had walked him east anyway. The knowledge, in both directions, had made no difference to the operation. That was what the word 'operation' was for.

She returned to the construction site. The two men had not asked her to clean it.

She picked it up.

A Mercator. The engineer's knife. Well-maintained, because Voss maintained everything. The blade was sharp. The grip was wrong. He had held it overhand. Elena could have told him: underhand, edge out, close to the body. She could have told him a dozen things that would have made the eleven seconds last longer and hurt more.

She closed the blade. The click was small and final. Her right hand—the one that had held his wrist—was beginning to ache. The ache would last three days.

She put the knife in her coat pocket.

Not evidence. Not a trophy.

A knife a man had pulled on her because she was taking him somewhere he did not want to go, and she took it from him the way she took everything from everyone—efficiently, professionally, without permission.

She walked back through the corridor. West. Through the American checkpoint, where the border officer waved her through with the same competent disinterest he had shown her that morning. She was a clerk with paperwork. The paperwork confirmed everything. The paperwork confirmed nothing.

The S-Bahn from Zoologischer Garten carried her back across Friedrichstraße at eighteen-forty-five, the border officer stamping the Katrin Berger passport for the second time that day. A second train took her on to Lichtenberg. Letting herself into the flat, she found the hallway light still on. She had left it burning that morning.

She sat at the kitchen table and wrote her report.

The report was brief. RETURN had been executed within parameters. The asset had been transferred to Eastern control. There had been a deviation—the asset had attempted to flee through a construction zone adjacent to the checkpoint corridor. The deviation had been contained. No injuries to the operative. No exposure. No witnesses outside the operational team.

She did not mention the knife.

She did not mention the eleven seconds.

She did not mention that Voss had carried the knife for fourteen days.

She did not mention the Trelleborg question, the Lübeck fallback, the Hitachi paper, the Schubert, or the instruction in the novel.

She did not mention the radiation-hardened logic chips.

Voss had been building brains for backpack-sized weapons missing from the NATO inventory since 1968. He had not known he was. Or he had. The chips were the second ledger's property, not Moscow's. So was the knife. So was the name in the novel.

She would keep all three in places the institution could not reach.

She finished the report. Sealed it. Dead drop for morning collection.

Then she took the Mercator out of her coat pocket and put it on the kitchen table.

A folded rectangle of black-painted steel. Thumb-thin. Three steel rivets. A single carbon-steel blade held open by a spring lock on the spine—the *Katzenmesser*, the slim working knife half the German working class had carried in its coat pocket for a century. A leaping cat stamped into the handle.

Voss had maintained the knife. Voss had maintained everything.

He had also, quietly, across the four weeks, been testing her. The phrase in the library margin. The Schubert reference on the walk. The novel in the café. The Hitachi paper at Charlottenstraße. Small probes. An engineer running continuity tests on a circuit.

She had passed them.

She had not noticed, at the time, that she was being tested.

Elena thought about what Bruhn's people would do to the things Voss had kept in working order—his circuits, his research, his security clearance, the flat in Erfurt. She thought about Zersetzung, and whether what waited for Voss was Zersetzung or something more direct, and whether the distinction mattered. Both produced the same result.

She picked up the knife and opened the blade. The mechanism was smooth. It locked with a clean click.

She stood up.

She opened the drawer beside the sink.

The drawer was shallow. It did not pull all the way out. She kept in it the objects that had no other category.

An empty matchbook from a café in Geneva in the spring of 1976.

A tram ticket from a May morning she had not been able to throw away.

A button from a coat she no longer wore.

A spare key to a West Berlin flat that would not be hers in January.

The drawer was the second ledger rendered in wood.

She put the knife in. It went beside the matchbook.

She closed the drawer.

The click of the drawer closing was the smaller twin of the click of the blade locking shut. Two mechanisms speaking the same sentence.

She stood with her hand on the handle for a second longer than the closing required.

In January she would return to London. She would carry the knife on the train through Helmstedt, in the inside pocket of the same coat she was wearing tonight. She would open the drawer beside the stove and place the knife beside the fountain-pen card, the Nagra reel, and the photograph of Kessler's *rothschildianum* that he would give her in January, three days before she left East Berlin.

Same shape of contents. Same architecture.

The two drawers were one drawer.

She would keep it there for years. Never use it, never explain it to anyone who saw it. If asked, she would say it was a kitchen knife. It was not a kitchen knife. It was eleven seconds on a gravel surface in October 1977, folded up and put in a drawer where she could find it when she needed to remember what she was.

She took the novel out of her coat and opened the inside cover.

Behind the endpaper, in pencil, in a hand that was not Voss's but a hand he had trusted, was a single name and a Leipzig address.

She memorized both. She closed the book.

She did not know yet whether she would carry the instruction out. The instruction was an accepted one but not a decided one. The name in the lining was another object on her table.

She let the deferral stand.

She opened the drawer and put the novel beside the knife.

Two objects. Two categories. One known, one not.

She closed the drawer.

She'd begun keeping notes.

Not operational notes. Those went to Bruhn and through Bruhn to Moscow. These were different. These were the things the operational notes could not contain—the shapes, the rhythms, the small wrongnesses that did not fit the institutional system. The notebook was the only surface in her life that was entirely hers.

She wrote in it that night.

Three entries.

The first was the phrase from the Italian inventory document Tom Hatch had laid in front of her in Geneva nineteen months earlier—*maintenance contact: to be determined*—followed by a single line in Russian: *Voss's file fits.*

The second entry was a single English word, written in Cyrillic transliteration: *easier.*

The third entry was a German line, followed by a date: *Die Forelle sieht den Fischer zu spät. 25 Oktober 1977.*

The trout sees the fisherman too late.

She closed the notebook and returned it to the false back of the wardrobe. Then she sat at the kitchen table in the dark.

The notebook was what she was—a woman who walked men in the wrong direction and disarmed them when they tried to change course and delivered them to systems that would dismantle them and did not look back. And, increasingly, a woman who failed to file the recognitions that would have helped the institution she worked for understand what was being done to it from above.

It was also—and this was the entry she had not yet written—a woman who had been seen.

Voss had seen her.

She was not accustomed to being seen.

Somewhere in East Berlin, in a room she would never see, Stefan Voss was beginning the longest night of his life.

And Elena was sitting in her kitchen thinking about orchids.

She was also thinking about the woman she had met that morning and a six-year-old boy she would never see again, after putting them on a courier's car at six in the morning in a Pankow flat. The mother would not see her husband. In perhaps a month the BND would bring her a cover story about a document room and an arrest, and she would believe it because believing was the only way to stay inside a life.

She was thinking about Kessler. About the *rothschildianum*. About seven years of patience producing a three-week flower. About the difference between growing something and dismantling something.

About how she was capable of both and how the capability was the same. The attention she'd given to Kessler's plants and the attention she'd given to Voss's wrist were executions of one architecture against different targets. She was the instrument.

This was the thing she could not file. Not because it was too painful. Because it was too true. She could touch a leaf with tenderness and break a wrist with precision. Neither action contradicted the other.

The knife was a knife.

She sat in the dark for a long time.

The drawer beside the sink held the knife and the novel. Her coat pocket was lighter than it had been that morning, and the part of her that was not the coat was heavier.

She slept above a basement she had never seen the inventory of. The next fizzle was statistically overdue. There was no operational extraction plan for that, and the operative who built one would have to build it alone.

She thought about Voss at his kitchen table in Erfurt, reading Fontane in the months he had been deciding, preparing three extractions—his family's to Malmö, his own to the corridor, and a third one he had put in a book lining for a translator named Katrin to carry to a journalist in Leipzig.

On Monday she would give up the West Berlin flat. The cover had done its work. Katrin Berger would not need to come back.

She thought about the name.

She thought about the journalist.

She did not decide what she would do.

The deferral was the decision the night could hold.

The Omega on her wrist covered the compass rose. Neither knew about the other.

Я научилась просто, мудро жить.

10

THE OFFICER AND THE GENTLEMAN

London—November 1977

The same autumn Elena was crossing the border with Voss. The same autumn the Mercator knife went into the drawer beside the stove. A different city. A different service. The same architecture.

James Calder was drunk.

Not the kind of drunk that announced itself. He had been building something inside himself for four years and had poured whisky over the structure tonight to see which parts held. Most of the structure held. The parts that did not were internal—a looseness behind the eyes, a warmth in the chest that was not warmth but the body's misreading of chemical damage as comfort, and a circling knowledge that had no address because the thing he knew did not yet have a name he was willing to use.

He started at the Special Forces Club on Herbert Crescent. The club smelled the way it always smelled—of old leather and wood smoke and the malt sweetness of whisky absorbed into carpet over decades. The radiators ticked. The ceiling was low enough that tall men developed a habitual stoop by their third visit, and the lighting had the amber quality of a room designed before electricity was expected to illuminate anything fully. Three whiskies, then a fourth. The fourth was the one he drank while reading the two files on the table beside him.

Both belonged to Century House. Neither was supposed to leave the building. The first was the Lillehammer archive—the Mossad catastrophe, the arrests, the aftermath. The second was a file he was not supposed to have at all: FEUERWERK.

The first file was about Lillehammer.

The second file was about something the Counter-Proliferation desk had given a one-word designation that Calder had never seen before and that he had been thinking about for four days the way you think about a word in a foreign language whose meaning you have only half-grasped.

The word was FEUERWERK.

Calder had spent his career tracking the things that moved in the spaces between governments—the fissile material that crossed borders without authorization, the weapons components that appeared in inventories where they should not have been, the small discrepancies that, seen from a distance, resolved into pictures no government wanted to look at directly. He had developed, over more than a dozen years, the particular instinct that Counter-Proliferation rewarded: the ability to look at a column of numbers and hear, in the rhythm of their spacing, the absence of something that should have been there.

The Lillehammer file was the public record dressed in classification. Norwegian police reports, Interpol summaries, MI6's own assessment of the Mossad operation that killed Rachid Hamidi in July 1973. Every officer of Calder's generation had studied the catastrophe.

But Calder was not reading the catastrophe. He was reading the footnotes.

Footnote 7, page 23: a Soviet defector named Grigor Petrov, living under a Norwegian identity, had been found dead in his flat two days after the Hamidi killing. Two gunshot wounds, small caliber, close range. Attributed to a burglary. The Norwegian police, overwhelmed by six arrested Mossad operatives, had given the case minimal attention.

A coincidence of timing. A footnote.

Calder did not believe in coincidences of timing. The Petrov killing had the signature of an operation—not Mossad's chaotic disaster, but something else. Quiet. Precise. Timed to exploit the chaos when every eye was looking the other direction. A Soviet operative. The KGB had reason to want Petrov dead. And they had the discipline to choose the one night nobody would be watching.

This was not new analysis. What was new—what had brought him to the club tonight, what the fourth whisky was for—was a hotel record from the Grand Hotel, Lillehammer, July 1973. A woman checked in 20 July, out 22 July. New Zealand passport. Alice Marsh.

Alice Marsh. Who had dark hair and a jawline like a propaganda poster and a tattoo in a script he could not read in the dark. Who said things that were occasionally too precise for her cover and caught herself saying them and caught Calder catching her. Who had been sharing his bed for four years and had never mentioned Norway.

He understood the danger of seeing patterns where none existed. Paranoia was the occupational disease. But he also understood the danger of not seeing them—of choosing to see the cover because the cover was beautiful and the alternative was a wound he was not prepared to open.

This was why he drank. Not the job. Not the pressure. Not the hours or the secrets or the institutional weight that the films got wrong and the novels romanticized. He drank because he was in love with a woman he could not verify, in a profession that required verification of everything, and the whisky was the only thing that loosened the lock on the room where he kept the knowledge he could not use. Four whiskies and the lock gave. Four whiskies and he could look at the thing directly. Four whiskies and the thing looked back.

The second file was thinner.

Eleven pages. A typescript with the particular grain of a document that had been generated on a manual typewriter at one of the older stations and had not been retyped for distribution. The covering memo had been written by someone whose initials Calder did not recognize and whose desk identifier—CP-Aux-3—corresponded to a Counter-Proliferation auxiliary section he had not been cleared to read from.

He'd been cleared to read from it on Tuesday afternoon, briefly, by a man named Hayward whose visit to Calder's office had taken less than three minutes and who had handed Calder the file with the unsmiling delivery of a man who had been instructed to deliver something to a particular pair of hands and to leave the room afterward without explaining why those hands were the correct ones.

The fragment described a discrepancy.

A discrepancy in a 1968 NATO inventory. Small atomic demolition munitions—deployed in Western Europe between 1962 and 1967 under a protocol no one had ever made public, and decommissioned, in 1968, under the same silence. The inventory said twenty-three destroyed. Someone, whose name was redacted from Calder's copy, had checked. The number confirmed destroyed was fewer than twenty-three. Calder read that sentence and sat with it for a long time.

The file did not say how many were missing, or where they had gone, or who was supposed to be holding them. It said only that there was a discrepancy, and that someone in Counter-Proliferation had given the discrepancy a name: FEUERWERK.

Parallel awareness. The phrase was the kind of phrase Calder's institution produced when it had a problem it did not yet want to admit it had. Parallel awareness meant: read this and remember it, and if you encounter anything that touches it, tell us, and meanwhile do not write it down and do not mention it in any meeting and do not acknowledge to anyone, including the person who handed you this file, that you have read it.

Calder had read it three times. He committed the eleven pages to memory. He had also, against his training and against the explicit terms of parallel awareness, gone further. He started, in his head, the kind of cross-reference he had been trained never to perform without authorization. He started looking for FEUERWERK shapes in every other file that crossed his desk. The shapes had not appeared. Not yet. But he'd looked, and the looking was the kind of action that, in Calder's profession, was the first step toward an investigation that could not be unstarted.

The second file had been in his briefcase since Tuesday. He carried it because he was beginning to suspect the two files were related, and the suspicion lived in the same pre-articulate region of his mind as the suspicion that Alice Marsh was not Alice Marsh. Both were generated by the same instrument. He did not know what to call it. He'd been trained to trust it.

He thought about 1968.

He had not thought about that year in years. He'd built the structure that prevented thinking about it with the same architectural discipline he applied to everything else, and the structure had held until tonight, when the FEUERWERK file had introduced into his briefcase a date—1968—that the file's redacted index had repeated three times, and the date had begun, slowly, to do what dates did when they wanted attention. The date had risen.

In 1968 he had been twenty-six and on his first overseas posting. Bonn. Junior to everyone in the station. He'd been sent into East Berlin one night in November on what had been described to him as a low-risk extraction—a defector, an electrical engineer, a man whose name Calder had been told to forget and whose name Calder had forgotten with the dutiful efficiency of a young officer who believed the rules were the rules. The operation had not gone as planned. The defector had not been at the rendezvous. The Stasi had been at the rendezvous. Calder had run—six blocks through Friedrichshain, the East Berlin district closest to the Wall, in the dark with a forged West German passport in his coat and the conviction that he was about to be killed in a foreign city for reasons his family would never be told.

He'd been pulled into a doorway by a woman.

The woman's name, she said, was Natalia. She'd pulled him into a doorway and up two flights of stairs into an apartment where she locked the door and pressed her finger to her lips and listened. Then she turned and said in soft German: you will sleep here. They will not look in the apartment of a woman who lives alone. She made him tea on a small electric ring. She did not ask who he was. He slept on her sofa and crossed back through Friedrichstraße before dawn. He never saw her again.

He'd reported the operation as a failure. He reported the route, the contact signal, the driver, the checkpoint configuration. He did not report the knife. He did not report the three steps he'd had to take in the dark to reach the fence. He did not report the expression on the woman's face. These were the things he kept in the private filing system he hadn't wanted to put paperwork on.

He went back into East Berlin three times in the years that followed. The operations succeeded. The men he pulled out —a hydrologist, a chemist, an engineer—went into the same private filing system. He had not spoken to any of them in years. He kept their addresses current.

He had not thought about her in years. The not-thinking had been a discipline. Tonight, with FEUERWERK in his briefcase and Alice Marsh in a Norwegian hotel register, the discipline had broken. The doorway and the mended cardigan and the tea she didn't apologize for were back, unbidden, in the front seat of Margaret's Rover at midnight. Natalia had nothing to do with Lillehammer or FEUERWERK. Natalia had to do with a night in 1968 when a stranger had decided an unknown man was worth six minutes of her life and four hours on her sofa, and had given those six minutes and those four hours without explanation, and had asked nothing in return.

He finished the fourth whisky. The glass was warm in his hand.

He came to the club tonight thinking he was looking at a KGB problem. He was not looking at a KGB problem. The Lillehammer hotel register and the FEUERWERK file were the same investigation, and the investigation was not about a service. The investigation was about a structure that had been hiding inside all four of his filing cabinets at once, and the outline of it was beginning to have a shape, and the shape had room in it for a woman with a New Zealand passport in a Norwegian hotel in 1973.

He put the Lillehammer file in his coat. He left the FEUERWERK file in his briefcase. He paid his tab. He walked out of the Special Forces Club into the cold November night and got into Margaret's green Rover, which was the car he was driving tonight because his own car was at the garage being looked at by a mechanic on the Old Brompton Road who had, two weeks ago, told Calder that the timing belt was a year past its replacement window and that the Rover was a perfectly serviceable substitute. The Rover was Margaret's. He was driving it home to Margaret. He was not driving it home to Margaret. He was driving it to Kensington.

He turned onto Cromwell Road.

The blue lights appeared in his mirror at 23:23. His first thought was: Alice. His second thought was: no.

They were unmistakable. The rhythmic pulse of a Metropolitan Police vehicle requesting that the driver ahead please pull over. The lights filled the Rover's interior with a cold strobing illumination that turned everything inside the car into a series of still photographs: Calder's hands on the wheel, the file on the passenger seat, the briefcase on the floor by the passenger footwell, the whisky's warmth receding rapidly as the adrenaline arrived.

Calder pulled over. He did this calmly, with the deliberate care of a man who was drunk enough to be pulled over and sober enough to know that the next three minutes would determine whether the rest of his career continued on its current trajectory or veered, irrevocably, into a category of event that the institution processed but did not forgive. He turned off the engine. He put his hands on the wheel at ten and two. He waited.

The officer approached the driver's side window. Calder could see him in the mirror—young, mid-twenties, moving with the careful procedure-following gait of a man who had been on the force perhaps eighteen months and who had developed, in that time, the composite suspicion of a generation of motorists who believed they were above the law and were regularly being shown they were not. The officer tapped on the window. Calder rolled it down. The cold air came in. The officer bent slightly to meet his eye.

'Good evening, sir.' The officer's voice was polite. London accent, but not strongly. South of the river, Calder guessed. Bermondsey or Peckham. The kind of voice that had worked to smooth itself without erasing its origins. 'I've been observing your vehicle for the last half-mile. You crossed the center line twice on Gloucester Road and you failed to indicate at the junction with Cromwell Road. Have you been drinking this evening?'

Calder looked at the officer. He looked at him with the appraising attention of a man calculating the fastest route through an obstacle and who had, in his inside pocket, the instrument that would remove the obstacle entirely.

'I've had a couple,' he said. His voice was steady. The voice was always steady. The voice was the last thing that went, and Calder was not drunk enough for the voice to go. 'Social occasion. I'm heading home.'

'I see, sir. Would you mind stepping out of the vehicle?'

Calder did not step out of the vehicle. He reached into his inside pocket—slowly, visibly, with the exaggerated deliberateness of a man communicating to an armed officer that the hand entering the jacket was retrieving a document and not a weapon. He withdrew the card.

The card was cream-colored. Heavy stock. It bore no name, no title, no institutional logo—only a telephone number and a six-digit reference code. The number connected to a Century House desk manned twenty-four hours a day. The code identified the cardholder as a serving SIS officer. The desk would issue the instruction the card existed to produce: release the cardholder. Do not log the stop. Do not record the interaction. Forget this happened. It did not happen.

Calder held the card out the window.

'I'd appreciate it if you'd radio this in,' he said.

The officer took the card. He looked at it. Calder watched the recognition arrive—not immediately, not the way it would arrive for an experienced officer who had seen the card before, but in stages. The officer read the number. The officer's eyes moved to the reference code. The officer's posture changed fractionally, a small tightening in the shoulders that said: this card is more than it appears. He did not know what it was. He knew it was something. He had been trained to recognize unusual credentials without being trained to know what the unusual credentials meant.

The officer looked at Calder. Then he looked at the card again. Then he walked back to his vehicle and radioed in.

Three minutes. Calder sat in the Rover and counted them. Three minutes of the young officer sitting in his patrol car with the radio to his ear, receiving instructions from a chain of command that went up and up and up past his sergeant, past his station, past his division, into the strange administrative country where cards like Calder's originated. Calder had made this call twice before. The procedure was standardized. A duty officer somewhere in Century House received the reference code, confirmed the holder, and issued a release. The motorist was released. The system operated.

The officer returned. He handed the card back through the window. His face had changed. Not dramatically. The earnestness was still there, the youth, the south London features that had not yet been weathered. But something behind the face had shifted. Something had been tested and had not quite broken but had bent, the way metal bends when you apply more force than the material was designed to bear.

'You're free to go, sir,' the officer said.

Calder took the card. He put it back in his pocket. His hands smelled like whisky. He noticed this the way he noticed everything tonight—too late. And then he did the thing he would think about for years afterward.

He was a prick about it. He did it anyway.

'Thank you, Officer,' Calder said. The thank you was the worst part. It was the thank you of a man acknowledging a service from a waiter.

The officer stood at the window. He did not move. He looked at Calder with an expression that was no longer the expression of a young police officer conducting a traffic stop. It was the expression of a man who had encountered something his training had not prepared him for and that his principles could not accommodate and that he was processing in real time, standing on the Cromwell Road at half-eleven on a November night, with the blue lights still pulsing behind him and the cold London air coming through the open window of a Rover driven by a drunk man who had just been told he was free to go.

The officer spoke. Quietly. Not for the record, because there was no record. Not as a Metropolitan Police officer, because the Metropolitan Police officer had been dismissed by the card and the phone call and the three minutes of radio that had erased the stop from institutional memory. He spoke as a man. A man in his twenties from south of the river who had joined the police because he believed in something and who had just been shown that the something he believed in had conditions he had not been told about.

'You should be ashamed of yourself,' he said.

He said it quietly. A fact stated to the air. Then he turned and walked back to his patrol car and got in and turned off the blue lights and pulled away from the curb and drove into the London night and was gone.

Calder sat in the Rover. The engine was off. The street was quiet. Cromwell Road at half-eleven: cars parked along the curb, the distant glow of the Natural History Museum, the sodium lights casting their orange wash over the pavement. A bus passed. Its windows were lit and nearly empty—two passengers visible, both staring forward with the blank interior focus of people traveling through a city they were not looking at.

You should be ashamed of yourself.

Calder sat with the sentence the way you sit with a diagnosis. The young officer had read him correctly. Had seen what Calder had performed and had, in one quiet sentence, named it.

Calder started the engine. He pulled onto Cromwell Road. He drove toward Kensington.

He parked on Alice's street at 23:47.

Her windows were on the second floor. Curtains drawn. No light. She was not home. She had not been home, as far as he could tell, for months, though the flat itself was maintained with the same quiet perfection Alice Marsh maintained everything.

He did not know what she did. Four years of her bed, her conversation, her body—and he did not know what Alice Marsh did when he was not with her. The surface was immaculate. The best he had ever encountered, and he'd encountered surfaces professionally for over a decade.

He sat in the car and thought about the flat. The second floor. The dark windows. The woman who was not behind them tonight and who had, for years now, been regularly not behind them on nights he was not there. He had never asked where she was on those nights. He had never asked because he had not, until the FEUERWERK file, been prepared to hear the answer.

He sat for twenty minutes.

He thought about the way her breath caught when he touched the tattoo on her ribcage. The way she said geraniums with an inflection that was not quite English and not quite anything else. The way she'd met Margaret in the bookshop and had been kind and looked at him across the shop with something in her eyes that might have been guilt or grief or the lonely sadness of a person standing inside a life they could not claim.

He thought about her hands. The way they were always steady. The way she held a wine glass—lightly, precisely. He thought about what other things those hands might hold with the same light grip.

He thought about Grigor Petrov. Two rounds. Close range. Professional.

He thought about Natalia in 1968. The thought arrived uninvited. Natalia had been a stranger in a doorway. Alice had been four years of his bed. The two had nothing in common except the thing they had in common, which was that both women had been kind to him inside machinery that did not reward kindness.

He did not go in. He drove home.

The house was dark. Chiswick, west London. The street smelled of wet privet and the particular suburban quiet of a neighborhood where the arguments happened indoors. A semi-detached where the neighbors were accountants and solicitors who came home at sensible hours and did not drive through London at midnight with classified files in their coats.

He went inside. The hallway smelled of rosemary and lavender sachets. The warmth of a house inhabited by a person who believed in the life being lived inside it. He hung up his coat with the Lillehammer file still in it. He set the briefcase with the FEUERWERK file inside the cupboard under the stairs, behind a box of Christmas decorations Margaret had been planning to take down from the loft for two weeks. He could have brought them down for her any evening. He had not. He stepped over the third stair from the top—the loudest one, the one Margaret said gave the house character, which was the word people used for flaws they had decided to love.

The bedroom door was open. Margaret was asleep.

Calder stood in the doorway and watched his wife breathe.

She was on her side, facing the door. Even in sleep there was something braced about her face—a faint tension at the corners of her mouth. She had started sleeping like someone expecting to be woken with news.

On the dresser, the charm bracelet she took off before sleeping was coiled in a small silver heap. He could see the charms in the half-light. The book. The cat. The heart. The letter M. And beside the M, the small empty ring that had been there since she bought it—darker at the clasp now, waiting. He did not pick up the bracelet to look more closely. The night had disqualified him from that kind of attention.

He looked at the bracelet for ten seconds. Then he looked away.

The room was quiet. The inhabited quiet of a house where someone was sleeping. Margaret's breathing was even. Slow. The rhythm of a woman who was not dreaming or, if she was dreaming, was dreaming of things that did not disturb the even slow pattern of her rest.

Calder stood in the doorway and felt the thing he had been trying not to feel for three years.

It was not guilt. Guilt was too simple. Guilt was the emotion moralists assigned to men who cheated on their wives, the categorizable feeling that could be confessed and absolved and managed. What Calder felt was not tidy. What Calder felt was the structural recognition that he'd built his life on two foundations, and the two foundations were incompatible, and the structure was developing cracks he could no longer fill with the quick-setting cement of compartmentalization.

Margaret was one foundation. Margaret who grew geraniums and taught Year Six English and made rosemary chicken on Wednesdays and who loved him in the way he had come to understand was specifically hers—steady, observant, uninsistent, the love of a woman who had decided a long time ago that love was a choice you kept choosing and that the choosing was the thing. Margaret who did not ask where he went or who he saw or why he sometimes came home at two in the morning smelling of the absence of her.

Margaret chose not to examine what she suspected, because examining would have required asking, and asking would have required an answer, and the answer would have required a decision. She had chosen not to force the decision. Her trust was not the naive trust of a woman who did not suspect. It was the deliberate trust of a woman who had weighed the evidence and decided that the evidence was less heavy than the alternative. Confrontation was a door she could not close once she opened it, and Margaret was a woman who understood doors.

Alice was the other foundation. Alice whose name appeared in a hotel register in Lillehammer. Alice whose hands were always steady. Alice who existed, for Calder, in the paradox of a woman he loved and a woman he suspected and a woman whose two selves he had decided, on a night in November 1977, not to collapse into one.

He watched Margaret breathe. He counted the breaths. Seven. Eight. Nine. Each breath was a fact. Each breath was the simplest, most irreducible evidence of the life he was supposed to be protecting. Calder's job—his real job, the one beneath the job title and the security clearance and the card in his pocket—was to protect things. National security. State secrets. The structures that kept the country functioning and the threats that would dismantle those structures if they were not identified and contained. He was a protector. That was the story he told himself. That was the foundational belief.

And he could not protect the woman sleeping in his bed from the man standing in the doorway watching her.

He undressed in the dark. He got into bed. He lay beside Margaret without touching her, because touching her would have been dishonest and not touching her was also dishonest and the distance between the two dishonesties was the distance he lived in now, the narrow uninhabitable space between the things he owed and the things he wanted and the things he was.

He did not sleep. He lay in the dark and listened to his wife breathe and thought about Alice's flat and the amber light around the curtains and the question he had not asked and the answer he was not ready to receive.

He thought about FEUERWERK. About the discrepancy. About the missing devices and the redacted dates and the thin file in the briefcase under the stairs and that the discrepancy and the hotel register in Lillehammer were two unrelated facts that were arranging themselves, in some part of his mind he had not authorized, into a single shape he could not yet describe.

He thought about Natalia in the doorway. He thought about her twice in one night, which was twice more than he'd thought about her in years.

The crack continued its slow silent journey through the glass.

In the morning, Calder returned the Lillehammer file to Century House. 07:15. The corridors were empty between shifts—the institutional twilight when a man could slide a classified file back into a cabinet without being observed. He locked it. He kept the FEUERWERK file. He had not been told to return it. Parallel awareness did not have a return procedure. The file was his to carry, in the sense that the file was his to be aware of in parallel. He put it in the locked drawer of his own desk where the most sensitive of his personal working documents lived.

He walked to his office.

A desk, a chair, a photograph of Margaret from their wedding. Both of them smiling. Both of them young in a way that seemed geologically distant from the man standing in the office with a hangover and the sick clarity that the morning after delivered free of charge.

He had been wrong before. That was the texture of the work—threads that turned out to be lint. He came back to the desk. The gap between FEUERWERK and ALICE had not changed. The gap never changed. It was the most patient space in the building.

He punched the wall.

Once. Not for an audience. A physical statement directed at the plaster beside the filing cabinet. The impact was solid. The pain traveled up his hand and settled in his wrist with the clean finality of a sensation that meant something.

The pain meant: this is real. The wall is real. The hand is real. Whatever else is uncertain—the woman, the file, the question he could not ask—this is real.

He flexed the hand. The knuckles were red. He would tell anyone who asked that he had caught them on a door. No one would ask. People in this building did not ask about bruised knuckles or the hollowed-out expression on a man's face the morning after he'd discovered something about himself he did not want to know.

He sat at his desk. He opened his morning briefing. He read the cables. He drafted a response to a station report from Berlin—routine intelligence assessment, the institutional language flowing from his pen without friction.

The machinery never cared. That was its function. That was its gift.

At nine o'clock there was a meeting. Calder attended. He contributed. He was sharp, focused, articulate—everything a thirty-five-year-old Counter-Proliferation officer was supposed to be at nine o'clock on a Wednesday. Nobody in the meeting room knew that he had punched a wall. Nobody noticed the minor swelling.

The meeting ended. He returned to his office. He sat at his desk. He looked at the photograph of Margaret.

He opened a new file.

He labeled it with a reference number that would not appear in any index and that corresponded to no official investigation. The file contained, at this point, a single document: a photocopy of a hotel register from Lillehammer, Norway, dated July 1973.

He labeled the file ALICE and locked it in his desk drawer.

The drawer now held two files. FEUERWERK, which he was not supposed to have. ALICE, which he had created without authorization. The two files sat next to each other. Calder looked at the gap between them for a long moment before he closed the drawer and locked it.

He thought of Margaret's bracelet on the dresser at home. The book, the cat, the heart, the letter M, and beside the M the small empty ring that had been waiting there for years. The bracelet was a drawer too. He had not understood this until now.

The gap was the question. The gap was what he was going to spend, he understood, the next twelve years working on. The question of whether the two files belonged together. The question of whether the hand he could not see in the FEUERWERK discrepancy was the same hand he could not see when he watched Alice Marsh hold a wine glass. The question of whether his wife's deliberate trust and his lover's precise observations and a 1968 night in an East Berlin doorway and a Norwegian hotel register and a missing inventory of atomic devices were all separate things or were, in the way the largest things in his profession were sometimes the same thing seen from too many angles, one thing.

He did not know yet.

For now, the gap was the gap. The drawer was locked. The card was in his pocket. The glass had been cracking since 1973 and he had been watching it hold, and the machinery hummed in the corridors of Century House, and somewhere in East Berlin a woman whose name was not Alice Marsh was, at this exact moment, sitting at her own kitchen table writing something in a small bound notebook that no institution would ever see.

Her London number was in the back of the small black address book he kept in the desk drawer at Century House. He had committed it to memory in October 1973 and had not called it since early 1975, when she had left for what she said was a New Zealand family visit. Three weeks ago he had been told, through the small accidental grapevine of a shared friend at Gerald's gallery, that she was expected back in the new year. He had been, for twenty-one consecutive days, deciding what he would do when she returned.

Calder looked at the photograph of Margaret on his desk.

Then he locked the files in his briefcase and walked home

through a London that had not changed and that he no longer recognized.

Three days later, on a Saturday morning when Margaret was at her sister's in Hampstead, he walked from the Chiswick house to a jeweller in Turnham Green he had never used before and bought a small silver charm in the shape of a key. He paid in cash. He gave a name that was not his.

That evening he waited until Margaret had gone upstairs. The bracelet was on the small dish in the hallway where she always left it. He opened the clasp, threaded the key into the small empty ring beside the M, and closed the clasp again. He set the bracelet back on the dish in exactly the position he had found it. The key caught the hall light once. He went into the kitchen and poured himself a whisky he did not drink.

ACT III

TEL AVIV

1978—1982

11

SARA LERNER

London / Tel Aviv—January—February 1978

She had been back from Berlin for nine days when Yuri set the meeting.

The Kensington flat smelled of Mrs. Aldridge's weekly airings and of nothing else. The camel coat was on the hook where she had left it in January 1975. Elena had taken it down on the first morning and put it on. It fit. The fitting was the new piece of information.

She had not seen Calder. He did not know she was back. The agreement when she'd left in January 1975 had been that they would not write. The agreement had held on her side and on his. Her body knew the route to his door. The not-appearing was the thing she was working her way toward, without being able to say to herself yet what she was working her way toward. There were two things in London first. Yuri.

Yuri had aged. A tightness around the eyes that had not been there before. He was fifty-eight now, wearing the same overcoat from the Bloomsbury café in 1973, except the cuffs had been re-stitched by a tailor who had not been asked to make the stitching invisible.

They met at a different café. Bayswater was burned. They met at an ABC tearoom in Marylebone, at a window table, on a Wednesday morning when the place was full of office workers and the waitress did not look at them twice.

Yuri put his teacup down. He looked at Elena across the table the way handlers looked at illegals when they were about to deliver a brief that the handler did not entirely understand and was not entirely comfortable delivering.

'Tel Aviv,' he said. 'February. You go in as Sara Lerner. *Maclean's* magazine, Toronto office. The credentials are with the Second Department. Real freelance relationship, real editor, four pieces a year. Mossad is interested in your European journalistic access. You will be interested in their view of the Lillehammer cleanup. The exchange is the cover. The assignment underneath is Step Two.'

'How long.'

'Indefinite. Years, not months. The assignment is Step Two of the Lillehammer-origin operation. You know what Step Two is.'

'Mossad's targeted-killing program. Mapping the chain of command, the operational cells, the European cutouts.'

'That is the version you will tell Mossad if Mossad asks. If they ask, you will of course not tell them, but the version you would not tell them is the version that exists.' Yuri's face did the small unhappy adjustment it did when he was about to say a thing he had been told to say but did not entirely believe. 'The actual brief is different. Moscow wants to know what Mossad knows about the European caches.'

Elena did not move. She lifted her teacup. She drank.

'Which European caches.'

'Moscow's instructions did not specify. The instructions said the European caches. They did not name them. They did not name the country. They did not name the inventory category. They told me to tell you that you would understand which caches when you saw what Mossad was tracking, and to proceed accordingly.'

'I understand the reference.'

'Good.'

He continued to look at the window.

Elena understood, in the silence between *good* and the next sentence Yuri did not yet say, that Yuri did not understand the reference. He had been instructed to tell her that she would, and he had been trusted to deliver that instruction without asking what it meant. His handlers had calculated that Elena would hear, behind Yuri's words, the thing Yuri did not know was there.

The rhythm of Yuri's briefing was not Yuri's. It was someone else's, mediated through Yuri. The hand that had written the script for this conversation was the same hand that had written the inventory Hatch showed her in Geneva. Elena could hear the hand in the pauses.

On the cover sheet of the briefing papers Yuri had brought, in pencil, was a small mark Elena had now seen three times. The mark on a Fitzrovia folder in 1974. The mark on a Geneva photocopy in 1976. The mark on this document now. That night she wrote a description of the mark in the small bound notebook—in pencil, the way the marks had been made.

'I will need a full medical kit and a backup set of credentials,' she said. 'I will need a contact in the Canadian embassy and a fallback in West Jerusalem in case Tel Aviv goes loud. I will need the *Maclean's* editor briefed on what Sara Lerner is permitted to ask and not ask. And I will need a standing instruction on what to do if I find that the caches Mossad is tracking are the same caches Moscow has already decided not to let Hatch publish about.'

'The last one was not in my briefing.'

'I am asking you to add it.'

Yuri looked at her. The look was tired. It was the tiredness of a man who recognized the question he had been hoping she would not ask, because he had not been given an answer and he was about to have to communicate the absence of an answer to an operative who would understand the absence as an answer in itself.

'There were no instructions for that contingency,' he said. 'Moscow assumes the contingency will not arise.'

'And if it arises.'

'You will report.' Yuri said this with the small forward lean of a man who was reading from a script. 'You will report what you have found, through the established channels, in the established cipher, through the established dead drops. You will not make the assessment yourself. You will not act on the assessment. You will report. Moscow will decide.'

Elena nodded.

She did not say any of this. She finished her tea. She paid for both of them, because Yuri had not brought enough and the small economic adjustment was the kind of thing she'd started to do for him in the past year without naming the doing of it.

She left the tearoom and walked back to Kensington in the cold January light, and she added to the ledger a line that read: *Yuri's overcoat has been re-stitched. Yuri does not know what he is briefing me on. The instruction came from above Yuri. The instruction came from above Moscow.*

The flat had not changed in three years. The Kensington plaster, the brass kettle, the small framed print of a Flemish drawing room, the table by the window where Alice Marsh had first chosen James Calder in the autumn of 1973 and written him into her life. The flat held its breath the way only London flats did—attentively, with the patience of rooms that had been furnished by several generations of women who were not always the ones to unfurnish them.

Elena opened the drawer beside the stove. The drawer had been growing since October 1973. Each object added without plan, without filing, without the institutional tidiness her training required. The diary she had never opened. The candle she had never lit. The pen she had not used. The three had been in the flat the day Alice Marsh moved in—Moscow's idea of the props a single woman would keep. Elena had used none of them and had not been able to bring herself to throw them away. Yuri's welcome card from the day she moved in: *Welcome to your new home—Y.* The Ronson lighter Yuri had passed across the Bloomsbury café table that November morning. The Nagra reel from the Paxton Gallery recording, at the back beneath the diary. Calder's first card—*the photograph of the Wall was better from the Eastern side—J.* And from Berlin, beside the reel, the photograph Kessler had given her of the *rothschildianum* in bloom.

From her handbag she drew the Mercator knife—the one with the cat stamped in the handle, the one she had not been able to leave in Berlin. She placed it at the back of the drawer, beneath the diary, beside the orchid photograph. A blade and a bloom in the same drawer. She did not think about what that meant. She would think about it later, in many rooms, for many years. The handle could not be seen if anyone opened the drawer to look for a candle.

She closed the drawer. On Tuesday afternoon she had tea at Tom Hatch's flat to meet his girlfriend.

Tom Hatch lived in a flat in Camden that smelled of damp paper, cheap coffee, and the particular determination of a man who had chosen his story over his comfort.

Elena had not been to the flat before. Their meetings since September 1975 had all been on neutral ground—the Free University reception, Amsterdam, a Geneva café in the rain, Zagreb. The Camden flat was the first piece of Hatch's private geography Elena had entered. Books stacked on the floor beside the sofa because the shelves had filled and Hatch was not the kind of man who rotated his library. A typewriter on a small desk by the window. A coat on a hook. The life of a man who had chosen his story over the rest of the story a life might tell.

The invitation had come the previous Friday, by phone, to the West London accommodation address Elena had been maintaining for Ingrid Lindqvist for two years.

'Claire wants to meet you,' Hatch had said. 'She's heard about you for three years and she says she would like to put a face to the name. Could you come Tuesday afternoon, around three? I make a passable tea.'

'I would like that very much.'

She said it without thinking. The without-thinking was the part that surprised her later. The Ingrid Lindqvist who had said *I would like that very much* had not stopped to consult Elena—the mark of a second identity that had begun to operate on its own autonomic nervous system.

She said yes. She hung up. She thought about it for ten minutes and decided the operational reasoning supported the visit. The stated reasoning was the cover under which the actual reason hid: she had wanted to meet Claire for two and a half years. Claire had been a person Elena constructed in her head from surveillance data, and the construction had acquired the kind of interior life constructions were not supposed to acquire—thoughts, preferences, the quality of attention Elena had decided she would recognize in a room.

She rang the bell at three o'clock on Tuesday afternoon.

Hatch opened the door. The flat smelled of damp paper and cheap coffee and, faintly, of whatever Claire was making in the kitchen, which Elena identified through the air as a sponge cake and the small, particular sweetness of a cake being made by a woman who did not bake often but had decided that this afternoon required a cake.

Claire was in the kitchen. Hatch led Elena down the short hallway and called out, and Claire walked through wiping her hands on the front of an apron, and for the first time Elena saw her in the same physical space she'd been occupying for the entire time Elena had been doing what she'd been doing to the man she shared a flat with.

Claire was thirty-one, the height the file had said, wearing wool trousers and a butter-yellow blouse and the apron over both. Brown hair pulled back at the nape. Her face was not beautiful in the symmetrical file-photograph way, but it was a face—a woman who had been paying attention to her life for long enough that the attention showed. Her gray-green eyes met Elena's with the directness of a woman who had been looking forward to this for three years and was not going to pretend otherwise.

Claire smiled. She extended her hand.

'Ingrid,' she said. 'At last.'

Her voice was warm. Her grip was firm. The handshake lasted exactly the right number of seconds. Everything Claire was doing was without performance. She had decided in advance to like Elena, and the deciding showed.

'Claire,' Elena said. 'Thank you for having me. It's lovely to finally meet you.'

Both sentences were true. They were also operational. The doubling did not bother Elena the way it usually bothered her. The doubling was, in this room, the only thing she had to give Claire that was not actively a betrayal, and so she gave both the truth and the work with the slight extra warmth of a woman who was offering the most honest currency she still had in her possession.

They went into the living room. Hatch made tea. Claire produced the sponge cake from the kitchen on a small willow-pattern plate that did not match the cups. The tea was strong and slightly oversteeped, the way Hatch always made it. Claire had stopped correcting him years ago. Claire poured. Claire arranged the cake on three small plates. Claire asked Elena about Berlin.

She gave Claire the Ingrid Lindqvist version of Berlin—freelance research, Stockholm via Hamburg, the weather in February. Claire listened with full attention, the way she listened to anyone Tom Hatch brought into the flat. Forty-five minutes passed. The cake was good in the way of a woman who baked from her grandmother's recipe.

Claire asked Elena if she had a partner. Elena said she did not. Claire smiled and said she understood.

Claire touched the small gold chain at her throat. On the chain was an enamel charm: a green hill, the Shropshire landscape where she'd grown up. Elena could not have known any of this from the file. Elena knew it now.

Three years ago, in a café on the Kurfürstendamm, Elena had written in her head the line Claire was patient and supportive and did not ask questions—qualities that made her both a good partner and a potential pressure point. The line had been the line of a professional.

The line had also been a small particular evil that Elena filed without naming, and the woman touching the gold chain at her throat in the Camden flat in January 1978 was the body the line had been written about. The body was real. The body had eyes. It had a small enamel charm with a green hill on it. It had baked a sponge cake for an afternoon visitor whose only function in the body's life was the slow systematic disassembly of the man the body shared a flat with.

Elena got through the next ten minutes. The discipline held. Ingrid Lindqvist enjoyed tea. Elena Vasilieva, underneath, filed the enamel charm beside the other things she was carrying that nobody could see.

At four-fifteen, Elena said she had to be going.

Claire walked her to the door. Hatch hung back in the living room, refilling his own cup. At the door, Claire took both of Elena's hands in both of hers. The gesture had no calculation in it. It was the unguarded warmth of a person who took goodbyes seriously.

'Tom thinks the world of you,' Claire said. 'He says you're the only person in his professional life who actually understands the work. I'm glad I finally got to meet you.'

'Thank you for having me, Claire.'

'Come again. When you're back in London. I'd like that.'

'I would too.'

Elena did not know which of those last two statements was the lie and which was the truth and whether the question of which-was-which was a question her body had any way to answer. She squeezed Claire's hands once and let go and walked down the stairs and out into the Camden afternoon.

She thought about Claire's chain. The green hill on the enamel. A woman who loved a man who was going to be destroyed, wearing a charm she did not know was evidence.

She added Claire's name to the ledger. The name went in beside Katarina's.

She walked home through Camden in the dark, past pubs she would not enter and couples whose lives did not require ledgers. She let herself into the Kensington flat. She did not open the drawer beside the stove. The drawer did not need to be opened. The drawer knew what it held.

Three days later she flew to Tel Aviv.

Tel Aviv—2 February 1978.

The Mediterranean light hit her at the terminal door—salt air, dry brightness, the warmth of an afternoon in February.

Sara Lerner arrived at Ben Gurion on the second of February 1978 with a Canadian passport, a commission letter, and three published clippings under her byline in real Canadian magazines.

The cover was solid. It had been built over time.

She inhabited it.

The flat on Bograshov Street was two blocks from the sea, in a Bauhaus building that had been white once and was now the color of old paper. A previous Sara Lerner had lived here—a different woman, a different cover, decommissioned and moved to Johannesburg in 1975. The Second Department had kept the flat warm. The furniture was Sara Lerner's. The small ceramic bowl on the kitchen counter holding dried lavender was Sara Lerner's. The life was waiting.

She unpacked and walked the neighborhood. She located the bakery, the post office, the kiosk that sold the *Jerusalem Post*, the small café on Bialik Street where she would file her dispatches over the next several years. She built the routines of Sara Lerner the way she'd built the routines of Alice Marsh in 1971—with the patient layered repetition of cover work.

She thought about Claire on the third day, while walking along the seafront promenade in the warm February afternoon. Claire was three thousand kilometers north and was, at this hour, finishing a Year Nine English class in Islington. The thought did not have anywhere to go. Elena let it pass through her and out into the Mediterranean wind and watched it go.

The Mossad work began in the second week.

The reception was at the Canadian embassy. A trade delegation from Toronto, the visiting Canadian deputy minister of industry, the kind of evening function that Sara Lerner could attend without effort or explanation because Sara Lerner was a freelance journalist with a *Maclean's* commission letter and the deputy minister's office had been pleased to add her to the guest list when her editor cabled to request the addition.

Elena arrived at seven. She wore a navy dress chosen by the same instrument that had chosen the silk blouse at the Ministry of Chemical Industry in October 1976—the instrument that selected for the impression she wanted the room to form before the room knew it was forming one. At this reception the impression was: Canadian journalist, credentialed, not ambitious, available to be approached but not seeking approach. The instrument was older than Elena.

She circulated and introduced herself to the deputy minister, the Canadian ambassador (whose name was Howard), and two trade attachés. She also met a young Israeli civil servant whose father had emigrated from Toronto in 1957; their three minutes of conversation were the most pleasant Sara Lerner had produced at a diplomatic function in six months.

Among the CIA contingent was the station chief, Caroline Kell—a name Elena had read in three files in Moscow. The KGB file said Kell was incorruptible. The Mossad file said her husband had died in 1971 and she was raising two children alone in a Tel Aviv suburb. The third file, which had reached Elena through a channel that did not officially exist, said Caroline Kell's name was on a list maintained by the same hand that maintained the FEUERWERK list.

She moved through the room.

In the corner near the window, she found Ambassador Oded.

He was retired. He'd been at the embassy in Oslo from 1971 to 1974, which placed him in Norway during the Lillehammer catastrophe. The kind of man a freelance Canadian journalist would naturally approach at an embassy reception.

She approached him and introduced herself.

He was delighted. The delight was not performed. Retired ambassadors at evening receptions were men whose social currency had thinned, and a young journalist expressing interest in the Norwegian-Israeli trade relationship was an audience Oded had stopped expecting.

They talked for fifteen minutes. Fish-export quotas, Oslo in winter, the pleasantries of a retired diplomat finding an audience. Oded raised the events of July 1973 himself, with the small unhappy professional gesture of a man acknowledging the central trauma of his Norwegian posting.

'A bad week,' Oded said. 'The worst week of my career, I think. Six of our people in custody. A dead Moroccan waiter. The Norwegian newspapers calling for our ambassador's recall. I was the deputy then. I sat with the ambassador for three nights without sleeping while we tried to decide what to tell the foreign minister in Jerusalem.' He looked at his wine. 'I was glad to be transferred out of Oslo when the time came. There are cities that hold what happened in them. Oslo held that.'

'I'm sorry,' Elena said. 'That must have been very difficult.'

'It was a long time ago.'

Elena stood three feet from him with the warm attentive expression of a woman listening to an older diplomat tell a story she'd asked to hear. She gave no indication that the story had been the ground beneath her feet for four and a half years. She was Sara Lerner. Sara Lerner's face did not change.

She stood three feet from the man whose worst professional week had been her Tuesday evening's work, and the filing system received it the way it received everything—accurately, without sound, and without instruction for what to do next.

Oded did not see her. Oded would never see her. He would not know that the freelance Canadian journalist who had asked him about Norwegian trade had been, on a rainy afternoon outside Lillehammer four and a half years earlier, the woman he had watched walk away from the catastrophe his service had authored. The world's smallness was its own weight, carried privately by the people who happened to be standing in it.

She thanked him for the conversation and wished him a pleasant evening. She moved on.

Dina was beside the long table at the back of the reception room, where the canapés had been arranged on three platters and where most of the room's moving traffic flowed past.

Elena noticed her on entry. She'd noticed her the way she noticed people who had the small particular stillness of professionals at evening functions—a stillness that was not the stillness of withdrawal but the stillness of attention that had been organized to conserve the appearance of social availability. The stillness was familiar. Elena had been performing the same stillness in dozens of rooms in dozens of cities. She knew it when she saw it.

Dina was thirty-four. She was wearing a charcoal suit of a cut that suggested it had been bought in Europe rather than in Israel. Her hair was short, dark, cut by a hairdresser who understood that the cut should not need any maintenance during a working day. Her eyes were the color of an olive tree's leaves. Her hands, when she lifted a small canapé from a platter, lifted it the way a surgeon lifted an instrument—small precise movements as the discipline a body owed to itself. Her fingernails were short and unpainted.

Elena moved toward her.

She did not have a pretext. The lack of pretext was the pretext.

'These are surprisingly good,' Elena said in English, lifting one of the canapés.

Dina turned.

The turn was not the turn of a woman startled. It was the turn of a woman who had registered Elena's approach twenty seconds earlier, calculated the trajectory, and let her come because the move was Elena's. Elena saw the calculation in the same second she saw Dina's eyes. The stillness was not Mossad's stillness. It was not Moscow's stillness. It was a stillness Elena had encountered before, and had not yet given a name.

'They are,' Dina said. 'The chickpea ones especially. I've been working my way through them for ten minutes. Do you know who made them?'

'I don't. The embassy probably contracted a local catering service.'

'It's a good catering service. I'll find out the name from the protocol officer afterward. I have a dinner party next month and I'm running out of ideas.'

The exchange took fifteen seconds. Dina was a woman who hosted dinner parties. Elena had been trained to read that as either cover or asset, and could not yet read Dina as either.

'Sara Lerner,' Elena said, extending her hand.

'Dina Sharabi.' The handshake was firm and brief. 'Foreign Ministry, strategic planning. You're the *Maclean's* journalist. Howard mentioned you when I came in. He said you were writing about trade.'

Dina's eyes dropped once to Elena's left wrist. The glance was a professional's—the speed and brevity of an assessment filed without being named. Elena noticed.

'I am.'

'Boring assignment.'

'Slightly less boring than I expected, actually. The fish-quota negotiations have an interesting structure. The negotiating teams are mostly the same people who were on the original 1968 working group, and they've developed a kind of generational shorthand that an outsider wouldn't recognize. I might write about that instead of the quotas themselves.'

Dina considered this. The consideration took two seconds. At the end of the two seconds, the answer was yes.

'That would be a more interesting article,' Dina said. 'Most journalists who come through here write the assignment they were given. They don't notice the people who would make the assignment worth reading.'

'I'm trying to.'

'You said it well.'

They talked for forty minutes.

Elena listened. She listened with the part of her attention that was Sara Lerner the journalist, and with the part that was Elena Vasilieva the operative looking for the seams.

Dina had no seams.

Elena could not find them. She looked through the forty

minutes with the patience of a woman whose professional identity was built on finding seams in thirty seconds, and she found nothing. The charcoal suit was not too expensive and not too cheap. The phrasing was natural. The pauses were the pauses of a woman thinking, not calibrating. The questions were the right questions, in the right order, with the right register of mild interest. They were also—Elena could see this only because she was looking for it—the questions of a woman running a quiet professional assessment of a foreigner whose presence in her country had not yet been categorized.

The assessment was not hostile. It was the quiet ambient assessment intelligence officers ran on every new acquaintance until they had been filed. Dina was running one. This was the thing, Elena recognized within the first five minutes, that she and Dina had in common: they were both running continuous assessments on each other while speaking pleasantly about catering.

Two locksmiths, Elena thought. Standing at a canapé table in a Canadian embassy in Tel Aviv, each pretending to talk about a dinner party, each running her fingers along the other's lock looking for the pin she could push.

Elena's pin was not findable in the forty minutes. Neither was Dina's.

The respect was involuntary.

The respect was also, Elena knew within the first fifteen minutes of finding nothing in the surface Dina was presenting to her, the most dangerous condition she'd been in professionally in years.

'I should let you go,' Dina said at the forty-minute mark. 'I don't want to monopolize you. Howard will be wondering where I've gotten to.'

'Of course.'

'Sara—coffee next week? The fish quotas are boring but you made them less boring, and I am selfish about people who can do that.'

The line was the operational opening of a relationship whose endpoint neither woman could currently predict.

'I would like that very much,' Elena said.

She'd used the same six words three weeks earlier in a Camden flat, to a woman in a butter-yellow blouse who had baked her a sponge cake. Both times the words had been true. Both times the words had been operational. In the Camden flat, the words had been the smaller danger, because Claire had been a person Elena was working against with no interior rebellion. In the Tel Aviv reception, the words were the larger danger, because Dina was a person Elena would be working both for and against, and the two would not hold apart.

They exchanged numbers. Dina's was a Foreign Ministry desk line. Elena's was the Bograshov flat. Dina put Elena's number in her jacket pocket. Elena put Dina's in the small leather notebook in her handbag.

Dina turned to leave. At the last moment she turned back.

'It was good to meet you, Sara.'

'It was good to meet you, Dina.'

Both statements were true. Both statements were operational. The doubling, in this room, did not produce in Elena the small interior horror it had produced in the Camden flat with Claire. The doubling with Dina felt like a shared language. Dina was doing it too. Dina was, Elena had understood somewhere in the first five minutes, in the same business Elena was in—not for the same service, not toward the same ends, but with the same tools and the same disciplines and the same cost.

Dina walked away. Elena watched her cross the reception

room. Dina did not look back. The not-looking-back was its own message: *I know you watched me leave. I am giving you the courtesy of pretending I did not notice.* She moved on.

Elena finished her wine. She circulated for another twenty minutes, made polite small talk with a Canadian trade attaché whose name she did not catch, and at nine-thirty walked out of the embassy and into the warm Tel Aviv night.

Her flat on Bograshov Street was three blocks from the embassy. She walked. The sea was audible two blocks away—the low continuous sigh of water against stone, with the orange streetlight glow particular to Tel Aviv in the evening. She thought about Claire's gold chain and the green hill on the enamel oval, Dina's charcoal suit, Oded's long sad anecdote about Oslo in winter.

She let herself into the flat. The lavender on the kitchen counter was still in its small bowl. She set an empty wine glass beside the sink. There was no glass. She had set nothing. Her body had performed the motion anyway, the way a body that had been holding a glass for an hour sometimes did. She noticed the absence and almost smiled.

She took the small bound notebook out of her handbag.

The notebook she'd bought in a Schöneberg stationer's the day after the Geneva meeting in March 1976, twenty-three months ago. It was now eighteen pages full and a hundred and four pages empty. She turned to a clean page.

She wrote three lines.

The first line was in Russian. *Claire wears a small enamel charm with a green hill on it. She touches it when she is listening.*

The second line was in English. *Oded does not know.*

The third line was in Russian. *Dina has no seams.*

She closed the notebook. She put it in the inside pocket of the handbag, which was where it would live in Tel Aviv because there was no false back of any wardrobe in this flat that she trusted yet, and the inside pocket of the handbag was the only place the notebook could go that would not be findable by a routine search.

The Mediterranean wind was moving in the courtyard below the flat and the shutters were making a small rhythmic knock she had not heard earlier in the day. She crossed to the kitchen counter and turned on the small shortwave radio the previous Sara Lerner had left behind, tuned it to the BBC World Service, and stood with her hand on the plastic housing while the set warmed.

The bulletin was late English. A Wednesday evening roundup. She listened without paying attention until the tone of the correspondent changed and she recognized, with the small body delay that preceded recognition, the subject before she had understood which word had triggered it.

A village in the Apennines.

Not the thirty-month piece she had watched in a Kensington flat in November 1973. A six-year-after segment. A radio correspondent filing from Rome was explaining that the petition the families of the 1971 victims had filed in the spring of 1973 had been dismissed by an Italian regional court in November 1977 on a procedural question. The appeal had stalled. One of the key witnesses—an engineer stationed at a civil defense post fifteen kilometers east of the village, whose testimony about a radiation reading he had taken that morning had been central to the petition—had died earlier that autumn of what the attending physician had classified as an atypical cardiac event. He was forty-eight. The BBC correspondent noted, in the small dry care of a man whose editors had told him to note without emphasis, that the engineer had been in good health the day before he died. The reading he had taken that morning—the families' lawyer told the BBC—had been recorded in a small black field notebook the engineer had kept in his coat pocket for nineteen years. The notebook had not been found among his effects.

The Rome correspondent returned to the mother.

The mother had died thirteen months before the petition was dismissed. Stroke. Sixty-three years old. She was survived by two sons and a daughter. The correspondent did not name the daughter. The daughter had been the one in the photograph. The daughter had been twenty-four. The daughter would be twenty-four permanently.

Elena's hand on the radio housing did not move. She felt the plastic warming under her palm, her own pulse in the tendons of her wrist, and behind her sternum the controlled drop in blood pressure her body performed when it understood a thing the conscious mind had not yet named.

Atypical cardiac event at forty-eight, in a man in good health. Stroke at sixty-three.

A compound. Developed in a basement laboratory at Yasenevo in the early 1960s. An arrhythmia indistinguishable from natural causes in any post-mortem that did not run the specific tests the standard European autopsy protocol did not require. She had been shown its profile in a briefing room at Yasenevo in the spring of 1972. She had read the authorized-use ledger. Three entries. A West German physicist, 1968. A Finnish border officer, 1971. A Turkish journalist, 1974. The ledger ended in 1974. Release required a signature at the level of the First Chief Directorate.

It had been used in the autumn of 1977 on a civil defense engineer fifteen kilometers east of Fanano. And thirteen months before him, on a sixty-three-year-old woman in a black cardigan who had cracked the first cover story open by writing two hundred letters.

Neither kill had entered the ledger. Neither had required the First Chief Directorate's signature, or possessed it, or been submitted for it. The compound had walked out of the basement at Yasenevo through a door somebody had held open, and somebody had been holding the door open for years, and the somebody was not in the chain of command the chain of command knew about.

She thought about the shape.

The first cover story had been the cover for the accident. The first cover had held for thirty months. Then a mother in a black cardigan had cracked it, in public, on Radio 4, at 22:48 on a Tuesday, and the cracking had been witnessed in a Kensington flat by a woman who had then been asked, six weeks before the witnessing, to manage the journalist the mother's letters were going to reach.

The second cover story was the cover for the people who had cracked the first. It had been written in the quieter register of medical bureaucracy. *Atypical cardiac event.* Stroke. The register depended on the absence of any investigator who would know to run the specific tests.

The first cover had protected a weapon. The second cover was protecting the first cover.

She did not permit it to arrive as a conclusion.

How many have I not seen.

She took the notebook out of the inside pocket of the handbag. She opened it to the page she had just closed. She added a fourth line, in Russian, beneath the three she had already written.

Fanano. Six years after. The mother dead. The engineer dead. Count is fourteen. How many have I not seen.

She closed the notebook. She put it back.

She turned the radio off. The courtyard wind continued in

the courtyard. The shutters continued to knock.

She made tea. She did not drink it.

Calder in London. Asleep beside Margaret, whose deliberate trust was the policy that allowed Elena to keep being what she was. She had been back three weeks and had not seen him. She'd walked past his street twice and had not gone to his door. Eighteen months of trying not to want to be seen by him. The want was a thing she had not yet named.

Calder. Margaret. The bracelet with the charms Margaret wore to bed. The weight of loving a man whose wife you were destroying and loving the wife whose husband you were using. She had not previously believed a person could carry a thing that had room for both kinds of love at once.

She thought about Claire's gold chain.

She thought about Dina's eyes.

She thought about the nine objects in the drawer in her Kensington flat, three thousand kilometers north: the diary, the candle, the pen, Yuri's welcome card, the Ronson lighter, the Nagra reel, Calder's first card from November 1973, the photograph of an orchid that had bloomed for three weeks in East Berlin, and the Mercator knife at the back beneath the diary. The entire archive of what she carried that could not be carried in any institution's file.

The drawer would have to wait. Tel Aviv was its own archive now. The notebook in her handbag was the only object she'd carried south, and the notebook would carry the archive until she could go home.

The drawer held everything now. Everything except the things she could not file.

12
THE TABLE

Tel Aviv—June 1980

Elena had been Sara Lerner for over two years. The Kensington flat was waiting. London was waiting.

Two years. Tuesday coffees with Dina at the café on Allenby—pretext at first, then habit, then something Elena did not have a category for. Once, early on, Dina had referenced a byline Sara had not yet filed, and Sara had absorbed the reference without naming the gap because Dina had moved on before the gap could be marked. Standing Friday dinners with Doron at the Bograshov flat, the wine still in his cabinet from Cyprus, the kitchen always half-cooked when she arrived. Yael at most of those dinners by the second year. Tel Aviv had moved Elena from operational to inhabited without her noticing the boundary cross.

Her original plan for Doron and Yael had been sequential. Doron first, then Yael. Two cultivations, two intelligence streams, two files. Together, they were two halves of an infrastructure Elena had been sent to map. Separately, they were manageable.

The plan failed in its second week because Doron and Yael were already sleeping together.

Elena discovered this at a Friday dinner at the apartment of a Tel Aviv University professor who collected journalists and diplomats the way some people collected stamps. Doron and

Yael arrived together. Elena registered not the fact of their arrival but the manner: the physical vocabulary of two bodies that had learned each other's geometry. Yael's hand finding the small of Doron's back as they navigated the crowded entryway. His quiet ease in its pressure.

Elena saw all of this in ten seconds. She revised her plan in twenty more.

The sequential approach was dead. You could not cultivate one without the other noticing.

The alternative was to cultivate them together.

No manual Elena had studied considered the possibility that the most effective approach to two people in love might be to become the third point of the triangle rather than the blade that severed it.

Not a honey trap—a transaction. An authentic intimacy that would generate the carelessness that generated the intelligence.

The design took two years.

Doron was thirty-six. Sabra, military service in a unit whose name he did not mention. Logistics manager for a defense-industries subsidiary.

Yael was thirty-two. Dark-haired, dark-eyed, with the coiled energy of a woman whose stillness was not calm but compression. She worked in a division of military intelligence she described, when pressed, as analytical.

Elena befriended them as Sara Lerner. Three meetings became a standing arrangement; she became the third person in a friendship that was, from the outside, exactly what it appeared to be. From the inside, it was also what it appeared to be. The cultivation and the friendship were the same activity, and the perspectives were converging. The liking was the tool and the tool was the liking, and she did not untie the knot. She let it tighten.

Two years.

She was having coffee with Dina Sharabi every other week. Dina did not know about Doron and Yael. Dina did not pry—and the not-prying was how Elena recognized a professional whose discretion was doctrinal, not personal. The compartments held. She suspected they would not hold forever.

The dinner was in June 1980. A Friday. Doron cooked.

He cooked the way he always cooked—with the focused abundance of a man who believed feeding people was a moral act.

The flat was in the Yemenite Quarter, a third-floor walk-up with tall windows open onto the warm Tel Aviv evening. The air was salt and jasmine. Doron was building lamb with pomegranate molasses and sumac.

Elena sat at the kitchen table and watched him cook and drank the wine Yael had opened—a Golan Heights Cabernet, dark and full. They were talking about a piece Elena had written about the Russian immigrant community in Bat Yam, and Yael was disagreeing with the granular specificity she brought to every disagreement.

'The piece was good,' Yael said. 'Too good. My mother read it. She wants to know if you want to come for *Shabbat*. She is convinced you understand Russians.'

'I do,' Elena said. 'Slightly. Canadians who grew up near immigrant neighborhoods develop a kind of tourist understanding.'

Doron looked up from the aubergine. 'Tourist understanding is the only kind that isn't useless. The rest of it pretends to know what it cannot.' He laughed—the loud laugh that filled rooms the way Doron filled them, generously and without apology.

The table was set with a white cloth Doron's mother had given them. This detail would matter later. On the cloth: plates, glasses, a bowl of olives, the bottle of Cabernet, a candle Yael had lit because she said that Friday dinner without a candle was just food and that food without ceremony was just fuel.

Elena watched Yael say this. The way she held her wine glass by the stem and turned it slowly while she thought. The compression in her body when she was making a point she believed in. Elena had noted these things as operational data. Sitting in the candlelight with the warm air coming through the windows and Yael's face animated across the table, she understood what she'd been cataloging was not data. It was attention.

They ate. The lamb was extraordinary. The conversation slowed.

Elena was aware of the intimacy. The mind was running its parallel process.

They cleared the table together. This was Doron's rule—the person who cooked did not clean. Yael and Elena stood at the small counter washing plates while Doron sat at the table with his wine. The kitchen was warm. The jasmine through the window was unchanged.

Yael's arm touched Elena's.

It was not an accident. Two women could stand at that counter without touching if they chose to. Yael's forearm stayed against Elena's. Bare skin against bare skin. The warmth of another person's body transmitted through the thin sensitive surface of the inner arm.

Neither moved.

Two years of Tel Aviv had changed her. The sun had found the olive undertone in her skin. The eyes had not changed. They never changed.

Yael had once told Elena that her eyes were the stillest eyes she had ever seen on a person who was not sedated. Elena had been unsettled by it, in the private place where she kept things that were true.

The touch was a question. The oldest question.

The answer arrived not from Elena's operational mind but from her body, which had decided, without authorization, not to pull away. The body had known for months—since the beach in April when Yael had emerged from the sea in a black one-piece and Elena had looked and had registered the looking and had not cataloged any of it.

Doron was watching. Elena could see him at the edge of her vision—sitting at the table, his wine glass in his hand, his body still. His expression was not surprise. It was not jealousy. It was attention. The focused attention of a man who was seeing something he had been waiting to see.

Elena had been cultivating them. They had been cultivating her.

The realization was so complete that Elena's operational mind did something it had never done before. It went quiet. There was no protocol for the moment the operative discovered she was not the operator but the operated upon.

The kitchen was quiet. Yael's arm was still against Elena's. The dishes were forgotten in the sink.

Yael turned.

She turned the way she did everything—with commitment, without second-guessing. She looked at Elena and Elena looked at her and the look lasted two seconds and contained no ambiguity. It said: I see you. Not Sara Lerner. You.

Yael kissed her.

Yael's mouth was warm. She tasted of Cabernet and of the salt on her skin from the sea air coming through the windows. Her hands came up to Elena's face—both hands, framing her jaw, holding her with a firmness that was not aggressive but certain. Her tongue found Elena's and the kiss deepened, unhurried, with the open confidence of a woman who had been thinking about it for two years and had decided, tonight, to stop thinking.

Elena kissed her back.

Her body was in command now. Yael's mouth against hers and Yael's hands on her face and the taste of wine and the smell of jasmine from the open window. The heat of Yael's body. The heat of the kitchen. The heat of a Tel Aviv night in June pressing against them through the windows like a third body already present, already involved.

Elena's back hit the table edge. The impact was solid—the table's wooden rim against her lower back. She leaned into it. Yael pressed into her. The cotton skirt Elena was wearing rode up her thighs as the position adjusted.

A wine glass tipped.

Elena heard it. The small musical sound of crystal losing its balance. Then the larger sound—the glass hitting the tablecloth and the wine spilling, red on white, the stain spreading outward from the point of impact in a dark irregular bloom that looked, in the candlelight, like something living.

Nobody caught it. Nobody cared.

Doron stood. He crossed the kitchen in three steps. He reached across the table and swept the remaining dishes aside. Ceramic and glass hit the tile floor.

He was behind Yael now, his body close enough that Elena could feel the heat of him through two layers of fabric, and the heat was the first time in years that Elena had felt a man's body without calculating what she was going to do with it.

Doron lifted her onto the table. The wine stain was beneath her.

Yael's mouth was on Elena's neck. Then the hollow between her collarbones where the pulse was visible, and Yael pressed her lips to the pulse and held them there, and Elena felt the double rhythm—her own heartbeat and Yael's mouth registering it.

Three bodies. Six hands.

Elena's shirt came off. She did not remember who removed it. The Akhmatova tattoo on her ribcage—the script she had worn since she was seventeen and that Calder had read with his fingers in a Fitzrovia flat—was visible now to Yael and Doron, who did not know the words meant *I taught myself to live simply and wisely* and that Elena had failed at both.

She was wet in a way that felt like a confession.

Yael's mouth moved lower, pausing to read the Akhmatova letters with her lips the way Calder had once read them in the dark—but unlike Calder, Yael understood what the words meant.

The kitchen light had been left on. It came through the doorway like a witness.

Yael's mouth reached the place it was going.

Elena's hand found the edge of the table. Her fingers gripped the wood hard enough to leave marks in the varnish. A moan she had not meant to make left her throat and traveled through the kitchen like something she had been keeping inside a drawer for nineteen years.

'Sara,' Yael said. Just the name. Just the breath of it.

The room was very warm.

She was focused. She was free. The two were the same thing now and had never been the same thing in seven years of trained breathing.

The sound that followed was not managed. It came from the place below selection, where the body simply told the truth, and the truth was: yes. this. here. Without the filing system. Without the performance. Without Alice Marsh or Sara Lerner or any of the other women she had built to stand between herself and the world. Just Elena, gripping the edge of a kitchen table in Tel Aviv, and the sound that was only hers.

Elena came apart.

The orgasm began in her thighs and moved upward through her body in a wave that she had, in fourteen years of performed intimacy, never permitted herself to feel arrive before. It arrived now. It kept arriving. Her body shook against Yael's mouth and against Doron's chest, and she did not know whose hands were where and she did not care, and the not-caring was the part that would haunt her afterward.

She came with Yael's mouth on her and Doron's arms around her and her hands gripping the edge of the table where the wine stain was still spreading, and the sound she made was loud and uncontrolled. It was the most honest sound she had produced in fourteen years.

Afterward.

Afterward.

Three bodies on the kitchen floor. Still. Breathing hard. The tablecloth beneath them, stained with wine and creased by the geometry of what had occurred on it. The candle on the table above, still burning, its light casting shadows on the ceiling that moved with the breeze from the windows.

Elena was between them. Yael's head on her chest. Doron's arm across her waist. Skin against skin against skin. The most honest silence Elena had inhabited in seven years of work.

She thought about what had just happened. The filing system had no category for it.

Yael spoke.

She spoke quietly, into the hollow of Elena's shoulder, with the drowsy post-coital intimacy of a woman who was talking because the silence had lasted long enough and because what she had to say was small enough to fit inside the silence without breaking it.

'There's a thing at work,' she said. 'A passport issue. Canadian passports.' A pause. 'Someone's been using them—our people, I mean. For operations.' She shifted against Elena's shoulder. 'It's become a problem because the Canadians noticed. There's a diplomatic situation and nobody wants to deal with it. Doron's shop is going to have to change the rotation again.' Her breath was slowing. 'Last week one of our people had a Canadian passport flagged at Athens customs. They ran it. Turned out the same passport had been used twice in two weeks by two different people. The consular service is going to make a stink. It's annoying.'

Elena's operational mind came fully alert.

She let it pass. She did not ask a follow-up question. She did not probe. She lay on the floor with Yael's head on her chest and Doron's arm across her waist and she said, 'Mmm,' the non-verbal acknowledgment of a woman who had heard what was said and was too satisfied and too sleepy to pursue it.

The Mmm was the most precisely calibrated sound she'd produced all evening.

Yael fell asleep with her head on Elena's chest a few minutes later.

Doron slipped into his own deeper breathing not long after that, and Elena lay between them in the kitchen with the candle still burning on the table above and the warm Mediterranean air coming through the windows and her mind running at the speed and clarity it always ran at when an operation had just delivered a fact she had not expected and would not be able to forget.

In the morning, Elena lay between two sleeping bodies and composed a report in her head.

The report would be clinical. It would describe the intelligence obtained—the Canadian passport operation—and it would provide context and assessment and recommendations for follow-up. It would be transmitted through the Nicosia channel within forty-eight hours.

Then she revised the timeline.

The report would not be transmitted within forty-eight hours. The decision did not arrive at the level of her operational mind, where decisions were weighed and documented. It arrived at the level beneath—the level where Sacco had been not-reported in March 1976 and where Voss had been not-reported in October 1977 and where the not-reporting had become, by 1980, the part of Elena's professional identity that was no longer asking permission of the part that wrote the reports.

The report would go to Moscow. Eventually. Six weeks from now, when the Canadian passport line could be folded into a longer assessment of Mossad's European operations.

Elena lay still. Yael shifted in her sleep, pressing closer. Doron's breathing was deep and even. The morning light came through the windows and fell across the stained tablecloth and the scattered cutlery and the three bodies lying in the middle of it all like survivors of something that had been, in its way, as violent as anything Elena had done in a checkpoint or an alley.

Calder. She had not thought about him during the table or the floor or the silence afterward. She thought about him now the way she always thought about him—at a distance, in the dark, with the loneliness that was the truest thing she carried.

Tuesday coffee with Dina. She would sit across from Dina and listen the way she always listened—with the complete attention of a woman hiding everything and the complete tenderness of a woman who was not.

The rope in the death strip. The *rothschildianum* leaf in Kessler's greenhouse. The Mercator knife in the drawer. The wine stain on the tablecloth beneath her now. All the things getting added to the archive that lived in no institution's filing system.

Elena closed her eyes. She did not sleep.

Later, before the sun came fully up, she wrote the Yael line in the small red notebook, in Russian, under the word withheld. It was the third entry under that heading. She knew, lying on a kitchen floor in Tel Aviv with two sleeping people against her, that she had just had, at the age of thirty-two, her first real sexual experience.

The sun rose higher. The city woke. The shawarma stand on the corner began its work, and the smell of roasting meat came through the windows and mixed with the jasmine and the salt, and Elena lay still and held the silence and let the morning arrive.

13

JAFFA

Tel Aviv / Jaffa—December 1982

Dina ordered the cardamom coffee because the cardamom coffee was what Dina had ordered every second Tuesday for five years.

They were at their usual café on Allenby, at their usual table by the window—Dina in the chair against the wall, Elena across from her—and the waitress had stopped asking them what they wanted in 1979 and now simply brought the cardamom coffee and the black Americano and set them down without pause. Five years of Tuesdays. The waitress had aged visibly in the interval. She would retire in six months. Dina had already arranged to attend the small party.

They did not talk about work. They talked about the novel Dina was reading—a Hungarian writer whose translator Dina thought was making small choices that shifted the register. They talked about Dina's sister who was getting divorced in Haifa and whose teenage daughter had begun sneaking out at night in a way that was either normal or a symptom, and Dina was too tired to determine which. Dina mentioned, in passing, a hotel bar she had started going to after work—a small place called the Cinema, near the Ministry—and that the barman had begun bringing her drink without her ordering. Dina had found this familiar in a way she could not quite place. They did not talk about the passport.

Dina asked, between the novel and the sister, whether Sara had been sleeping well lately. She asked it the way a friend asks. Her eyes were on her cup. The asking was so casual that Elena registered it only on the second pass a week later, in the notebook she maintained for observations that did not fit anywhere else. Elena had not mentioned, to Dina or to anyone, that she had not slept well for three weeks. There was no way Dina could have known.

At the end of the hour, Dina paid. It was Dina's turn. They had kept track, loosely, for five years.

On the pavement outside, Dina touched Elena's elbow—a small gesture, established years ago, the handshake they had built in lieu of the handshake neither of them could give the other.

'Tuesday next week?'

'Tuesday next week.'

Elena walked home along the seafront. The wind was off the water, colder than the calendar. A Tel Aviv winter was not quite a winter, and the city performed it half-heartedly. She passed a residential tower on Ha'Yarkon whose sub-basement she had begun to suspect since her first week in the city, and the archive did what it always did, and on the fourth-floor balcony a child was watching the seabirds the way small children watched moving objects, and she did not look up at the windows.

The consular report was waiting on her kitchen table when she arrived home.

The discrepancy was small. The kind of thing most people would not have noticed, because most people did not maintain a photographic inventory of every document connected to their cover identity.

Elena noticed.

She sat back down at the kitchen table with a second cup of coffee. The radio was on, turned low. A muezzin call from three streets over sliding through the window. The cup was Alice Marsh's cup—she'd brought it from Kensington in 1978 because the woman who had acquired it in 1974 had reached for it every morning without thinking, and the reaching had become part of the cover the way breath became part of a body. Sara Lerner drank from Alice Marsh's cup. Neither of them was Elena.

A Canadian passport in the name of Sara Lerner had been flagged at Athens International Airport on 14 September 1982. A border control officer had recorded the document's serial number and photograph. The photograph did not match the bearer. The name did. The passport number was within the block Canadian passports had been issued from during the months the real Sara Lerner's documentation had been assembled by the Second Department. It was, operationally, a perfect duplicate.

Elena had not been in Athens on 14 September. She had been in Tel Aviv, in her flat on Bograshov Street, writing a dispatch about the Lebanese refugee community. The dispatch's dateline and the editor's records established, with documentary certainty, that Sara Lerner had been in Israel on the day Sara Lerner's passport had been used in Greece.

Someone else was traveling on her passport.

Two and a half years earlier, in a kitchen in the Yemenite Quarter, Yael had told her in a sleepy post-coital sentence that Mossad was using Canadian passports for operations. Elena had said Mmm. She had filed Yael's sentence. She had not reported it to Moscow for six weeks, and when she reported it she had folded it into language that allowed Moscow to read it as ambient gossip rather than operational lead. The folding had been the third withholding in her career and the moment she formally recognized herself as a defected operative who had not yet defected.

The September flag was the same operation. The thread Yael had touched in 1980 had now grasped the most personal piece of paper Elena owned.

She read item thirty-one a second time. Then a third. The third reading was not for comprehension but the way a body processed information it had already understood but had not yet accepted.

She accepted it now.

Elena did not report it.

Not to Nicosia. She did not encode a priority signal. She did not activate the emergency channel that existed for exactly this kind of contingency. She sat in her flat and held the consular report and did not do the thing her training, her professional protocols, and every instinct she'd developed over eleven years of intelligence work demanded that she do.

The paper was thin. The typewriter the Nicosia desk had used was one she recognized from the ribbon's slight shift to the left. A machine had typed the word flagged, and the word was now in her hands, warm from the courier's briefcase.

Reporting it would trigger a response she could not control. Moscow would extract her, shut down the Sara Lerner identity, close four years of operational investment in Israel, and write off Dina and Doron and Yael and the slow patient circuit of trust Elena had built around herself in Tel Aviv. Moscow would not want to understand why a Mossad passport operation had touched Sara Lerner specifically. Moscow would want to be clean of it.

Elena did not want to withdraw. She wanted to investigate.

The withholding was the fourth in five years. Sacco. Voss.

Yael's sleepy passport line. And now this—the largest yet, because this was not a single fact omitted from a single report. This was an entire off-books investigation she would run alone, against Mossad, with no weapon and no backup. The withholding was no longer a small interior rebellion. It was the operation now.

She began work that afternoon.

Three weeks of solitary work.

The first lead was wrong. Five days on a warehouse that resolved to a Sony distributor and a merchant family's tax structure. Fatigue asked her, more insistently than before, whether the passport flag was worth this. She did not permit it the hearing.

On the fourteenth day she found it.

An Ottoman-era building on Yefet Street. Three stories, ground-floor spice shop, upper floors shuttered. The building's lease was held by a shell entity registered at an address six blocks from the Mossad complex on King Saul Boulevard. The shell entity had been created in 1976. The lease had been renewed twice.

She did not visit the building in daylight. She visited it after sunset on two separate evenings, from different approach directions, and confirmed on the second visit what the first had suggested: the spice shop closed at eighteen-thirty, but the upper floors showed intermittent light through the shutters until nearly midnight, the pattern consistent with the rotating presence of operators who arrived, worked for a period, and left.

She located the observation post on the third reconnaissance. A vacant flat across the narrow street, one floor higher than the safe house's top floor, with a sightline through a gap in the shutters on the building's south window. The vacant flat's door was padlocked. Elena opened it in twenty seconds.

She set up on the evening of the eighteenth.

No electricity. No running water. A sleeping bag rolled into the corner where the floor had settled. The Nikon FM on a small tripod, loaded with Tri-X 400, the lens a 180mm telephoto she had acquired through Sara Lerner's photographer contacts years earlier. A contact microphone taped to the inside of the shutter frame and connected to the Nagra in her coat pocket. The Mercator knife in her other pocket, the weight of it familiar now, five years in a pocket instead of a drawer.

The microphone was the kind of improvisation Moscow would have forbidden. Contact microphones picked up building vibration, not conversation, but a trained ear could read vibration the way a trained eye read a face. Elena's ear, over eleven years, had become trained.

She watched for three nights.

The Jaffa nights had their own particular character. Cats on the harbor wall, the occasional fishing boat leaving the marina, distant radios playing Arabic-language broadcasts. The smell of the sea, of the fish market's concrete being hosed down at four in the morning, of nine hundred years of stone.

Nights one and two passed without event. Arrivals around nine, departures before midnight. Different men each time, different sedans, Israeli civilian plates. She photographed from the shutter gap. No movement in the adjacent rooms. Routine maintenance presence, safe house dormant. She returned at dawn. She slept four hours. She went back.

Night three was the night that mattered.

At 21:47, she nearly abandoned.

A cat came across the tiles behind her. Orange, thin, moving with the silence cats produced when their own hunger had educated them in movement. But Elena's body registered the footfall as human before her ear corrected the information, and her hand had already found the Mercator knife in her coat pocket before her mind had finished assembling the data. The body was still wired for Kessler's cat on the fire escape in Lichtenberg years earlier—a stillness that ran faster than thought. The body knew it was a cat. The body had reached for the knife anyway. This was what eleven years had done to her.

She moved her hand off the knife. The body was louder than the cat.

At 23:40, two men entered the safe house from a dark sedan. Different men. Different sedan. The compact trained build of operators whose bodies had been maintained for the work. She shot twelve frames in the time it took them to cross from the car to the door. The upper-floor lights came on in a pattern that was different from the previous nights—two rooms lit simultaneously, which had not happened before.

At 00:15, the voices started.

Not shouting. The contact microphone picked up the rise and fall of the voices. A male voice, heavy, pressing a question. Another male voice, lighter, evading. The acoustic shape of a debriefing that had become an interrogation.

In her coat pocket, the Nagra was running. Through the wool she could feel the tick—the small mechanical defect she'd concealed from Yuri in October 1973, nine years old now. A nick on the metal spindle that pulled the tape past the recording head. Each time the spindle turned, the nick caught the tape and scratched it, and the scratching made the click. Every click was also a permanent mark on the recording. Recording or playback—the nick did not know the difference. A reel listened to twice carried twice the damage. One per four seconds. The mechanism was failing the way old precision instruments failed—not catastrophically but cumulatively.

Someone was walking in the room above. Back and forth. The pacing of a man who was not yet certain whether he was the interrogator or the interrogated.

Then the pacing stopped.

For eight seconds there was no footfall. No chair. Only the building's ambient frequencies and the Nagra ticking one per four seconds in her coat. Elena counted. At the end of the eighth second she felt the temperature of the lit window change in the way temperature changed when a man had stopped performing and had begun being.

At 00:23, the gunshot.

A single report. Muffled by the walls but unmistakable. Her body went still—not frozen, still. The professional stillness of assessment.

Where. How many. Threat level. One round from the safe house. No follow-up. The dense silence of a space in which something irrevocable had just occurred.

And then the detail she would carry: half a second after the report, the flat concussive sound of a body meeting tile. Not the muted thump of carpet. Tile—which could be cleaned in the hour that would follow, and carpet could not.

The safe house was not only a safe house. It was a kill room, fitted out for exactly this.

She held position. The pacing resumed. A chair scraped. The heavier voice was still audible on the contact microphone. The lighter voice was not.

One round. Close range. Small caliber. The kind of round a professional administered when the subject of a debriefing had become its obstacle.

The silence had a specific shape. She had heard it before. In

Fanano in 1971. In the minister's file. In the hotel-register thinning that had preceded each of the magistrates whose warrants had been about to touch the Livorno manifest. It was a housekeeping protocol with a name only inside the hand that ran it. Tonight the protocol had visited Yefet Street.

At 00:26, the men left fast. One carried a document case he had not been carrying when he entered. The other's hand was in his jacket pocket in the shape of a hand holding a weapon. They did not check the street. They drove north.

Their walk was the deliberate, even walk of technicians whose work had reached its expected conclusion. She logged the gait.

Elena memorized the registration. She shot five frames of the departure. The sedan turned left at the top of the street and was gone.

She did not move.

She counted to one hundred and twenty.

Then she saw the rooftop.

A figure at the parapet of the building one structure east. Male, dark-clothed, stillness that had been still longer than her own. Binoculars or a long-lens camera aimed directly at her window. He had been there the entire time. He was raising a small object to his mouth.

A radio.

The radio meant: I have her. Send the team.

In Lillehammer, nine years earlier, Elena had sat in a bar and watched a Mossad team and had read them in three minutes. Team size. Communication methods. Positioning. Timing between surveillance and execution. By most professional standards they had been very good. By hers they had been legible. She had cataloged them the way a naturalist catalogs a species—with the patient thoroughness of a woman who had never imagined that the naturalist was being cataloged in turn, by someone in another window, in a language the naturalist did not know existed.

She had been someone else's species.

Elena had perhaps ninety seconds. The observation post was compromised. The street was compromised. The team was already in transit, coordinated through the watcher's radio frequency.

Her body began to do the work her mind was still assembling.

She did not pack the camera. She pulled the Nikon off the tripod, extracted the roll, fed the film into the interior pocket of her coat beside the two exposed rolls she had already completed. She left the body on the tiles. The Nagra kept turning in her coat.

She went down the back staircase three steps at a time.

She had walked the route four times in the last three weeks. She had walked it twice at night. She picked the first alternate exit in the service yard in eleven seconds—a wooden gate with a padlock older than she was. She went through. She padlocked it behind her.

Behind her, footsteps. Two sets, possibly three. The runners were professionals. Their pace was the controlled tempo of men who knew that pursuit at full sprint exhausted the pursuer faster than it caught the pursued. They knew Jaffa. They knew the alleys.

At the mouth of the narrow passage between two buildings she caught movement at her six o'clock and turned her head three degrees, no more, without breaking her pace. A man was standing at the entrance she had come through thirty seconds earlier. Dark jacket. Dark cap. Not running. Not pursuing. His face came up into the yellow light of the lamp above the passage for half a second and she saw the scar. The scar was on the left cheekbone. The shape was the shape her Nikon had caught through the shutter an hour ago. He had followed her out of the observation post. He was not trying to catch her. He was standing at the mouth of the passage and watching her leave it. The allowing was the whole operation. The scar was its face.

Elena walked the old city for exactly this contingency.

She ran the route she'd memorized during four years of cover maintenance walks. Through a courtyard, through the abandoned kitchen of a shuttered restaurant, over a wall, through a tailor's shop she picked open in eleven seconds. Out the front door onto a street that ran perpendicular to the street the runners were searching.

She walked. She did not run. A woman running through Jaffa at one in the morning was a woman who attracted a policeman's attention. A woman walking through Jaffa at one in the morning was a woman who had worked late at a nearby restaurant, and the policeman who saw her would decide not to stop her because stopping her would require a report he did not want to write.

She walked west for six blocks. The Nagra ticked in her coat. The tick had accelerated. Not one per four seconds anymore but closer to one per two. The nine-year-old defect was compounding in real time while she was running for her life, and she noticed the compounding the way she noticed everything tonight—automatically, and the instrument she'd been carrying for nine years was running out of time alongside her.

The Fiat 127 was parked on the coast road near the first beach entrance in Bat Yam.

She had not chosen the car. The car had chosen itself by being unlocked, by being old enough that its ignition could be shorted by any hand that had been trained on pre-1974 Italian wiring, and by being parked with the steering wheel turned so that the front tires had cleared the curb, which meant the owner had left in a hurry and was unlikely to return before morning.

Nine seconds from approach to ignition. Even in a hurry she cataloged the interior as she drove—a rosary on the rearview, a child's drawing in the footwell, an empty water bottle under the passenger seat. Elena would abandon the car somewhere she could leave it running with the keys in the footwell, to minimize the damage to a life she would never know the shape of.

She drove north along the coast road. The Mediterranean was black on her left. The city slept at a different frequency than the one that had produced the gunshot in Jaffa.

She abandoned the Fiat in a beachfront parking lot in Bat Yam, windows cracked and keys in the driver's footwell so that whoever found it first would treat it as a car left for someone else to collect. The owner would find it in the morning, be annoyed, then relieved, and forget about it by the end of the week. Elena walked the coast road for eighteen minutes until she flagged down a private car driven by a young Russian-Israeli moonlighting as a taxi.

She paid him in cash. She got out two blocks from her flat. She walked the rest of the way.

She let herself into her Bograshov flat at 02:50.

In the silence of the flat, she could hear the Nagra's tick.

Thirty per minute. The mechanism would not last another year. At thirty, the spindle was still holding—the tape still moved at the speed it needed to move to make recorded sound intelligible. But the margin was narrowing. Each tick was the nick cutting deeper, by the fraction of a millimeter that had become the fraction of a centimeter that was becoming something worse.

She listened. The tick was not outside her anymore. It had moved inward over the drive back, and now it was in her sternum, one per two seconds, running in parallel to her pulse without asking permission. The Nagra had been with her for nine years. She had carried it through four cities and every cover identity she'd worn and had concealed its single mechanical defect from three different handlers, because the defect was the thing that made it hers. Tonight the apparatus was finishing.

She set the machine on the kitchen table. She watched the reel turn.

She thought about the drawer. Just the one reel from October 1973. Geneva, Berlin, the long evenings in Kensington when she'd recorded her own assessments—all of those she had listened to once and burned. The drawer kept only what could not be burned—and what she had not played a second time, because a second playback would have left a second pattern of scratches across what the first had already marked. The reel Calder's voice was on. The reel she had recorded in her clutch bag at the Paxton Gallery the night she met him. The reel whose tick Yuri had once heard and had dismissed as weather in the recording, because weather was the explanation a handler reached for when the alternative was to acknowledge that his illegal was using a faulty instrument to record him.

Her recordings could only be heard by the machine that had made them, and the device on her kitchen table was the one failing. Other Nagras existed, but borrowing one meant producing the reels, and producing the reels meant explaining what was on them. If the mechanism died, the drawer died with it. The recordings and the woman who made them had that in common—both trapped inside something that was not going to last.

She would not report the failure. She had not reported it in 1973. She would not report it in 1982. The decision was the same decision, made nine years apart, by women who understood themselves to be different women.

She switched the Nagra off. The reel stopped. The tick stopped with it.

The flat was quiet in the particular way a borrowed city was quiet at three in the morning. She heard the ceiling fan in the flat above hers, which the woman who lived there ran every night because the sound helped her sleep. She heard the distant traffic on Dizengoff. She heard, through the open kitchen window, a single scooter accelerating and then diminishing into the city's northward sprawl. The sea she could not hear at this hour because the sea was an absence at three in the morning—a pressure against the coast that the ear registered as silence.

She took off her coat. She emptied the pockets methodically, the way the Institute had taught her to empty pockets after a field action—smallest item first, largest last, each item placed in a specific location before the next was removed, so that if anything went missing she would know exactly when it had gone.

The three rolls of Tri-X. The contact microphone. The reel from the Nagra. The pick. Her wallet. Her notebook. A key that was not her key.

She looked at the key.

A small brass key, Yale profile, attached to a plain steel ring with no fob. Not her flat key. Not her mail key. Not the key to the observation post she had padlocked behind her. She did not recognize it. She had not put it in her pocket.

She held the key in her palm and thought about the last twelve hours and tried to identify the moment at which a key had entered her coat pocket without her awareness, and she could not identify it. The coat had been in the observation post from 19:00 to 00:26. She had worn it on the exit. She had not removed it during the Fiat or the sherut.

The watcher.

The watcher with the radio. The watcher who had been on the rooftop when she left.

The watcher had not been alone. The watcher had been the visible member of a team. Someone else had been closer to the observation post than Elena had registered—close enough, at some point during the three hours before she exited, to plant a key in a coat she had hung on a hook inside the observation post at 19:30 while she was rigging the contact microphone at the shutter.

Elena stared at the key.

Her breathing changed. Not dramatically. By one cycle, the long exhale operatives practiced until the exhale registered as calm even when the chest underneath had stopped registering as hers. The calm was institutional. The chest underneath was not.

She set the key down. She picked it up again. The weight was negligible. Four grams, perhaps five. A key was made to fit a lock, and fitting the lock was all a key was for. This key, held in this hand, in this kitchen, at this hour, was a key that had been chosen to be held. Chosen by someone who had stood near enough to her coat to reach inside it.

She thought, for the first time in eleven years of operational work, about the distance between her body and another body in a room she had not registered contained one. She reviewed it. The contact microphone at 19:30. The forty-five seconds with her back to the door. The ninety seconds adjusting the telephoto. The sixteen minutes at the binoculars before she left. Every interval in which a small efficient person could have entered the observation post, placed an object in the coat hanging on the hook three meters from her, and exited —and had exited, because the coat had not moved and she had not cataloged any of it.

She had been within reach.

The reach had not closed.

Her hand, holding the key, was warm. The kitchen was cold. The body was still operational because the operators who had chosen not to dispose of it were running an operation that required the body to continue.

The filing system came back on a fraction of a second later. But the fraction in which it had been off was the interval in which Elena had learned, in her throat and her hand and her breath, the thing her training had never permitted her to learn and that she had been attempting not to learn since Lillehammer: that she was not, and had not ever been, the only operator in the room. The rooms she had been working in had always contained others. The others had been declining, for reasons of their own, to show themselves.

Tonight one of them had shown himself by the length of a coat sleeve and the weight of a Yale-profile key.

A key was not a kill. A key was not a tag. A key was a message. The message had been left by an operator who had been close enough to eliminate her and had chosen not to. The message was: we see you. We have seen you for a long time. We are letting you continue.

She set the key on the table beside the Nagra.

The key was brass. The Nagra was steel. Both caught the kitchen light with the hard clarity small manufactured objects produced at three in the morning, when the body's eye saw with the resolution it reserved for information it could not afford to misread.

She did not know who the watcher had been. She suspected she would never know. But the key in her palm was evidence that whoever had marked the pencil dots on the Fitzrovia folder in 1974 and the Geneva photocopy in 1976 and Yuri's briefing papers in 1978 had now found her physically, had stood in a room she had occupied, had left an object in a coat she had touched, and had allowed her to walk out.

She had been recognizing. Tonight she had been recognized. The hand that had dropped the key had been near her in the dark. She had not heard the breath. She had been the watched one for she did not know how many years.

The allowing was its own statement—the shape of the thing she had been tracing. The shape did not want her dead. The shape wanted her aware.

The Mossad officer in the upper room had been investigating the same pattern. Someone at King Saul Boulevard had been pulling the thread from its own side. The hand had let him get close enough to be eliminated in a Mossad room at a Mossad hour by operators a Mossad officer would not have recognized until they were already in the building. Elena had spent nine years believing the design was four services arrayed behind four flags with one hand reaching between them. Tonight the hand had killed an investigator inside one of the services. The four services had been, for longer than she could yet measure, one instrument. She had been one of its components. The thought arrived quietly. She did not write it in the notebook. The notebook was not ready to hold a sentence that large.

She developed the Nikon rolls in the kitchen sink with chemistry from a local photography shop where Sara Lerner had been a regular customer.

The photographs from the third night were grainy but usable. Two male faces, mid-thirties, compact, trained. One distinguishing feature on the taller man: a scar on his left cheekbone, the kind edged weapons left and time did not erase. The scar's shape was not the shape of a training exercise. The shape was the shape of a blade held by a person who had intended damage.

The registration number produced nothing through channels available to a Canadian journalist. Accessing the KGB's vehicle database would require reporting the investigation to Moscow, and reporting it to Moscow would end it.

She filed the photographs inside the lining of her suitcase. She used the same cotton thread she had used to install the lining years ago, the same needle. The stitching was invisible to any observer who had not installed it. The photographs joined a slim set of documents that had lived inside the suitcase lining since 1978—a duplicate of the Sara Lerner passport, a typewritten list of telephone numbers, a small envelope containing four one-hundred-dollar bills. The Mercator stayed in her coat pocket where it always stayed.

She put the key inside the envelope with the cash and the blade. The envelope went back inside the lining. The lining was re-stitched.

Century House, London. The same morning.

On the morning Elena sat at her Bograshov kitchen table with the key and the Nagra on the wood between her, James Calder was reading a cable in his office on the fifth floor of Century House.

The cable was from Ottawa.

It had reached his desk through the slow gravity of institutional routing—Ottawa to the UK High Commission, from there to the Foreign Office, from the Foreign Office to the SIS liaison officer whose job was to identify which cables might interest which stations, and from that officer to Calder's Counter-Proliferation desk because Calder had, two years earlier, circulated an informal note requesting sight of any cable mentioning unusual Canadian passport patterns. The note had been ignored at the time. It had not been deleted.

The cable summarized three separate incidents in which Canadian passports had been flagged at airports in Athens, Larnaca, and Rome between August and November 1982. The bearers' photographs had been recorded and the passport numbers were from a block issued in 1975 to Canadian External Affairs for operational use—low-profile, not diplomatic, the kind of documentation available to intelligence services that Ottawa chose not to scrutinize too aggressively. One of the bearers had passed through Athens on 14 September.

Calder read the cable twice.

Then he stood. He walked to the locked drawer of his desk, the drawer that held the FEUERWERK file and the file labeled ALICE. He unlocked it. He added a single sheet of paper to the bottom of the ALICE file—the cable, photocopied, the Commonwealth stamp visible in the corner, the yellow note still attached.

He did not know what the cable meant. He did not know that three thousand kilometers south-east, in a kitchen on Bograshov Street, a woman named Sara Lerner had, three days earlier, set down a cup of coffee without looking at it. He would not know. The drawer was full of things he did not yet know and that he was not, in December 1982, able to see the connections between.

But he filed the cable.

The ALICE file was now seven items deep. One was a hotel register from Norway. One was a note in his own hand recording a remark Margaret made at a dinner in 1974, about a woman he was meeting for the first time who had held a wine glass by the stem in a way Margaret had not seen a New Zealander hold a wine glass. One was an Observer byline from 1976 that did not quite match the Observer's stylebook. One was a scrap of his own handwriting—Hatch, Geneva, March '76, the word Sacco in parentheses—that he had filed without yet understanding why. Three were photocopies of margin marks, identical, from three unrelated documents across four years. The cable was the latest item—not evidence of anything involving the woman in his bed, but a shape at the edge of his professional attention that, he suspected, was the same shape that had left a woman's name in a Norwegian hotel register in 1973. The file was not evidence. The file was the shape of a question.

He did not know what the cable meant. Not yet. Outside, the December afternoon had already started to fail.

He closed the drawer. He locked it. He went back to his desk. He drafted a response to a station report from Ankara that was due before the end of the day. He did not, that morning, permit himself to think about the cable he had just filed, because thinking about it would not help him. The work did not care about the cable in the drawer or the woman in his bed or the gap between what he knew and what he was allowed to know.

The gap was still the gap. The drawer was locked. The work continued.

Three days later, Elena met Dina for coffee again.

The Tuesday meeting had been last week. This one was off-cycle. Elena had asked for it. The asking had been small—

a note left at Dina's office through a courier Elena had used twice before and that Dina would not have to acknowledge if the moment needed to go unacknowledged. Dina had sent a single-word reply. Yes.

They met at the usual café on Allenby. Same table. Same waitress. Elena liked the coffee meetings the way she liked Kessler's greenhouse visits and Doron's Friday dinners—as genuine experiences nested inside operational contexts, real warmth surrounded by professional ice.

Dina's chair was angled toward the door, the way Elena's was. Two professionals at a table on Allenby, each having taken the seat from which she could watch the room without thought, without asking. Elena had been seeing it and had not let herself see that she was seeing it. Today she saw it.

Elena reached for her coffee. As she lifted the cup, her watch shifted on her wrist—a millimeter, no more—and Dina's eyes dropped to the gap. The glance lasted less than a second. It took in the edge of the compass rose, the black ink against the inside of Elena's wrist. Then Dina's eyes returned to Elena's face. She did not ask.

Today, something was different. Dina's scanning pattern had changed—not the scan of a woman monitoring her environment but of a woman processing a problem whose processing was leaking into her physical behavior. They performed the friendship. Coffee. Pastries. The political situation. The weather, which in Tel Aviv was a brief topic because the weather in Tel Aviv was always the same.

Then Dina said something that changed the shape of Elena's entire investigation.

She said it casually, the way she said everything—with the flat direct delivery that made it difficult to distinguish between gossip and intelligence. A bureaucratic annoyance at the Foreign Ministry. A passport issue. A mess.

'Canadian passports,' Dina said. She was stirring her coffee. Her eyes were on the cup. 'Someone in operations has been using Canadian documentation for field work. The Canadians are starting to notice. It's becoming a headache.'

'Messy,' Elena said. Her tone was appropriately light. The weather of her face had not changed. 'Canadians are particular about their documents.'

Dina lifted her cup. She did not drink. 'So are Israelis,' she said. 'About other people's.'

Elena's operational mind activated with the same total engagement she had felt on Doron's kitchen floor when Yael had mentioned the same subject. The same thread. Arriving through a different channel.

'That sounds like a mess,' Elena said. Sara Lerner's voice. Sympathetic. Mildly interested.

'It is a mess,' Dina said. 'The kind of mess that someone should have anticipated and that nobody did because the people who use the passports and the people who manage the diplomatic consequences operate in different buildings and don't talk to each other.' She paused. 'Institutional failure. You'd think we'd be better at this by now.'

Elena heard what Dina was not saying: that Dina had been assigned to clean up the mess. Dina was pulling the same line Elena was pulling. From the opposite direction.

Two women sitting at a café on Allenby, drinking coffee, performing friendship, each investigating the same mystery from a different side. Elena drank her coffee. She made a joke about bureaucracy. Dina laughed. The laugh was real. The conversation moved on. The moment passed.

They paid and walked out into the Allenby afternoon together for half a block before their directions diverged. At the corner where they parted, Dina turned to Elena and said, in a voice calibrated for a register neither of them had used with each other before:

'Be careful, Sara. The people who use those passports are not careful. And the ones who issue them are less careful still.'

Elena nodded. She did not ask how Dina knew to warn her. She did not ask what Dina had assessed during the forty minutes in the café. She did not ask whether the warning was professional courtesy or something closer.

The not-asking was its own answer. Dina received the not-asking. Dina walked north on Allenby. Elena walked south.

Elena put the moment in the place where she kept the things Moscow would never see. Dina was circling the same mystery from the Mossad side. The stolen identity, the duplicated passport, the safe house on Yefet Street, the body on the tile floor, the watcher with the radio, the key in her pocket—all of these were different views of a single object, and the object was bigger than either of their services had been briefed to acknowledge.

That night she opened the small bound notebook and turned to a clean page. She wrote five lines.

The first: The men with the case had a scar. I have the photographs.

The second: The Nagra is at thirty ticks per minute.

The third, in English: Dina is pulling the same thread.

The fourth: A key was left in my pocket. I do not know whose. I know what it meant.

The fifth was the line she'd been carrying since the kitchen on Yefet Street: I am keeping my own secrets from everyone now. The institution does not know it has lost me. The not-knowing is the only protection I still have.

She closed the notebook. She sat at the kitchen table for a long time. Outside, the Mediterranean breathed against the shore. The Nagra sat beside her, silent, the reel motionless, the tick stilled by the absence of motion but waiting. The mechanism would not last another year. She knew this now.

She thought about Doron and Yael. The Friday dinners had continued—quieter now, two and a half years on, the cultivation having settled into something that resembled friendship from the outside and was, from the inside, a third thing for which she did not have a name. They had not asked where she had been on the night in Jaffa. They were good at not asking.

She thought about London. She had crossed back as Alice Marsh four times since 1978—a Christmas, two summers, and a week in March 1981 when Margaret was at her sister's in Hampstead and Calder had been alone in Chiswick. Each crossing brief. The Kensington flat exactly as she had left it. Calder asking nothing she had not volunteered. The relationship survived on the discipline of unanswerable questions, both of them practicing the same restraint.

She thought about Dina's sleep. She envied it—the sleep of a woman whose interior architecture did not need to monitor itself in unconsciousness because the honesty had been built into its center. Elena had not slept that sleep since she was nineteen. She did not expect to sleep it again.

Sleep did not come. She did not ask it to.

In the morning she would be Sara Lerner again. But tonight she was Elena. Only Elena. The woman who kept her own files now.

The photographs were in the suitcase lining. The key was in the envelope with the photographs. The notebook was in her handbag. The Nagra reel was in the drawer three thousand kilometers north, in a flat where the drawer was still open and had been for four years. The archives had begun to split. One of them was hers.

ACT IV

THE CAMPAIGN AGAINST CALDER

1983—1985

14
THE DINNER
London—March 1983

The walk from the Tube to the Chiswick house took eleven minutes through residential streets that smelled of privet hedge and wet brick. March had turned the front gardens gray. A cat sat on a wall two doors down, watching Elena with the flat professional attention of a creature that understood surveillance. A Conservative window poster had been put up in number 14, the same poster Elena had seen in three other windows on the walk down. The general election was three months away. The houses were already deciding.

Margaret was gone. Not permanently—not yet. But the house had begun to register her withdrawal the way a garden registers drought: slowly, starting at the edges. Elena knew it before Calder opened the door.

Elena knew it from the hallway. The hallway of the Chiswick house where Margaret had grown geraniums and made rosemary chicken on Wednesdays and loved her husband with the deliberate policy-based trust of a woman who had decided that suspicion was less important than marriage. On Elena's previous visits it had smelled of cooking and lavender sachets and the inhabited warmth of a house that was cared for by someone who believed in the life being lived inside it. It smelled different now. It smelled clean. Not warm-clean, the clean of a house in use. Cold-clean. The clean of surfaces maintained by habit in the absence of the person the habit was for.

Calder opened the door. He was wearing an apron. Margaret's apron. The apron was ridiculous—blue and white stripes, purchased without consideration. He was holding a wooden spoon. He looked, in the doorway of his own home, like a man impersonating domesticity with the same competent fraudulence he brought to all his impersonations.

'Alice,' he said. He had a tea towel over his shoulder and rosemary on his fingers. 'Come in. The lamb is almost ready.'

Elena stepped inside. She scanned the hallway in the three seconds between the threshold and the coat hook. The lavender sachets were gone from the cupboard. The coat hook held two coats instead of four. The small table by the door, which had previously held Margaret's keys and Margaret's post and a small ceramic dish that Margaret had bought at a craft fair in Hampshire, held only Calder's keys. The ceramic dish was gone. The space where it had been was visible—a faint rectangle of lighter paint on the table's surface, the ghost of an object that had been there long enough to protect the wood beneath it from the slow, uniform fading that sunlight and time applied to all exposed surfaces.

Calder did not mention Margaret. He would not mention her tonight. The silence had the practiced quality of a subject declared off-limits—the kind that required both parties to sustain it. Elena would sustain it. It was easier to sustain an off-limits subject than to construct a lie about one.

Margaret's ghost was everywhere. Not Margaret—Margaret's absence, which was louder than her presence had ever been. The absence was in the gaps. Gaps on the bookshelves where her novels had been. A tidiness in the sitting room that only a man's tidiness produced, the kind that mistook arrangement for order. Elena noted the absence in thirty seconds the way she cataloged everything—automatically, without visible attention, the intake running on a channel her face did not advertise.

'How was Paris?' he asked.

'Rainy,' she said. 'The Musée d'Orsay is being renovated. The scaffolding is obscene.'

She had not been in Paris. She had been in Tel Aviv. She'd arrived in London that morning from Ben Gurion via a routing that took her through Paris for six hours—long enough to purchase a Métro ticket, visit the Musée d'Orsay, and collect the sensory details required to support the lie. The scaffolding at the Musée d'Orsay was real. Elena saw it. The scaffolding was her evidence—the truth that supported the lie, the genuine stone at the foundation of the false building.

Calder nodded. 'I've never cared for the Impressionists,' he said. 'Too much light.' He turned back to the kitchen. 'Too much happiness.'

Elena followed him into the kitchen. It was the one room that looked approximately the same as it had before Margaret left, because kitchens were functional spaces and Calder, whatever else he was failing at, was maintaining the function. The lamb was in the oven. A salad was on the counter. Wine was open—a Bordeaux, good but not extravagant, already half gone, the wine of a man who knew wine without needing anyone to know he knew wine. Two place settings on the table. One set of towels hanging by the sink.

One set of towels. Elena noted it with the clinical attention of a woman who understood domestic archaeology. Margaret had taken her towels. Or Calder had put them away. Either interpretation confirmed the same fact: the marriage was over, or suspended, or in the indefinite deferral the English applied to emotional crises the way they applied it to constitutional reform—not resolving the problem but agreeing, through silence, that the problem would not be raised.

They did not discuss Margaret. They had never discussed

Margaret. Margaret existed in the conversation the way dark matter existed in the universe—invisible, detectable only by the way other things bent around her.

'I need the bathroom,' Elena said. 'Long journey.'

'You know where it is,' Calder said. He was plating the lamb. His attention was on the plate and on the arrangement of meat and vegetables with the focused precision of a man who was transferring his professional competence to a domestic surface because the work surface was the only one he trusted. 'Take your time.'

Elena's handbag was on the hallway table. She'd placed it there when she came in. The bag was a structured leather satchel, dark brown, the kind a woman carried when she wanted to look professional without looking expensive. Inside the bag: wallet, lipstick, keys, a paperback novel, the small red notebook bound in cloth she'd been carrying since March 1976, a pen, and a hotel receipt from the Dan Tel Aviv Hotel in the name of Sara Lerner, dated four days ago.

The receipt was a mistake. Not a careless one. Elena did not make careless mistakes. Two cover identities occupying the same operational space, documentation from one leaking into the personal effects of the other. Sara Lerner had checked out of the Dan Tel Aviv and placed the receipt in her bag. Alice Marsh had picked up the same bag at the safe flat in Paris. The receipt had migrated. A piece of Sara Lerner's existence, folded inside Alice Marsh's bag, traveling to London like a stowaway.

The notebook was not a mistake. It was Elena's most valuable possession, and it traveled with her the way some women's grandmother's ring traveled with them—close to the body, on the assumption that distance was a worse risk than proximity.

Elena was in the bathroom upstairs. The door was closed.

Elena was not using the bathroom. Elena was standing at the medicine cabinet above the sink, which she'd opened with the silent practiced motion of a woman who had been opening other people's medicine cabinets for eleven years and who understood that the contents of a medicine cabinet were, for an intelligence officer, more revealing than the contents of a desk. Desks contained what people chose to display. Medicine cabinets contained what people needed to survive.

Calder's medicine cabinet contained: aspirin, a razor, shaving cream, dental floss, a half-empty bottle of antacid tablets, and a prescription. The prescription was in a white pharmacy bag, folded, tucked behind the shaving cream with the half-hearted concealment of a man who had placed it out of sight but not out of reach.

Elena unfolded the bag. The prescription was for diazepam. Five milligrams. Thirty tablets. The prescribing physician was listed as Dr. R. Hargreaves. The dispensing pharmacy was listed as the Boots two streets from Century House.

Elena memorized everything. The drug, the dose, the quantity, the physician's name, the pharmacy location. Three seconds.

The physician's name was the critical detail. Dr. R. Hargreaves was not a civilian physician. Elena knew this because she maintained a mental database of known MI6 medical panel doctors, compiled over years of operational targeting—physicians cleared to treat serving officers, physicians whose patient records were classified and whose prescriptions were dispensed through pharmacies near intelligence facilities. The Boots two streets from Century House.

She also had something else: evidence that Calder was not well. Diazepam, five milligrams, half the bottle gone. The man downstairs plating lamb with surgical precision was managing something the institution had sanctioned through its medical panel.

Elena replaced the prescription behind the shaving cream. She closed the medicine cabinet. She flushed the toilet, ran the tap, dried her hands. She looked at herself in the mirror. Alice Marsh looked back. Elena went downstairs to eat lamb with her lover and lie about Paris.

While Elena was in the bathroom, Calder opened her handbag.

He did it in the kitchen. He had approximately three minutes—the estimated time between the bathroom door closing and the toilet flushing, the window of opportunity any experienced intelligence officer could calculate by subtracting the time required for the social performance of using a bathroom from the time the person spent in the bathroom. Three minutes. Plenty.

He moved from the stove to the hallway in four steps. He opened the bag. His hands were practiced—the unhurried efficiency of a man who had searched personal effects professionally for years and who understood that speed was less important than method and that method meant replacing every item in its exact original position so that the bag's owner, upon retrieving it, would find nothing displaced.

He found the receipt in eleven seconds. It was in the interior pocket, folded once, tucked beside a tube of hand cream. He unfolded it. He read it.

Dan Tel Aviv Hotel. Sara Lerner. Check-out: four days ago.

Calder's face did not change. What changed was a quality of stillness that settled over him like a temperature drop. He was holding a hotel receipt that placed his lover in Tel Aviv under a different name on dates she'd told him she was in Paris. The receipt was the second piece of physical evidence in nine years—after the Lillehammer register—and he added it to the file labeled ALICE with the patient attention of a man building a case against the person he most wanted to be innocent.

Sara Lerner. A second name. A second identity. A second life running parallel to the life she'd been sharing with him.

He photographed the receipt. The camera was a Minox—a miniature intelligence camera, the size of a lighter, the standard-issue tool of field officers who needed to copy documents without removing them. He carried it the way other men carried a pen—habitually, automatically, in the inside pocket of whatever he was wearing, because the habit of being prepared for intelligence collection was not a habit he could turn off and did not want to turn off and had not turned off even in his own kitchen while his lover was upstairs using his bathroom.

Two photographs. Front and back of the receipt. The Minox's shutter was silent.

He would develop the film himself in the darkroom under the stairs. He had been doing his own developing since 1971. The photographs in his life were not photographs he trusted to a commercial lab.

He should have stopped. The receipt was enough. But the bag had an inner compartment he had not yet opened. His hands had been searching bags for years. The hands moved before the assessment.

The inner compartment held the small red notebook.

It was bound in cloth. The cloth was worn at the corners in the way books were worn that had been carried by the same person across many cities and many years. The kind a stationer in a German-speaking country would have sold cheaply—three or four marks at most. Calder had owned three like it himself across twelve years of intelligence work.

The tradecraft staple of operatives whose institutions did not know everything about them.

He opened the notebook.

The pages were full. The handwriting was small and precise. The handwriting was in Russian.

Calder's breath did not catch. His training did not permit catching breaths inside other people's houses while photographing other people's notebooks. But the air in his chest changed quality—as air changes quality when a body recognizes something it has been waiting nine years for. At the base of his neck, where the vagus ran close to the skin, his pulse acknowledged what the training was denying. The handwriting was Russian. Alice Marsh wrote in Russian. Alice Marsh, who taught herself Italian for art-historical research and whose German was the German of someone who had studied it at university and whose French was the French of a New Zealander who had spent a year in Paris in her twenties—Alice Marsh kept her private notebook in Russian.

He turned the pages. His fingers turned them with the lightness of a man who knew that the bag's owner would notice any disturbance and that the disturbance had to be minimal. Most of the pages were Russian. Some were English. A few entries had place names in Italian and German that he recognized. Lichtenberg. Schöneberg. Kreuzberg. Pankow. The geography of East and West Berlin.

One page was different.

It contained, near the top, a single Italian word: Fanano. And beneath the word, in pencil, a small careful sketch of a mountain profile—three peaks, the middle one tallest, the outline drawn with the attentive hand of someone who had spent time looking at a mountain rather than looking at a map of one. Below the sketch, in Russian: a single line Calder could not read but whose Cyrillic letters he could transcribe by sight.

He photographed it twice—once for the sketch, once for the line of Russian. The Minox's shutter was silent.

Fanano. The word meant nothing to him. He filed it as a placeholder for an investigation still in progress—the meaning would arrive in its own time, as long as he had the picture and the page reference and the certainty that the page existed in a notebook in his lover's handbag, written in the language of the country whose intelligence service was, possibly, paying her salary.

He sat for one second in the silence between the photograph and the closing. The last nine years rearranged themselves around him. The rearrangement took less than a second. He noted the speed of it. The speed was the cost of having been a professional all those years.

He closed the notebook. He returned it to the inner compartment, at the same angle, with the same orientation. He closed the receipt back into the interior pocket. He closed the bag. He returned to the kitchen. He finished plating the lamb. He opened a second bottle of wine.

His hands were always steady.

The toilet flushed. The tap ran. Footsteps on the stairs.

He lit the candle.

Dinner.

The lamb was excellent. It was roasted with rosemary—Margaret's recipe, Elena realized, though she did not say this and Calder did not mention it. He was cooking his estranged wife's recipe for his lover, which was either a sentimental act or a hostile one or both, and Elena cataloged it as both and ate and complimented the lamb and poured the wine and settled into the sustained performance of a woman enjoying dinner with a man she cared about.

Calder was performing too. His performance was flawless—warm, attentive, funny in the dry understated way English intelligence officers were funny, with the timing and the restraint and the careful placement of warmth at intervals calibrated not to reveal. He was performing the role of a man having dinner with his girlfriend. The word *girlfriend* had never been used between them. Its absence had not been accidental on either side.

Every sentence had two meanings.

They spoke in the code of people who knew the other was lying and had agreed, without agreeing, to maintain the surface.

Every pause was a calculation.

The pause after he mentioned a colleague who had recently returned from Norway was a calculation. Norway. Lillehammer. He dropped the word into the conversation like a stone into a pond and watched for the ripple. Elena's face produced no ripple. Alice Marsh had no reason to react to Norway. Alice Marsh had never been to Norway. The passport that had been to Norway was in a drawer in a flat Calder did not know about.

'Thornton,' Calder said. 'From the Berlin desk. He came back from Norway last week. Skiing, apparently. A stag weekend for a man he went to school with. He's older than either of us. I don't know why he was on a stag weekend.'

'I don't ski,' Elena said. 'I tried, once. In the Alps. Austria. I was bad at it.' She refilled his wine. 'More lamb?'

'Please.'

The pause after she asked, casually, whether his work had been stressful lately was a calculation. Stressful. The diazepam in the medicine cabinet. She was pressing the bruise without appearing to touch it, the conversational equivalent of *Zersetzung*—a question designed to produce a response that would reveal the shape of what was being concealed. Calder's response was perfect: a slight shrug, a half-smile, the words No more than usual delivered with the calibrated lightness of a man who was taking five milligrams of diazepam daily and who was not going to allow the medication's existence to surface in a conversation with the woman who might be the reason he needed it.

She thought, briefly and involuntarily, of the Nagra. It was at home in Kensington, where it had stayed more often than it had moved these past three years. The dinner was the kind of evening she would once have recorded for her own archive, because the evenings she recorded were the evenings that contained information the official channels would not hold. But the Nagra's defect had passed the point of usefulness years ago. She was older than the instrument. She had been keeping records in her head since.

They ate. They drank. They talked. Two people who had just searched each other's belongings sat across a candlelit table eating lamb and drinking Bordeaux with the impeccable manners of a couple whose relationship was built on mutual attraction and mutual suspicion and the exhausting discipline of maintaining both simultaneously.

The candle burned. The wine went down. The evening aged.

At eleven they moved to the sitting room. Calder put on a record—Coltrane, *A Love Supreme*—and poured whisky, and they sat on the sofa Margaret had chosen and that was, like everything else in the house, still Margaret's in ways neither of them mentioned. They did not talk. They listened to Coltrane. They held hands. They drank their whisky the way couples who had been together a long time drank whisky—in quiet parallel, each alone with whatever they were thinking about and not pretending otherwise.

The not-talking was, for the first time in nine years, a relief, because talking required the double performance and the double performance was exhausting and the silence was the one space where they could be near each other without the nearness being a contest.

They went to bed. The bedroom was different without Margaret's things—sparser, the surfaces cleared of the small accumulations a woman's presence deposited in a shared space. The bed was the same bed. The sheets were different. Calder had replaced them—a detail Elena noted and that communicated, in the domestic language men did not know they spoke, that the bed was no longer Margaret's territory and was now a neutral space, or a new space, or a space that had been deliberately cleared of one woman's residue in preparation for another woman's occupation.

They made love. It was different from the Fitzrovia flat nearly ten years ago. Different because of what they had each found during dinner—the receipt, the notebook, the things neither of them would mention. But different too because each of them knew the other knew something, and the knowing had changed the vocabulary. They were not making love to each other. They were making love to the last version of each other that had been possible before dinner.

Afterward, Calder slept. Elena did not.

At 4 AM, Elena got out of bed.

She moved with the silent precision of a woman who had been getting out of beds without waking the person beside her for eleven years and who had developed, through the repetition of the maneuver, a technique that was less a technique than a quality of movement—a lightness, a redistribution of weight that allowed her to transition from horizontal to vertical without disturbing the mattress springs or the blankets or the ambient sound profile of the room. Calder was on his side, facing away. His breathing was the deep even rhythm of genuine sleep, not the performed sleep of a man who was awake and pretending. Elena could distinguish between the two. She had been distinguishing between the two for nine years.

She went downstairs. The house was dark. She did not turn on a light. She moved through the hallway and into the small room that Calder used as a study—a room she'd been in before, a room she'd examined before. Never at 4 AM, never after confirming her lover was a serving MI6 officer, never with the operational intensity she brought to this examination.

There was a file on the desk surface. Not in a drawer. On the surface, beside the blotter, in a manila folder of the kind the British civil service used for working documents that were supposed to be kept under physical control by the officer to whom they were assigned. The folder was unlabeled on the front. Calder had been working on whatever was inside it earlier in the evening, before Elena arrived, and he had not put it away when he'd left the study to begin cooking. The leaving-it-out was not a security failure. It was the small carelessness of a man who lived alone and who had stopped expecting his work to be observed in his own home by anyone whose observation could matter.

Elena opened the folder.

Inside: a photocopied set of pages from what looked like Italian Carabinieri reports—the typography was unmistakable, the paper was carbon copies of carbon copies, the pages had been generated in the seventies and reproduced through the photographic chain of evidence preservation that intelligence services applied to documents they intended to keep for years. The reports were about bombings in northern Italy. Piazza Fontana. The 1972 attack on a Carabinieri car at Peteano. A magistrate killed in Palermo in 1974. Calder's handwriting was in the margins of two pages—small annotations in pencil, the marginalia of a man working through a problem he had been working on for some time.

The Gladio file. Calder's working Gladio file.

And folded into the file, between two of the photocopied pages, was a single sheet that did not match the rest. Better paper. Newer. Typewritten in a format Elena recognized—the same format she had been receiving through the Nicosia channel for years. The same rhythm. The same institutional authority that belonged to no institution she could name. Below the heading, a list of European cities arranged in a column.

Milan

Bologna

Modena

Vienna

Brussels

Frankfurt

Strasbourg

The first three cities—the Italian cities—were circled in pencil. The circles had been drawn freehand, by Calder, trying to make a pattern visible to himself.

She did not catch her breath. But the air changed quality the way air changes when a body crosses a threshold it cannot uncross. She was looking at a list of cities, and the list was what the cadences and the Sacco document and the Canadian passports and the dead man in Yefet Street had all been pointing toward.

Four services. One architecture. Two people inside two of those services had found it from opposite sides, and the two people were sleeping in the same bed, and neither of them could say so.

The Italian cities were circled. Milan, Bologna, Modena. Elena understood the circling. Calder was working through the geography of the operations he had attributed to the FEUERWERK architecture—tracking which cities the network had used and which it was moving through next. The other cities on the list were not yet circled. They were the cities Calder was watching.

She stood in the dark study and placed the three circled Italian cities against the list she had been carrying in her head since 1973. Milan where Piazza Fontana had been. Bologna where the station bombing still had no acknowledged author. Modena the closest city to the Apennine village where twelve had died in what the state had called a mining accident. The pencil circles were not analysis. The pencil circles were a man with a desk lamp in Chiswick beginning to see the shape she had been tracing alone for nine and a half years, and the shape had teeth, and the teeth were sixty pounds each and had been missing from the NATO inventory since 1968.

She thought, with the small clear precision that arrived in moments like this: the British know.

Not all of it. Not the way Elena knew it. They did not have Sacco. They did not have the Geneva document. They did not have the Cyrillic Fanano entry in the small red notebook in her handbag in the kitchen. But they had the shape. James Calder, sitting at this desk in Chiswick with a pencil in his hand, was doing the same thing Elena was doing in her Bograshov flat in Tel Aviv: assembling fragments of an operation that no one had told either of them existed, into a picture neither of them had been authorized to see.

The two of them were running parallel investigations against their own services, in two different cities, on the same target, for seven years now, without knowing about each other's investigation.

Until tonight.

In her handbag in the kitchen was the small red notebook. On one page of that notebook was a sketch of three peaks in pencil and a single word in Italian—Fanano—and a line of Russian that Calder had photographed twice before dinner and that he had filed, he had told himself, as a placeholder. She had drawn the three peaks in 1976, from memory, from a report. She had never been to Fanano. The mountain she had drawn without seeing was now in Calder's camera, and the camera was in his coat pocket, and the coat was hanging on the hook beside the door. The operations that had circled each other for seven years had just produced their first physical exchange, and neither of them could yet see what they had traded.

She replaced the FEUERWERK page between the two photocopied pages where she'd found it. She closed the folder. She left it on the desk surface, at the same angle, with the same orientation. She moved to the bottom drawer of the desk.

The drawer was locked. The lock was a standard Chubb lever. Elena opened it in nine seconds with two tools from the lining of her handbag.

The bottom drawer contained another unlabeled folder. The unlabeled folder, beneath the insurance documents, was the file Elena had been afraid she would find before she ever opened the drawer.

She opened the folder.

Inside: photocopies. Norwegian police reports. Dated July 1973. Lillehammer.

Her breath caught.

The response was physical, involuntary, absolute. The body

preparing for a threat that was not physical but existential. Her hands went numb at the fingertips in the exact pattern they went numb before long surveillance operations, and the numbness spread up the tendons into the palms, and she understood that she was being readied by a body that had rehearsed this preparation for a threat the body had always known was coming.

Calder had the Lillehammer files.

She read the photocopies in the dark, by the streetlight that came through the study window, tilting each page to catch the sodium glow that turned the white paper orange and the black text into something that looked like it had been written in a dying language. Norwegian police reports. The Hamidi investigation. Witness statements, surveillance photographs, the arrest records of the six Mossad operatives.

One photocopy was marked. A yellow highlighter—fading, old, the mark of a man who had been studying this material for a long time. The highlighted section was a footnote. Footnote 7. The footnote about Grigor Petrov. The Soviet defector found dead in his flat two days after the Hamidi killing. Two gunshot wounds. Close range. Small caliber. In the margin beside the highlight, in pencil, was the same small mark.

She had seen that mark five times before. Fitzrovia paper, 1974. A Geneva photocopy, 1976. A Marylebone brief, 1978. A Nicosia directive, three months ago. A page in her own handbag she had seen at her kitchen table in Tel Aviv the night she had recognized the Yasenevo compound in a BBC bulletin about a dead engineer. Tonight the mark was in Chiswick, on a photocopy in a desk drawer in a Counter-Proliferation officer's home. The mark was not Calder's. It was the same mark. Which meant the photocopy in Calder's drawer had reached him through the same channel Elena's directives had reached her. Calder had not been pulling a thread the hand had failed to notice. Calder had been pulling one the hand had placed in his hands. The hand had been running two operations on the same target from two services, and the two operations had—as the hand had presumably intended—been permitted, over nine years, to converge on this room.

Elena stared at the highlighted footnote and she thought: *he knows. Not everything. Not yet. But the shape. He knows the shape of what I am.*

Beneath the photocopies, in the bottom of the folder, was a sheet of paper that was not a photocopy. A single sheet, typed by Calder himself, on the typewriter she'd seen on the side table in this study on her last visit. The sheet was a list. A list of dates and locations she recognized:

Lillehammer—July 1973

Bonn (Foreign Office reception)—November 1974

Berlin (academic conference)—September 1975

Geneva (private meeting)—March 1976

Press reception, West Berlin—May 1976

He'd been mapping her movements. Not all of them—some of these were dates Elena did not associate with anything Calder could know about. But enough. Enough to see a shape. The shape would not yet be a name. It would be a set of coincidences that were becoming, over the months of Calder's patient observational work, too numerous to be coincidences.

The shape was Elena. The shape was a woman who had been in Lillehammer and in Tel Aviv and who operated under multiple names and who was sleeping in his bed while he assembled the evidence that would identify her as the thing she was.

But the shape was also something else, now. The shape was the reciprocal of a shape that lived in a different file in this same desk—the FEUERWERK file in the unlabeled folder on the desk surface, with the Italian city list circled in pencil.

The two files were the same investigation seen from two sides. One was Calder looking at her. The other was Calder looking at the thing she had been looking at for nine years.

Elena replaced the photocopies. She closed the folder. She returned it to the bottom drawer, beneath the insurance documents, at the same angle, with the same orientation. She closed the drawer. She locked the desk. She returned the picks to the lining of her handbag.

Elena stood in the dark study and she breathed.

She got back into bed. Calder had not moved. His breathing was the breathing of a man who was not asleep but who was performing sleep with the competence of a professional. She lay beside him and performed the same competence. Two performers. One bed. No audience except each other.

She did not file a report. Not to Moscow. Not to Nicosia. Not to anyone.

She was keeping her own secrets now. From everyone. Including the man breathing beside her, whose secrets she had just read by streetlight in a room that smelled of his books and his ink and the faint persistent ghost of Margaret's lavender.

In the morning, she would make coffee. She would kiss him. She would say something about Paris. She would leave. She would walk through Chiswick in the early morning light and she would carry the FEUERWERK page in her memory the way she carried everything: precisely, completely, in the archive that no institution could access and no search could find.

The thread was tightening. Calder was pulling it. It led to her. And past her, the thread led to the men who had rotated FLAMINGO out of the index, and those men had been tolerating Calder's inquiry the way a predator tolerated a tracker, for exactly as long as the inquiry did not graduate from history into names.

But Calder did not know that the thread he was pulling led to a woman who was pulling it from the other end. The pulling was being done by both hands of the same operation. The operation was the only operation either of them was running that mattered. And neither of them could yet tell the other what they had found, because telling the other meant telling the institution, and telling the institution meant losing everything.

Elena closed her eyes. She did not sleep.

Calder breathed.

The candle on the dinner table had burned down to nothing. The wine was finished. The lamb was cold on the plates they had not cleared. The house was dark and quiet and full of ghosts—Margaret's ghost, and the ghost of the marriage, and the ghost of the future that was coming toward both of them through the dark like a shape they could feel but not yet see.

Tonight, in the dark, they were just two people in a bed, each holding a piece of the other's proof, each lying beside the evidence of their own destruction, each pretending to sleep while the truth moved through the house like a draft from a window neither of them had the courage to close.

In the morning she told him the gallery needed her early. He nodded over coffee. He did not ask which gallery.

She took the Northern Line to Hampstead. On the Tube she was thinking about the FEUERWERK page on his desk. She was still thinking about it when the doors opened at Belsize Park and closed again with her still in her seat.

She had ridden past her stop.

She got off at Chalk Farm. Doubled back. Arrived at the dead drop four minutes late. Serviced it. Walked back through Hampstead in the thin March light.

15

THE APARTMENT IN OTTAKRING

Vienna—August 1983

The directive came through the Nicosia channel in the second week of August 1983. Three pages, arriving at Bograshov Street in the hot stillness of a Tel Aviv August afternoon, with the rhythm Elena had been counting and had, by that summer, stopped pretending to herself she would ever hear in Yuri's prose. She had heard this rhythm before. She would count it from now.

The directive named one man. Andrei Lebedev, fifty-eight, Soviet-born, defected through Vienna in 1978, currently employed by the International Atomic Energy Agency in its analytical-services section. The directive specified a three-day window in the second week of August. It specified the apartment: Wien-Ottakring, Koppstraße, fourth floor, rear. It specified the means.

The directive specified that Lebedev had been, since 1981, pursuing a private correlation of European industrial-radiological incidents and had recently requested access to IAEA source documents whose access denial had produced, in his correspondence with a Swiss colleague, a specific phrase the directive had highlighted: *the incidents are not random.*

Elena read the directive three times. She burned the sheet over the kitchen sink. She made her travel arrangements.

She flew into Vienna on the Tuesday morning. Canadian passport, press card from *Maclean's*, two small pieces of luggage. Sara Lerner, freelance, assigned to a piece on nuclear non-proliferation for the IAEA's public information office. The cover had been built in three days and would survive the kind of routine scrutiny Austrian intelligence applied to credentialed foreign journalists. It would not survive the kind of scrutiny that would follow a murdered IAEA consultant in his own flat. That kind of scrutiny would not begin. That was the operational assumption.

She checked into the Hotel Imperial on the Ringstraße. Alpine courtesy at the front desk. She went up to her room. She unpacked a leather-bound reporter's notebook and set it on the small desk by the window. She did not open it. She did not need to. The wire had been threaded through the binding in Tel Aviv, between the endpaper and the spine, so that the binding itself felt no different than any other notebook until a hand knew where to pull the seam apart. The technician who had done the threading had been a man in his late sixties who said nothing while he worked and who left the room the way a man who had been doing this since 1955 left rooms: without acknowledgment that the room had held anything worth acknowledging.

Piano wire. Eighteen inches. Two small hardwood toggles at the ends. A length short enough to be tied around a wrist under a cuff, long enough to compass a man's neck.

She set the notebook on the desk. She did not touch the binding.

She spent Tuesday and Wednesday reporting. Two interviews at the IAEA. She walked Lebedev's neighborhood on Wednesday evening—the entrance to Koppstraße, the service door at the rear, the angle from the courtyard, the back staircase that came up to the fourth-floor landing with a single turn. She did not see Lebedev. She did not need to. The file had given her the shape of his week. Tuesdays and Thursdays he came home at 18:42. Wednesdays and Fridays he stopped at a wine bar nearby and came home at 20:15. Monday he sometimes visited his daughter in the nineteenth district and did not come home until after ten.

Thursday was the day.

She spent Thursday morning in the hotel room writing the piece on nuclear non-proliferation. By noon she had eleven hundred words that would, when filed, satisfy her editor in Toronto and constitute the paper trail the cover required. She filed it by telex at two. She took lunch at a brasserie on the Kärntner Straße. She walked the long route back through the Stadtpark. She returned to the room at three-fifteen. She changed clothes. Dark slacks, a dark blouse, soft-soled shoes. Nothing a witness could describe that would not also describe a third of the women in Vienna in any given week.

She took the notebook.

She entered Koppstraße 14 at five forty-five.

The front entrance was kept unlocked until eight in the evening; a child's wooden toy was wedged between door and frame in the kind of Viennese apartment-house arrangement the tenants tolerated rather than repaired. She climbed the service stairs to the fourth floor. She listened. The floor was quiet. Lebedev's door was the third on the right. The lock was a 1962 Austrian deadbolt of a make Elena had been trained to open with a tension wrench and a rake in under forty seconds. She opened it in thirty-one.

The flat was two rooms. A kitchen-and-sitting room at the front. A bedroom behind. Books in stacks. A small desk at the window overlooking the courtyard. A photograph on the wall of a woman in her forties, dead eleven years according to the file. An empty dish on the counter. A newspaper folded in half. The domestic inventory of a widowed academic who had not expected company.

Elena closed the door behind her. She set the notebook on a chair in the entryway. She stepped out of her shoes. She walked the flat in silence—assessed the bedroom closet (narrow, would not fit her body), the bathroom (too small, no line of retreat), the kitchen pantry (best option). She opened the pantry. She stood inside it with the door not quite closed.

At six forty-one she heard the key in the lock.

Lebedev came in at 18:44. Two minutes late. Elena heard the key turn from inside the pantry, and she heard the small pause between the lock turning and the door opening—a half-second of hesitation, the way a careful man checks the air of his own apartment before crossing into it. The pause resolved. He came in. He closed the door. He slid the chain.

He had a string bag of groceries in his left hand and a slim folder under his right arm. He set the bag on the counter without looking at it; it landed with the soft sound of bread on Formica. He set the folder on the desk beside a small stack of handwritten pages held down by a glass paperweight, and he aligned the folder to the edge of the desk with the care of a man who had already decided where in his evening this folder was going to sit before he walked through the door.

He took off his jacket. He hung it on a cast-iron hook in the shape of an oak leaf—a hook chosen, presumably, for pleasure, by a man who lived alone and was permitted small pleasures. He put the kettle on the stove. He turned the gas. He struck a match.

The match did not catch.

He struck a second.

Elena watched all of this through the half-inch gap she had left in the pantry door. She watched his hands. Engineer's hands, small and competent, the way they handled the second match—the slight resettling of grip a man learns from forty years of small mechanical tasks. The instructor in 1971 had said: the only people who survive this work see hands without feeling anything about them. Elena had thought she understood. She had been wrong about that for fourteen years.

She took the breath she had been taught to take.

Elena took the notebook from the chair. She pulled the seam. The wire came out in her hand. She wrapped the toggles in her fingers. She crossed the six feet between the pantry and the stove in the time it took Lebedev to reach for the matches.

He was turning as she reached him. He was faster than the file had suggested. The file had said he was an analyst with a slight stoop from a back injury sustained on a Baltic fishing boat in 1969. The file had not said Severodvinsk 1963—the same training floors Elena had stood on twelve years later, some of the same instructors, including the woman who had taught Elena the wire and had presumably taught Lebedev the wire too, in a different decade, when he had been a different kind of man. Lebedev had been thirty-five years old in 1963. The defection through Vienna was fifteen years away. He had not yet decided that he was going to spend the second half of his life counting radiological events in pencil on numbered pages.

Lebedev saw her.

He saw her the way a man sees something he has been waiting to see. Not surprised. Not afraid in any sense Elena could feel through the wire. He understood the wire before it was at his neck. He got his left hand up.

The left hand went between the wire and his throat.

He had done it correctly. Four fingers and the thumb at the angle Severodvinsk had taught both of them was the angle.

The wire bit into the hand instead of the throat. Lebedev produced a small sound—not a cry, the controlled expulsion of a man calculating, in the quarter-second the wire had bought him, whether to go for the knife on the counter or drive her backward into the stove.

His eyes met hers.

She saw the recognition land in him. Not the recognition of her—they had never met—but the recognition of what she was. The training. The institution. The thing he had walked away from in 1978 and had been trying, in pencil on numbered pages, to dismantle from the outside. He saw the institution standing in his kitchen with a wire around his hand. He understood, in that quarter-second, that the institution had read his pages.

He chose the stove.

He turned hard. His body was heavier than Elena had planned for. She lost her footing against the tile. Her shoulder struck the corner of the counter and a hot spike of pain went up the back of her neck. The wire tightened on his hand—on the meat of the thumb and the two fingers he had gotten between the loop and his neck—and drew blood along the web. The blood was warm. She felt it on her own knuckle.

He tried to pull her forward to headbutt her.

The training said: do not let him take you forward. The training said: release. Elena released the left toggle. The wire went slack on his hand. She let the slack become a full second of his weight committing to a direction he had calculated by the resistance she had been providing. Then she pivoted under his arm, re-tightened the wire by wrapping the loose toggle around her wrist, and brought the whole loop—now half around his throat and half through the fingers of his own trapped hand—upward into the carotid groove beneath the jaw.

She took his weight onto her back. Her feet found the floor. She lifted.

Lebedev's own body weight drew the wire into his throat. On the desk past his shoulder, twelve handwritten pages lay neat beneath a glass paperweight. The trapped hand was no longer on the wire's path, because the wire was now above the hand, cutting on a different vector. She held him for the count she had been taught to hold. Fifteen. Twenty-two. Twenty-six.

His feet stopped moving at twenty-eight.

His weight became weight only.

At thirty she lowered him to the floor.

She lowered him slowly. The training had said do not drop the body. The training had said the body was a thing whose final dignity was the person who put it down. Elena did not know, anymore, whether she still believed the training said that, or whether she had been telling herself the training said it for fourteen years.

She waited. She had been taught to wait. Thirty more seconds. The body did what bodies did. She unwrapped the wire from his neck. The cut was thin and precise except where his hand had been, where the skin had torn in the slipping.

Lebedev's eyes were open.

She closed them. The instructor at Severodvinsk had taught both of them to close the eyes of the people they killed, because not closing them was a kind of leaving the room messy that operations could not afford. Elena had not thought about that woman in years. She thought about her now.

Elena stood up. Her shoulder hurt. Her right hand had a small abrasion where the toggle had pressed into the palm. Her breath was short but under control. The kettle on the stove had not yet whistled, because the kettle had only been on the flame for forty-three seconds when Elena had come at him from the pantry.

She turned off the gas.

The kitchen settled into its silence. Above the sink, a clock kept the time Lebedev had wound it to that morning, and would go on keeping it until someone noticed.

She looked at him for a single controlled breath. She filed the face. She logged the position of the hand. Then she walked to the desk.

The handwritten pages under the paperweight were the thing she had come for after the thing she had come for.

Lebedev wrote in Russian. His hand was neat. The pages were a running summary—twelve pages dated across the previous eleven months—of incidents in Western Europe that Lebedev had identified as probable unacknowledged radiological events. He had cross-referenced newspaper reports, regional health-data anomalies (which he had obtained through an IAEA colleague at the WHO's Copenhagen office), and a set of industrial bulletins that a state security service somewhere had made available to him under terms Lebedev did not specify in the pages.

Three pages in, the argument became clear.

Lebedev had counted seven candidates since 1971. Five he had rated as probable. Two he had rated as confirmed, on the strength of isotopic signatures reported in small specialist journals. The two confirmed were the 1971 Apennine village and a site in the Moselle valley Lebedev had dated to the late spring of 1985.

The late spring of 1985.

The date was forward. Lebedev's text was dated June 1983. The Moselle valley event he was describing had not yet happened.

Elena held the page in her hand.

She read it a second time to confirm the tense of Lebedev's sentences. He had written it in the future. He had written it as a prediction.

She read further. Lebedev's theory was not that the incidents were maintenance failures on an aging stockpile. His theory was that the incidents were operationally selected—dates chosen, wind windows calculated, cover stories pre-written, the events staged to produce small civilian casualty counts at a rate consistent with maintaining a continental-scale political climate of ambient radiological anxiety. The anxiety, Lebedev argued, serviced a broader architecture. States chased shadows. Populations held their breath. Certain institutional actors, within services but operating between them, retained their budgets and their unaccountability by supplying the shadow and then being paid to chase it.

The last sentence of Lebedev's penultimate page:

the fear is the product. The bomb is the marketing.

Elena read it twice.

Lebedev had a schedule.

On the twelfth page, in pencil, in a hand that had gone from the neat academic register of the body of his text into something tighter and more private, was a column of codes. FN-71 he had crossed out—the date in parentheses after it was 1971, and Elena understood FN was the Apennine village, the first on the list. TR-85 was the Moselle event he was predicting. Beneath TR-85 were eight more codes. FH-nn, BZ-nn, MG-nn and so on. The second halves were dates Lebedev had not committed to; he had written question marks. The first halves were cache designations in a system Lebedev had reconstructed from fragments.

FH-87 was the fourth entry down. The date after FH-87 had been written and then erased and then written again more faintly: *scheduled, unconfirmed.*

Elena did not know, in August 1983, what FH stood for. She carried away from Koppstraße only the shape of a column of codes and the date 1987 hovering in pencil next to FH.

She took Lebedev's twelve pages. She folded them twice. She put them inside the notebook where the wire had been.

She left the flat by the back stairs at six fifty-eight. She walked east through Ottakring. She caught a tram on the Gürtel. She rode four stops and got off. She walked two blocks west. She boarded a second tram. She rode it to the Hotel Imperial. She went up to her room. She showered. She washed the small abrasion on her palm. She put the notebook in the hotel safe with her passport and her press cards. She went down to the restaurant and ate dinner.

At eleven she came back up. She opened the notebook. She read the twelve pages once more.

She wrote two lines in the small red cloth-bound notebook she had carried in from Tel Aviv.

The incidents are not random.

Lebedev was seeing what I had been refusing to see.

She closed the notebook. She put it in her handbag. She did not write the codes down. The codes were in Lebedev's pages. The pages were in the hotel safe. The codes would travel back with her to Tel Aviv in the binding of the reporter's notebook, beside the wire, which had been cleaned and re-threaded into the spine in the bathroom under the running shower.

She turned out the light.

She did not sleep for a long time. Her right palm pulsed with the small residual ache of the toggle. Her shoulder ached from where the counter had struck it. Her throat was dry. She thought about Lebedev's hand between the wire and his neck. She thought about the quarter-second in which he had decided to go for the stove instead of the knife. She thought about the training they had shared. She thought about the instructors who had been theirs both.

She thought about what Lebedev had been writing in a quiet flat in Ottakring in the summer of 1983, alone, because no one had listened when he had spoken out loud.

She thought about the hand that had put a pencil mark against his name.

She thought about the hand that had used her.

She thought about the phrase Lebedev had used, which had landed in her chest the way certain phrases did—*the fear is the product, the bomb is the marketing*—and the thought went into the body and found, there, a room she had been keeping empty for ten years because she had not had a name for what would go into it.

Now she had a name.

She slept eventually. She did not dream.

Before she packed, she opened the notebook to the page she had not opened in seven years. Geneva, March 1976. Two lines in her own hand: *Sacco said Petrov was the template.* And: *an unregistered link always has a cleaner.* In 1976 they had been fragments—what Hatch had told her, what she had not yet known how to file. After last night they were architecture. Petrov had been the template because Petrov had been the test of the protocol. The cleaner had been Elena. She closed the notebook. She did not write anything new. The old lines had become new lines on their own.

She flew back to Tel Aviv on the Friday afternoon. She resumed the cover. She worked the Mossad access she had been cultivating for five years. She filed her reports in Yuri's rhythm and did not write a word in her own. The pages in the suitcase lining stayed in the suitcase lining. The pattern was accelerating. She had been counting cadences for seven and a half years. The fourth would arrive in November.

16

THE FOURTH CADENCE

London—November 1983

The second directive arrived on a Tuesday.

It arrived through the standard channel—a dead drop on Hampstead Heath, a hollow beneath a bench near the Kenwood boundary where Elena had been collecting instructions for six years with the weekly regularity of a woman visiting a post office. The bench was patronized by dog walkers and retired couples and the occasional student reading a paperback, none of whom had any reason to notice a woman in a gray coat sitting for three minutes and leaving with something in her pocket that had not been there when she arrived.

She walked the route three times. She sat with a paperback on her knee for the full window. Her right hand moved once.

She did not look back.

The envelope was the size of a credit card. She could feel it through the lining of her coat. It weighed almost nothing. It was, by its weight alone, indistinguishable from the hundreds of other pieces of paper she had carried out of this park.

It was not indistinguishable. She knew that before she reached Highgate. The preamble Yuri sometimes attached to high-priority instructions had been there when her finger brushed the top edge inside the envelope. The preamble was a single folded sheet—smaller than the cipher, thicker paper.

Her hand identified it by texture before her mind identified what its presence meant.

She read it at the kitchen table in Kensington forty minutes later, with the kettle boiling because Alice Marsh made tea when she came in and Alice Marsh was performing her afternoon.

Asset's reporting on Target Nine has become less operationally detailed than her access level and duration of engagement would suggest. Recommend enhanced monitoring of asset's operational compartmentalization.

Elena read the paragraph three times.

The language was institutional. The meaning was not.

Someone had been reading her reports on Calder—not for the intelligence they contained, but for the intelligence they did not contain. Someone had noticed the shape of the gaps. Someone had measured the silence in her reports and found it was exactly the size of a man.

The kettle began to whistle. She turned it off. She did not make the tea.

The cipher was clean. Elena decoded it at the kitchen table where Alice Marsh drank Earl Grey and read exhibition catalogs, working with the mechanical precision decoding required—each symbol converted to its letter, each letter assembled into its word, each word arriving at her consciousness with the flat factual weight of institutional language performing its institutional function: converting a human being into a target and a target into a task and a task into eleven sentences on a single sheet of paper.

The first sentence identified the target: James Calder, MI6, recently promoted to Deputy Head of Section, Soviet Desk.

The second sentence described the threat: Calder's new position gave him access to materials that could compromise the KGB's Illegal network in Western Europe. Specifically, he was now authorized to review the files of suspected Soviet penetration agents operating under non-diplomatic cover—the files that contained the patterns and anomalies that, if studied with sufficient attention by a man with sufficient intelligence, could lead to the identification of operatives like Elena.

The third through ninth sentences described the operation: full Zersetzung protocol. Systematic psychological destabilization through environmental manipulation, social isolation, professional undermining. The patient erosion of the target's confidence, relationships, and capacity to function, conducted over a period of twelve to eighteen months. The objective was not to eliminate Calder but to neutralize him—to reduce his professional effectiveness to the point where MI6 would remove him from the sensitive position that made him dangerous, reassigning him to a role where his access to the files that could expose the Illegal network would be revoked.

Between the seventh sentence and the eighth, she realized she had stopped pressing the pencil against the decoding pad. The pencil was suspended a millimeter above the paper. She had been holding it there for an undetermined interval. She lowered the pencil and continued decoding.

The tenth sentence assigned the operation to Elena.

The eleventh sentence was the authorization code.

She noticed the rhythm on the third sentence.

The rhythm was not that of the London residency encoding officer. He had a rhythm Elena had been reading for six years—he favored short declarative units, he front-loaded his operational nouns, he had a particular way of structuring conditional clauses. His sentences landed a certain way.

These sentences landed a different way. These sentences had the cadence Elena had been counting. Geneva, 1976 —Hatch's four pages. Marylebone, 1978—Yuri's Tel Aviv briefing. Bograshov Street, 1983—the directive through the Nicosia channel that had named Lebedev. Kensington, to-night. Four instances in seven and a half years. The same rhythm each time, the same pressure in the commas, the same mind placing the weight of the sentence one syllable before the reader expected. Four cadences. One voice. A voice that had been handling her since 1976 from behind the service that officially handled her, and that was, tonight, issuing an instruction through the same channel Yuri used.

Geneva. Marylebone. Bograshov Street. And now, at a kitchen table in Kensington where Alice Marsh drank Earl Grey, the fourth.

Seven years and eight months since Geneva. The pattern was accelerating.

Elena put down the decoding pad.

She sat at the kitchen table and looked at the eleven sentences as they had begun to form on the page. The directive in her hand had not originated at Moscow Center. It had been whispered into Moscow Center by the same voice that had whispered the Lebedev directive into it three months ago.

The voice had whispered that Calder's promotion to Deputy Head, Soviet Desk, made him a threat to the Illegal network—which was true, but was also an excellent cover.

The real threat Calder posed was not to the Illegal network. The real threat was to the FEUERWERK investigation Calder had been conducting in his Chiswick study with a pencil and a list of European cities circled in a folder on his desk surface that Elena had seen eight months ago in the dark at 4 AM.

The network wanted Calder removed. Not killed—removed from the position where his unofficial investigation could do damage. The Zersetzung directive was the network speaking through Moscow's voice, using Moscow's methods, to solve the network's problem.

And Yuri was also an instrument.

Elena had not understood this until the fourth cadence. She understood it now. Yuri had received the directive from Moscow Center and dispatched it to the Hampstead Heath dead drop with the institutional competence of a handler executing his part of the chain. He had not known—had never known—that the rhythm passing through his office for years did not originate from Moscow. That he was being used by a service that was not his service, to transmit orders that were not Moscow's orders, to operatives who were being asked to do things that were not the KGB's operations.

Yuri was the same shape Elena was.

Two people inside one service, taking instructions from a second service neither of them could see, executing operations that served the second service without knowing the second service was the beneficiary. The difference was that Elena knew it and Yuri did not. The difference was that Elena was counting cadences and Yuri was not. The difference was that Elena had been on a kitchen floor in Tel Aviv for forty-five minutes years ago and had come apart in a way that had never fully reassembled and had, in the incomplete reassembly, developed the capacity to notice things her training had been designed to prevent her from noticing.

Yuri, as far as Elena knew, had not had a comparable experience. Yuri was still assembled in the original configuration.

The KGB was not running this operation. Neither was MI6. Neither was anyone with a flag flying above their building.

The operation was the shape of the thing that had been running them all, and the thing had no flag, and the thing had been patient for decades.

◆◆◆

She finished decoding the directive.

On the cover sheet, in the upper margin, in pencil, was the mark. The same mark. The fifth time she had seen it.

The mark was small. A pencil dot, slightly ovoid, placed a centimeter from the upper edge, two millimeters to the left of the fold crease. It could have been a printer's registration mark. It could have been a smudge from a pencil resting on the page. It was not. She had seen it four times before and she knew the weight of the impression and the specific oval shape the pressure produced, and the mark was what the hand left when the hand wanted a piece of paper recognized by eyes that knew to look for it.

She had begun, in the eight months since the FEUERWERK page, to think about the hand that made the marks. The hand had a steadiness she could read but no name she could give it. She imagined it sometimes—a right hand, male or female she could not tell, holding a pencil at the particular angle the mark required. The owner of the hand was the voice behind the rhythm—the name she did not yet have.

She burned the sheet.

She held the paper over the kitchen sink and lit it with a match and watched it curl and blacken and reduce itself to ash, and the ash fell into the basin and she ran the tap and the water carried the ash down the drain, and the directive was gone. Physically gone. Irretrievably gone. The only copy that remained was the one in her memory, and the copy in her memory was the one that would stay.

She turned off the tap.

She stood at the kitchen sink. She looked through the window at the Kensington street below, where the afternoon was doing what London afternoons did in November—being gray and damp and committed to a specific kind of darkness that was not night and that was not day and that was, at four in the afternoon, the light under which the English conducted most of their winter lives.

A woman walked a dog. A delivery van idled at the curb. An old man with a shopping bag waited at the bus stop with the patient uncomplaining posture of a person who had spent a lifetime waiting for things that arrived on schedules he did not control.

Elena stood at the window and she did not react.

She did not react because there was no reaction adequate to what had just arrived in her kitchen. An institution she'd stopped believing in six years ago—itself the instrument of another institution she'd spent four cadences beginning to suspect—had just asked her to destroy the one man in the world who was pulling the same thread she was.

Anger was insufficient. Grief was insufficient. Horror was insufficient. The directive exceeded the scale that any single emotion could accommodate. So she produced no emotion. She stood at the window. She watched the street. She was composed, still, present in the room the way a piece of furniture was present in a room—occupying space, solid, without interior activity.

The training had won. Not in this moment—the training had won years ago, the day she walked into the Red Banner Institute and began the process of learning to contain what she felt inside a system designed to prevent feeling from interfering with function. The machinery had been winning every day since—every operation, every cover, every seduction, every report that omitted the thing she felt.

Her blood had gone cold in the Chiswick study at 4 AM months ago. Her blood did not go cold now. Her heart maintained its normal rate. Her breathing maintained its normal rhythm.

The directive had not created a new situation. It had named an existing one.

Elena had been destroying Calder for nearly ten years—through the simpler, more comprehensive destruction of loving him under a name that was not hers. The Zersetzung directive did not ask her to start. It asked her to convert the slow unintentional destruction into the fast intentional kind. The difference was between a building that collapsed because its foundations were flawed and a building demolished by a professional. The people inside were harmed either way. Moscow—or the voice behind Moscow—was asking her to make it a project.

She sat at the kitchen table.

She did not move for a long time. The November afternoon outside darkened the way November afternoons darkened in London—not in stages but in a single slow continuous dimming that a person watching the street could not quite catch in the act of happening. The streetlights came on at 4:32. The woman with the dog came back in the other direction. A car started somewhere down the terrace and drove away.

She thought about refusal.

Refusal was not an option the architecture permitted. The KGB did not issue directives with a menu of responses—accept, decline, negotiate. The KGB issued directives the way physics issued laws: as descriptions of what was going to happen, not proposals for what might happen.

Elena could refuse. Elena could send a signal through the Hampstead Heath dead drop declining the assignment. The signal would be received. Elena would be recalled, debriefed, subjected to the institutional consequences the KGB applied to operatives who declined orders. The second ledger would freeze. And whoever was running the hand above Yuri would continue. With another operative. On a different case. The institution did not accept declines. It accepted postponements.

If she refused, someone else would be assigned the Zersetzung campaign. Someone who did not know him. Someone who would approach the campaign the way Elena had approached the campaign against Hatch—clinically, methodically, without the intimate knowledge of the target that ten years of proximity had provided. Someone less effective than Elena but also someone without Elena's operational reason to soften the execution.

If Elena ran the campaign, she could build the failure points in. She could design Phase One to look devastating and produce damage that was recoverable. She could front-load the social isolation and hold back the professional undermining. She could choose which connections to sever and which to leave intact. She could execute the campaign with the precision of a woman who knew exactly where the load-bearing walls were—and who could therefore, with the same care, avoid cutting them.

No one else could do this. No one else had the map.

The campaign was going to happen. The only question was who would hold the pencil that drew the demolition plan.

Elena could be the instrument and also, quietly, work to ensure the man it was dismantling survived.

She accepted.

The acceptance did not arrive as a decision. It arrived as the recognition of a condition that had been true for some time and was only now being named. She accepted because she was still inside the structure the Red Banner Institute had built for her at nineteen, and the structure did not contain a door marked *out*. She accepted because refusing would have removed her from the only position in which she could see the hand. She accepted because the person who had written the directive wanted her to accept, and the wanting carried a weight she understood now that she could not have understood in 1973.

She knew only that the voice was asking her to remove Calder, and that the asking was the fourth cadence, and that the cadence was the only intelligence she had, and that the intelligence would be lost if Elena was no longer operational. She understood, sitting at the kitchen table with the ash of the decoded page in the basin behind her, that the hand above Yuri was asking her to eliminate the one man outside her own head who was pulling the same thread she was. The request was not an accident. The request was a test. The hand was finding out whether Elena would protect the thread or protect herself.

She arrived, that November, at the condition she would occupy from here on. The condition was not loyalty and it was not defection. It was the narrow space between them, where an operative continued to execute orders she no longer fully trusted on behalf of an institution she no longer fully served, while quietly maintaining the investigations and the withholdings and the off-books documentation that amounted, cumulatively, to the construction of a private service of one that would, eventually, produce the evidence required to name the voice behind the rhythm.

She did not yet know what she would do with the evidence when it was complete. She knew only that she would be the one who assembled it, and that the assembly would continue inside the Zersetzung campaign, and that the campaign would therefore have two purposes: the one Moscow—or the voice behind Moscow—had assigned her, and the one she was assigning herself.

The two purposes were in tension. The tension was the condition. The condition was her work now.

◆◆◆

That evening she went to Calder's flat.

She took the Piccadilly Line from Gloucester Road and walked from Green Park to the small flat on Half Moon Street he had taken in the autumn—the second flat now, the weeknight one, after a year of Margaret spending her weekends in Salisbury and the Chiswick house emptying around him in slow degrees. The flat was a weeknight residence, not a move; Chiswick was still home on paper, still home on weekends, still home where the post arrived. Half Moon Street was the small geometry of a man whose marriage had not yet ended and whose week had stopped fitting inside it. The flat was not decorated. It was furnished. The furniture had been bought in a single afternoon at a shop in the Fulham Road by a man who did not want to spend additional afternoons buying furniture. The flat smelled of ink and old books and the faint mineral cold of a space a man had been sleeping in alone.

He opened the door. He was wearing the charcoal wool trousers and the blue shirt he wore in the evenings when he was not expecting to go out again. He had been drinking. One glass. He kissed her.

The kiss was the familiar kiss of ten years—warm, brief, the kiss of a man who had stopped calibrating because the calibration was no longer necessary. She returned it. Her lips registered the taste of whisky and the slight rasp of the stubble he had not shaved since morning, and the two registers—the operative cataloging the sensory input and the woman receiving a kiss from the man she had just been assigned to destroy—passed through her in the same second without distinguishing themselves.

'Come in. I was making dinner. Lamb again. I know.'

'Lamb again is fine.'

He had been getting better at the lamb. The rosemary was more confident, the timing more precise, the product of a man who was learning to cook the way he'd learned everything else: through repetition, through attention, through the application of systematic intelligence to a problem most people solved through intuition.

He poured her wine. He served her the lamb at the small table by the window. Candles, because Calder had decided that the small compensations of domestic performance were, after Margaret, the part of the English evening he was going to keep. Elena ate the lamb. She complimented the lamb. She drank the wine he poured and she sat across the table from him in the candlelight and she looked at his face and she thought: *I am going to take this apart.*

Not the dinner. Not the evening. Not the face across the table.

The life. The frame. The structural integrity of James Calder's professional confidence and personal stability and the connections between the two that Elena had spent ten years mapping and that she was now going to use—the map becoming the demolition plan, the knowledge becoming the weapon, the intimacy becoming the instrument of its own destruction.

He asked about her day. She told him about a painting Gerald had decided not to acquire, which was a real story—the kind of story Alice Marsh would tell, operationally true and personally irrelevant, the social currency that filled the space between two people who had been sleeping with each other for ten years and who therefore no longer had to work at conversation. He told her about a committee meeting. She asked two questions. He answered them with the calibrated minimum of a man who was not going to discuss his work with a woman whose interest in it he could not fully account for.

He smiled at her across the candle. The same smile for ten years. Warm, guarded. A man who knew she knew, and who had decided the hiding was part of the arrangement. The smile said: I see you. I don't know what you are. I love you anyway.

Elena smiled back. The smile that had worked for ten years. The smile that would work for another eighteen months while Elena dismantled the man behind the smile on the other side of the candle.

They cleared the plates. They washed up. She stood at the small sink in his small kitchen and dried the plates he handed her, and he stood beside her with his sleeves rolled to the elbow washing the pans, and the domestic choreography of two people who had been doing this for a decade produced the particular silence in which no words were needed and no words would have been accurate to what was happening inside the silence.

They went to bed.

The routine was the same. Everything was the same. The lamb, the wine, the candle, the man, the woman, the bed, the dark. Everything was the same except the eleven sentences in Elena's memory and the absence in Elena's chest and the campaign that would begin tomorrow.

Elena lay in the dark beside Calder. She listened to him breathe. She counted the breaths.

She counted them the way he'd counted Margaret's breaths from the doorway years ago—as evidence of the life she was supposed to be protecting and was about to destroy.

She did not cry. She had not cried since she was nineteen. The machinery had trained out crying, and the comprehensiveness of the training was, tonight, beside a man she was going to demolish for a voice she could not identify, the most violent thing that had ever been done to her. Not the most violent thing done to her body. The most violent thing done to the part of her the machinery denied.

The part that was, even now, alive.

Alive enough to recognize what the directive was asking. Alive enough to know that what she was about to do was unforgivable. Alive enough to choose to do it anyway, the way she chose every lie—because the alternatives were worse and the logic was impeccable and the lie was functional. Alive enough to feel the absence where the horror should have been.

Alive enough to know that the absence was the horror.

Elena lay in the dark. The rope. The napkin. The fourth rhythm, and the intervals compressing, and the voice behind the rhythm whose name she did not yet have but suspected she would.

Calder breathed beside her. She counted his breaths.

Tomorrow the campaign would begin. Tomorrow she would start building the machine that would take apart the man breathing beside her, and the instrument would be the most precise thing she had ever constructed. The precision would be love's negative image—the same knowledge, the same attention, the same intimate understanding of every load-bearing wall, applied not to support but to demolition.

She had eight weeks to design Phase One. She started designing it in the dark, beside him, while he slept.

She was about to apply the same patience Kessler had applied to a different kind of cultivation. The same daily attention. The same careful adjustments to light and temperature. The same understanding that living things responded to consistency rather than force.

The difference was that Kessler's patience produced beauty. Elena's patience would produce rubble.

She placed the distinction in the archive beside the rope and the napkin and the orchid leaf she'd touched with tenderness and the wrist she'd broken with precision. The archive did not judge. The archive only held.

Outside Calder's flat the November rain began, soft at first and then insistent, the rain of London winter settling in for its long stay, and Elena listened to the rain through the window above the bed and counted the man's breaths and thought: I can no longer tell whose orders I am following. The not-telling is the working condition I am going to live inside from now on.

On Sunday, Elena went to Helen's for biscuits.

Helen's flat smelled of butter and Radio 4 and the particular warmth of a woman who kept her heating on for guests. Helen was in the kitchen making tea. The Sunday papers were spread across the sofa cushions the way Helen always left them—sections interleaved, supplements sliding onto the floor, the comfortable disorder of a woman who read the news as company rather than information.

Elena sat down and moved a section of the *Observer* to make room.

Beneath it was a Reuters wire clipping Helen had torn from the *Telegraph* and left on the cushion, the way she left things she intended to mention and then forgot. Two lines. A Soviet diplomat named Alexei Volkov, posted to New York under cultural-attaché cover, had died of pneumonia in a Moscow military hospital. The hospital had issued no further details. The diplomat's age was thirty-four.

Elena read the two lines. She read them again.

Alexei had been at the Red Banner Institute with her. Two years behind. Quiet, careful, the kind of operative who filed his reports early and never argued with his handlers. She'd liked him. He played piano badly—the wrong notes hit with such confidence they almost sounded right. He had a wide shy smile and a habit of cleaning his glasses when he was thinking.

He was not the courier Dmitri Volkov from Hampstead Heath—the Soviet Union produced Volkovs the way Iowa produced corn. He was a different Volkov, and he was dead at thirty-four of a disease the Soviet Union did not officially acknowledge existed.

Helen came in with the tea.

Elena folded the clipping and placed it beneath the *Observer* supplement where she'd found it. Helen asked about the gallery. Elena told her Gerald was considering a new acquisition. The shortbread was good. The afternoon was the afternoon.

She walked home through Chelsea in the late light. The two lines on the Reuters wire sat in her chest beside the three-page directive and the rhythm that was not Yuri's, and the distance between the directive and the death was the distance between the woman who built the lie and the man the lie was built over, and the distance was closing.

The flat on Kensington Church Street was where she had left it that morning. The bookshelf with the Gombrich. The kitchen with the drawer beside the stove. The bedroom with the narrow bed and the chair she had stopped using two years ago because it had matched too closely, in its position, with the chair in the observation post on Yefet Street.

She checked the door telltale before she unlocked it. A single dark hair, three inches long, glued to the frame with saliva at 08:40 that morning. The hair was still there. The glue was intact. The door had not been opened.

She unlocked the door. She entered. She closed it behind her. She removed her coat.

She walked to the kitchen.

The kitchen was the kitchen she had left. The kettle in its place on the stove. The tea tin beside the kettle. The two cups she had washed that morning inverted on the draining board. The drawer beside the stove, closed.

She opened it.

The nine objects were in their places. Diary, candle, pen, Yuri's welcome card, Calder's first card, Ronson lighter, Nagra reel, orchid photograph, Mercator knife. She did not move any of them. Her eye crossed them in the order her memory filed them, and in the third second her eye registered the one wrongness.

The Ronson was oriented three degrees off.

Not dramatically. Not the kind of wrongness a casual observer would detect. She had placed the Ronson, four days earlier, with its hinged cap facing the left wall of the drawer and the baseplate flush against the photograph of the *rothschildianum*. Today the cap was still facing the left wall, but the baseplate was rotated three degrees—rotated with enough precision that a person replacing the Ronson had been attempting to match her orientation and had failed by a margin only she would see.

She picked it up.

The weight was unchanged. The screws were tight. The cap opened and closed with its proper click. She pressed the third striker pawl twice, carefully, without burning a frame. The shutter actuated silently. The mechanism was operational.

Only the orientation was wrong.

And: the metal was warmer than the other objects in the drawer. By the amount a small brass-and-chrome object becomes when it has been held in a human hand for between twenty and ninety seconds and then placed back in a cold drawer, four to six hours earlier.

The drawer had been the one place. The flat she could lose. The cover she could shed. The body she would, eventually, surrender. The drawer had been the one place that had belonged to no one else. They had been in it. They had been precise enough to put the Ronson back wrong by three degrees on purpose. The wrongness was the message. The message was that the drawer had never been hers.

Elena placed the Ronson back, cap toward the left wall, baseplate flush against the orchid photograph—the way she had placed it four days earlier.

She closed the drawer.

She stood at the kitchen counter for a full minute.

She did not check the door telltale again. She did not search the flat. Whoever had been in her kitchen had come through the front door—the telltale had been designed to detect forced entry, not entry by a person in possession of a working key.

The trace said: we have been here before. We will be here again.

Elena made tea. She drank it standing at the window, watching the Kensington street darken into November evening. A milk float. A woman walking a poodle. Two teenagers kicking a football against a garden wall.

She went to bed early.

She did not write in the notebook.

Some things were not for the notebook.

17

MARGARET

London—January—June 1984

The letter to Margaret was the first action.

The January light in the Kensington flat was the color of used dishwater. It came through the kitchen window at an angle that illuminated surfaces without warming them. The radiator under the window ticked as it heated.

The gold Omega on her left wrist—Calder's gift, covering the compass rose—caught the dishwater light as she sat down. The same hands that had filed the Ronson's burr and held still for eight seconds over a microdot reduction lens were about to type a letter that would end a marriage. The hands did not distinguish between precision and destruction. They never had.

Elena wrote it at the kitchen table on a second-hand typewriter she would use only once. Each keystroke was louder than it should have been. Each keystroke echoed off the walls like a whisper amplified into speech. On the radio in the corner the four o'clock summary was running, low: a closed facility outside a small Bavarian town, no casualties listed. The shape of the language was a shape she had been reading for ten years. The count was twenty-three. She did not stop typing. Between the fourth sentence and the fifth, she lifted her fingers from the keys and held them above the carriage for the length of one breath. She lowered them. She finished the sentence. The typewriter would go into the Thames at

Putney Bridge that evening. Her hands would not shake until later and the letter would arrive without a source—truth with no author.

The letter was addressed to Margaret Calder at the school where she taught.

The letter said:

Dear Mrs. Calder,

I have been trying to decide whether to write this for some time. I don't know your husband well, but I've seen him often enough to recognize him. I've seen him with a woman—dark hair, about his age—at restaurants near Kensington Church Street on more than one occasion. The most recent was last month. They were not behaving like colleagues.

I may be mistaken about what I saw. I hope I am. But I don't think I am, and I thought you should know.

I'm sorry to write something like this.

Unsigned. A lie built on truth—the same architecture she used for everything. The affair was real. The restaurants were real. The multiple occasions were real. The only lie was the author—an anonymous concerned citizen who had witnessed the potential affair and felt compelled to inform the wife.

The circularity was precise. Elena was informing Margaret about Elena. The snake eating its own tail. The weapon striking the wielder. The operation consuming the operator.

She sealed the letter. It was warm from her hands as she addressed it. It would be posted from a postbox in Paddington, three miles from her flat, at a time of day when the collection would place it in the postal system's Tuesday morning processing stream, which would deliver it to Margaret's school on Wednesday. Wednesday was the day Margaret had staff meetings and would therefore open her mail in the staffroom where colleagues might notice her reaction. Every detail was designed. Every detail was Zersetzung.

On the walk back she passed a florist. The front window had bunches of early crocus and paperwhites in narrow buckets, the flowers leaning toward the street like they were asking for something. She stopped. She stood in front of the window for perhaps four seconds. Margaret liked paperwhites. Calder had mentioned it once, in 1978. Elena walked on.

The Paddington postbox cleared at 17:30.

Elena was in her kitchen at 17:30 because she had walked back through Hyde Park and had timed her arrival to the same minute the collection van made its stop. She was standing at the sink with a glass of water in her hand. She had filled the glass without intending to. Alice Marsh filled glasses of water. Elena was standing inside Alice Marsh and Alice Marsh was holding water.

The letter was now in the system. It would arrive in the morning. The institution that moved it was the British Post Office. The institution that had written it was a woman in a Kensington kitchen. The two institutions had collaborated, and the collaboration could not be reversed by any motion available to the woman in the kitchen.

She threw the glass.

It struck the wall above the radiator. The water went everywhere—the wall, the floor, the front of the cupboards. The glass shattered into pieces that her training would have catalogued automatically as evidence to be removed. Her training did not catalogue them. Her training had stepped, for one half-second, outside the room.

She stood at the sink. She did not move. She watched the water she had thrown find its way down the wall toward the skirting board. A small pale crater had appeared in the plaster where the glass had hit—not from the glass, which had broken too cleanly to dent the wall, but from the corner of the metal radiator, where her aim had been off by an inch in the half-second she had not been managing her aim.

She would not repair the crater. The decision arrived as a fact rather than a choice. She would leave it. She would walk past it every morning she stood at this sink. The crater was the only physical mark in this kitchen of the operation she had launched, and the operation was not allowed marks anywhere else.

She knelt and gathered the glass. She wiped the water off the floor. She did not wipe the wall.

Her hands were not steady. For seven minutes after she stood up they did not return to steadiness. At the eighth minute they did.

Elena composed the Phase One report at the kitchen table on the Sunday after the letter went into the postbox. Subject Calder. Period December 1983 through February 1984. Classification restricted, handler eyes only. Phase One: environmental preparation. Anonymous communication delivered to subject's spouse on 18 January, designed to confirm her existing suspicion and prevent reconciliation. Concurrent action: letter to Senior Officer Halford, timed to coincide with the operational failure at the Berlin station, styled in internal memorandum language. Subject's flat entered on three occasions; items displaced below the threshold of conscious detection. Subject exhibiting early-stage disorientation. Recommend continuation.

The seven sentences had taken eight weeks to execute.

Elena had studied MI6's internal communication style for seven years—the specific vocabulary, the sentence structures, the blend of bureaucratic formality and clubhouse jargon that characterized memoranda between senior officers. She absorbed the style.

The letter raised concerns about Calder's recent performance. It cited a failure at the Berlin station—a failure Elena had engineered through a separate channel and that had, by the time it reached Halford's desk, attributed itself to Calder's misjudgment. In the same week she fed a drinking narrative into three independent routes: a reception comment to a junior officer, a cultivated observation at Calder's club, a worried aside to a mutual acquaintance. Three routes. Three confirmations. Circular citation. The technique she had used on Hatch, now refined and applied to a man whose lamb she would eat that evening.

The flat entries were the worst part.

Elena had duplicated Calder's house keys in December—the keys from his trouser pocket while he slept, Waterloo's twenty-four-hour machine, the originals back in the pocket before he woke. She entered the Chiswick house three times in February. Each entry lasted between twelve and twenty minutes. The house smelled like him. Coffee and wool and the faint cedar of the wardrobe.

First entry: three books reversed on the living room shelf. A Deighton between a le Carré and a Fleming, a Greene moved one shelf down, two Ambler novels out of order. Second entry: the top desk drawer left open by two centimetres. Third entry: the kitchen window unlatched. An open window was a statement. An unlatched window was a question. She performed each with the steady hands and steady heartbeat of a woman who had been trained to compartmentalize and who was compartmentalizing now with a thoroughness that would, she suspected, cost her something she could not yet calculate.

She also noted, on the third entry, what the campaign was not doing. The FEUERWERK working file on his desk had grown by sixty pages since January. The handwriting in the margins was still steady. He was breaking professionally and not breaking operationally. The two were not the same.

The cost would come later. The cost always came later.

The forged document was Phase Two's centerpiece.

Elena had obtained a blank MI6 internal assessment form through a contact at the Government Communications Headquarters in Cheltenham—a filing clerk who believed he was providing documents to a journalist investigating government waste.

The form was genuine. The content Elena would add was not. She was going to forge an internal assessment questioning Calder's fitness for duty and plant it in the briefcase of a junior MI6 officer named Patterson, who would carry it into Century House, where it would be discovered during a routine security audit and appear to have originated from within the service's own personnel division.

The draft arrived through the Hampstead Heath dead drop on a Tuesday in March—not the forged document itself, which Elena would type, but a guidance from Moscow specifying language and tone and the specific concerns Moscow wanted raised about Calder. Elena read it the way she read every institutional communication: at the words, and at the negative space around them.

The kitchen was cold. She had not lit the ring. She read standing up, with her coat still on.

The mark was in the upper margin, in pencil. This time she read the pressure. The pressure was steady. The slight tremor in the line was the tremor of a hand past sixty. The hand was older than she'd thought.

On the fourth read she noticed the line.

It was buried in the paragraph about Calder's analytical reliability—a single sentence, twenty-three words long, recommending that the assessment flag inconsistencies in subject's handling of counter-proliferation materials, specifically the FEUERWERK working file maintained on subject's home desk.

Elena read the sentence three times.

She also read, for the fourth time, the paragraph above the sentence. The paragraph described Calder's psychological profile in language that was specific in a way that external intelligence should not have been. It knew which room in the Chiswick house he used as a study, with the desk facing the window rather than the door. It knew he kept the FEUERWERK file on the desk surface rather than in a drawer. This was not the language of a service observing a target from outside. This was the language of a service that had read the target's own institution's internal assessment—or that had written it.

She read it three times because the sentence was a bomb and she needed to be certain of what kind of bomb it was.

FEUERWERK was the word. The same word Elena had seen on the single typewritten sheet in Calder's Chiswick study in March 1983, in a manila folder between two photocopied pages of Italian Carabinieri reports. The sheet that had made Elena understand, for the first time, that the British knew.

The word had never appeared in any communication Elena had received from Moscow before—no directive, no briefing. Elena had been carrying it privately for eleven months, in the archive behind the archive, in the place where she kept the noticings she had not yet named. And now the word was in a piece of paper that had been delivered to her through her own service's standard operational channel, as part of the guidance for an operation the fourth cadence had told her the network was running, and the word was instructing her to insert it into a document that would enter MI6's institutional memory as a line a British analyst had raised about his own colleague.

Her pulse was suddenly present in her throat. Not in the bruising way a pulse registered under threat but in the specific way a pulse registered when a body had been noticed by something it had been assuming did not notice it. Someone above Yuri had been watching Elena watch FEUERWERK. They had not said so. They had not warned her. They had simply included the word in a directive, letting Elena understand the inclusion as a private message: *we know what you are looking at. We know you have been looking at it for eleven months. Write the sentence, and you are ours. Refuse it, and you are a problem we resolve.*

The sentence, if written into the assessment, would harm the FEUERWERK investigation. Either MI6 would chase the apparent Soviet leak back toward Elena herself, or they would bury their own inquiry under the institutional response to a penetration that did not exist. Either outcome reached the same place. The hand above the hand was operating through her pen. Her hand had been Elena's for forty-one years. It was now also the network's pen.

Elena knew only that the sentence was not going into the assessment.

She took out her pen and crossed out the twenty-three words. She crossed them out with a single clean line and replaced them with twenty-three words of her own: a generic observation about Calder's analytical caution becoming hesitation in allied-service liaison. Bureaucratic enough to serve the Zersetzung purpose. Bland enough to avoid planting the word she was not going to plant.

She typed the assessment on a Remington at the gallery she

managed as Alice Marsh, one whose characters she'd confirmed would not match any machine registered to Century House. The assessment was complete in forty minutes. She folded it into the newspaper she would carry to the Waterloo pub that evening.

Her hands were steady.

Her hands had been steady through worse things than this. The steadiness was different now. She had not refused the order—she had edited it. Twenty-three words removed, twenty-three words her own. The first time in twelve years of operational service that she had not executed a directive exactly as received.

She was not yet ready to decide what the refusal was. She was only ready to do it.

The exchange was scheduled for a Thursday evening at the Hole in the Wall in Waterloo—a narrow crowded pub favored by commuters and intelligence personnel from nearby Century House. Patterson would be at the bar at 18:00. Elena would arrive at 18:05, order a drink, drop her bag, and exchange the folder for Patterson's receipt in the five seconds it took to retrieve the spilled contents.

Elena arrived at 18:15. She ordered a drink and positioned herself at the bar, two seats from Patterson, who was drinking lager and talking to a colleague about cricket with the specific numbing enthusiasm the English applied to a sport whose primary function was to facilitate conversations about nothing.

Then she saw the MI5 officer.

He was standing near the door. Not drinking, not talking. Doing what MI5 officers did in pubs where MI6 officers drank: watching. His cover was adequate—a pint in his hand, leaning against the wall—but his eyes were doing the thing surveillance officers' eyes did when they were on the job: the systematic sweep that covered the room in quadrants and returned, with metronomic regularity, to a single point. The single point was Patterson.

MI5 was watching Patterson. The counter-intelligence service had him under surveillance. The reasons were unknown and, at this moment, irrelevant. What was relevant was that the pub was not clean, that the exchange could not proceed as planned, and that Elena had approximately thirty seconds to decide whether to abort the operation or adapt it.

She adapted.

The adaptation required removing the forged document from her newspaper and inserting it into Patterson's briefcase without the MI5 officer—or Patterson—detecting either. The newspaper was on the bar. The briefcase was on the floor beside Patterson's stool. The MI5 officer was twenty feet away, with a sightline to Patterson but not to the floor beneath the bar, because the bar itself occluded the lower third of the room from his position.

Elena dropped her bag. The contents spilled—lipstick, keys, compact mirror, the choreographed debris of a woman's handbag hitting the ground. The lipstick rolled toward Patterson's stool. Elena knelt to retrieve it, placing herself in the dead zone between the MI5 officer and the floor. 'Let me help,' Patterson said, bending to pick up the compact mirror. In the two seconds his body was turned away from his briefcase, Elena's left hand opened the briefcase's side pocket and inserted the folded document with the speed of a motion practiced until it required no conscious direction.

She straightened, thanked Patterson, and collected her bag's contents. The entire sequence had taken eleven seconds. The MI5 officer had not moved. His eyes had registered the spill, assessed it as irrelevant, and returned to their quadrant sweep. Patterson's briefcase was on the floor, closed, containing a document that would enter Century House in the morning and that would, within a week, add another layer to the atmosphere of doubt Elena was building around the man she went home to.

She finished her drink and left the pub. Waterloo station. The Tube to Kensington. The flat. The door closed behind her. She put down her bag and did not turn on the lights. She sat in her kitchen in the dark for an hour.

She did not think about the pub. The pub had been flawless—the adaptation, the extraction, the eleven seconds of precision that had saved the operation and that would, she knew, be described in her report as a minor deviation managed within parameters. The pub was not the problem. The twenty-three words that Moscow had asked her to write were not the problem either, because she'd already dealt with them, and the dealing had been, whatever else it was, final.

The problem was Margaret.

Ealing—Wednesday, 18 January 1984.

The letter was in Margaret Calder's pigeonhole at the staffroom of St. Anne's Junior School on the Wednesday morning between the union newsletter and a parents' association mailing about the summer fete.

She did not open it immediately. She marked the morning register. She walked to the staffroom at break, made a cup of tea, and stood at the window. Then she sat at the small corner table and opened her post.

The letter was unsigned. Three pages. The handwriting was careful—not anonymous in the way of an angry stranger, but anonymous in the way of someone who had thought about what they were doing. Margaret read the first half-page and understood she was holding the answer to a question she had stopped asking herself in the autumn of 1976.

Restaurants in Fitzrovia. Multiple occasions. The names of two restaurants she had been to with James. A description of a woman whose physical specifics did not match anyone Margaret recognized but whose existence she did not doubt.

She read it twice. The second reading was for confirmation that she had read what she thought she had read.

She did not cry. She had used up her crying years ago, in a different staffroom, on a different Wednesday, when she had decided that her marriage would continue and that the continuing was the choice she would make every morning whether or not the morning made it for her.

She folded the letter once. She folded it again. She placed it in her bag, between the geography textbook she was returning to the library and the lunch she had not yet eaten.

Janet came in to make tea. Margaret asked about Janet's daughter's audition for the school play. Janet said it had gone well. Margaret said that was good news. The exchange lasted four minutes. Margaret's face did not change.

The bell went. Year Six. They were doing comprehension that hour. The passage was a description of a Cornish village in winter; the questions asked the children to identify what the writer had felt about the village and how they could tell. Margaret read the passage aloud. Her voice did not change.

At the end of the day she walked to the bus stop in the rain. She sat on the upper deck. She watched London move past the window in the gray light particular to early February in a January that was already failing. She thought, quite clearly, about a Wednesday morning in October 1973 when she had asked James whether the gallery opening had been interesting and he had said it was and the saying had not quite matched the way he was buttering his toast.

She had added an entry to her fourth column that morning, in private, with the staffroom empty. She had been adding entries for ten years.

The letter was the last entry. The column was now closed.

When she arrived home she did not show James the letter. She did not mention it. She made rosemary chicken because it was Wednesday. She watered the geraniums. At nine she said good night and went up the stairs to bed.

She continued.

The continuation was what would do the damage. She had decided this in the staffroom, at the window, before she had opened the post. She had been deciding it for ten years.

Margaret had received the letter on Wednesday, as Elena had designed. Margaret had read the letter in the staffroom, as Elena had predicted. Margaret had not reacted visibly, which was not what Elena had predicted—Elena had expected tears, or a sharp intake of breath, or the specific public distress the staffroom setting was designed to amplify. Margaret had done none of these things. Margaret had read the letter, folded it, placed it in her bag, and continued her day.

Elena knew this because she had a source at the school —a teaching assistant named Janet whom Elena had befriended at a parent-teacher event attended as a friend of the Calders, and who reported, without knowing she was reporting, on the small details of Margaret's daily life. Janet had mentioned, in a phone conversation, that Margaret had seemed quiet on Wednesday. That was the word. Quiet. Not upset. Not distressed. Quiet. The quiet of a woman who had received information she had been expecting and who had processed it not with surprise but with the heavy confirmation of something she'd already known and had been carrying alone.

Margaret had known. Margaret had always known.

She knew the way women knew things their husbands did not tell them—not through evidence, which was James's language, but through atmosphere, which was hers. The atmosphere in the marriage had changed early on. Not dramatically. The way a room changes when someone opens a window you cannot see. She knew. She did not have the name. She did not need the name. She had the temperature.

Elena had taken that option away. Elena had taken it away deliberately, precisely, as part of an operation designed to isolate Calder by removing his domestic support structure. The operation had worked. Margaret was going to leave. Not because of the letter—Margaret had been leaving for years, slowly, incrementally, in the way people leave when they cannot admit they are leaving. The letter had not caused the leaving. It had accelerated it. It had removed the last structural support that kept the marriage standing—the possibility that Margaret could continue to trust without examining what she was trusting. Elena had made the trust impossible to sustain. The marriage had done the rest.

Chiswick—a Sunday morning in late May 1984.

Before she left, she said it to him.

Not in anger. Not in the register of a confrontation. She waited until a Sunday morning in late May, when the light through the kitchen window was the light that had been in the kitchen for twelve years of Sundays, and she waited until he was standing in the doorway with his first coffee, and she said it the way she read the register at school.

'I hope you'll be kind to whoever it was.'

That was all. She did not say it was over. She did not say that she knew. She said only that she hoped he would be kind, and she used the word *was* instead of *is*, and the tense did more work than any sentence with her name in it could have done.

James did not speak. She had known he would not speak. The sentence had been constructed to require nothing from him except the hearing of it. Margaret had spent two years constructing sentences that required nothing of the hearer and that contained, inside their refusal to require, everything the hearer had been missing for two years. The sentence was the best she had made. She had made him stand in the kitchen doorway to hear it because the doorway was a threshold and the sentence was a threshold, and the geometry of the morning arranged itself, without her needing to arrange it, into a room she was leaving.

She turned back to the sink. She finished rinsing the teapot. She did not look at him again that morning.

He left for Century House at eight fifty-five. The door closed behind him the way it always closed. Margaret stood at the sink with her hands in the warm water and the charm bracelet on her left wrist clicking gently against the porcelain rim. The silver key caught the window light.

She had not decided, that morning, when she would leave. She had decided only that she would, and that the sentence she had just said was the moment the decision became a fact the house would remember after she was gone. The house did not yet know what she had done. She knew. And from that morning onward, the knowing was hers alone, which was the condition she had required of herself before she could begin doing the work of leaving.

Chiswick—a Saturday in June 1984.

Margaret left in June 1984.

She did not leave dramatically. She left the way she'd lived in the marriage—quietly, practically, with the dignified competence of a woman who understood that the situation was what it was and who was not going to demean herself or her husband by pretending otherwise.

She collected the last of her things from the Chiswick house on a Saturday. She chose Saturday because Saturday was the day she always deep-cleaned the kitchen. Margaret Calder was the kind of woman who would deep-clean the kitchen of a house she was leaving because leaving a dirty kitchen was, in her private moral code, worse than leaving a marriage. She cleaned the oven. She descaled the kettle. She watered the geraniums on the windowsill—the geraniums she was leaving behind because they belonged to the house, and the division of property did not extend to living things that had rooted themselves in the soil of a life she was walking away from.

'I'm going to water the geraniums before I go,' she said to no one. The house was empty. She spoke to it anyway.

She paused at the kitchen counter. The blue pot was on the shelf above the kettle—the Portobello pot, the pot she'd bought the week after their wedding, the pot that had made tea every morning for twelve years. She reached for it. Her hand closed around the handle. She held it for a long time. Then she put it back. The pot belonged to the kitchen. The kitchen belonged to the house. The house belonged to James. The pot would stay.

She would buy a new pot. A different color. A different weight in her hand. A pot with no history. The thought of a pot with no history was, Margaret understood, the saddest thought she had ever had about an object, and the sadness was not about the pot.

Then she did something she had not planned to do.

She went upstairs to the bedroom she had not slept in for a year. She opened the small drawer in the dressing table where she'd kept the charm bracelet James had given her for an anniversary. The bracelet was still there—she had not taken it when she left the first time, because taking it would have been a decision she was not ready to make, and leaving it had been its own decision in the way that not-leaving was. She picked up the bracelet and looked at the charms. The book. The cat. The heart. The letter M. The silver key.

The silver key was the newest charm. It had arrived on the bracelet nearly seven years ago, in November 1977, without explanation. Margaret had not added it herself. James had not mentioned adding it. For weeks she'd thought about asking him where it had come from and had decided, in the end, not to ask, because the way the key had appeared—silently, in the place where a charm belonged—had the quality of a message from a man who did not say the thing he wanted to say out loud and who had chosen, for reasons of his own, to put it in the bracelet instead.

Margaret had her own theories about what the key meant. She'd never told anyone her theories. She'd never asked James to confirm them. She had lived for nearly seven years with a silver charm she had not chosen and a private catalog of interpretations she had not spoken. It was possible to love a man who was trying to tell you something without words. Loving him required accepting that the telling would not arrive as language.

Now she was leaving. She put the bracelet in her pocket. Then she reached for the notepad on the dressing table and a pencil and she wrote one line on a piece of paper.

The silver key.

That was all. Three words on a small square of paper. She did not write what the words meant. She did not write what she thought the key was for. She wrote the three words and she folded the paper at the word *key* and she put the paper in the inside pocket of her handbag, beside her reading glasses, and she zipped the pocket closed.

She did not know why she was taking the note with her. She knew only that she was going to take it with her and that she was not going to throw it away and that someday—probably not for years, probably for longer than that, probably at some moment she could not yet predict—she was going to need it.

She went back downstairs. She watered the geraniums carefully. She spoke to them, the way she always had—not words exactly, but the small encouraging sounds people made to plants and cats and children who were too young to understand language but who responded to tone. The sounds were, if anyone had been listening, the most honest Margaret had been in months. The geraniums did not require performance. The geraniums did not lie.

She left the keys on the hallway table—the same table where the ceramic dish had been, the table Elena noted on her first visit, the table that was now bare. Margaret left the keys and she left the house and she left the marriage and she did not leave a note, because the absence of a note was the note, and the note said: I knew. I always knew. And I'm done choosing not to know.

But the other note—the three words on the folded paper—was in the inside pocket of her handbag, traveling with her into whatever came next.

Calder came home to an empty house. An emptier house. A house that had been partially empty since January 1983 and that was now completely empty, not of furniture but of Margaret. The absence of Margaret was, as it had been since the beginning, louder than Margaret's presence had ever been.

Elena learned about the departure from Calder. 'Margaret's gone,' he said. He said it the way you say something you've been rehearsing and that still comes out wrong. The same flat understated delivery. Margaret had decided. The separation was permanent now. He said it the way he said everything—with the controlled composed professional management of information that his training required. But his hands, when he reached for his wine glass, were not steady. For the first time in ten years, Elena saw Calder's hands shake.

His hands had always been steady. She had known them to be steady since the night in the gallery in 1973—the way he had held the photograph, the way he had held a wine glass. The precision had been the first thing about him to identify him to her. The precision was failing now.

She reached across the table and held his hand. Alice Marsh's hand, holding the hand of the man Alice Marsh loved, steadying the shake Alice Marsh had caused. The weapon had struck the wielder. The operation had consumed the operator.

Elena held his hand and she thought: *I did this. The letter was mine. The departure was mine. The shake in your hands is mine. Everything that is happening to you is happening because of me, and you are holding my hand because you do not know this, and I am holding your hand because I cannot tell you this, and the holding is the most honest and the most dishonest thing I have ever done simultaneously.*

18

THE ASSASSINATION MANUAL

London—February 1984

The document arrived in February—through an intermediary in Washington, a KGB officer under diplomatic cover who had obtained it from a filing clerk at the CIA's historical archives division. It reached Elena's kitchen table in Kensington while she was, in the same month, writing the letter that destroyed Calder's marriage, moving books on his shelves, and running a Zersetzung campaign whose work continued in her absence.

A Study of Assassination. CIA, 1954. Nineteen pages, typewritten, classified, never intended for public release. A manual. A document that described, in the flat procedural language of an institution that had decided killing was a professional skill rather than a moral event, the methods by which a human being could be made to stop being a human being.

She read it on a Tuesday afternoon, with a cup of Earl Grey going cold beside her and the gray London light coming through the window.

The manual was organized like a cookbook: method, technique, complexity, each category arranged for appropriate use. Even murder, when it was institutional, required proper formatting.

The accidental category described methods of killing designed to appear as something other than killing. Falls. Car accidents. Drowning. They did not require confrontation. They required arrangement—the patient manipulation of the target's environment until the environment became the weapon, and the weapon's action looked like circumstance.

Elena closed the manual.

The Stasi liaison was Markus. Thirty-eight, East German, cultural attaché at the GDR embassy—the cover nobody bothered to believe. He handled the day-to-day mechanics: dead drops, the Pimlico safe flat, local servicing. Yuri remained her handler of record on paper, but three months ago he had been quietly removed from the channel between Elena and the field, in the same week the Zersetzung directive passed through his office. She noted it: the network does not want Yuri close to me anymore.

Markus was a technician—a man who understood the mechanics of intelligence without understanding its art. He was also attracted to her—contained, carefully managed, but Elena could see it. She did not exploit it. She did something else.

She taught him.

The session happened that evening in a Pimlico safe flat. Table, two chairs, a lamp, and the stale air of rooms occupied only for purposes.

They were there to discuss operational methodology. East Berlin wanted a psychological assessment capability for the London station. Bruhn's old desk had heard about Elena's profiling work and asked for it to be taught. Markus had been assigned as the student. Elena as the teacher.

That was the official version. She began suspecting a different version about eight minutes into the session.

The first wrongness: Markus had a notebook open, the blankness of a man instructed to keep the page empty until the subject produced something worth recording.

The second: his chair was eleven inches further from the table than it should have been—the distance an interrogator put between themselves and the person across the table when the interrogator wanted the person to feel slightly exposed. Students leaned in. Markus was not leaning.

The third completed the assessment. Markus's attention was the attention of an examiner, not a student. He was sitting with the flat composure of a man who was not waiting to absorb but waiting to record. He was preparing to take an inventory.

Elena was the inventory.

She took a breath. Markus was not here to learn profiling. Markus was here to profile her. The notebook, the eagerness, the questions—all designed to produce the kind of extended demonstration that would give his real handlers enough material to assess whether Elena was still the woman they thought they had assigned the campaign to.

Markus had been chosen for a reason. He was the instrument the network used when it wanted to read its own operatives. He had read others before her. Some of them were no longer alive.

She had a second and a half to decide. She could abort. She could perform as instructed. Or she could perform a version—the operative Markus's handlers expected to find, with the small wavering interior corrections left out, and let the one it did not expect remain in the notebook in the inner pocket of the handbag at her feet.

She chose the third.

'Tell me what you see,' she said.

She was sitting across from him. The lamp was between them, casting light upward, illuminating their faces from below in the dramatic way upward lighting produced—shadows in the hollows, brightness on the planes.

'What do you mean?' Markus said.

'Look at me,' Elena said. 'Not at the materials. At me. Tell me what you see.'

Markus looked at her. He performed the looking competently. He described her features—jawline, dark hair, eyes—the way a man described a woman he found attractive: noting what he wanted and ignoring the rest.

Elena shook her head.

'You're looking at what you want to see,' she said. 'Look at what's there. The jaw is relevant—but not because it's shaped a certain way. Because of how I hold it. The set of the jaw tells you what I'm feeling about this conversation. Right now I'm holding tension in the left side. You can see it if you look—the masseter is slightly contracted. That means I'm concentrating, or I'm frustrated, or I'm managing an emotion I don't want you to see. Your job is to determine which.'

Markus leaned forward. She could smell his cologne—institutional, forgettable. The distance was professional. The charge in it was not.

She demonstrated the false smile and the real smile, the muscles around the eyes that distinguished one from the other. The demonstration was technically perfect. It was also, for the first time in her career, missing something—the small wavering that would have signaled she knew what the techniques cost. She withheld it. The wavering was evidence, and evidence was what Markus had been sent to find.

'The best operatives don't fake emotions,' she said. 'They produce real ones. They find the genuine feeling inside themselves and they deploy it. The deployment is calculated. The feeling is real. The combination is what makes it undetectable.'

Markus was looking at her face with an intensity that had shifted, over the course of the lesson, from the attention of a student to the attention of an examiner who had also become a man attracted to the woman he was examining. Elena let her smile go warm.

She had located the genuine feeling inside herself: pity for Markus—a competent man being used by his service to study a woman he had no instrument to reach. The pity was real. The smile was real. The deployment was calculated.

'Now,' she said. Her voice had dropped. Not dramatically. By a quarter-tone, a reduction in volume that brought the conversation from the register of instruction to the register of confidence. 'I'm going to profile you. In real time. I'm going to tell you what I see when I look at you, and I'm going to tell you what it means. This will be uncomfortable. That's the point.'

Markus nodded. He did not speak.

Elena profiled him. He was afraid. He was managing the fear with competence, which was the most dangerous combination in intelligence work. The photograph in his wallet was a daily measurement—the distance between the man in the photograph and the man holding the wallet was getting larger. The daughter would, at sixteen, know the difference. Elena watched each truth land.

Markus's hand moved toward his jaw. He stopped it. Elena saw the stop. The stop was confirmation. The stop was the lesson.

In the same half-second Markus looked at her with the unguarded expression of a man who had seen something he was supposed to be the only one looking for. Elena saw the expression. Markus saw her see it. Neither of them adjusted. The professional courtesy was the not-adjusting.

She held the silence. The silence was warm and full and charged with the specific electric vulnerability of a man who had been opened like a file and who was sitting across from the woman who had opened him.

'This is what profiling does,' Elena said. Her voice returned to its instructional register. 'It creates the feeling of being known. The feeling of being known is the most powerful emotional experience a human being can have. People will do anything for the person who makes them feel known.'

'This is why profiling works. This is why everything we do works. We make people feel known, and then we use the knowing.'

She delivered the closing line of the lesson—the line about the cost—but she delivered it with the slight tonal distance of a senior officer warning a junior officer about a future risk, rather than a woman currently living inside the risk and barely surviving it.

'The danger,' she said, 'is that the knowing goes both ways. You cannot truly know someone without being changed by the knowing. The instrument is altered by the measurement. The profiler is profiled by the profiling. This is a thing senior operatives have been telling junior operatives for as long as the work has existed.'

She paused.

'Most of them mean it. Some of them mean it more than others.'

She heard herself say it. The sentence had arrived as instruction and landed as confession. She moved on before Markus could hear the difference. She was two and a half years past the threshold the warning was meant to protect her from, and Markus had just filed her, by the small precision of her qualifier, on the right side of it.

The session ended. Markus looked at her one second longer than debriefing protocol required. They put on their jackets. They left the Pimlico flat separately—Markus first, Elena twelve minutes later.

She thought about the report Markus was going to file. The report would say: subject fully professional, no indication of personal compromise. The report would satisfy Moscow. Moscow would pass it onward, by whatever path the network used, until it reached whoever the voice belonged to.

The hope was the operation she was running for herself.

Elena walked home through London. The Akhmatova line on her ribcage was cold against her skin. The tattoo was the oldest document in her possession. She had taken it at seventeen because it was a poem and because the poet had survived.

She walked past the turning for Half Moon Street. She did not take it. Not tonight. Tonight she had just spent four hours learning, with institutional patience, how to administer the kind of death that left no evidence of having been administered. Tomorrow she would see him. Tomorrow she would kiss him. Tomorrow she would continue what she had begun three weeks ago—the campaign already running underneath every dinner, every lamb, every steady hand—and she would add to it, by increments so small the body could not detect them, the slow reduction of the man she loved to a set of symptoms his doctor would attribute to work stress and middle age.

Markus's hand moving toward his jaw and stopping. The stop. The confirmation. The moment when the student-who-was-not-a-student discovered that the teacher had been right about him.

She thought about the marks. Eleven years of marks, on documents from four services, in the same pencil. The hand was older now—she'd read the tremor on the FEUERWERK guidance—and she'd begun, without evidence she could share with anyone, to suspect that the hand wore a ring. She did not know where the suspicion came from. She held the suspicion under observation.

Tonight she had not told it to Markus. His job had been to find evidence that she knew. The evidence she'd given him had been chosen to look like a woman who had heard the warning and managed it—not one who had been broken by it years ago and had been operating ever since on the structural integrity of the breakage. Markus had tested her on the profiling. The manual in her bag had taught her the accidental kill. She had been holding both instruments all along.

She went home. She let herself into the Kensington flat. She did not turn on the lights. She sat at the kitchen table in the dark and she took the small red cloth-bound notebook out of the inner pocket of her handbag and turned to a clean page.

In Russian:

The cost of seeing people clearly is that you can never stop seeing them. They live in you. All of them. Even the ones you destroyed. Especially the ones you destroyed.

She closed the notebook. She replaced it in the inner pocket of the handbag. She did not move from the kitchen table for a long time.

She did not dream. She never dreamed.

But in the dark, behind her closed eyes, she could see them. All of them. Calder and Hatch and Kessler and Margaret and Claire in her butter-yellow blouse and Voss and Doron and Yael and Dina and Markus and Lebedev on the kitchen tile and the boy in the death strip and the man in Lillehammer and Alexei Volkov dying in a Moscow military hospital with the staff in masks and every person she had ever mapped and filed and known and used. They were there. They would always be there. They were the cost.

Nobody told you about the cost.

She turned the page.

19

PHASE THREE

London—August—November 1984

Elena had filed the Phase Two report in June, the week Margaret left. She had sealed it. She had placed it in the dead drop package for Hampstead Heath. Two months later she still had not stood up from what she had filed.

Then she sat in her kitchen in the dark. For longer than an hour. She sat until the street went quiet and then silent and then, in the small hours, produced the sounds that preceded dawn—a milk float, a rubbish lorry, the first bus.

Calder's hands. The shake. The moment when the glass trembled and the wine inside it moved and the surface of the wine reflected the candle flame in a distorted unstable pattern. Distorted. Unstable. Reflected in surfaces he used to trust.

Margaret. The quiet. The letter had told Margaret nothing she didn't know and had taken from her the one thing she'd left: the choice not to know. Elena had removed that choice with a typewriter and an envelope.

She thought about the report she had just filed. The clinical language. Subject's domestic support structure has been eliminated. Nine words. Nine words that described the end of a marriage and the departure of a woman who had loved a man for twelve years and who had finally been cornered into admitting that the love was not enough and that the choice not to know was no longer sustainable.

Domestic support structure. Eliminated.

This was the thing she could not file. Not the actions. She'd filed worse actions. Not the results. Worse results had been filed too. The thing she could not file was the simultaneity. That she loved him and was destroying him at the same time, in the same rooms, with the same hands. That the love and the destruction used the same knowledge. That the most intimate understanding of another person she had ever achieved was being deployed as a weapon against the person she understood.

She took out the notebook.

She opened to the page where, in November 1983, she'd written a single line: the lie that looked like mercy and functioned as permission. She looked at the line for a long time. It was still true. It had been true the night she wrote it and it was true now, nine months later, and the truth had not softened with time the way most truths softened. This truth had hardened. This truth had become a small stone Elena carried in the notebook that she carried in the handbag she carried everywhere, and the stone did not rattle but it was heavy, and the weight was the only thing she still fully trusted about her own interior.

She added a new line beneath the first. In Russian. I removed the FEUERWERK line from the assessment today. The removal was the first sentence of the work I am doing for myself.

She closed the notebook.

She sat in the dark until dawn. The kitchen smelled of plaster dust from the mark on the wall.

In the morning she made coffee. She showered. The water was too hot and she did not adjust it. She dressed in Alice Marsh's clothes. The clothes fit the way they always had. The woman inside them did not. She went to the gallery where Alice Marsh worked. Gerald had acquired a small oil the previous week—a street scene, Antwerp, late nineteenth century, unsigned—and had placed it on the wall beside the reception desk with the satisfaction of a man who had found something at a price his clients would not know to question. He asked Alice what she thought of it. She looked at the painting for the correct number of seconds. She told him the composition was stronger than the handling of the light. He agreed. He said he was pleased with it. She said she was too. She typed two letters on the Remington and answered the telephone three times and drank a cup of tea brought to her at eleven. She performed the life.

That evening, she went to Calder's flat. He was making spaghetti and had forgotten where he kept the salt—Margaret had kept it in the cupboard above the stove; he had, in the months since, moved it twice and now could not remember where he had moved it to. He stood in the middle of the kitchen turning in a small confused circle. Elena did not point at the counter. She went to the cupboard where the salt used to be, as if she had never seen it in any other place, and said 'It's not here.' He said 'No, I moved it.' He found it behind the kettle. He did not ask her how she had known to look in the cupboard first. They ate. He opened wine. They went to bed. She lay beside him and listened to him breathe and she did not count the breaths because counting had become a thing she could not do anymore without thinking about what she was counting down to.

The campaign continued. Phase Three was next.

Chiswick—a Thursday in November 1984.

On a Thursday in November, with Calder at Century House and the Chiswick house empty, Elena let herself in with the key she had duplicated in December. She was not there to plant anything. She was there to retrieve.

The bathroom cabinet on the landing had been cleared. Margaret had been thorough. The shelves were bare except for a bar of soap wrapped in wax paper, a small can of talc, and —wedged behind the razor Calder still kept on the middle shelf—a single strip of foil-backed tablets. Ten pills of thirty remaining. The label read MRS M. CALDER, 14 GROVE PARK ROAD, 5mg, dated April 1983. Margaret had either missed it or left it. Elena could not tell which, and the not-telling was the point at which her hand was already reaching.

She put the strip in her handbag between her lipstick and her notebook. She locked the house behind her. She took the Tube back to Kensington without looking at her bag. She did not look at it while she made tea. She did not look at it while she sat at her kitchen table. She took out her notebook and looked at the pale mark on the wall. The mark had not changed.

She opened the notebook to the next clean page. She wrote four lines. In Russian.

Phase Three. Diazepam at sub-therapeutic dose, introduced through tea at his own kitchen table. Interval: every fourth evening. Duration: until the subject describes his own memory as unreliable.

She read the four lines once. The clinical language performed its institutional function: converting the dosing of the man she loved into a schedule. She thought about the promise she had written into the operative report the week before. She had written the promise as a clinical line in a classified document because that was the only register in which she knew how to make it. That it had been written in that register did not, she understood, make it a promise.

She had no feedback mechanism. She had administered compounds before, in training, to controlled subjects on known baselines; Calder's baseline was not known. She was introducing a variable into a system she could not fully model and watching the system and calling the watching control.

The calling it control was the lie she needed to proceed. She had told herself worse lies. None of them had been quite this precise.

This was the push.

She did not cross out the lines.

She closed the notebook.

She took the strip of pills from her handbag and placed it in the drawer beside the stove. In the spring she had moved the Jaffa key from the suitcase lining to the same drawer. The key and the strip sat together now between the Ronson and the Mercator knife—two objects she had taken from other people's lives and held until she found a use for them. The strip was the residue of the marriage she had ended: a Chiswick doctor's prescription to a woman who had grown geraniums for six years.

Elena composed the report at the kitchen table on a Sunday in November. She wrote in the institution's voice because the institution's voice was, by this point, hers. Subject Calder. Period June through November. Classification restricted, handler eyes only. Campaign within parameters. Domestic isolation complete. Subject functional. Collateral assessment: capacity for recovery moderate. Threshold of irreversible psychological damage not reached. Recommendation: proceed to Phase Three.

She read it before she sealed it. She read it twice. The second time, she read the line about collateral assessment—the line that said Calder's capacity for recovery was moderate and that he had not reached irreversible psychological damage. She'd written this line deliberately, inserting it into the operational report as a clinical observation, because the clinical observation was also a promise she was making to herself: she would not cross the line. She would take him to the edge.

She would not push him over.

The promise was the second lie she told herself that year. Like the first, it was the kind of lie that looked like mercy and functioned as permission.

The system was operational. It never stopped.

In the kitchen, a mark was on the wall where she had thrown a glass in January—the night the letter to Margaret cleared the Paddington postbox and she had understood, standing at her own sink, that the thing was now in the system and could not be recalled. A small pale crater in the plaster, the size of a ten-pence coin. She had not repaired it. She was not going to repair it.

And the distance between Elena and the system had closed to zero.

Or: the distance had always been zero, and Elena had spent fifteen years pretending it was something else.

20

THE GLASS IN THE KITCHEN

London—March 1985

The update arrived through the Hampstead Heath dead drop on a Thursday in March 1985. It was a single line appended to the operational summary for the Calder campaign—the kind of administrative addendum Moscow's filing system produced when a previously reported development required a status change. On the cover sheet, in the upper margin, was the mark. Elena had stopped filing the marks as noticings months ago; the marks were a routine part of her reading now.

The line said: Subject's spouse has filed for divorce. Separation confirmed as permanent. Domestic isolation complete.

Domestic isolation complete. Three words. The institutional language performing its institutional function: converting the end of a marriage into a status update. Twelve years of Margaret Calder's life reduced to a line item in a file in Moscow. The file would never contain that Margaret had grown geraniums in Chiswick, had taught Year Six English, had loved a man with the deliberate trust of a woman who had decided that suspicion was less important than marriage. She had been right about the suspicion. Wrong about the importance.

Elena read the line. She read it once. She placed the decoded message on the kitchen table. She stood up. She walked to the cabinet above the sink. She opened the cabinet. She took out a glass. Plain, clear, ordinary.

Elena held the glass in her right hand. Three seconds. She turned toward the wall.

Her arm did not release.

Four seconds. Five. The arm that had never failed her in any room she had ever entered did not know what to do in this one.

Then it released. A jerky, graceless motion. The glass left her hand at the wrong angle and hit the wall two feet from where she'd been looking.

The glass broke.

The sound was brief—a sharp percussive report followed by fragments scattering across the floor.

Elena stood in the kitchen. The wall had a mark where the glass had hit—a small pale impact point on the cream-colored paint, a divot no larger than a coin. Not the first mark on this wall. The first was eight inches north of this one, from January of the year before: the night she had confirmed the letter was in the postal system. She had not repaired that one. She would not repair this one. The kitchen was holding both of them now. The floor was covered in glass. What remained was the ringing absence that followed a sudden sound in a quiet room.

Elena stood for perhaps ten seconds. She looked at the glass on the floor. She looked at the mark on the wall.

She got the dustpan.

She swept the glass methodically, starting at the perimeter and working inward, the technique everyone learned eventually, either by instruction or by stepping on a missed fragment at 3 AM. The methodology was the machinery and the system did not shut down for a broken glass. The sweeping was precise in the way the throwing had not been. The precision was what held her together.

She emptied the dustpan into the bin and checked the floor for remaining fragments—two, one against the baseboard, one beneath the table. She picked them up with her fingers and placed them in the bin. She wiped the floor with a damp cloth, rinsed it, and returned the dustpan to its hook beside the refrigerator.

The kitchen was clean. The glass was gone. The mark on the wall remained.

She did this. She wrote the letters. She designed the architecture of his collapse and she watched it perform, and the Red Banner Institute would have called it a textbook execution, and the success tasted like ash in the back of her throat, and the ash would not go away.

That evening Elena sat at her kitchen table and took the small red cloth-bound notebook out of the inner pocket of her handbag.

She opened to a fresh page. She picked up her pen. She wrote a single word.

Proportional.

She looked at the word for a long time. *Proportional.* The word was doing more work than a single word should have to do. She drew a line through it. The filing system was where feelings went to die.

Proportional. The word was a lie. It was the institutional language that converted what she felt into something she could file.

But the notebook was not a report. And what she meant, when she wrote *proportional,* was: I destroyed a marriage. And the response years of institutional conditioning allowed me to produce was another glass. Thrown at a wall. Swept up. Disposed of. The kitchen is clean. The marks on the wall remain.

Proportional.

Elena drew a single line through the word. Precise. Controlled. The line was thin and straight and final.

She did not replace the word. The word visible beneath the line. The line visible across the word. Both present. Neither sufficient.

She closed the notebook. She returned it to the inner pocket of the handbag.

She caught her reflection in the bedroom mirror as she passed it. The woman in the mirror was thirty-seven years old and looked it. The face was thinner than the Moscow file photograph. The body underneath the shirt was the body of a woman who had been converting herself into function for nineteen years and whose function was now, for the first time, uncertain of its purpose.

She lowered her shirt. She went to the kitchen. She looked at the marks on the wall. She did not repair them. She would not repair them for the years she had left in this flat. The marks would be there when she packed Alice Marsh's belongings for the last time. One broken glass. One crossed-out word. Two marks on a wall she chose to leave—the accumulated honesty of a woman who had been dishonest about everything else.

Elena did not tell Calder.

She took a half-tablet of Margaret's diazepam from the strip in the drawer beside the stove—Margaret's prescription, left in Chiswick when she moved to Salisbury, retrieved by Elena in November. She crushed it on waxed paper with the back of a teaspoon. She folded the powder into a small envelope and put the envelope in the inside pocket of the handbag she would carry to Chiswick. The dose was 2.5 milligrams. His own prescription had been escalated twice since Hargreaves handed him to a civilian psychiatrist in 1984. Combined with the wine he would drink with dinner, the half-tablet would tip the accumulation into the quality of next-morning fatigue his psychiatrist would file as further evidence of worsening depression. The evidence was the point. She did not know what the accumulation looked like from inside. She had never known. That was the part the notebook entry had not contained.

She washed her hands. She rinsed the teaspoon. She put the teaspoon back in the drawer. The teaspoon was, by her reckoning, the ninth object in the kitchen's domestic surface that had been recruited, that evening, into the operation against the man she loved.

She saw him two days later. Dinner. The flat. The lamb. The routine. He mentioned the divorce. He mentioned it the way he mentioned everything connected to Margaret—with the flat controlled delivery of a man managing information rather than experiencing emotion. The divorce was proceeding. The solicitors were communicating. The house would be sold. The proceeds would be divided. The sentences had the quality of a briefing—structured, sequential, delivered to a listener who required the information for administrative purposes rather than to a partner who was implicated in the event the information described.

Then he said one more thing. 'She told me, when she left, that she hoped I would be kind to whoever it was. She said it in the hallway, with her hand on the door, in the same voice she used to read register at school. She did not raise it.' He looked at the candle. 'That is the only sentence I have not stopped hearing.'

Elena listened. She made the sounds listening required. She

held his hand. The mark on the wall was still fresh and the crossed-out word in her notebook was still drying.

She held his hand. He held hers. They sat at the table with the candle and the wine and the ruins of the lamb and they held hands across the wreckage and neither of them said the thing they were both thinking, which was that the wreckage was the relationship and the relationship was the wreckage and the two had become indistinguishable, the way a fire and the thing it burns become indistinguishable at the moment of greatest heat.

That night, in bed, Calder said something he'd never said before.

'I don't know what's happening to me,' he said.

He said it into the dark. Not to Elena. Not to Alice. Into the dark, the way people spoke when they were not addressing a listener but releasing a statement into the air because the statement had been held inside for too long and the holding had become heavier than the releasing. He was lying on his back. His eyes were open. He was looking at the ceiling.

'I don't know what's happening to me,' he said. 'I can't trust my own memory. Things in the flat are wrong. I'm drinking too much. Halford is asking questions. Margaret is gone. I can't—' He stopped. The stop was not a decision to stop. It was an inability to continue. The sentence had run out of language. The experience it was trying to describe had exceeded the vocabulary available to describe it, and the excess was the space where *Zersetzung* lived—the space between what was happening to a person and what the person could articulate about what was happening to them.

Elena lay beside him in the dark. She listened to the sentence and the stop and the silence that followed it. She lay beside the man she was destroying and she heard him describe the destruction without understanding it and she said nothing.

There was nothing she could say that would not be a lie. There was nothing she could say that would be the truth. The space between the two was the space she lived in, and the space was the width of a kitchen table and the width of a bed and the width of a life.

She put her hand on his chest. She felt his heartbeat. She held it. She did not say: *I know what's happening to you. I am what's happening to you. I am the books and the drawer and the window and the letter and the circular citation and the Berlin failure and the forged assessment and everything else, I am all of it, every piece of the machine that is taking you apart, I am the machine. I am lying next to you with my hand on your chest holding your heartbeat while the machine runs.*

She said: 'You're going to be all right.'

Calder turned toward her. He put his arm around her. He held her the way drowning people held things—not with affection but with necessity, the grip of a man who was losing his hold on the surfaces he had trusted and who had found, in the body beside him, the one surface that still felt solid.

The surface was Elena. The surface was the machine.

She held him. She held him in the dark in the bed in the flat where she had moved his books and opened his drawers and unlatched his windows. Her body knew the route. She held him and she breathed with him and she did not sleep and she did not cry and she did not break anything else.

Calder slept—eventually, the way people slept after releasing sentences they had not meant to release, a shallow unrestful sleep. Elena lay beside him in Chiswick with her hand still on his chest where she had placed it when she lied to him. She did not move the hand. Moving the hand would have been its own kind of departure, and she had not yet decided which kind of departure she was going to perform in the morning.

The light came gradually, in the way early-March light came in Chiswick, filtering through curtains Margaret had chosen in 1979. The bedroom was still furnished with the choices of a marriage that had ended. Calder had not replaced anything. The not-replacing was the same kind of honesty the two marks on her own kitchen wall had become.

At six-twelve she slid her hand out from under his and rose. He did not wake.

The stairs in her bare feet. The second stair from the bottom squeaked; she had learned the squeak in April 1978 and had walked around it ever since. She walked around it now.

The kitchen was cold. Margaret's geraniums were on the windowsill—one pot, the others gone to Salisbury. The remaining geranium was doing what geraniums did: surviving without comment. Elena filled the kettle and set it on the gas. The flame ticked.

Through the open kitchen door, on the hallway table, the ghost rectangle where the ceramic dish had been. The lighter paint. The outline of an absent object. She had noted it in January. It was still there. Calder had not moved anything onto it. The outline was the shape of a thing the flat had adjusted to.

The kettle began its rise. Elena heard, without deciding to hear, the sound it had made in her own Kensington kitchen the afternoon before—the kettle she had turned off at the gas without looking at it when she threw the glass. Two kettles. Two kitchens. One woman listening to them.

She turned this kettle off before it whistled.

At the window with the unpoured water: a neighbor's cat was on the wall, unmoving, its attention on something Elena could not see. She watched the cat for perhaps thirty seconds. The cat did not move. The stillness was instructive.

Her hand, holding the kettle, was steady.

She had expected it to shake. She had been waiting, since she rose from the bed, for the shake to arrive—the physical release the body was supposed to produce after a night of sustained unreleased pressure. The shake had not arrived. The hand was steady. The body was not going to release anything. The body had learned, over nineteen years, not to.

The steadiness was the cost Markus had been sent to measure. It was also, she understood now, the cost she had refused to admit to him. The profiler was profiled by the profiling, and the profiling had produced a hand that did not shake when it should.

She set the kettle on the hob. She did not pour the tea. The tea had been the pretext.

Upstairs, Calder was asleep on his side, facing the window, his breathing the shallow breathing of a man who had released a sentence in the dark and whose body was still processing the release. She watched him for fifteen seconds. She memorized the angle of his shoulder, the place where his hair met his neck, the line of the blue dressing gown hanging from the back of the door. She did the memorizing the way she had done it with Petrov—directly, without flinching. This was the small respect owed to people you had turned into outcomes.

He was not yet an outcome. He was an outcome in progress.

She dressed quietly. She left before he woke. Passing the hallway table, she set her hand on the ghost rectangle for one second. The table was cool under her palm. The absent object was not there. She had not expected it to be. She withdrew her hand.

She let herself out of the Chiswick flat.

She reached her own Kensington flat at half past eight. The kitchen was as she had left it the previous afternoon. The dustpan on its hook beside the refrigerator. The bin holding the glass. The mark on the wall—the new one, coin-sized, two feet from where she had been looking when her arm finally released—exactly where she had left it, eight inches south of the mark from February 1984.

She stood at the kitchen threshold and looked at the two marks together. Two marks. Two releases. Two kitchens—hers and his—in which the wrong thing had failed to happen and the right thing had failed to happen and the interval between them had been a night.

She went to the cabinet above the sink. She took out a glass. Plain, clear, ordinary. She filled it with water from the tap and drank it standing at the sink, looking at the two marks, not looking at the window, not looking at the clock, not looking at anything the kitchen contained that had been chosen.

She finished the water. She set the glass on the draining board. She did not throw it. The not-throwing was the day's first operational decision.

One glass. One word. One line through the word.

Proportional.

21

TWENTY-ONE

London—May 1985

Alice Marsh kept Alice Marsh's hours through April—the gallery on weekdays, shortbread with Helen on Sundays, milk at the corner shop on the way home. The mark on the wall dried into the plaster by the second week. The lie she had told Calder in the dark held. Spring arrived in Kensington. She watched it from the inside.

On a Wednesday in the last week of the month she saw Calder at a distance, coming out of a chemist in Marylebone. He did not see her. She did not cross the street. She stood for perhaps four seconds in the doorway of a stationer's and watched him unfold a prescription receipt and consult it, the way a man checks that what he's received is what he expected. He refolded it. He put it in his inside pocket. He walked on.

The walking was slightly wrong. Not a limp, not slowness—a small hesitancy in the rhythm, the half-second pause between the thought of a step and the step itself, the pause that surfaced in patients whose proprioceptive architecture had begun to consult itself before every motion. She had cataloged the pause in a Koppstraße neighbor, the retired physics teacher whose Tuesday mornings she had timed because the building's schedule had required it. The pause was not Parkinson's in Calder. The pause was the cumulative interior friction of a man whose drawers had been moved and whose books had been re-shelved and whose windows had been unlatched and who had been medicated into the category of man-whose-body-did-not-trust-the-floor.

She walked back to Kensington the long way. The long way was two stops further on the Tube and a quarter-mile of damp pavement. She took it because the long way gave her the seventeen minutes of walking she needed to not do anything with the pause.

She had built the pause. The pause was an output.

She filed the pause.

In the flat, the two marks on the kitchen wall had begun to feel less like writing and more like a set of architectural specifications. Two such marks, eight inches apart. The pattern was predictive.

That afternoon she took the leather case down from the top shelf of the wardrobe. She switched the Nagra on. The tick came at two seconds, slightly worse than the last time. She switched it off and put the case back.

Two weeks later, the telex arrived through Moscow channels.

It was not addressed to Elena. It was a routine industrial-safety bulletin from the Federal Republic, intercepted by Moscow and forwarded in the weekly digest of West German incident reports. Elena read the digest through her Sara Lerner cover—a standing arrangement with the GDR cultural office that gave her a plausible reason to receive paperwork that included, on its third page, information no press card was supposed to obtain.

The bulletin was a single buried paragraph. It described an *anomalous radiological event* at a water treatment facility outside Trier, on the West German side of the Moselle valley, in early May 1985. The language was West German industrial-safety bureaucracy—measured, careful, designed to leak nothing. The event had been classified a *minor unintended release*. The facility had been *temporarily evacuated*. The release had been contained. The cause was *under investigation by the relevant authorities*.

Somewhere in a basement no bulletin would name, a metal sphere had stopped doing what metal spheres were supposed to do.

Elena read the paragraph twice. Then she read it a third time, very slowly, because the third time was the time when the rhythm of the language separated from the content of the language and revealed what it was concealing.

The rhythm was the rhythm of a cover story.

She knew it the way she knew the tells—by pattern, by repetition, by what the language refused to describe in the space where a description should have been.

The paragraph was a Fanano paragraph.

Elena learned the Fanano shape from the Sacco document Hatch had laid in front of her in Geneva. The four pages described a *mining accident* in northern Italy that had killed twelve workers and been attributed to a mercury seam. The cover story was competent but visible to anyone who knew what to look for. *Mercury seam. Routine excavation. Twelve workers.* The shape of a small explosive event buried inside an industrial-accident category that a casual reader would accept and a careful reader would not. Elena had been the careful reader. The recognition was the moment her career pivoted.

The Trier paragraph was the same shape.

A second nuclear demolition munition had fizzled. Not detonated—fizzled. The same signature as Fanano in 1971. A partial release beneath a civilian area, buried in industrial-safety language, investigated by nobody. The investigation was suppressed because the suppression protected the operation, and the protection was a higher institutional priority than the truth.

She took Lebedev's twelve pages out of the suitcase lining. She had not looked at them since Vienna. She turned to page eleven. *TR-85. Moselle valley. Late spring 1985.* He had written it twenty-one months ago, in the neat academic hand of a man nobody had listened to when he spoke out loud. He had been right to the month. She turned to page twelve. The column of codes. FN-71 crossed out in his pencil. TR-85 she crossed out now, in hers. Beneath them, eight more codes with dates in pencil and question marks. FH-87 was the fourth entry. *Scheduled, unconfirmed.* Twenty-one months from tonight. She did not know what FH stood for. She knew only that Lebedev's predictions had started arriving.

Elena placed the digest on the kitchen table. The paper was still warm from the courier's briefcase.

She did the arithmetic. Twenty-three minus Fanano minus Trier. Twenty-one. And they were moving them—knowing the weapons had aged past safe handling, doing it anyway.

The Fanano fizzle had killed twelve people. The Trier fizzle would kill some smaller or larger number that the West German cover story would not disclose and that Elena would never know. The casualties were absorbed by the cover. The cover absorbed the casualties because that was what covers were for.

Children walking home from a school. A man at a kitchen radio. A woman at her sink. Whatever number had been in those buildings on the morning of the fizzle was a number that would not be published. The not-publishing was a service the West German state was performing for the same architecture the Italian state had performed it for in 1971. Twice in fourteen years. Elena was not waiting for a third instance. She was waiting for the first one that did not fizzle.

She thought about the mark on the wall. The distance between throwing a glass in March and reading this paragraph in May was the distance between knowing in your body and knowing on paper. Both were now true.

The ledger in her head adjusted from twenty-three to twenty-one. The ledger was getting heavier, because this weight was the weight of explosive devices currently in the ground in cities where children were going to school.

She took the notebook out of the inner pocket of the handbag. She turned to the page where she'd written *proportional* and crossed it out. She turned the page. She wrote one new line in Russian.

Trier. May 1985. The count is twenty-one. They are willing.

The last two words were the new piece of information. *They are willing.* The network was willing to accept civilian casualties. The distinction between a threat and an intention was now, for the first time, visible.

She closed the notebook. She returned it to the handbag.

She did not throw a glass. The glass had already been thrown. The mark on the wall was still there.

The kitchen was quiet. The London evening came through the window. Outside, the city did what cities did in the long British twilight—held its shape, waited for night, continued without comment on the events being processed inside any particular flat by any particular woman with any particular ledger.

The ledger was twenty-one. The campaign against Calder was running. The notebook had a new line. The mark on the wall had a new context.

The mark was a kind of writing. Elena was the only reader. The reading would continue.

The marks in Europe would continue too. The Trier water plant. Whatever next month's paragraph was going to call by another managed name. The same hand was running both campaigns—the domestic one against Calder in a Kensington flat, and the continental one against whatever civilian category the ADMs were about to graduate into. The methods had converged. She was the seam. She had been the seam since she opened the Geneva folder in 1976 and had been paid for her silence in every currency the institution had left to pay her with.

After Trier, she did not sleep. She lay in the dark. The mark was on the wall and she counted the things that had happened since November 1983—the directive, the sabotage of the FEUERWERK line, the Pimlico session with Markus, the cost she had refused to admit to him, the divorce, the glass, the *proportional*, the line through the *proportional*, the dinner with Calder, I don't know what's happening to me, *you're going to be all right,* the worst lie she had ever told, and now Trier, and now twenty-one, and now *they are willing.*

The list was eighteen months long and getting longer at an accelerating rate. The intervals between entries were compressing the way the intervals between the four cadences had compressed. The ledger was getting heavier. The mark on the wall was the only object in the flat that did not get heavier with time.

ACT V

THE NETWORK REVEALS ITSELF

1985—1987

22

THE DOSING

Vienna—October 1985

Katya was late.

This was unusual. Katya had been Elena's courier—the Nicosia channel, the one that bypassed Yuri—for two years and had never once been late. The precision of her arrivals had become, for Elena, a kind of metronome.

Today the metronome was off. Katya was seven minutes late. Elena sat at a corner table in a Viennese coffee house on Wollzeile and counted the minutes. Patterns deviated for reasons.

The coffee house was two hundred years old. High ceilings, cracked marble, waiters who moved with the unhurried certainty of men who had been carrying trays since the Anschluss. Elena chose it because the acoustics were terrible—every surface hard, every word dissolving into the architecture before it reached anyone worth worrying about.

She was here because Moscow had requested a face-to-face. Not demanded—requested. Moscow demanded routine meetings; Moscow requested the ones that mattered. The request had arrived through Hampstead Heath three weeks ago, encoded in the standard cipher, providing a single sentence Elena had decoded and burned and carried since: *Assessment meeting. Full cooperation required.*

Assessment meeting. The phrase belonged to the KGB's internal review vocabulary—the language used when the institution wanted to evaluate an officer by a human being rather than a file. Elena had never been subject to one. The decision to deploy a human being instead of a file was an escalation.

She drank her coffee. Katya arrived at nine minutes past the hour.

She was younger than Elena expected. Their exchanges for two years had been dead drops and brush contacts; Elena had imagined Katya as middle-aged, solid, the female equivalent of Yuri. The woman who sat down across from her was perhaps twenty-eight. Dark hair cut short. A face that was intelligent rather than pretty—the bones too strong for conventional attractiveness, the eyes set at an angle that gave her a quality of permanent assessment.

She was wearing a coat that was wrong for Vienna—Soviet fabric, Soviet cut.

'Sara,' Katya said—the cover name, signaling that the café was a stage. She had the unconscious authority of a woman accustomed to being attended to. Katya was something with rank.

'You're late,' Elena said, in Sara Lerner's mildly annoyed tone. Katya's coffee was already on the table. She had not touched it.

'The flight was delayed.' Katya smiled—practiced but not false. She opened her bag and placed a thin folder on the table. 'Your assessment.'

Elena did not touch it. Katya had not touched her Melange, and was watching her with an intensity that exceeded the requirements of delivering a folder. She picked up her coffee and drank.

It was the last clear thought she had for approximately six hours.

◆◆◆

Forty minutes later, the room moved.

Not dramatically. Not the cinematic hallucination of a room spinning or walls melting. The room moved the way a room moves when you have been staring at it for too long and the depth perception shifts by a millimeter. Everything was in its place. Everything was also slightly imperceptibly wrong.

Elena recognized it. LSD-25. The compound that had sent Frank Olson through a window. Katya had put it in the coffee.

She could feel the compound in her throat—a faint metallic sweetness beneath the bitterness of the Melange.

The professional assessment arrived first: 100 to 150 micrograms. Peak in two hours. Six to eight hours ahead.

The personal assessment: the institution she'd served for fourteen years had decided to dissolve the perceptual architecture of one of its best operatives without her knowledge or consent. The institution had done to her what the CIA had done to Frank Olson.

The filing system was the only difference.

She did not panic. The training—the thing that had converted her feelings into data for fourteen years—was still running beneath the drug.

Elena performed.

Moscow had dosed her. Moscow was watching her through Katya. Moscow wanted to know whether Elena was still reliable.

Or—the thought arrived in the fourth second—or this was not Moscow at all. Four rhythms had taught her that every Moscow operation that mattered had originated outside Moscow. The dosing was designed to dissolve the architecture she'd built around the things she was not filing, and see what came out.

Elena understood all of this in three seconds. In the fourth she performed the expected breakdown.

Elena knew the expected breakdown. Confusion, distortion, anxiety, panic, loss of environmental confidence, emotional flooding—and in subjects with strong defenses, *fortress behavior,* the mind holding position while the compound assaulted the walls. Elena gave them everything except the fortress.

She widened her eyes. She set down her coffee cup with a deliberateness that communicated motor uncertainty. She looked at her hands the way a person looked at their hands when the hands had felt like they belonged to someone else.

'Something's wrong,' she said. Sara Lerner's voice, trembling. The trembling was calibrated. Enough to communicate distress, not enough to communicate performance.

Katya leaned forward. The concern on her face was professional. The eyes behind the concern were recording.

'What do you mean?'

'The room,' Elena said. She let her gaze drift. The compound was asserting itself, and the millimeter of displacement was now a centimeter, and the centimeter was growing.

Elena let the compound work on the surface while she maintained, beneath the surface, the cold continuous assessment the training had installed in her.

The wonder was the compound's gift. The fear was the performance—what whoever stood behind Moscow expected to see: a woman losing control, a woman whose defenses were being dissolved.

Elena was going to show them a woman. The woman was a

performance. The performance was the last thing the system could do.

Katya moved her to the hotel.

The hotel was on the Kärntner Ring—old, marble-fronted, the kind of establishment where intelligence services preferred to conduct meetings whose nature did not match the declared purpose. Katya had the key. The room was on the fourth floor, already booked. A bed, two chairs, a low table, a window overlooking the Ring. A faded burgundy carpet with a small repair at the seam by the window where someone had matched the threads imperfectly. A lamp on the writing desk with a green glass shade. A coffee service on the low table, untouched.

Katya helped her sit on the edge of the bed. Elena's motor function was decoupling from her motor intent—the lag between the decision to lower the body and the execution of the lowering was widening as the compound climbed.

'How do you feel?' Katya asked. Her voice was quiet. The professional quiet of a handler managing an asset in distress.

'Strange,' Elena said. She said it with Sara Lerner's vulnerability—the openness of a woman who was afraid and who was allowing herself to show the fear because the fear was expected and the showing was the performance and the performance was the last controlled thing she could do while the compound took apart everything else.

'That's normal. It will pass.'

The lie was smooth. The lie was kind. The lie was the same lie Elena told every target she had ever managed: *it will pass. The situation is temporary. You are going to be all right.* The words were designed to produce compliance through reassurance. Elena recognized the architecture because she built it. She built it in Hatch's 2 AM kitchen and in Calder's rearranged bookshelves and in the bed in March beside the man whose marriage she had ended where she'd said the same words into the dark.

Katya had come for something. Whoever stood behind Katya had come for something. The dosing was not random —chemical resources were not wasted on random assessments. The dosing was targeted. Designed to dissolve Elena's professional composure and see what was underneath. What was underneath Alice Marsh and Sara Lerner and all the other names.

Elena gave them what they wanted. She gave them confusion and fear and the gradual staged dissolution of a woman's professional composure under the influence of a compound she did not know the name of. She gave it because Katya expected it, because the literature expected it, because the compound itself was asking for it. The giving was performative, but the performance was costless because the body was already producing the raw material—trembling, a faster heartbeat, a sense that the room had acquired observers. Elena performed at the edge of what the compound was producing, which was the place the trained performance always stood.

Beneath the performance, the system continued. Cold. Continuous. Assessing.

She was thinking about Frank Olson. A man who fell from a window in New York thirty-two years ago because the same institution that employed him decided to dissolve his mind to see what would happen. A window shade pulled down before the glass broke. A man who pulls down the shade before jumping is either performing a final act of modesty or is not the one doing the jumping.

Elena closed her eyes. The compound was peaking.

The peak was a country she'd never visited.

With her eyes closed, the visual field did not go dark. It went somewhere else. Patterns moved the way the death strip sand moved when it was raked: parallel lines, orderly, disrupted by something that crossed them. A footprint. A body. The rope.

The rope was also the mountain sketch over Fanano, and both were the same shape seen from different distances, and the compound was showing her the distances simultaneously.

This was what the drug did. It dissolved the walls between the compartments—each operation from every other operation, each feeling from every other feeling, each identity from every other identity—and the contents flowed into each other. The flowing was the thing Elena had spent fourteen years preventing, because the flowing was the truth.

She opened her eyes. Katya was closer. Katya had moved from the chair to the edge of the bed. Katya's hand was on Elena's forehead—the back of the hand, the way a mother checked a child's temperature, the gesture ancient and involuntary and warm.

'You're all right,' Katya said. 'I'm here.'

The warmth entered her through the skin of her forehead, and the compound took the warmth and amplified it. The amplification was chemical. It was also something else.

It was also the touch of a woman touching another woman's face. And the compound could not tell the difference. And Elena could not tell the difference. And the inability to tell the difference was the most terrifying thing that had happened to her since the death strip, because Elena's survival depended on always knowing the difference. Between the real and the performed. Between the genuine and the operational. Between the person and the officer.

The drug took that away.

◆◆◆

What followed was not an operation. Or it was an operation. Or it was both.

Katya's mouth was on her collarbone. Elena did not know how this had happened. Between the hand on her cheek and the mouth on her collarbone was time, but the time was not linear, and the compound had suspended whatever would have told her how long it had been.

Elena's body responded with a rawness she had not experienced since before the Red Banner Institute—the rawness of a body that had not yet been converted from a site of experience into an instrument of collection. The response was not operational. That was the horror of it and the relief of it and the confusion that would live in her memory for years afterward. Fully. Involuntarily. Without the intermediary of consciousness deciding what the communication meant.

Katya's hands were on her ribcage. On the tattoo. Katya could read Cyrillic. Her fingers traced the letters the way Calder had traced them in the Fitzrovia flat twelve years ago, in the dark, without asking what they said. But Katya could read them, and her lips moved against Elena's skin, shaping Akhmatova's words—the act either intimacy or surveillance, the compound refusing to let her distinguish.

I taught myself to live simply and wisely.

The drug heard the words and did what the drug did to everything—it removed the container and left the contents exposed. The contents were grief. The grief was pre-institutional. It belonged to a girl in Leningrad, not a woman in London. The body was in charge now, and the body did not file.

Elena made a sound. The sound was not performance. The sound was the sound she'd made on Doron's kitchen floor in Tel Aviv five years ago—the sound that had no professional category because it was not operational. The sound came from the place beneath the covers, beneath the training, beneath the fourteen years of learning to convert experience into data. The sound was Elena. Not Alice Marsh. Not Sara Lerner. The girl who had chosen the tattoo at seventeen. The girl who had read Akhmatova under the covers with a penlight. The girl who existed before the machine claimed her and who was, apparently, still in there, still alive.

Katya heard the sound. Elena felt her hear it—felt the quality of the attention change, felt the handler's clinical assessment falter for a fraction of a second, felt the woman beneath the handler surface the way Elena was surfacing beneath the operative.

There was a moment when Elena cried. There was a briefer, more dangerous moment when she said a name—not Alice, not Sara, a name she had not spoken aloud since 1970. The compound had opened a door the training had sealed, and the contents were under pressure and the pressure had nowhere to go except out.

It was the first time Elena had cried since she was nineteen years old.

Katya held her. Katya held her while she cried and the holding was either professional or personal and Elena could not tell and the inability to tell was, she understood even through the compound's dissolution of understanding, the point.

Then the door opened.

Elena would not be able to reconstruct, afterward, the interval between the sound she made and the sound of the door. The compound had erased the connective tissue that linked one moment to the next, the way a fire erased the floorboards but left the joists. There were the joists. There was the door.

Between them was the gap.

The door opened and a man entered the room. Or two men. Or three men. Elena would, in the days that followed, try to count them. She would not succeed. The count was the first thing the compound took and the last thing it returned, and what it returned was not the number but the certain knowledge that there had been more than one.

The man who spoke first spoke in Russian. He was middle-aged. He wore a dark suit. His face was—and here her memory would, even three days later, even two weeks later, even at the end of her life—fail in a way her memory had never failed before. Her memory could give her the suit, the watch (Patek Philippe, silver dial), the cologne (sandalwood), the shoes (English, hand-stitched).

Her memory could not give her the face.

'Get up,' the man said. In Russian. The voice was calm and educated. The voice did not match any service Elena had ever encountered. The Russian was not Moscow's Russian. It was older Russian, the Russian of a generation that had learned the language before the Revolution standardized it—not a reconstruction, not an émigré inflection, but the Russian of an institution that had simply never updated. Not KGB. Not GRU. Something beneath Moscow. Something that had been using Moscow's channels for longer than Moscow had existed. The voice had the cadence—the same cadence—that Elena had been counting for nine and a half years. Geneva, Marylebone, Bograshov, Kensington. This was the fifth instance, and the fifth instance was a voice in a hotel room in Vienna, attached to a man Elena's memory was already failing to retain.

Katya rose from the bed. Her professional surface had returned in the moment between the door opening and the man's instruction. She did not look at Elena. She moved to the chair where her coat was draped and she stood beside it with the posture of an officer awaiting orders.

Elena sat up. The compound made the sitting up a slow event. She sat up at the speed the compound permitted, which was the speed of a body that had recently been elsewhere and was returning by stages to the room.

The man—*the men, possibly two men, possibly three*—moved to the chairs by the low table. They sat. Elena's eyes saw them and failed to retain them. The failure was not the compound. The compound was global—it softened everything. This failure was local. Specific. Something in the room was being unseen on purpose, by an architecture she could feel operating against her vision the way she could feel cold air from a draft she could not locate.

The first man—or the first voice—spoke. In Russian.

'Tell us about Calder.'

Elena's training said: *do not answer.* The compound said: answer. The compound was louder. The compound had dissolved the wall between the question and the answer, and the answer was already moving up through her body toward her mouth before she'd decided whether to permit it.

She told them about Calder. She told them in fragments. She told them about the directive of November 1983, which they already knew. She told them about the campaign, which they already knew. She told them—and this they did not already know—that she had been modifying the directives. That she had been sabotaging her own operation from inside. That she had removed one sentence from an assessment, and had let Calder see a file she was supposed to have burned, and had failed to observe him at three moments she could have observed him and should have.

The voice—the second voice now, in German, accented in a way Elena could not place—said: *Gut. Und Hatch?*

She told them about Hatch. About the four pages in Geneva in March 1976. About the rhythm of the prose that had not been Hatch's. About the moment she'd recognized that the document had originated somewhere outside Hatch, outside Sacco, outside any service she could name. She told them she'd filed the recognition for nine and a half years and had counted the cadences and arrived, in November 1983, at the formal recognition that the cadences were the same voice and that the voice was not a Moscow voice and that the voice belonged to whoever was asking her this question now.

The third voice—in English, with the accent of a man who had learned English from other educated men whose first language was something else entirely—said: 'And the Italian fragments.'

She told them about the Italian inventory fragments. About the six tactical nuclear demolition units in shared custody with a maintenance contact left undefined. About the Fanano page in her notebook and the mountain sketch with the three peaks and the ledger she'd been maintaining since 1976 that had stood at twenty-three for nine years and had dropped to twenty-one in May. She told them about Trier. She told them she'd recognized the cover-story shape and that the recognition had told her the network was actively moving the weapons and was willing to accept civilian casualties to do so.

She told them all of this because the compound had dissolved the wall between *what she knew* and *what she said,* and she couldn't stop the saying without an act of will the compound had also dissolved.

There was a silence after she finished. They weighed what she had said against whatever they had brought to the room as the assessment criteria. Elena lay on the bed in the half-undone state Katya had left her in and waited for whatever came next. The compound was peaking now in a different way than it had peaked with Katya. The peak was not perceptual. The peak was the recognition that she had just told the network everything she knew and that the telling had been involuntary and that the involuntary had been the point of the dosing.

The first voice spoke again. In Russian. The voice was even and unhurried.

The instrument that knows it is an instrument, the voice said, *is more valuable than the instrument that does not. We have known about your investigation for some time. We have not corrected for it because the correction would have required removing you, and you are difficult to replace. The investigation is permitted to continue. The continuation has uses. We will tell you what the uses are when we are ready to tell you.*

Elena listened. The compound made the listening into a kind of physical experience—the sentences arrived at her body as much as at her ear, and her body received them the way a body received warmth, with no defense and no commentary.

You will not remember this conversation in detail, the voice said. *You will remember that we spoke. You will not remember our faces. We have been speaking to operatives like you for thirty years and the operatives never remember the faces. This is not pharmacological. This is structural. The structure exists for reasons you will not be told and that would not change your operational behavior if you were told.*

Continue your campaign against Calder, the voice said. *Complete it within parameters. Continue your withholdings from Moscow. We approve the withholdings. The withholdings have value to us in ways the institution has not assessed and would not assess correctly if it tried.*

We will not contact you again, the voice said, *until we have something we need from you that the standard channels cannot provide.*

A pause. Then, softer:

The orchid in the photograph in the drawer beside the stove in your Kensington flat is a particularly good print. Tell Kessler when you next see him. He will be pleased.

The compound, which had been processing the voice as physical sensation, paused and produced a single clear flash of cold sober terror. The terror lasted approximately one second. It was the terror of a woman who had just been informed that the private archive she had been maintaining for twelve years—the notebook, the drawer beside the stove, the operational recognitions she had filed where no institution could reach them—was not private. The voice had been reading her private archive for some time. The voice was informing her of the reading now because the informing was itself the operation.

The men rose. Or the man rose. The room contained their motion and her memory failed to record it. They moved to the door. The door opened. The door closed. They were gone.

Or they had not been there. Or they'd been one. Or they'd been the room itself, briefly arranging itself into the shape of human figures to ask her questions, and then disarranging itself back into a room when the questions were done.

Elena lay on the bed. Katya was gone—Katya had left when they did, or before they came, or when they were already in the room, or had never been in the room at all. The bed was unmade. The compound was beginning its slow descent. The light in the green-shaded lamp was the only light in the room.

In the descent, when she could focus her eyes, she saw the one thing her memory would keep.

It was on the low table. Beside the coffee service. A small object the man—*one of the men, the speaker, the voice that was not Yuri's and not Hatch's and not anyone she could name*—had placed on the table during the conversation and had not retrieved when he left. Or it had been there the whole time. Or it had appeared only because the compound had decided, in the descent, that one detail needed to be visible, and this was the detail.

A signet ring. Small. Gold. Old gold, the kind that had been worn by the same finger or the same family of fingers for decades. The device on the face of the ring had been worn smooth by what looked like a century of handshakes. It was no longer legible as any specific symbol. It was just an oval of slightly raised gold on a ring that had once meant something to the people who knew what it meant and that now signified, to anyone who did not know, only that it had once signified something.

The oval was the wrong shape for any heraldry Elena could place. It was, perhaps, what remained of a circle that had been worn down by something at the center—a point that the centuries of handshakes had pressed back into the gold until only the perimeter remained. The perimeter was almost the perimeter of a compass rose. Almost. Elena did not know whether the almost was the compound's contribution or the truth.

The ring was on the right side of the table, between the cup and the small jug. It was the only object in the room Elena's memory would record from the encounter with the men, and her memory would record it with the comprehensive eidetic precision that her training had developed. She could see, in the descent, the worn place at the inside of the ring where decades of contact with the same finger had polished the gold. She could see the small dent on the rim of the bezel where the ring had been struck against something hard at some point in its long life. She could see the warmth the ring still held from having been on a hand a moment ago.

The ring was on the table. The hand it belonged to was gone.

The hand had never been there—the hand was the absence the architecture inhabited, and the ring was the only piece the design permitted her to retain.

She closed her eyes. When she opened them again, the ring was gone.

Morning.

The light came through the window with the gray-gold quality of Viennese October dawn. Elena was alone in the room. Katya was gone. The bed was made—or remade. The coffee service had been removed from the low table. The repair at the seam in the carpet by the window was where she remembered it. The lamp was where she remembered it.

Elena lay still and let the system rebuild. The compartments came back on slowly, in stages, the way power came back after a blackout. Assessment returned first. She could assess the room again. The marble was marble. The carpet was carpet.

Then she tried to assess what had happened.

The Katya part was clear. The Katya part was a memory she could organize chronologically—the hand on her forehead, the hand on her cheek, the hand on her ribcage, the mouth on her collarbone, the sound, the crying, the holding. The memory was vivid and emotionally complete and she would carry it for the rest of her life, and the question of whether the encounter had been operational or personal or both would never resolve into an answer, because the compound had taken the answer with it when it receded.

The men part was different.

She could see the suit, the watch, the shoes, the cuff where it emerged from the jacket. She could not see the hand inside the cuff, the wrist, the throat, the face. Everything around the man and nothing of the man himself—the negative space around an object removed from a photograph.

She tried for three days afterward. She produced nothing. The absence was not compound damage. Her memory had, in this one specific instance, failed to record what it was supposed to record. The architecture of unseeing had operated against her eidetic recall, and it had won.

She had told them about Calder. About the FEUERWERK line she had removed from the 1984 assessment. About the Italian fragments. About the ledger at twenty-one and the mountain sketch and Trier. About the cadences—the full nine and a half years of private investigation she had never filed with Moscow or Bruhn or anyone. The compound had taken the wall between *what she knew* and *what she said,* and the saying had been total and unrepeatable.

She had not been able to stop it. This was not the same as not having done it.

The question she would carry out of Vienna, unfiled, was not whether she had told them too much. The question was whether they had already known—and whether the private ledger she had been keeping for nine years had been, from their side of the architecture, not a liability they had tolerated but the shape of an asset they had been quietly building.

The one detail her memory kept was the ring.

The small gold signet ring on the right hand's little finger of the man who had been the speaker—the ring she'd seen in the descent on the low table beside the coffee service. The ring she could draw. The ring she could describe down to the worn place on the inside and the small dent on the bezel rim and the warmth of the gold and the precise angle at which it had been set down.

The line she had been keeping between her life and her work was, she now understood, a line only she had been pretending was still there.

She filed the ring in the private ledger under *the one visible thing.* It was not yet clear what the ring meant or why it was the only object her memory would keep. She suspected she would see it again—in some other room, on some other day, when the network produced its representative and her memory failed in the same specific way. She did not know when. She did not know where. She knew the seeing would be the next step in whatever they were preparing for her, and that what came next would be larger than anything before it.

The orchid in the photograph in the drawer beside the stove in your Kensington flat is a particularly good print.

The voice had been in her flat. The voice or its instruments. It knew about the drawer. It knew about the photograph. It was telling her, in the politest possible way, that her private archive was not private, and that the visit had occurred without her detecting it. No further proof of the network's reach was going to be required.

She could see, for the first time, the wall behind the performance. The compound had not destroyed the wall. It had made the wall visible. The wall between herself and her experience, the wall she'd been living behind since the Red Banner Institute, the wall that made everything possible and everything false. She could see it the way you could see a glass wall after someone threw a ball at it. The wall was intact. The impact point was visible, a star-shaped fracture, and the fracture would be there forever, and the light would come through it differently from now on.

She left the bathroom. She sat on the bed. She removed the small red cloth-bound notebook from the inner pocket of her handbag. She opened to a fresh page. She wrote one sentence in Russian.

The difference between us and the Americans is the filing system.

She looked at the sentence. It was the coldest expression of the truth she had arrived at in years of service. The KGB and the CIA used the same compounds on their own operatives. The filing system was the only difference.

She added a second sentence.

There were two of them. Or three. Or one. The ring was on the right hand's little finger. Old gold. The device worn smooth.

She added a third.

They have been in my kitchen.

She added a fourth.

They are willing to come back.

She closed the notebook.

She would carry the notebook for the rest of her operational life. The notebook had begun as the place where she kept the things she could not file. It was now the only place where she kept the things she could not even prove had happened.

She left Vienna that afternoon. A flight to London via Zurich. She sat in the window seat and watched the Alps pass below—white and angular and ancient, mountains that had existed before any intelligence service.

The sound she'd made. Had it been real, or had the compound manufactured it? She could not tell. The inability to tell was a crack in the foundation of everything she had built—the compound's lasting damage, not the perceptual distortion, which had passed, but the question itself.

She thought about the men. About the absence of their faces. About the ring on the low table. About the orchid in the photograph in the drawer in her Kensington kitchen, and the voice that had known about the photograph. Her private archive was not private. The mark on the wall had been observed by another reader, and the reader had let her know.

In her bag, the notebook held four new sentences. In her body, the fracture held the light.

In London, the drawer waited. Calder waited. The campaign waited. The machinery waited.

It always waited. It never stopped.

She opened her eyes. The plane was landing. She put on Alice Marsh's face. She prepared for London. The cover closed around her like a coat in cold weather, familiar and necessary and no longer, after Vienna, entirely sufficient.

She took the train to Kensington. She let herself into her flat. She locked the door.

She opened the drawer beside the stove and removed the orchid photograph. The *Paphiopedilum rothschildianum*. The cool waxy bloom. Kessler's nine years of patience produced as evidence.

She turned the photograph over.

On the back, in the lower right corner, in pencil, was a small mark she had never put there. Three peaks. The middle one tallest. The same shape she had drawn in her notebook in 1976 to remind herself of Fanano.

The voice had been in her kitchen. The voice had wanted her to know that the voice had been there.

The voice had been in her kitchen for years. It had read the notebook. It had watched the drawer fill. It had known which orchid, which photograph, which page. It had been waiting, across years of quiet observation, for the one Vienna hotel room in which the telling could be arranged without being asked for. The arrangement had happened. The informing was the purpose.

Elena replaced the photograph. She closed the drawer. She

made tea and drank it standing at the window, watching the street darken. Operational. Composed. The weapon the institution had built.

She was also still lying on a bed in a hotel room on the Kärntner Ring with the compound in her blood, listening to a voice she could not remember describe a photograph she would find in her own drawer that evening.

Both were true. Both were Elena.

The filing system could not hold both.

23

BRIXTON

London—March 1986

The call came at 14:07 on a Tuesday in March, and Elena knew what it was before she answered because the phone that was ringing was not Alice Marsh's phone.

Alice Marsh's phone was in the kitchen, mounted on the wall beside the fridge, a cream-colored rotary that rang several times a day with the polite domestic trill of an appliance designed for grocery lists and dinner invitations.

The phone that was ringing was in the bedroom, behind the wardrobe, in a space between the wall and the skirting board that was accessible only if you knew which section of skirting was loose and how to lift it. Elena had installed the phone herself in September 1979. She had not used it in six years and six months. The phone was the burn line. The phone was the line that rang only if a safe house had been compromised.

Elena was in the kitchen making tea when she heard it. The sound was muffled by the wardrobe and the wall, reduced to a faint buzzing vibration most people would have attributed to pipes or traffic. Elena was not most people.

She set down the kettle. She walked to the bedroom. She removed the skirting board. She answered the phone.

'Crossword,' said the voice on the line. Male. English accent—west of London, the kind that had been at university and was still carrying it. Not someone she knew. '*Seven across. Twelve letters.*'

'I'm listening,' Elena said.

'The house has visitors coming. Forty-five minutes, possibly less. The front door is being watched. Recommendation is a full spring clean.'

The line went dead.

Elena replaced the phone. She replaced the skirting board. The Brixton safe house. MI5 in forty-five minutes. The front door was under surveillance.

A full spring clean meant: sanitize everything. Leave nothing. Burn what you cannot carry.

Forty-five minutes. Possibly less.

Elena looked at the clock on her bedside table. 14:08. She had until 14:53. Possibly less.

She moved.

Elena left the flat at 14:11. Three minutes to process the call, change her shoes, and collect two items from the hall closet: a canvas bag of tools she'd maintained for exactly this contingency, and a darker heavier coat with deeper pockets and a modified lining.

She walked to South Kensington station at the pace of a woman running a routine errand. Fifteen years of practice was in her muscles.

She boarded the District Line, changed at Victoria, and took the Victoria Line southbound. Eleven minutes. She ran the assessment.

The safe house contained four sets of backstopped emergency identity documents, two partially-used cipher pads for the Hampstead Heath channel, three drawers of correspondence dating back to 1981, a shortwave radio tuned to Moscow's emergency frequency, and the Brixton log: dead drop dates, courier protocols, the bookkeeping of the clandestine network. A prosecution could build a network map from it.

All of it had to burn by 14:53.

She ran the second assessment in parallel. The one she'd been running automatically since Vienna. *Who actually wants this raid to happen?*

MI5 did. But the timing was wrong. MI5 did not arrive at safe houses with forty-five minutes of advance warning conveniently leaking through a phone line that ought to have been beyond their reach. The warning had come from a network that had known MI5 was coming before MI5 had finished deciding to come.

Elena understood this on the Victoria Line between Pimlico and Vauxhall. The network had triggered the raid. They had also warned her through Moscow's own channel. The two actions were two halves of the same operation, and the purpose was not to expose her but to *force her to burn her Moscow infrastructure herself.* To leave her with only the cover identities, the routine channels, and the things she'd built privately, off books, in the inner pocket of her handbag.

The raid was a curation. The network was curating Elena's dependencies. Vienna had established that she belonged to them.

The Tube reached Brixton. Elena got off.

She reached the safe house at 14:27. Twenty-six minutes remaining. Possibly less.

Railton Road was a Brixton terrace still scarred by fire. The 1985 riots had passed through like a weather system and left a quality of wariness that had not dissipated.

The safe house was number 47, ground floor. The landlord—

a retired plumber in Croydon who had never met his tenants —believed the flat was occupied by a quiet man who worked in insurance. Neither of them did.

Elena approached from the south. She walked past the flat without slowing. She scanned the street the way she scanned every street—automatically, comprehensively, cataloging vehicles, pedestrians, sightlines, anomalies. The scan took four seconds.

Two anomalies. A white Ford Transit van parked forty meters from number 47, facing south, the windshield condensation telling her someone had been inside for at least an hour. And a man on the opposite pavement walking a Border Terrier, his pace too slow for a destination and too steady for aimlessness—the pace of a man covering ground at a rate determined by how long he needed the walk to take.

MI5. The van was surveillance; the dog walker was a static observer. Somewhere nearby, probably around the corner on Atlantic Road, was the entry team—four or five officers in plainclothes with a warrant and a locksmith.

Elena did not go to the front door.

She walked to the end of the terrace. She turned left into the service alley that ran behind the row of houses—a narrow unpaved lane used by dustmen and foxes and, on this Tuesday afternoon, by a woman who had mapped it seven years ago, on the day the safe house became operational. The alley was the second exit. Every safe house had a second exit.

The back door of number 47 was accessed through a padlocked wooden gate. A Squire combination lock, four digits, set by Elena, known to no one else. She opened it in three seconds. She crossed the garden. The back door had a Yale and a deadbolt. She carried both keys for seven years on a ring in the lining of the darker coat she was wearing now.

She entered the safe house at 14:31. Twenty-two minutes remaining. Possibly less.

The flat was cold. The March afternoon had entered through the single-glazed windows and settled into the plaster and the floorboards. The kitchen light was the same dishwater gray it had been on the Saturday she wrote the letter to Margaret, two winters ago. The same angle. London winter light did not change. It endured.

Elena did not turn on the lights. The front curtains were drawn, which was standard protocol. The back windows were frosted glass, admitting gray light without permitting observation. The flat was dim. Elena did not need it to be bright.

She set the canvas bag on the kitchen table. She opened it.

Inside: two thermite canisters, military grade, Soviet manufacture. Thermite burned at 2,500 degrees Celsius. It could not be extinguished. In sufficient quantity it could convert a steel filing cabinet into slag that no forensic laboratory could reconstruct.

Elena had two canisters. One for the filing cabinet. One for the document safe in the bedroom closet.

She also had a hammer, a screwdriver, a roll of gaffer tape, a box of matches, and a stopwatch, which she now started.

Twenty minutes. Possibly less.

She worked fast. Not frantically—fast. Frantic was fear. Fast was a plan she'd rehearsed every month for seven years.

The filing cabinet was in the living room. She placed the first thermite canister on top of the papers in the middle drawer, where the heat would direct upward and downward simultaneously.

The document safe was in the bedroom closet behind a false panel Elena had installed herself in 1979. Four screws. She opened the combination and confirmed the contents.

She removed one item from the safe before placing the second canister inside. A photograph—a second print of Kessler's *rothschildianum* that Frau Lentz had sent her in 1978 through a quiet Berlin channel. She kept it at the Brixton flat because she hadn't been able to bring herself to put two prints of the same orchid in the same drawer in Kensington, and she hadn't been able to bring herself to throw either of them away.

She put the photograph in her coat. Her hand had made the decision before her mind authorized it. The hand knew what the thermite was for and the hand knew what the photograph was for and the hand had chosen.

She placed the canister in the safe, closed it, replaced the false panel, replaced the screws.

She checked the flat one final time. The shortwave radio was in the kitchen, on a shelf behind tinned food. She opened the housing and removed the frequency crystal—a quartz element the size of a postage stamp, tuned to Moscow's emergency channel. She put the crystal in her pocket. She left the radio.

She swept the flat with her eyes. No fingerprints. The flat was as clean as it could be.

She looked at the stopwatch. Eleven minutes remaining. She struck the first match.

Thermite ignition was quiet. A match touched a magnesium fuse. The fuse burned fast and bright and white. The thermite did what thermite did—an exothermic reaction at a temperature that exceeded the melting point of structural steel.

The filing cabinet glowed. The seams of the metal began to warp inward where the heat had found them. The papers inside were not burning. They were being consumed at a level beyond burning—seven years of correspondence becoming a fine black residue chemically indistinguishable from any other ash.

Elena watched for four seconds. She confirmed the reaction was proceeding within parameters. The bedroom. The closet. She pulled the false panel. She struck the second match.

The safe's canister ignited. Contained by the steel walls, the heat was concentrated—the identity documents, the cipher pads, the notebook, all of it being erased at the molecular level, reduced to slag that would tell MI5 nothing except that someone had used a military-grade incendiary to destroy something.

Elena could feel the heat through the closet wall. The smell was the chemical tang of aluminum oxide—a smell that did not exist in nature and that Elena associated with the institutional smell of evidence being unmade.

She walked to the kitchen. She picked up the canvas bag. She moved toward the back door.

Then she heard the front door.

Not the knock. MI5 did not knock on the doors of suspected Soviet safe houses. What Elena heard was the sound of a lock being worked—the metallic probing sound of a locksmith's tools engaging with the Yale mechanism, the sonic signature of a professional defeating a residential lock with equipment designed for the purpose. The sound was quiet. It was professional. It was approximately six minutes ahead of schedule.

MI5 was early.

Or—and the thought arrived with the same precision as the

recognition on the Victoria Line—*the network had wanted MI5 to arrive six minutes early.* The network had calibrated the operation so that the MI5 entry would coincide with the active thermite reaction. The calibration was not a coincidence. The warning had been designed not merely to save her but to demonstrate the depth of access the source possessed. Either interpretation served them. Elena could not, in the six seconds available, determine which was the operative one.

Her body responded before her mind completed the assessment. The body moved toward the back door. The body's movement was not flight—it was the trained automatic execution of the exit protocol designed for exactly this contingency.

She was at the back door when the front door opened.

She heard it—the specific sound of a door opening into an environment it was not supposed to open into. The front door opened into the hallway. The hallway was connected to the living room. The living room contained a filing cabinet that was currently burning at 2,500 degrees Celsius. The air that rushed through the newly opened front door met the superheated air of the living room and the meeting produced a deep percussive thump.

The windows blew out.

Not all of them. The living room window—the large single-pane Victorian window that faced the street, the window behind the drawn curtains—blew out. The glass departed the frame in a single sheet, propelled by the overpressure wave from the living room. The sheet broke as it left the window, fragmenting into the street in a pattern that would have been fatal to anyone standing within six meters of the building. There was no one standing within six meters of the building. Brixton in March, at three in the afternoon on a Tuesday, did not produce pedestrian density along a residential street that went nowhere.

Elena felt it as a hot punch in her shoulders—the air shoving her forward into the doorframe, the back door swinging outward with the force of the compression. She caught the frame with her right hand. Her palm registered heat she had not expected from a door at the back of a house whose front was on fire.

The thermite had run its reaction faster than the parameters predicted, or the network's forty-five-minute calibration had had another purpose Elena had not been briefed on. Either explanation was operational. Neither was comforting.

Elena did not look back.

Through the back door. The garden. The gate. The alley. She was walking—not running, because running in an alley behind a row of houses during what was rapidly becoming an observable event was the fastest way to convert a clean exit into an arrest. She was walking at the pace of a resident who had heard a noise and was leaving the area with the sensible unhurried urgency of a person who understood that noises in Brixton were best investigated by someone else.

Behind her, the safe house was burning. The contents, not the building. The filing cabinet was slag. The safe was slag. The seven years of paper and crystal and clandestine bookkeeping that had sustained Elena's operational infrastructure in London were being converted, at 2,500 degrees, into evidence that proved nothing except that someone had been very serious about not being found.

She reached the end of the alley. She turned right onto a residential street whose name she did not know because she'd never needed to know it—she'd mapped the route by landmarks, by turns, by the physical sequence of left-right-left that carried her away from Railton Road and toward the bus stop on Coldharbour Lane.

The 35 bus arrived at 14:49.

Elena boarded it. She showed her Travelcard to the driver. She walked to the upper deck. Emptier. Better sightlines. The upper deck of a London bus was, for reasons she had never fully understood, a space where people did not make eye contact.

She sat in the third row from the front. She placed her canvas bag—now empty of thermite canisters and containing only the hammer, screwdriver, tape, and matches, none of which would attract attention in a random bag search—on the seat beside her.

She picked up a newspaper. Someone had left it on the seat —a copy of the *Daily Telegraph,* folded to the sports section. Elena opened it. She read about cricket.

She did not know the rules of cricket. Fifteen years in England and she had never learned.

She read about a county match between Surrey and Hampshire that had been delayed by rain and had produced, in the two days of play the weather permitted, a result the article described as a resolute draw. *A resolute draw.* A result achieved through the determined principled refusal to produce a result. This was England.

She did not think about the safe house. She did not think about the windows blowing out or the MI5 entry team that had arrived six minutes early. A facial expression on a bus was data, and data was evidence, and evidence was what she had just spent twenty-two minutes destroying.

The bus moved through Brixton.

Her hands were always steady.

Fourteen minutes. Flat to bus. Twenty-two minutes inside the safe house. Thermite lit at minute eighteen. Windows at minute twenty. Alley at minute twenty-one. Bus at minute twenty-two. Newspaper at minute twenty-three. Cricket at minute twenty-four.

The most efficient destruction of evidence Elena had ever conducted, executed for an institution that was not the institution she'd thought she was working for, on the orders of a voice she could not remember the face of. The machinery, as always, did not pause.

She went to her flat first.

She changed her coat. She removed the gloves. She washed her hands—not because they were dirty but because the washing was the ritual, the transition between the operative and the performance, the physical act that separated the woman who had just burned a safe house from the woman who was about to eat dinner with a man she was simultaneously loving and dismantling. She washed her hands and she looked at them and they were clean and the cleanness was, like everything else about Alice Marsh, a surface.

Then she went to the drawer beside the stove.

She opened it. The contents were as she'd left them: the small archive that had been growing in the drawer since October 1973, thirteen years of keeping, none of it filed anywhere but there. She removed the *rothschildianum* photograph. She turned it over. The Fanano pencil sketch was there in the lower right corner—three peaks, the middle one tallest, drawn by a hand that had been in this kitchen and had handled this photograph and had returned it to this drawer in October.

She placed the rescued Brixton photograph beside it on the kitchen table. The two prints of the same flower, taken by two different people during the same brief bloom in the winter of 1977-78, one given to her by Kessler in his back room and one sent to her months later by Frau Lentz through

Bruhn's quiet channel. One flower. Two photographs. One photograph carrying a mark she had not made. The other clean.

She turned the rescued photograph over. The back was unmarked. Frau Lentz had not signed it. A flower without commentary—the photograph she would have taken herself if she'd been Frau Lentz, with the photographer's instinct for the leaf placement and the petal angle and the small adjustment of the focus that brought the burgundy spots into perfect specificity. The two photographs were the same flower seen by two women who had loved it for two different reasons. Elena loved it because it represented Kessler's patience. Frau Lentz had loved it because it was the closest thing to a child the greenhouse had produced in nine years of waiting for the right pollination to take.

Elena placed the rescued photograph in the drawer beside the marked one. Two prints of the same flower. The drawer was the same drawer it had been in 1976, but she now understood the institution had known about its contents for at least four months.

The drawer was no longer private. The drawer had been demonstrated to be reachable. But the demonstration had been left in only one place—on the back of the original photograph, in pencil, in the corner where the network had wanted Elena to find it. The rescued photograph had not been marked. The Brixton flat had been targeted for destruction, not for observation. The two photographs in the same drawer were now the two ends of the network's communication with her: the marked one said *we are here,* and the rescued one said *we have just removed your other infrastructure for you.*

She closed the drawer.

She put on Alice Marsh's camel coat. She left the Kensington flat. She took the Tube to Chiswick.

◆◆◆

She rang the bell. Calder opened the door. He was wearing the striped apron. He was holding a wooden spoon. He looked like a man impersonating domesticity, which he was, in the same way Elena was impersonating normality, and the two impersonations met at the doorstep and recognized each other without acknowledgment, the way two professionals in the same field recognized each other's technique without discussing it.

'Alice,' he said. 'You're early. I'm still cooking.'

'I can help.'

She stepped inside. The hallway smelled like rosemary. The lamb. Margaret's recipe. Calder was still cooking Margaret's lamb, two years after Margaret had watered the geraniums and left. The recipe was a haunting. The lamb was the ghost of a marriage, served on plates Margaret had chosen, eaten at a table Margaret had bought, in a kitchen Margaret had arranged and that Calder had not rearranged because rearranging would have been an acknowledgment that the arrangement had changed.

Elena hung up her coat. She went to the kitchen. She poured herself a glass of wine from the bottle Calder had already opened. She sat at the table. She watched him cook. The watching was both operational and genuine, because everything between them was both at once, and the both was not a contradiction but a condition, the permanent condition of two people who loved each other and spied on each other and who had been doing both for so long that the doing had become indistinguishable from the being.

'How was your day?' he asked.

'Quiet,' she said. 'The gallery was dead. Gerald is threatening to close on Tuesdays.'

'That's a shame.'

'He won't do it. Gerald threatens things the way the Foreign Office issues communiqués. Strongly worded. No follow-through.'

Calder smiled. The smile was genuine. Elena's observation about the Foreign Office was the kind of thing Alice Marsh would say—sharp, slightly irreverent, the humor of a woman who was smarter than her job required and who expressed the surplus intelligence through observations that were accurate enough to be funny and innocuous enough to be safe.

They ate. The lamb was good. The wine was good. The conversation was good in the way their conversations were always good—two intelligent people talking about things that did not matter while the things that did matter sat in the room with them like uninvited guests whose presence both acknowledged and neither named.

At nine o'clock, Calder turned on the television.

The news was the news. The sofa was the sofa. His shoulder against hers was the warmest thing she had felt since Brixton. Elena sat on the sofa with her wine glass and watched without watching.

Then the Brixton item.

The newsreader's voice changed. The modulation was subtle—a shift from the conversational register of domestic news to the slightly heightened register of an event. Behind the newsreader, a photograph appeared: a terraced street, emergency vehicles, the visual vocabulary of a London incident—blue lights, police tape, the uniformed presence of men and women whose job was to stand at the boundary between the event and the public and ensure the boundary was respected.

'—fire at a residential property in Brixton this afternoon,' the newsreader said. 'The Metropolitan Police have confirmed that the fire, which caused significant damage to the ground floor of a house on Railton Road, is being treated as suspicious. One person was treated at the scene for minor injuries. The fire is believed to have been caused by an incendiary device. Police are appealing for witnesses.'

One of the entry team. She had calculated no one would be in the six-meter radius. She had been wrong by approximately three feet.

The photograph changed. A closer shot. The front of number 47. The window was gone—a dark rectangle, the brickwork above it blackened. The interior was visible: charred, gutted. The filing cabinet was a dark shape in the wreckage. No longer a filing cabinet. A form that could not be opened, could not be read, could not be entered into evidence.

Elena watched.

She watched the way she watched everything—with attention, without visible reaction, the observational intake running beneath the social performance of a woman sitting on a sofa with a glass of wine watching the evening news with the mild detached interest of a citizen who lived in a city where things occasionally burned.

'Brixton again,' Calder said. He was in the kitchen doorway, drying a plate with a tea towel. 'Never a dull moment.'

'Incendiary device,' Elena said. She was looking at the screen. 'That sounds dramatic.'

'Could be anything. Brixton's had a rough few years. Could be political. Could be criminal. Could be a gas main and the Met are covering because they don't want to admit the infrastructure's falling apart.'

Elena nodded. She sipped her wine. She did not say any of the things she knew about the fire. She said nothing because the saying would have been a confession and the not-saying was the last operational discipline she had left.

She watched the news. She drank her wine. She sat on a sofa in the house of a man she was destroying, watching a report about a fire she'd started. The wine. The lamb's residual scent. The man in the kitchen doorway with the tea towel. The normality was so complete that Elena felt the vertigo of performance and reality occupying the same space so precisely the space could not tell the difference.

The star-shaped fracture from Vienna. The light coming through it differently now. She could see the performance from both sides simultaneously. She could see herself on the sofa. The woman on the bus reading about cricket. The woman in the safe house striking the match. The woman on the Victoria Line who had understood the raid was the network's. All four of them were her. The filing system could hold them in separate compartments, but the walls were thinner than she'd believed, and the thinness was permanent.

Calder put the plate away. He came into the living room. He sat beside her. He put his arm around her. The gesture was automatic—the muscle memory of a man who sat beside a woman on a sofa and put his arm around her because that was what you did. The gesture was the shape of domestic intimacy.

Elena leaned into him. She felt his warmth. She smelled the rosemary on his hands. She closed her eyes.

On the television, the weather forecast confirmed what everyone already knew: tomorrow would be gray, with a chance of rain. London would be London.

In Brixton, number 47 was cooling. The filing cabinet was slag. The safe was slag. The seven years of paper that had documented Elena's Moscow infrastructure were atoms now

—carbon and iron and trace elements of aluminum oxide, dispersed through the atmosphere of a city that absorbed everything and forgot everything and continued everything without caring what had been consumed.

The two *rothschildianum* photographs were in the drawer in Kensington, twelve miles from where Elena sat with Calder's arm around her. One was marked. The other was not. The drawer held everything now—the small archive of a woman who had been listening.

She was alone now. Moscow was gone—not in the sense that it no longer existed, but in the sense that she no longer belonged to it. Moscow's safe house was ash. Moscow's cipher pads were ash. Moscow's ledger was ash. The infrastructure that had connected her to Moscow Center had been removed in an afternoon, and the removal had been arranged by the network, and they had used Moscow's own emergency channel to warn her so that she would execute the removal herself.

She had no service now. She had only them, an organization that had not asked her to join it and had been operating her for years anyway. The Brixton thermite had narrowed her institutional choices to one. And she had the things in the drawer beside the stove. The two photographs. The knife. The reel. The cards. The diary that did not contain entries. The notebook in her handbag with the four lines from Vienna.

It was not a defeat. It was a narrowing. She had been narrowed into the position the network wanted her in since 1973 when a man she had not yet met had written her name into a FLAMINGO-adjacent file, and the narrowing was now complete. She was inside the architecture that had been arranging her for twelve years. The design was not visible from outside. It was visible only from the place she had been delivered to, and the place was the ashes of a Brixton safe house and a Kensington drawer and a sofa in Chiswick with James Calder's arm around her shoulder.

Calder's arm was warm against her shoulder. The arm did not know what the woman it was holding had done at three in the afternoon. The arm did not know what she would do tomorrow morning at the gallery, or next month at the Pimlico flat, or in the two and a half years that were coming. The arm trusted her. The trust was the warmest thing in the room. The trust was also what she was using to maintain the professional composure the news report required of her. She let herself feel the warmth for the eleven seconds the weather forecast lasted. Then she put it away.

She opened her eyes. She looked at the screen. The weather map showed a cold front approaching from the Atlantic.

'More rain,' she said.

'Always more rain,' Calder said.

They sat together on the sofa. The news ended. A sitcom began. They did not change the channel. They watched something they were not watching, in a house that was not hers, in a life that was not real, on an evening that was, in every way that mattered, the most ordinary evening in the world.

Elena's hands, resting in her lap, were steady.

They were always steady.

And the machine, after today, was no longer Moscow's.

24

THE NUCLEAR FILE

East Berlin—June 1987

Fifteen months after the Brixton fire, the instruction arrived through the Hampstead Heath dead drop in the second week of May. It was three lines long. It told her to travel to West Berlin on a particular Thursday, to cross into East Berlin at Friedrichstraße station on foot at 13:45 using the Alice Marsh documents, to proceed to an antiquarian bookseller's shop on Prenzlauer Allee and to present a specific request for a Rilke first edition. The bookseller would respond, or he would not respond, and the responding or not responding would determine what happened next.

Elena read the instruction once. She decoded the cipher. She burned the sheet over the kitchen sink in Kensington, in the same place she had been burning every piece of paper that needed to not exist since the Brixton fire. She watched the ash go down the drain. She replaced the kettle on the hob and made tea, because Alice Marsh always made tea after a long afternoon.

She thought about the cipher. The cipher had been correct —current, properly keyed, transmitted through the channel that Moscow had been using for fifteen years. The instruction had come through Moscow's apparatus. The instruction had also, she understood with the precision she'd been deploying since November 1983, not originated at Moscow. The rhythm of the instruction's prose was the same cadence she had been counting for eleven years. Geneva, Marylebone, Bograshov, Kensington, Vienna. This was the sixth. The intervals had compressed and then held: twenty months between the most recent and this. The compression had slowed. She did not know what the slowing meant.

Elena knew what the instruction meant. The instruction meant that the network was preparing to look at her again, in the same way it had looked at her in the Vienna hotel room twenty months ago, and that this time the looking would be conducted in sobriety, in East Berlin, and that the briefing officer would be—she suspected, although she could not prove—the same presence she'd encountered in the Kärntner Ring hotel room. Or a different presence performing the same function. The two were operationally indistinguishable. That was the point.

She made the travel arrangements. Nine years of Sara Lerner had made the choreography automatic: airline, editor, hotel, cover assignment. She traveled with one suitcase and the notebook in the inner pocket of her handbag. The orchid photographs stayed in the drawer. They were the things she would come back to.

The instruction had specified Thursday, 13:45, Alice Marsh documents, Prenzlauer Allee. Elena would arrive a day earlier, two hours earlier, on Sara Lerner's transit, at a bookstore she had located herself on Karl-Marx-Allee. The bookseller would still be the bookseller. The signal would still be the signal. The rest of the choreography she would conduct on her own terms. The instruction had come through Moscow's apparatus. The apparatus, she understood now, was where her details went to be sold.

She flew from Heathrow to Tegel on a Monday afternoon. She slept at the Kempinski. She crossed at Friedrichstraße at 11:30 the next morning, on the standard journalist transit document the GDR issued to Western press personnel. The crossing was uneventful. The border guard who stamped her papers was approximately twenty-three years old and was watching a fly on his desk lamp. Elena passed beneath the gaze of an empire that no longer paid attention to its own perimeter.

The smell hit her on the eastern side of the checkpoint. Lignite. The same sweet chemical thickness that had lived in the back of her throat for two years in the mid-seventies, when she'd been twenty-seven and learning Zersetzung from Bruhn in the offices on Normannenstraße. Twelve years later the GDR was still burning the same coal. The smell had not changed. The Unter den Linden was the same gray processional, the trees twelve years larger, the pedestrians twelve years more tired, the flags on the government buildings faded from red to a particular exhausted pink.

Elena walked east through central East Berlin. She crossed the Spree. She reached Karl-Marx-Allee by early afternoon. The bookstore was on the south side, between a stationer's and an Intershop that sold imported Western luxury goods to East German citizens with hard currency. The stationer's window contained pencils. The Intershop's window contained a bottle of Johnnie Walker Red Label and a tin of English Breakfast tea. The bookstore's window contained the collected speeches of Erich Honecker in a uniform binding that suggested institutional procurement rather than retail enthusiasm.

Elena entered the bookstore.

The shop was dim and smelled of glue and old paper and the specific mineral cold of an East German interior in summer that had not been heated since April. A clerk was behind the counter. Two men browsed the politics section. An older woman examined a children's book near the front.

Elena walked to the third shelf. The shelves were arranged by subject, in the order an East German bookstore arranged subjects: politics first, then philosophy, then history, then literature. The third shelf was history. She located the third book from the left. It was a hardcover edition of *Die Geschichte der Arbeiterbewegung in Deutschland,* Volume 7, published by Dietz Verlag in 1968 and showing the fading of a binding that had been on the shelf for nineteen years without ever being read. Elena removed it. She inverted it. She replaced it on the shelf with the spine facing inward.

She moved to the next shelf and pretended to look at a volume of nineteenth-century German poetry. The pretending lasted four minutes. The two men in the back finished looking at the politics section and left. The older woman with the children's book paid for it and left. The clerk did not look up.

At 14:06, the door opened. A man entered. He was perhaps fifty, broad-shouldered, with the heavy rumpled overcoat of a Soviet citizen who had been issued his coat in 1979 and had not yet been issued a new one because the issuing of coats was governed by a schedule that did not concern itself with the conditions of any individual coat. He had a thinning hairline. His face was unremarkable in the way the faces of intelligence officers were often unremarkable—the trained averageness that allowed a man to occupy public space without registering on any observer's memory. He was carrying a briefcase.

He walked directly to Elena.

'You must be the journalist,' he said. In Russian. The voice was warm, slightly tired. A handler's voice. 'I am Mikhail. I am your handler now.'

Handlers did not give their names unless the meeting was significant.

Yuri was gone. She did not ask where. Handlers of thirty

years' standing did not retire into gardening; they were moved into quiet rooms inside Yasenevo and given cold tasks for as long as their memory was useful to the institution that had once trusted them. Elena had not seen Yuri since the re-stitched cuffs. She suspected she would not.

'Mikhail,' Elena said. Sara Lerner's voice. Mildly puzzled, in the manner of a journalist who had been given an unexpected appointment. 'I'm sorry—I think there's been some confusion. I'm here for a piece on—'

'There has been no confusion,' Mikhail said, in Russian, smiling slightly. 'We can speak in Russian. The clerk is one of ours and the rest of the customers are gone. There is a car outside. We have a meeting in twenty minutes. I will explain on the way.'

Elena dropped the cover. The dropping was a small physical relief. She had been Sara Lerner for nine years and the dropping of the cover was a movement her body made with the same gratitude a body made when it took off shoes that were a half-size too small.

'Where are we going?' she said. In Russian.

'Friedrichshain,' Mikhail said. 'To meet a man you have met before. He has asked for you.'

The car was a Lada, dark green, standard Soviet diplomatic transport in East Berlin. Mikhail drove. Elena sat in the passenger seat. She watched East Berlin pass by the window in the gray afternoon light.

'I know who you are meeting,' Mikhail said. He did not look at her. He was watching the road.

'I do not know who he is. I have not met him personally. The orders came through Moscow Center, classified at a level above my normal clearance.

'I am telling you this because you are about to meet a man who exists in a category Moscow Center does not have a name for, and I want you to know that I am not the man, that I do not know the man, and that I am as much of an instrument in the meeting that is about to happen as you are.'

Elena turned her head to look at him. Mikhail was perhaps a year older than Yuri had been when she had last seen him in 1983. The same air of professional resignation, the same careful courtesy. The difference was that Mikhail was telling her, openly, in the front seat of a Lada in Friedrichshain, that he understood his position in the operation he was about to participate in.

'How long have you known?' Elena said.

'That something is operating beyond Moscow's reach? Eleven years. Since a directive came through my office in 1976 about an Italian colonel I was supposed to authorize the funding for and that I had no record of having previously been on our books. I asked the question once and was told to stop asking. I stopped asking. I have been carrying the not-asking for eleven years.'

He kept his eyes on the road. His hands on the wheel were large, the knuckles slightly swollen, the hands of a man who had been driving for forty years.

'I tell you this in the car because I will not be able to tell you in the room and because someone needs to know that I am not your enemy and that the man we are about to meet is not, in any sense Moscow recognizes, your friend.'

Elena filed it. Two operatives. Two suppressed knowledges. The first conversation between them, in a car in Friedrichshain.

'Do you know where the meeting will be?' she said.

'An apartment building. Residential. The basement is the

meeting place. After the briefing, the man you are meeting wants to show you something in the sub-basement. I do not know what it is. I have been instructed not to enter the sub-basement. I have been instructed to wait in the lobby and to bring you back to the bookstore when the showing is complete.'

'And then?'

'And then I will drive you to Friedrichstraße and you will cross back into the West and you will return to London and you will continue the work you have been doing. The instruction includes a phrase I am to relay to you when we arrive. I will relay it then. I do not know what it means and I do not want to know.'

Elena watched East Berlin through the window. They had turned off Karl-Marx-Allee and were moving north into the residential streets of Friedrichshain. The buildings were five-story residential blocks from the 1950s, the kind of socialist housing that always looked, regardless of paint or maintenance, like the buildings in Leningrad where her childhood had happened. She had not been home in twenty-three years. She was not home now.

Mikhail parked the car on Pettenkoferstraße. The building was on the south side. Number 14. Five stories. A pre-war building that had survived the bombing, with a façade re-rendered in the sixties. A woman in her seventies came out as they approached, carrying a small dog on a lead. She nodded to Mikhail without recognizing him. The woman turned right at the corner.

'He is in the basement,' Mikhail said. 'Down the stairs at the back of the lobby. I will wait by the noticeboard.'

Elena entered the building.

The lobby was small and clean in the way East German residential lobbies were clean—mopped floors, polished brass, walls painted in the pale institutional green the GDR had been using for thirty years.

Mikhail stayed by the door. Elena walked through the lobby toward the staircase at the back. As she passed the notice-board mounted on the wall beside the radiator—the standard *Mieterversammlung* announcement board where building meetings were posted and where residents pinned the small notices of communal life—her eyes registered the contents automatically. Three official notices in identical Dietz Verlag typeface, two handwritten cards announcing a lost cat and a children's sewing circle, and, in the lower right corner, pinned with a single rusted thumbtack, a child's drawing.

She paused.

The drawing was on a piece of rough grayish A4 paper—the kind East German schools used. A house with a yellow sun. A tree. Three figures holding hands—a tall one in a triangle dress, a smaller one in trousers, a child between them. The labels were not present, but the figures were unmistakable.

In the lower right corner of the paper, in pencil, in a child's careful handwriting: *Anneliese, 2B.*

Two floors above the weapon. The child had signed her name and her address.

Elena looked at the drawing. A square house. A smiling sun. A family on the lawn. The universal vocabulary of childhood, drawn by a child who lived above a basement Elena was about to enter.

The plutonium beneath her bedroom had a half-life of twenty-four thousand years. The drawing had been pinned to the noticeboard for eight months.

She looked at the drawing for perhaps four seconds. Then she walked to the staircase at the back of the lobby and descended.

The stairs were unlit. Mikhail had said the basement. Elena knew what was there. She knew because of the rhythm and because of Vienna, and the knowing was the only protection she had against what would happen in the room she was about to enter.

She reached the bottom of the stairs. There was a door. She opened it.

The basement was unlit until she stepped into it. Then a fluorescent light came on overhead, activated by a switch she had not touched. The lighting was on a relay; someone had been waiting and had turned the light on at the moment she crossed the threshold.

The room was a basement. *Kellerraum*, in the GDR's residential vocabulary. A small concrete-floored room with white-washed walls and a low ceiling. A folding table had been set up in the middle of the room. Two folding chairs flanked the table. A briefcase sat on the table. Behind the table, in one of the chairs, sat a man.

The man was wearing a dark suit. The suit was English in cut, German in fabric, the kind of suit that had been made by a tailor in some city Elena could not identify and that had been worn by the same man for long enough to acquire the soft shape of a particular body. His tie was dark. His shoes were Church's, polished with the patient attention of a man for whom polished shoes were hygiene rather than vanity. He had entered the lobby through a door she had not seen him use.

The man's face was there.

She was looking at it. The basement was lit. The compound was not in her bloodstream. The conditions of perception were ordinary. She was looking at a man's face from approximately three meters away, in adequate light, with the trained composure of an intelligence officer in her sixteenth year of service whose visual recall had been measured by her instructors at the Red Banner Institute as the highest in her cohort.

Her visual recall was failing.

The failure was specific. She could see the suit, the shirt, the tie, the hands on the folding table, the watch, the cologne in the air. The watch was a Patek Philippe with a silver dial—the same one she had seen on the man's wrist in Vienna twenty months earlier. The cologne was sandalwood. The shoes, when he had crossed the lobby to her, had been English and hand-stitched. The details matched the Vienna details the way the members of a regiment matched: not identical, but issued from the same supply. She could see everything except the face. Her brain was processing the man as a presence rather than as a person, cataloging him as *administrator* and refusing to record the features. The details below the neck were permitted. The face was not.

The features were being not-recorded in real time, while she was looking directly at them. The compound in Vienna had been the cover. The architecture of unseeing was the function itself.

Bruhn had described the principle to her once in Normannenstraße—the systematic averaging of appearance, the trained neutrality by which public figures learned to become invisible in crowds. The Stasi had studied it as a defense. The unit had reversed it and was operating it against her now.

She would write it in the small red cloth-bound notebook that evening.

'Sit down, Elena,' the *administrator* said.

He spoke in Russian. The voice was the same voice from the Vienna hotel room. She knew the voice the way she knew the tells and the directives and every other piece of institutional language that had passed through her professional life and that had originated from the same place. This was the sixth instance. The voice was still speaking to her.

She sat down in the folding chair across from him.

He looked at her—or his face turned toward her, the orientation of the head consistent with looking, the absence of features consistent with the architecture. On the right hand's little finger was a small gold signet ring. Old gold. The device on the face of the ring worn smooth by what looked like a century of handshakes. It was the same ring she had seen in Vienna—or one indistinguishable from it.

The ring belonged to the hand she had been filing since Hamar in 1973—the morning her pen did not hesitate. The hand had arrived in the room.

In the second minute of the briefing, she filed a new and unsettling thought.

The ring may not be his. The ring may be the function's—a livery, identifying the office without identifying the officer. *We are the same thing across encounters, even though we are not the same body.*

Elena looked at the ring. She could not look at the face. She looked at the ring.

The *administrator* opened the briefcase.

He laid three documents on the table.

The first was a single sheet of paper, typewritten in German, with a NATO classification stamp at the top in red ink that had faded to brown. The classification was *Cosmic Top Secret—Special Handling Required.* The date at the bottom was 1962.

'In 1962,' the *administrator* said, 'NATO authorized the placement of twenty-three tactical atomic demolition munitions across European cache sites.

'Yields between one hundred tons and three kilotons each.

'The purpose was to provide a tactical nuclear stay-behind capability in the event of a Warsaw Pact ground invasion of Western Europe.'

He turned the page. The folder was a folder; the page was a page; he turned them both with the unhurried patience of a man for whom the briefing was the thousandth of its kind.

'The weapons were placed by joint teams from the United States, the United Kingdom, France, and West Germany. The placements were selected for plausible deniability and rapid access by special forces units trained in their use.

'You can read the German if you wish.'

A pause. He smiled very slightly.

'The German was the operational language of the placement teams. The teams were most often hosted by the West German Bundeswehr.'

He paused.

Elena's hands were flat on the folding table. The concrete floor was cold through the soles of her shoes. She could feel the building above her—the weight of five stories of residential life pressing down through the structure toward the room she was sitting in.

'The placements were intended to be temporary,' he said. 'They were intended to be removed during the gradual reduction of NATO's tactical nuclear posture in the 1970s. They were not removed.'

He laid the second document beside the first. It was a longer document—six pages, in English, with a different classification stamp. The stamp was NOFORN—UKUS EYES ONLY and the date at the bottom was 1968.

'In 1968,' the *administrator* said, 'the four governments transferred custody to a joint technical unit. The paperwork was destroyed within the year. The unit was never given a name. It existed in the gaps between the four services, drawing members from each, reporting to none. Each government has been told one of the other three has custody. None of them do. The unit operates the weapons.'

The unit was new. The administrators of the unit were not. They had filed paperwork under different names, for different governments, since before 1947. The work was older than any of the names.

He laid the third document on the table. This one was a single page of typed numbers and dates—a manifest. Twenty-three entries. Each entry had a code, a date of placement, and a country identifier. IT. FR. DE. BE. AT. NL. UK. DK.

Elena's eye went to the codes first. FLAMINGO was there. She had watched it drop out of the supply-chain index from her Kensington kitchen the autumn before Berlin and had understood, even then, that the dropping was reclassification rather than decommission. Fourteen years later, in a basement in Friedrichshain, FLAMINGO was still on the manifest. It had never been decommissioned. It had only been hidden from the people who were authorized to know about it, and named to people who were not.

Twenty-three entries. The Geneva document had shown her six—the six in shared custody that the Sacco page had called a maintenance contact undefined. She had been counting the six for eleven years without knowing the six was a fraction. The ledger she had maintained since 1976 was not the whole ledger. It was a partial accounting of a partial disclosure, and the fuller number was three times larger and was laid out in front of her now in typed columns with country codes and dates of placement.

The Italian entries were marked with small handwritten symbols beside them: a cross beside one, a question mark beside another. Elena recognized the cross. The cross was the entry for Fanano, 1971. The fizzle. The first reduction of the count.

'The count of the original twenty-three has been reduced twice,' the *administrator* said. 'The first reduction was in 1971. The cause was a partial release during a routine inspection at the Fanano site in northern Italy. Twelve people died. The cover story attributed the event to a mercury seam encountered during mining operations. The cover story was constructed by the unit. The local Italian authorities accepted it because the alternative was to acknowledge a category of events the Italian state was not prepared to acknowledge.'

He paused. Elena heard the cadence. The same cadence as the Sacco document in Geneva, eleven years ago. The same speaker. The cold arrived at the base of her neck—the small physiological tell twelve years of training had not been able to eliminate. The network had been talking to her since 1976. She had not understood until now.

'The second reduction,' the *administrator* said, 'was in May 1985. A water treatment facility outside Trier on the West German side of the Moselle valley. A second partial release during a routine relocation. The casualty count is restricted. The cover story was an industrial-safety bulletin classifying the incident as an anomalous radiological event. You read the bulletin at the time. You recognized the cover-story shape. You filed the recognition in your private notebook on the night of 9 May 1985. The notation in your notebook reads: *Trier. May 1985. The count is twenty-one. They are willing.*'

Elena's right hand moved a quarter-inch on the table. It was the only movement she made. The movement was involuntary.

The *administrator* had just quoted, verbatim, a line she'd written in the small red cloth-bound notebook in the inner pocket of her handbag. The notebook that no one but her had ever opened. The notebook that lived in the handbag at her feet, six inches from her right shoe, in a basement room in Friedrichshain in June 1987.

The voice that had been in her kitchen had read her notebook. The reading was complete. There was nothing in the notebook the voice did not know.

'You may continue to write in the notebook,' the *administrator* said. The voice was even and unhurried. 'We have no objection. The notebook has analytic value to us. You are an unusually careful observer and the observations you produce when you believe you are producing them privately are of higher quality than the observations you produce in your reports. We have been reading both for some time.'

He moved on.

'The remaining twenty-one weapons,' he said, 'are the leverage. They are distributed across cache sites whose locations are known only to the unit. The weapons are aging. Plutonium degrades. Pits develop hot spots that change the criticality calculations in ways that the original designers did not fully account for. The fizzles in 1971 and 1985 were a direct consequence of pit aging. We anticipate additional fizzles. We have decided that *the rate of additional fizzles is acceptable* in light of the operational uses to which the weapons will be put.'

Elena did not move. She did not speak. The *administrator* waited.

The phrase *the rate of additional fizzles is acceptable* settled into her body the way the warmth of Katya's hand had settled into her body in the Vienna hotel room twenty months ago. It went somewhere her training did not have a category for, and it stayed there, and the staying was the part of the briefing she would carry permanently.

'I want to show you one of the weapons,' the *administrator* said. 'There is a relevant operational reason for the showing, which I will explain afterward. The weapon is one floor below us. The cache site is the building you entered when you came in. The building has been kept active as a cache site since 1964. The unit has rotated the weapon at this site twice in twenty-three years. It is currently a 3-kiloton variant.'

He stood. He walked to a door at the back of the basement that Elena had not noticed because she'd been looking at his face and at his hands and at the documents on the table. The door was painted the same color as the wall. There was no handle. The *administrator* pressed a section of the wall beside the door and the door opened inward, releasing the cooler air of a deeper space below.

'Come,' he said.

The stairs went down twenty steps. The second basement was deeper than any residential building required and had been excavated, Elena understood, at the time of the original placement, for the specific purpose of hosting the cabinet below. The walls were raw concrete with a pale efflorescence of mineral salts where groundwater had, across decades, pushed through the pores of the aggregate. The floor was concrete with a shallow drain at one end. The lighting was fluorescent. The air was cold—deliberately cold, maintained at a temperature designed to keep the plutonium pit within its engineering tolerance.

In the center of the room was a piece of equipment.

It was the size of a small filing cabinet. Painted institutional gray. Stencilled on the side, in German, in the sober technical lettering of GDR municipal infrastructure: *WASSER-AUFBEREITUNGSANLAGE—MOD. 4-B—VEB BERLINER WAS-SERWERKE—INV. 1973-417.* Water treatment unit. Model 4-B. Manufactured by the Berlin water utility. Inventory number from 1973.

Elena had spent eleven years assembling, in her head, a thing she had imagined larger than any room. The room was bigger than the thing.

'It is plumbed,' the *administrator* said. 'The inlet and outlet are connected to dummy pipes that run into the building's actual water system. The unit performs no water treatment. If a building inspector ever opened it—and no building inspector ever has—the inspector would see what looked like a malfunctioning municipal filtration unit and would fill out the paperwork to have it replaced. The replacement order would be intercepted within the unit's own logistics chain and rerouted to a maintenance crew that does not exist. The crew would not arrive. The order would lapse. The unit would continue.'

He walked around the cabinet to its back. He opened a panel Elena had not seen.

Inside the cabinet, where the water treatment mechanism would have been in a real Model 4-B, was a metal sphere approximately the size of a basketball, mounted in a steel cradle, surrounded by a black ceramic shell with cooling vanes and a small electronic control unit attached to one side. There were three cables coming out of the control unit. The cables ran to a small steel box mounted to the inside of the cabinet door. The box had a single keyhole. The keyhole was the kind a small barrel key fit into.

Elena was looking at a 3-kiloton atomic demolition munition in the basement of an apartment building in Friedrichshain. Her mouth had gone dry. The dryness was the body's first honest response to the briefing. The weapon had been in this cabinet since 1964. Twenty-three years. The plutonium pit at its core had a designed shelf life of twenty-five years. After twenty-five, the physics became a question. After thirty, the question became urgent. The Fanano fizzle had not been a transport accident. It had been a weapon reaching the outer edge of its operational life—the pit degrading, the geometry shifting, the line between controlled and uncontrolled narrowing to a tolerance that depended on the network's eighteen-month maintenance cycle and on two-man teams who were the only human beings on earth who knew the weapons existed.

FH-87. The fourth entry on the twelfth page of Lebedev's twelve pages, folded into the notebook she had carried out of his Ottakring kitchen in August 1983 after forty seconds with a piano wire. F—H. Friedrichshain. The code had been waiting four years for its address, and the address was three feet from her. *Scheduled, unconfirmed.* Lebedev had written scheduled because the fizzle was scheduled by metallurgy. The unit was accepting the schedule. The next inspection was four months from tonight. If the pit decided not to wait four months, Friedrichshain would be the next Fanano at three kilotons, and the forty or so people upstairs would be the first paragraph of the cover story that would be written about them by people who had already written it.

The ledger in her head opened. Twelve years of entries arranging themselves, for the first time, around a physical object she could see and touch.

Piazza Fontana: the NATO convoy diverted, the container whose weight did not match its departure weight—the container had been carrying one of these. The magistrate in Palermo who had been three weeks from a warrant when his car exploded: the warrant would have traced a shipping manifest that would have traced a device like this one to a port it should never have reached. The minister outside

Rome whose audit had found numbers that did not match the 1968 baseline—the baseline was twenty-three, and the numbers were fewer, and the fewer was in this cabinet and in cabinets like it.

Hidden beneath apartment buildings across a continent whose governments did not know they were sleeping above the thing their treaties had been written to prevent.

Lebedev's line returned without invitation: *the fear is the product, the bomb is the marketing.* It had arrived in her notebook in 1983 as theory. It was not theory. The product was the silence the network had spent twenty-five years cultivating. The marketing was three feet from her, drawing standby current.

Elena's hands were at her sides. She had not moved them since the *administrator* opened the panel. The concrete floor was cold through her shoes. She could hear, very faintly, a child's footsteps two floors above—running across a hallway, the light rapid percussion of a life being lived above a weapon designed to end forty thousand of them.

Voss's radiation-hardened logic chips. The chips were for the control unit attached to the side of the sphere—the small electronic brain that converted a key-turn into a detonation sequence. The chips degraded. They needed replacing on the same eighteen-month cycle as the plutonium maintenance. Voss had been manufacturing replacements without knowing what he was manufacturing replacements for, and the BND had been receiving his intelligence about the replacements without knowing what the intelligence was intelligence about, and the network had been running both sides of the transaction from behind both services' walls.

The four pages Hatch had shown her in Geneva in March 1976 had described the logistics chain for this kind of maintenance. Not the weapon. The chain. Hatch had been three paragraphs away from describing the object in front of her.

The network had sent Elena to make sure he never wrote the fourth paragraph.

Elena stood in the sub-basement in Friedrichshain and understood what she had been assembling for twelve years. The picture was a basketball-sized sphere in a fake water-treatment cabinet. Thirty feet above it, the residents were cooking dinner and watching television and putting their children to bed.

Twenty-one of these weapons sat in basements across Europe. Above each one, a building full of families. Above each building, a government that did not know it existed as anything other than a residential address. If the maintenance cycle failed, the weapons would not announce themselves by detonating. They would announce themselves by degrading past the point where the fissile material could be contained—a radiological event in a residential neighborhood in a European capital, on the morning news, and no government on earth knew it was there.

She did not move. Her training did not produce a response, because her training had no protocol for this. Nothing had prepared her for standing three feet from a tactical nuclear device while a man whose face her memory was refusing to record explained that the unit was willing to accept additional fizzles.

The *administrator* closed the panel.

'Fanano looked exactly like this,' he said. 'Trier looked exactly like this. The other twenty-one are in identical units, in identical cabinets, in basements like this one in twenty-one buildings whose addresses are stored in a single document in a safe in a building in a city I will not name. The unit visits each cache site once every eighteen months for inspection and pit calibration. The visits are conducted by two-man teams. The teams report through a chain that terminates at a desk that is staffed by a person whose name appears in no service's personnel records. The arrangement has been operating for twenty-five years. It will continue to operate.'

He paused.

'There are people in this building,' Elena said. The voice was Elena's. Not Alice Marsh's. Not Sara Lerner's. Elena's own voice, speaking in Russian, in a basement in Friedrichshain, in a register her training had no category for.

'There are people in this building,' the *administrator* said. 'Forty-three people, currently. Four families with children. Eleven elderly residents. The *Hauswart* and his wife. Two students from the Humboldt who rent the small flat on the third floor.'

Elena's jaw set. Somewhere above them, along a pipe in the wall, water moved—somebody on the second floor running a tap. A woman, perhaps. A kitchen sink. The sound arrived through the concrete the way all sounds arrived in this room, compressed and slightly flat, and it continued for three seconds and stopped.

'The building has been a residential one since the cache was placed in 1964. The placement was deliberate. Residential structures generate ambient population presence, which provides better operational cover than industrial sites. The criteria specified that the weapons be installed in buildings that contained children, because government response to an incident involving children would be slower and more cautious than response to an industrial-site release. We have benefited from the slowness for twenty-three years.'

He looked at her—or his face oriented toward her without becoming a face.

'I am telling you about Anneliese in 2B,' he said, 'because the question you are about to ask, and that you are not going to ask out loud because the asking would compromise your operational composure, is the question of whether the unit understands what it is doing. The answer is yes. The unit understands. The understanding does not change anything. The arrangement is necessary. Anneliese's drawing is on the noticeboard upstairs. You looked at it on your way in.'

Elena had not told him she'd looked at the drawing.

He had known she looked at the drawing. That was the most precise demonstration of the network's reach Elena had ever encountered. The *administrator* had been watching her on the stairs. Or the building had. Or the woman with the dog. The same mechanism that prevented her from registering his face. The mechanism observed. The mechanism remained unobserved.

'Take the drawing when you leave,' the *administrator* said. 'I have been told by the people who told me to give you this briefing that the taking is permitted and that the drawing's removal will not be replaced. It will simply be missing from the noticeboard. The *Hauswart* will assume the wind took it.'

He turned and walked back toward the stairs.

Elena followed him. The 3-kiloton weapon in the cabinet stayed where it was. The cooling vanes continued to dissipate heat. The firing circuit continued to draw its small standby current. The basketball-sized sphere of plutonium-239 continued to be what it had been since 1962. Elena climbed the stairs out of the second basement and into the first, where the table and the documents and the briefcase still waited, the briefcase open on the table the way the *administrator* had left it.

He sat back down. He gestured for her to sit. She sat.

Then he said:

'The instrument that knows it is an instrument is more valuable than the instrument that does not.'

Elena had heard the line before. In a Vienna hotel room,

twenty months earlier, while a hundred and fifty micrograms of LSD were dissolving the wall between her observation and her experience. She filed it then as language she could not verify because she could not remember the speaker.

The speaker was speaking now. In sobriety. In a basement in Friedrichshain. The line was the same line, and the function that had wanted her to hear it again wanted her to understand what she had not understood the first time.

The line was not a compliment. The line was an assignment. She was about to be deployed.

'Continue the Calder campaign,' the *administrator* said. 'His investigation is now within twelve to eighteen months of producing a piece of analysis that, if it reached MI6's formal product stream, would identify the unit and the cache sites. You have been managing the dismantlement competently. We want you to complete it. The completion matters to a larger settlement I will not describe. Your continued presence is the operational fact we are protecting.'

He paused.

'One more thing,' he said. 'What the Stasi called Zersetzung, the Americans called COINTELPRO. Same architecture. Different filing system. Bruhn understood this. He died in 1983.'

Elena had not known Bruhn had died. She had not heard. The Frau Lentz channel had stopped delivering small communications about Berlin people in the autumn of 1983, and Elena had assumed at the time that the channel had been compromised and that the silence was protective. She now understood that the channel had stopped because there had been no one on the Berlin end who was permitted to send. Bruhn had been kept inside an institutional silence that had outlasted him. Bruhn had died in the silence and Elena had not been told. He had taught her the silence himself.

She did not allow her face to register the new fact. She would think about Bruhn later, on the train back to West Berlin, in the small private room of her interior where she kept the people the machinery had taken. Irina had occupied the room for seventeen years. Bruhn would take the chair beside her without disturbing the arrangement. There had always been another chair.

'Complete the Calder campaign,' the *administrator* said. 'We will contact you again in approximately fourteen months, by the same channels. Mikhail will continue to be your handler of record. He will not be present at the next meeting. The next meeting will be with someone else. The someone else will, like me, be unmemorable to you. The ring will be the same ring or a ring indistinguishable from it. You will know when you are in the room with us by the ring.'

He closed the briefcase.

The briefing was over.

She climbed the stairs back to the lobby. Mikhail was beside the noticeboard, looking at the postboxes with the affected interest of a man waiting for a meeting he was not supposed to be in to end.

Elena passed him. She walked to the noticeboard. She removed the thumbtack holding Anneliese's drawing. She removed the drawing. She folded it once, in half, the way you folded a piece of paper you intended to put in a coat pocket. She put it in the inside pocket of her coat. The pocket was empty. The notebook she usually kept there was in the handbag at her feet. The drawing fit the coat pocket with the soft light precision of paper finding a place that had been waiting for it.

She walked toward the door. They left the building and got

into the Lada. Mikhail drove away from Pettenkoferstraße without looking at her.

'He gave me a phrase,' Mikhail said, after they'd been driving for two minutes. 'He told me to relay it to you when we were alone. The phrase is: *Kessler asked us to thank you for keeping the photograph.*'

Elena's breath did not catch. She'd become very good, in the months since Vienna, at not letting her breath catch when the network produced these small intimate pieces of demonstration. She knew what the phrase meant. She'd known the moment Mikhail spoke it. The phrase meant: *Kessler is alive. Kessler knows we are talking to you. Kessler knows you have the photograph in the drawer. Kessler is part of this. Kessler may have always been part of this.*

The orchid grower in the greenhouse in the death strip in 1976. The man who had taught her that the growing was the relationship. The man whose patience she'd carried for nine years as the small private warmth her professional life could not justify keeping.

Either Kessler had been the network's eye on her since 1976, or Kessler had been a real orchid grower who knew nothing about it and they were using his name to demonstrate that they could. Elena could not determine which. The inability was the day's third operational fact, after the warhead and the architecture of unseeing in sobriety.

Mikhail drove for another minute in silence. Then he said:

'I have a question I am going to ask you and that I would like you to answer if you can, and that I will not write down, and that nothing about the answer will appear in any report I file. The question is for me. I have been waiting eleven years to be permitted to ask it.'

'Ask it,' Elena said.

'What is the difference,' Mikhail said, 'between us and the Americans?'

Elena thought about it. The thinking was brief. The answer had been in her notebook for two years, in Russian, written in October 1985 on the morning after the Vienna dosing. The answer was:

'The filing system,' she said.

Mikhail smiled. The smile was a small precise expression of grief—a man hearing a thing he had been waiting to hear and that, hearing it, did not relieve him in the way he had expected.

'Yes,' he said. He put the car in gear. 'We lose.'

He did not elaborate. He did not need to. The losing was not the Cold War. The losing was older than the Cold War and was going to outlive it, and Mikhail, who had been a KGB officer for twenty-two years, was the only man in the car who understood which institution had actually won.

He drove her the rest of the way to the bookstore. At the bookstore he stopped and said: 'I will not see you again. I will continue to be your handler on paper. The paper handlers and the operating handlers have not been the same people for some time.'

She got out of the car. She walked to Friedrichstraße. She crossed back into the West.

West Berlin—that evening.

That evening she sat in her room at the Kempinski with the small red cloth-bound notebook open on the bed and Anneliese's drawing of the house with the yellow sun pinned to the wall above the writing desk.

Anneliese was the people the instruments were used against.

Anneliese was the lobby and the *Hauswart* and the small dog and the woman in her seventies who had walked past Mikhail without recognizing him. Anneliese was the building. Anneliese was the cache site. Anneliese was the *operationally acceptable rate of additional fizzles.*

Elena turned to the small red cloth-bound notebook. She opened to a clean page. She wrote one sentence in Russian.

The Wall is not a border. It is a blast radius.

She added a second sentence beneath the first.

The administrator was the same voice. The face was unrecorded again. The architecture worked in sobriety. The ring was on the right hand's little finger. The ring is the uniform. The uniform is worn by no one in particular.

She added a third.

Forty-three people. Four families with children. Anneliese, 2B.

She closed the notebook. She put it back in the inner pocket of her handbag.

She unpinned Anneliese's drawing from the wall above the desk. She held it for a moment. She thought about the child who had drawn it and the apartment the child lived in and the basement beneath the apartment and the cabinet labeled *Wasseraufbereitungsanlage* and the basketball-sized sphere of plutonium-239 dissipating its small continuous heat through cooling vanes the unit had installed in 1962 and continued to maintain because the maintenance was the leverage.

She folded the drawing and placed it beside the notebook. Both would travel to London in the morning, into the kitchen drawer beside the stove—the drawer that was becoming the only physical archive of her actual professional life. Moscow's archive was ash in a Brixton garden. The network's archive was held in rooms whose doors she could not find. Her own archive was a kitchen drawer and a notebook and a thirty-by-twenty centimeter piece of East German school paper with a child's drawing of a house with a yellow sun.

She lay down on the bed in her clothes. She did not get under the covers. She looked at the ceiling of the Kempinski room and thought about where the chain of command above her terminated.

The chain terminated in a hotel room whose location she did not know, occupied by a presence with a face her memory was not permitted to record, wearing a ring that was a uniform, speaking in a cadence she had been counting for eleven years—the casual authority of a function that had been operating across four major intelligence services for twenty-five years without ever being put on a piece of paper any service was prepared to read.

She was not sure she was still working for anyone she could name. She had not been sure since the Brixton thermite in March of last year. The not-sure was now, after Friedrichshain, the only operational fact about her institutional position that she could verify.

Outside the window, West Berlin produced the ambient sound of a Western European city at night—the small constant traffic, the distant tram, the murmur of a bar two streets away. A normal evening in a normal city in a normal year.

In Pettenkoferstraße, four kilometers east, in a sub-basement Anneliese's family had no idea existed, the cooling vanes of a 3-kiloton atomic demolition munition continued to dissipate the small continuous heat of an aging plutonium pit. The dissipation was monitored by a control unit drawing electricity from a meter that did not appear on any building service register. The monitoring would continue for eighteen months, until the next two-man inspection team arrived and filed whatever report it filed. The report would go to a desk staffed by a person whose name appeared in no service's personnel records, and the archive would grow by one page in a building in a city the *administrator* had not named.

The machinery would continue.

But Elena was carrying a child's drawing in the inside pocket of her coat now, and the drawing was the first physical object she had ever taken out of the network's territory, and she did not yet know what she would do with it or what it would do to her, but she knew the carrying was the beginning of something and that the something was the only thing she still belonged to.

Elena closed her eyes. She did not sleep.

She rarely did, anymore.

ACT VI

THE END BEGINS

1989—1990

25

9 NOVEMBER 1989

London—9 November 1989

The television had been on since half past nine.

Alice Marsh had stopped watching television in the evenings years ago. Alice Marsh read—novels from the shelves in the second bedroom, art books from the small library upstairs at the gallery, the quiet unobjectionable reading of a single woman of forty-one who had chosen the gallery life over the obvious alternatives and who no longer had to justify the choice to anyone. Alice Marsh was reading a novel in the chair by the window with a cup of tea at her elbow when a phone rang in the flat below and a voice shouted something a woman ought to shout once in her life. The shout came through the floor. Elena turned the television on.

She had not acted on what she had seen in Friedrichshain.

Two and a half years. Nine hundred mornings. The coat with Anneliese's drawing in the inside pocket had gone out the door each morning and come home each evening to the hook in the Kensington hallway. The drawing had traveled with the coat. The drawing had said nothing, because drawings did not speak. Elena had said nothing, because she had been trained not to.

She had filed the regular reports. She had photographed the regular documents. She had serviced the Hampstead Heath drop on the seventeenth of every month. Moscow had continued to believe she was Moscow's. The network had continued to pay her. The drawer beside the stove had grown, and the notebook in her handbag had grown, and the not-doing had grown alongside them—the largest of the three, and the one with no object to contain it.

Elena had told herself she was waiting.

Now the waiting was ending.

Tonight the television was on. The radio was off. Elena sat at the kitchen table with a cup of tea going cold in her hand and watched the images that BBC1 was transmitting out of West Germany with the particular stillness of a woman who had been watching one version of the world for sixteen years and was now watching it end.

A young woman was standing on top of the Berlin Wall.

The woman was perhaps twenty-two. She was wearing a dark coat and a red scarf and she was standing with her arms raised above her head in the posture that human bodies produced when they were celebrating or surrendering or signaling the arrival of something. In her right hand, she was holding a bottle of champagne. The champagne was uncorked. Foam was running down the side of the bottle and across her wrist.

Behind her, more people were climbing onto the Wall from both sides—from the East, where they were being helped up by hands extended from the top; from the West, where they'd been waiting. They had decided, collectively and within the last two hours, that the Wall was no longer the object it had been since August 1961.

The young woman with the red scarf threw her head back and shouted something. The BBC microphones did not pick up the shout. The shout was absorbed into the general ambient roar of the crowd that was now occupying the space in front of the Brandenburg Gate and that was, if the BBC's estimates were to be trusted, approximately a hundred thousand people strong and growing.

Elena watched the shout. Her throat closed around something she did not have a name for.

She watched the shout the way she watched everything—with the forensic attention she'd learned at the Red Banner Institute and with the second, deeper attention she'd learned at a folding table in a sub-basement in Friedrichshain. The second attention did not respond to political geography. It responded to architecture. The architecture that had been sleeping inside European governments was waking up, and the waking was a problem its makers had been preparing for. Tonight was the problem. Tonight was the day the alibi expired.

Elena had made such a sound once. On Doron's kitchen floor in Tel Aviv in June 1980. Again, five years later, on a hotel bed in the Kärntner Ring in Vienna, under a compound that had dissolved the wall between the sound and the self. Twice in sixteen years. The young woman on the Berlin Wall on the television screen was making the sound now, into a crowd of a hundred thousand strangers, with the uninhibited public fullness of a woman who did not yet understand that the sound was not supposed to be made and who was therefore making it freely.

Elena envied her for it. The envy sat in her chest like a held breath. It was clean and did not belong to any operational category.

The Wall had been over for about ninety minutes.

Elena had been watching for ninety minutes and she had not moved from the kitchen table, and the tea in the cup had gone cold and the tea was still in the cup and the cup was still in her hand, and the hand was still.

Her hands were always still.

This was what the machine had built. And now the thing it had been built to outlive was ending on a television screen in her kitchen, and Elena's body did not know what to do with the information, because the body had been trained to hold the position and the position was dissolving in front of her and no one had sent the order to stand down.

The dead drop had been dark for three weeks.

Elena had serviced the Hampstead Heath drop on 17 October and had found nothing—no message, no cipher, no acknowledgment, none of the routine confirmations Moscow Center had been sending through the drop for sixteen years with the steady institutional rhythm of a bureaucracy that filed everything. She serviced it again on 24 October. Empty. 31 October. Empty. 7 November, two days ago. Empty.

Four consecutive empty drops. Four weeks of Moscow silence. This was unusual. Moscow had gone briefly silent before—the Brezhnev funeral in 1982, a cipher compromise in 1984—but four weeks of unexplained silence had happened only once in her career, during the November 1983 transition from Yuri to Markus. She had not seen Yuri since.

Moscow was not in a normal transition tonight. Moscow was watching the Wall fall. Moscow was watching, from a building in Yasenevo that had been built to outlive the state it served, the collapse of the reason it existed. The KGB's First Chief Directorate had been organized for decades around the proposition that the Warsaw Pact states were the forward perimeter of Soviet security. Tonight the proposition had been voided by two words. *Ab sofort*. Immediately. A phrase Günter Schabowski had not been authorized to use—the load-bearing word in the collapse of a political object that had been constructed over forty years.

Moscow was not answering Elena's drop because Moscow was, at this moment, no longer Moscow. Not in the sense of having been dissolved, but in the sense of having had the institutional foundation pulled out from under it without warning, and the pulling had produced a state of suspended function during which the normal operational tasks of a long-term illegal in London were not being processed because the part of Moscow that had been processing them had not yet been told what its new job was.

Or—Elena considered the alternative—*the channel had been cleanly compromised.* MI5 had found the Hampstead Heath drop. MI5 was watching the drop. MI5 was waiting for Elena to service it one more time, and the one more time would be the arrest. This had always been a possibility in the operational life of an illegal and Elena had prepared for it at the level of abstract contingency planning. She had not considered it an active possibility until the third empty drop, when the pattern had become statistically meaningful.

Or—the third possibility, arriving with increasing clarity—*the machine was stopping.* Not because it had been caught. Because the service it had been built to serve was evaporating, and the evaporation was happening faster than the service could generate new orders. The machine had been built on the assumption that orders would always arrive.

Three possibilities. She had been running them against each other for three weeks.

Tonight she understood, in the way she had been understanding since November 1983, that all three possibilities were simultaneously true. The channel had been compromised. The service was rebuilding. And the silence was the network's—because the Wall coming down was precisely the moment the network had been arranging for across three decades, and the dropping of her dead drop was the network's signal that the next phase of operations would not require her signal of readiness to begin. The phase had begun without her. She was no longer a sender. She was a recipient.

Moscow was not going to answer the drop. Not next week. Not the week after. The drop was going to stay dark and the darkness was going to become, over the next eighteen to twenty-four months, the permanent condition of the channel.

Elena was being released.

The release was not being conducted by a decision. The release was being conducted by the institution's quiet failure to continue. There would be no notification. There would be no severance. There would be no handler who sat down across from her in a Pimlico safe flat to tell her that her services were no longer required. There would be only the continuous absence of the instructions that had structured her professional life for sixteen years, and the absence would, by the ordinary operation of institutional entropy, become the new structure.

For the first time in her adult life, she did not have handlers. She was a serving illegal whose service had ended without notice and whose handlers had stopped answering and who was, tonight, watching a young woman celebrate on a wall that had been the architecture of her career. Elena considered, briefly, whether this was the thing she had been waiting for since November 1983. It was not. That thing had not yet arrived.

She stood up to refill the kettle. She was halfway to the hob before she understood that she did not know which of them had stood, or which of them was going to pour. Alice Marsh's routine had been the cover for Elena for sixteen years. Tonight the cover and the person were, for a moment, indistinguishable in a new way. She sat back down without filling the kettle.

She drank the cold tea. It tasted like tea that had been left too long.

She thought about the warheads.

She did the arithmetic in her head, slowly, the way she'd done it in May 1985 at the kitchen table in Kensington when she'd read the Trier bulletin and dropped the count from twenty-three to twenty-one.

Twenty-one atomic demolition munitions. Distributed across cache sites in buildings chosen for their residential population density and for the presence of children. Operated by a technical unit that crossed the membership of all four major services and that reported to none. Maintained by two-man inspection teams on eighteen-month rotations. The unit's continued function was not affected by the dissolution of the state the Wall had been defending, because the unit had never belonged to the state. The unit had belonged to the network, and they were something else.

The fall of the Wall tonight did not reduce the count. It did not relocate the warheads. It did not change the condition of the plutonium pits, which were continuing to age at the rate of plutonium pits.

What the fall of the Wall did change was the network's deniability. Before tonight, there had been services to hide behind. After tonight, the services themselves would be under investigation. They would need to move their assets before the archives were opened. The arrangement had been designed for exactly this contingency.

The warheads were about to become fully deniable.

The GDR had been the network's thickest layer of institutional cover. After tonight, the GDR would not exist. The archives would be opened. The cover names would surface. And their assets—the weapons, the personnel, the infrastructure—would need to be moved before the investigators arrived.

The network had been preparing for tonight for forty years.

The preparation had always included Elena. Her usefulness to the network had been bounded by the cover's existence. The cover was the Cold War. Inside the Cold War her parallel ledger had been a tolerated risk because no investigator into either service would ever find it. Outside the Cold War her parallel ledger was the thing that could destroy what the network had built. Elena was sixteen years of accumulated knowledge that the network would now need to move into a position from which the knowledge could not return. There were two such positions. One required her cooperation. One did not.

The Wall was coming down. The basements were not.

Three weeks before the Wall came down, a report had arrived through the Hampstead Heath dead drop. Single page. Encoded in the format Elena had been using for sixteen years. The report described the emergency relocation of a warhead from a cache site in Vienna to a secondary location in southern Germany. The relocation was described as imminent. The report contained a specific detail—a railway routing number for a freight car departing Südbahnhof on 14 November—that had the texture of actionable intelligence and the weight of something she was supposed to act on.

Elena read it twice. The signature was wrong.

Not wrong in the way Yuri's rhythm had been wrong in the Lebedev directive. Wrong in a different way—too precise, too specific, too actionable. Real intelligence about warhead movements did not arrive in single-page reports with railway routing numbers. Real intelligence arrived in fragments, over months, through the slow accumulation of details that had to be assembled into a shape. This report arrived preassembled. The shape was already there. Someone had built the shape and placed it in the dead drop the way you placed a baited hook in water—not to inform but to see what surfaced when the bait was taken.

She'd mentioned the Vienna report to Dina at their next Tuesday coffee. Not the details. The shape. She'd mentioned the shape because the shape was the kind of thing Dina, with her Mossad access, could verify or dismiss. Dina had listened. Dina had said she would look into it. Dina had looked into it.

Elena understood this with the clarity of a final assembly—thoughts she'd been holding separately for years clicking into position like tumblers in a lock. The network was the system working as designed. The weapons were leverage. Leverage only worked if the people being leveraged did not know it existed.

And then, following the Dina thread back, the rest of it arrived. Doron's unexplained summer in Scandinavia in 1973. Yael's June 1980 passport line—a fragment delivered through sleep, on a kitchen floor, to a woman her service had instructed to cultivate. Hamidi in a Lillehammer restaurant, killed by thirteen rounds. Petrov three streets away, killed by Elena, while every officer in town ran south. The chaos had been engineered. The wrong-man fiction had been the cover for a target the machine had needed removed. The Mossad team had not been a blunder but an instrument. The Wrath of God was itself a cover. Some of its operations had belonged to Israel. Some had belonged to the network. The operators had not been told which.

She did not know if Doron had been in Lillehammer or only near it. She did not know if Yael had known. She suspected—with the same clarity that had assembled the rest—that those were the wrong questions. Doron and Yael had loved her. They had also been used. The two facts did not exclude each other.

Somewhere in Europe—Elena did not know where, had never known where, would never know where—a man with a gold ring on the little finger of his right hand was having breakfast.

Three documents waited in his briefcase by the door. He would sign all three with the same pen, in the same hand, with the same measured script he had been using for thirty years. The signatures would be identical. The pen would not distinguish between a storage unit and a hog barn and a human life. The man would not distinguish between them either. That was not cruelty. That was administration. The machine did not require cruelty. The machine required consistency, and consistency was what the man with the gold ring provided, the way a clock provided time—not by caring about the hours but by marking them.

Elena sat at her kitchen table in Kensington and watched a young woman with a red scarf celebrate on top of a wall. The champagne was being uncorked above twenty-one bombs in twenty-one basements. Tomorrow morning the residents would walk their children to school over blast radii none of the map-makers knew existed.

The celebration was real. The celebration was also operating on a geopolitical surface that had been quietly undermined for decades by a mechanism whose representatives wore livery rings and occupied rooms whose architecture did not permit faces to be recorded. The young woman with the red scarf would live the rest of her life inside the first fact and would never encounter the second.

The purpose was not the warheads. The warheads were the insurance. The four services believed they were acting independently. None of them were. The threats were curated. The responses were anticipated. The anxiety was the product.

Elena filed the arrangement beside the other things she was filing tonight. The filing system had never needed Moscow; it had needed Elena. Elena was still in the kitchen.

At twenty-three minutes past eleven the BBC cut from the Wall to the news ticker. *Industrial accident reported in central Germany. Residential evacuation underway in a Hessian municipality. Federal authorities investigating an anomalous chemical release at a closed facility outside the village. No casualty figures released. Federal Environment Ministry asking residents within four kilometers to remain indoors.* The item ran for eleven seconds. The footage cut back to the Brandenburg Gate.

The bulletin was managing.

Anomalous chemical release. Closed facility. Hessian municipality nobody had heard of until tonight. The shape was the Fanano shape. The shape was the Trier shape. A small explosive event filed inside a civilian-incident category that the late-evening editor of the BBC newsroom would not look at twice on a night when the Wall was coming down.

Elena dropped the count.

The drop was a small mechanical adjustment in the ledger that tracked the twenty-three. Twenty-three minus Fanano minus Trier minus tonight. Twenty. The drop was real-time. The bulletin was eleven seconds old. The cover had been written for the most distracted news night in European history.

Berlin was the cover for Hessen. The Wall had been used as a shroud.

She did not know whether tonight's event was the Friedrichshain weapon moved, or one of the eight codes Lebedev had never filled in with a year. The H could have meant Hessen as easily as it had meant the building on Pettenkoferstraße. The not-knowing was the condition.

Twenty was still twenty. Twenty European cities under

buildings whose residents did not know what waited beneath their children. The Cold War was ending tonight. The weapons placed for it were not.

The shape was older than the bulletin. A dead man's pencil had drawn it already.

The network had not waited for her to decide. They had moved a weapon tonight. The movement was already producing casualties whose count would never reach the BBC because the cover had absorbed them.

The weapons were moving.

The question was what she was going to do about it.

She thought about running. Leave Kensington tonight, use one of the emergency identity sets in the Geneva cache, fly to Canada or Australia, disappear into the civilian life of a woman who had once sold paintings. The identity sets were three deep. Each could hold for years. None were known to Moscow. None were known, she believed, to anyone. But the believing was the problem. *None were known* was the sentence an operative told herself before discovering that at least one had been known the entire time. Anneliese's drawing had made the sentence unsayable. The drawing was in the drawer. The drawing had been in her kitchen for thirty months. The network had been in her kitchen.

She thought about publishing—the cadences, the Sacco pages, the Fanano sketch, the assassination manual in her study. Sixteen years of material, in principle enough to force four Western governments into a formal investigation. She ran the sequence forward in her head: the *Guardian*, a select committee, a front-page story, seventy-two hours of coverage, and then the network's response, which she could predict with the precision of a woman who had been studying those responses for thirteen years. The weapons would move. The disclosure's authors would die. Elena within a week. Hatch within two. The warheads would still be in basements.

That left staying.

Staying was not a choice in the way the other two had been choices. Staying was the continuation of a motion Elena had been inside since November 1983—since the campaign against Calder, since the FEUERWERK line she'd withheld from the Moscow assessment, since the performance for Markus and the fire at Brixton and the sentence in the Friedrichshain basement that the *administrator* had called an assignment. The motion had been running underneath her operational life for six years.

On the television, a BBC correspondent was trying to be heard over the crowd at the Brandenburg Gate. His voice kept cutting in and out. People were singing. A boy on someone's shoulders waved a flag Elena could not identify. Behind him the floodlights turned the concrete the color of old teeth.

Tonight, watching a young woman in a red scarf being handed down the eastern side of the Wall on a television in a Kensington kitchen, Elena formalized what the motion had been saying the whole time: I am the instrument that knows it is an instrument. I am staying in the position because the position is the only instrument I have.

She did not run. She did not publish. She continued.

The choice was not moral. The choice was tactical, and the tactic was: wait.

Wait for the network to do the next thing. Wait to see what the next thing was. Continue to live in the kitchen where the notebook could be kept. Continue to have Sunday lunches with Helen and threatening-to-close-on-Tuesdays conversations with Gerald and occasional dinners in Chiswick with the man whose mind she'd been dismantling for six years.

Continue to be Alice Marsh. Continue to be inside the one vantage point from which they had chosen to let her observe their operations, because the vantage point was the only asset she currently possessed and abandoning it would be abandoning the only chance she had to do anything with what she knew.

The *administrator* in Friedrichshain had told her the sentence was an assignment. Elena had understood at the time that the assignment was to finish Calder. Tonight she understood the assignment was longer than Calder—that the finishing of Calder had been the first of a sequence of assignments the network would issue, and she would execute, and that the execution would eventually bring her to the place they wanted her to be.

She did not know where that place was. She did not know whether, when she arrived at it, she would still be useful or would have become inconvenient. Either outcome was survivable for the network. Neither was particularly survivable for her.

Elena accepted this. The acceptance was clean and belonged to no category Moscow had ever needed.

At some point in the next hour, the fox crossed the street.

Elena saw it through the kitchen window. She'd walked to the window at about ten o'clock to refill her tea and paused there—her own face faintly visible in the glass, superimposed on the Kensington street like a ghost haunting its own neighborhood. The face was forty-one. The jawline was still there. The mouth was still there. But something behind them had thinned. She looked at the reflection and the reflection looked back and neither of them blinked. Her tea had gone cold in her hand. She had not noticed.

Then the fox emerged from the area steps of number 34 and

trotted diagonally across the road toward the small garden opposite. The fox was thin in the way London foxes were thin in November—muscular rather than starved. Its coat was a reddish-brown that the sodium light rendered as a warmer orange, and its tail was held low and slightly to the side, and its ears were rotated forward in the focused attention of an animal that was occupying a street at an hour when the street belonged to it.

Elena watched the fox cross. The crossing took perhaps four seconds. The fox did not look at the window. The fox had mapped this street over many nights and had classified Alice Marsh's window as functionally inert, because Alice Marsh was usually asleep at this hour.

Tonight Alice Marsh was awake and the fox did not know it. The fox had crossed on the assumption of an empty observer at the window, and Elena was the empty observer—producing neither movement nor intention, the categories the fox was detecting.

The fox reached the opposite pavement. It slipped into the garden of number 27 and disappeared behind the low hedge. The crossing was complete.

Elena stood at the window and thought about the fox. It had adapted to human infrastructure the way she had adapted to institutional infrastructure—by learning the gaps, the timing, the routes nobody watched. The fox was an illegal. The fox was very good at its job.

Elena saw herself in the fox for the first time.

She had not previously thought of herself as a fox. She'd thought of herself as an instrument, as an operative, as a weapon system shaped like a woman, as a filing system with a body attached. She had not thought of herself as a small wild animal using human infrastructure for its own purposes without believing in the infrastructure.

The fox's model of the street was Elena's model of London. Sixteen years of moving through the city the way the fox moved through the street—mapping the surfaces, using them competently, not sharing the beliefs of the people who had built them. She'd used them. The using had been expert. The using had never been belief.

The fall of the Wall tonight did not change her belief structure because she did not have a belief structure. She had only the using. The using would continue as long as the infrastructure that could be used continued to exist. The fox would adapt. The fox would continue to cross at dawn. The fox would survive because the fox was not invested in any particular configuration of the human surfaces.

She thought: *continue as Alice Marsh. Cross the street at dawn. Do not believe in any of it.* The thought was not exhortation. It was description. It was what she'd been doing all along, and tonight she was only recognizing that she'd been doing it.

She turned from the window. The fox was gone. The street was empty. The sodium lights were doing what sodium lights did, which was to produce a yellow wash that flattened shadows into a gentle institutional uniformity, the color of a London night in a borough that had been designed to be decorous at every hour of the day. On the television, the BBC was replaying the earlier footage of the first Trabants crossing at Bornholmer Straße. The young woman with the red scarf would be on a loop for the next forty-eight hours. The Wall would continue to not exist.

She went to the kitchen drawer beside the stove.

She opened it. She had not opened it all evening, and the not-opening had been a kind of restraint, the small discipline of a woman who did not allow herself to consult the archive except when the consultation was operationally necessary. Tonight the consultation was not, by that measure, necessary. Tonight the consultation was a different kind of necessary—the necessary that applied to the moment when an assembly finally took its final form and required acknowledgment.

The drawer contained:

The diary, empty, purchased when she moved into the flat for the single purpose of occupying space beside the recipe book and looking like the kind of object a woman called Alice Marsh would keep in a kitchen drawer. It had never been written in. Its pages were still blank after eighteen years. The blankness was operational. The blankness was the pretext for the drawer's existence and the cover for everything else the drawer contained.

The recipe book. *Mrs Beeton's Book of Household Management,* 1968 edition, with the inscription Margaret on the flyleaf. She had bought it for the inscription. The inscription was still doing its work. The book had two bookmarks—a receipt for a bottle of olive oil and a landscape photograph Alice Marsh had clipped from a magazine. Neither bookmark marked an actual recipe Elena had ever made.

The small white candle, unused, bought in 1973. A pen, a blue Bic, also from 1973. Yuri's card—the welcome card, the one that had been in the drawer since the day she moved in, Welcome to your new home—Y. And beside it, the fountain-pen card Calder had sent her in November 1973, the first invitation, in the handwriting she had been reading for sixteen years.

The Ronson lighter Yuri had passed across the same Bloomsbury café table that November morning—chrome, ordinary in appearance, the F-21 Ajax film camera concealed beneath the baseplate. One hundred and seventy-eight frames remaining. The instrument had not been carried operationally in twelve years. It was waiting.

The Mercator knife she took from Voss in 1977, cleaned, returned to working order, blade closed. The folded steel handle that had once held a man's body weight now sitting quietly in a kitchen drawer.

The brass key from Jaffa, dropped into her coat pocket on the Yefet Street night in December 1982 and moved from the suitcase lining to the drawer in the spring of 1984 when the suitcase had begun to be used too often for legitimate travel. She had never learned what it opened. She had stopped needing to know. It was the one object in the drawer that was not evidence of anything, and the drawer needed one such object.

The Nagra reel, the one with the defect she'd concealed in 1973—progressing on schedule for sixteen years, now at thirty ticks per minute, not going to survive another year of use. When the mechanism failed, the recordings in the drawer would become permanently unreachable. Like names on a headstone. The words there, the meaning gone.

The *rothschildianum* photograph Kessler had given her in his back room three days before she left East Berlin, taken during the brief bloom in the winter of 1977-78. On the back of it, in the lower right corner, in pencil, three peaks with the middle one tallest, drawn by a hand that had been in her kitchen in October 1985.

The second *rothschildianum* photograph, taken by Frau Lentz during the same brief bloom and sent to Elena through Bruhn's quiet channel months later in 1978 and kept in the Brixton safe house until March 1986 and rescued from the thermite at minute twenty-one and placed in this drawer on the evening of the same day. The back of this photograph was clean. No pencil mark. No message.

The small folded piece of A4 paper. East German school paper, slightly grayish. A child's drawing of a house with a triangular roof, two windows, a chimney, a tree, three stick figures, and a yellow sun with a face and eight rays. In the lower right corner, in a child's careful handwriting: *Anneliese, 2B*. Taken from a noticeboard in the lobby of number 14 Pettenkoferstraße on a Tuesday afternoon in June 1987 and carried from Friedrichstraße to the Kempinski and from the Kempinski to Tegel and from Tegel to Heathrow and from Heathrow to Kensington and placed, the day after her return, in the drawer beside the stove where it had lived for two and a half years.

And the small red cloth-bound notebook. Bought at a Schöneberg stationer's in March 1976 for seventy-five pfennigs. Kept in the inner pocket of her handbag since 1978. Removed tonight, for the first time in weeks, and placed in the drawer for the consultation she was about to perform.

Elena stood at the kitchen counter and looked at the contents of the drawer.

She'd told herself, for sixteen years, that the drawer was an archive. The archive of a woman whose covert life did not permit the keeping of objects, and who had kept them anyway, and who had kept them because the keeping was the warmth a professional life was not supposed to retain but did. The drawer was Elena's interior made external. The drawer was what Alice Marsh had instead of a self.

Tonight, in the half-dark of her kitchen with the television replaying the woman on the Wall, Elena understood that the drawer was not an archive.

It was a dossier.

Every object in the drawer was evidence. Together they were the only case file that existed against a network nobody else had identified. The drawer was not a drawer. It was an indictment that had never been filed.

And the dossier was Elena's. Not Moscow's, because Moscow was gone. Not the network's, because they had taken only what they had wanted Elena to know they had taken and had left the rest. Not MI5's or MI6's, because neither service had ever suspected the drawer existed. It belonged to her, in a way that no institutional object had ever belonged to her before. It was the first thing she had ever fully owned.

A dossier required a recipient. She did not yet know who the recipient would be. She suspected the recipient was a man whose name she had been refusing to write down for sixteen years and whose address she had passed three times this week without knocking. She suspected the recipient was also herself. Both required the same act, in the same room, in the same hour. She did not know which room. She knew the hour was coming.

She looked at it for a long time. She did not touch anything. She did not rearrange anything. She stood at the counter in the half-dark of her kitchen and she let the drawer be what it had become.

Then she closed it.

She went back to the sitting room. On the television, the BBC was showing the young woman with the red scarf again. The foam was running down the bottle. The crowd was still roaring. The sound was still inadequate.

Elena sat down. She picked up the tea that had been cold since nine o'clock. She drank it anyway, because the drinking was what Alice Marsh would do. She watched a young woman celebrate on a wall above a blast radius that the young woman did not know about, in a city where the century was ending eleven years before its calendar date, and she waited for the next thing the network was going to do.

The next thing would arrive in its own time.

But the dossier was in the drawer, and the drawer was in the kitchen, and the kitchen was hers, and the hers was, for the first time in sixteen years, a word that meant something she could verify.

At eleven o'clock the BBC began a new analysis segment. Elena turned off the television.

She thought about Yuri. She had not thought about him in months. He had been her handler from October 1973 until the network removed him from her channel in the autumn of 1983. She did not know whether he was alive. She did not know whether anyone in Moscow tonight remembered his name. His welcome card was in the drawer beside the stove, beside the things she had carried. The card had been the first thing she had ever filed in that drawer. The drawer had not been a drawer yet, then. It had been a drawer with one card in it.

From somewhere outside, faintly, the sound of people singing. The flat was quiet in a way it had not been quiet before tonight. Sixteen years of quiet, and none of it had been this quiet. The quiet was the quiet of a room in which the world had changed and the furniture did not know.

Outside, somewhere in Kensington, the fox was crossing another street.

26

THE OTHER ARCHIVE

London—early December 1989

The man with the gold ring arrived on a Wednesday afternoon in early December, twenty-eight days before the room in Bermondsey was due to be entered.

Elena was at the kitchen sink. She did not hear him enter. She heard him cough, behind her, in her sitting room.

She finished rinsing the teacup. She dried her hands. Then she turned.

He was in her armchair.

For one second the room was the wrong room. The hook by the door, the drawer beside the stove, the two marks on the kitchen wall that she had not repaired and was not going to repair—none of these were arrangements that included a man in the armchair. The armchair, with him in it, was a piece of furniture she had never seen before. The wrongness lasted one second. Then her training closed over it the way it closed over everything, and the room was her room again.

Late fifties. Charcoal suit cut by a tailor. The little finger of his right hand wore a small gold signet ring with a worn place on the inside and a small dent on the bezel rim.

She had drawn the ring once, in a hotel room in Vienna, years before.

'Mrs. Marsh,' he said. The voice was English, educated, soft.

'I have brought you an offer. You have approximately four weeks before the people I work with conclude that the silence we have been extending you since the ninth of November is not a silence you intend to honor. I am here to extend the silence. The terms are these. You continue to operate. You continue to be Alice Marsh. We have new work that requires the patience you have demonstrated for sixteen years. The work will, in a shape I am not yet authorized to describe, rearrange post-Cold War Europe in directions you have already, in your private ledger, identified as preferable. We have read your ledger.'

Elena said nothing.

'The alternative,' he said, 'is the alternative.'

She looked at the ring. The ring she had drawn in a hotel room in Vienna and seen again from a basement table in Friedrichshain. The ring that had a name somewhere—in a cemetery, she was certain of it now, in a box, in pencil, waiting. She did not have the name yet. She had the ring.

'I know your ring,' she said. 'Vienna, October 1985. Friedrichshain, June 1987.'

A small flicker at the corner of his mouth. He had not expected the recognition.

'Yes.' He paused. 'My name is Thornley,' he said—the way a man of process offered information from a position of advantage. 'Laurence Thornley.'

'I am not coming back.'

He looked at her for a long moment. The look was not angry. It had the composure of a man who had been told that sentence several times in a long life and had a procedure for it.

'Then you understand what is going to happen.'

'I have understood since the ninth of November. I have been waiting for you to come and tell me how much time I have.

Four weeks is more than I expected. It is still less than I require.'

'You will not get more.'

'I know.'

He stood. He smoothed his jacket—a vain, automatic gesture—and moved toward the door. He paused. He turned. He considered something. He decided against it.

'Two others were offered before you. Both accepted. One is alive. One will, in three years, be a member of a government you would recognize. The offer was real.'

'I believe you,' Elena said.

He nodded once and let himself out the way he had let himself in. The lock made the small precise click of a man who knew how to open and close it without sound.

Elena did not cross to the chair. She washed the teacup a second time, although the cup was already clean.

She had been wrong. He had not come to deliver a verdict. He had come, with a courtesy that had nearly worked, to offer her one more chance to choose differently. The choice was between the work she had been doing on the wrong side of an account she had not been permitted to see, and the work she now had twenty-eight days to do on the right side of one nobody alive had been permitted to see.

She chose the second.

The day before the man with the gold ring arrived, the bell rang at 19:47 on a Tuesday.

Elena was at the kitchen table with the television on low and the lamb she had not eaten cooling beside unopened wine. She'd been doing this for three weeks. Since the Wall came down she'd been performing the small unhurried rituals of

Alice Marsh's evening with the precision of a woman who no longer knew whether the rituals were cover or habit. Walk back from the gallery. Make tea. Cook. Not eat. Watch what Eastern Europe was becoming.

Eastern Europe was becoming a sequence of crowds. Prague, Sofia, Bucharest. From this distance the crowds had a uniform texture and only the city changed.

Elena watched them. The drawer beside the stove had not changed since the Wall came down. The rhythm had not stopped. The network that needed the Cold War to justify its existence had not, as far as she could determine, noticed that the Cold War was over.

Her front door rang.

The bell was the building's, not the flat's. Visitors had to be buzzed in. Elena did not have many visitors. Helen on Sundays for biscuits. Gerald twice a year for accounts. Helen had brought biscuits two days ago. Gerald was not due. None of these visitors arrived without phoning first.

Nobody had called this evening.

Elena rose. She crossed to the intercom. She did not pick up. A neighbor locked out. A delivery person with the wrong flat. A canvasser. These were the explanations a bell at 19:47 on a December Tuesday produced in the lives of women whose lives were what they appeared to be.

The bell rang again.

Twice was deliberate. Twice meant the person at the door had a reason to be at the door and was not going away.

Elena picked up the intercom.

'Yes,' she said. Alice Marsh's voice. Mildly inquiring. The voice of a woman whose evening had been pleasantly interrupted.

'It's Dina Sharabi,' said the voice on the line. 'I am sorry to come without calling. I would not be here if it were not necessary. Please.'

The voice was Dina's voice. The voice in the intercom had eleven years of recognition behind it. The voice was not the voice of a Mossad officer arriving with operational intent. The voice was the voice of a woman asking for entry.

Elena pressed the buzzer.

She did not move from the door. She listened to Dina come up the stairs. The footsteps were slower than they had been in Tel Aviv. Elena placed her hand on the latch. She waited until the footsteps reached the landing and the knock came—three taps, conventional—and then she opened it.

Dina was wearing a charcoal coat that was not heavy enough for London December. Her hair was shorter than the last time Elena saw her, in October at a press café on Sheinkin. There were small new lines at the corners of her eyes that had not been there in October. She was carrying a leather shoulder bag and a small brown paper parcel tied with kitchen string.

'Hello,' Dina said. Her voice was steady. Her hands were not.

'Hello,' Elena said.

They looked at each other across the threshold of an English flat in Kensington in December. Dina's hand was still on the doorframe. Elena's was still on the door. Three seconds passed. Neither hand moved. The three seconds contained the thing that had not been said for eleven years and that was now going to be said.

'Come in,' Elena said.

Dina came in. She removed her coat. Elena hung it on the hook behind the door beside Alice Marsh's camel coat, and the two coats hung beside each other on the hook with the easy domestic adjacency of garments belonging to women who had been arriving at this flat together for years, although Dina had never been at this flat before tonight.

'Tea?' Elena said.

'Please.'

Elena went to the kettle. Dina followed her into the kitchen. Elena did not look at her while she filled the kettle and lit the gas, because looking at her would have required Elena to choose which of the two sets of muscles in her face to use —the Alice Marsh muscles or the other ones—and Elena was not yet ready to choose.

Dina did not sit. She stood in the kitchen door and looked at the room. She looked at the table. She looked at the cabinet above the sink. She looked at the small framed Flemish print. She was cataloging the flat the way Elena had cataloged Lebedev's flat years earlier—the observational intake running on a channel her face did not advertise. Elena watched her catalog. Elena did not comment. Two operatives in a kitchen in Kensington, each taking the measure of the other's domestic surface.

'You broke a glass against the wall,' Dina said. Quietly. Not as a question.

'In 1985,' Elena said.

'And you did not repair it.'

'No.'

Dina nodded once, the small nod of a woman acknowledging information she did not need to ask the meaning of.

'Sit,' Elena said. 'Please.'

Dina sat at the kitchen table. She placed the leather shoulder bag on the chair beside her. She placed the small brown parcel on the table in front of her, equidistant from her hands, with the careful neutrality of an object that was waiting for the conversation to reach it. The kettle whistled. Elena made tea—Earl Grey, no milk, because Earl Grey was what the kitchen had—and brought two cups to the table. She sat across from Dina. The wine she had not opened was beside her left elbow. The lamb she had not eaten was on the counter behind her.

'I have been in London since Saturday,' Dina said. In English. 'I had to wait until I was sure no one had followed me from Heathrow. I think no one followed me from Heathrow. I am not certain. I came tonight because I cannot wait any longer to be certain.'

Elena nodded.

Dina switched to Russian.

'Elena Vasilieva.' The name sounded different in an Israeli accent—harder consonants, the stress in the wrong place. The rhythm was the rhythm of a sentence long rehearsed. 'I know who you are. I am not here to expose you. I am here because there is a thing I have been carrying since 1981, and I cannot carry it alone.'

Elena did not move.

The room was quiet. The television in the next room was still on, low, the BBC's evening news producing the soft murmur of presenters describing crowds in cities Elena could no longer travel to. The kettle was silent. The tea was steaming. Dina's hands were on the table on either side of the brown paper parcel, palms down, the universal gesture of a person who wanted to demonstrate that she was holding nothing.

Elena assessed the situation in two seconds. No extraction team. No handler. Dina had come alone, and the aloneness meant this was not operational. The voice across the table was the voice of a woman making herself vulnerable. Elena had known the sound of that voice in other women in other rooms. The sound was not faked. And the year: Dina had said since 1981, and 1981 was the year the Berlin channel had gone silent, and the coincidence was not a coincidence. The fourth layer was the parcel.

A woman flown from Tel Aviv alone with a parcel she had been carrying for eight years was entitled to a certain foreplay.

And Dina said, without preamble, 'The mark on the wall is bigger than it looked from the street.' She said it the way a person remarks on the weather. Elena filed it. She had a parcel in front of her and a decision to make, and the filing would wait.

Elena looked at the parcel. It was small—twelve centimeters square, perhaps two centimeters deep. It was wrapped in plain brown paper of the kind Israeli post offices sold for parcel mail. It was tied with kitchen string knotted in a single knot, which meant the contents were not fragile and were not the product of a wrapping that needed to deceive a mail clerk. It was sitting on the table with the patient neutrality of an object that had traveled from Tel Aviv in a suitcase and that had been waiting for a kitchen table in Kensington to arrive on.

Elena answered Dina in Russian.

'I have been counting the cadences since March 1976,' Elena said. 'Six. Geneva. Marylebone. Bograshov. Kensington. Vienna. Friedrichshain.' She paused. Her hands were flat on the table. 'I have a notebook in my handbag. I have a drawer beside this stove. The drawer has photographs and a knife and a tape reel and a drawing made by a child who lives above three kilotons of fissile material. I am not the woman Moscow thinks I am. I have not been her for thirteen years.'

She looked at Dina.

'You are the second person I have said any of this to. The first was a handler in a Lada in Friedrichshain who told me he had been carrying the same recognition for the same eleven years.' She breathed. 'I am telling you because I have known since our third coffee that you were running the same operation against the same ignorance. And because tonight the not-knowing has nowhere left to go.'

She stopped.

She had not spoken Russian in two and a half years. The last time had been in the basement on Pettenkoferstraße. The Russian came back with the easy fluency of a language that lived beneath every other language she had ever used and that was the only language her mother had spoken to her in the kitchen of a Leningrad apartment in 1953. The Russian was the language she'd been told, at the Red Banner Institute in 1968, that she would have to forget to become useful. She had not forgotten it. The not-forgetting had been the first withholding.

Dina was watching her with an expression Elena recognized but had never seen on Dina's face before. The expression of a woman who had released a sentence she'd been holding for so long that the holding had become the shape of her mouth.

'Six,' Dina said. 'I counted three.'

Elena did not say anything.

'I did not get to Friedrichshain,' Dina said. 'I did not get to Vienna. The cadences I caught were inside Mossad. Three of them. An operation in Beirut in 1983 that used a Mossad team but was not a Mossad operation. A weapons transfer in 1985 that passed through a Mossad logistics channel without Mossad authorization.'

Elena nodded once. She did not speak.

'And a man—a handler who was running a relay whose terminus nobody at Mossad was permitted to ask about. I asked once. I was told to stop. The Wall came down. The structure the not-asking was supporting has nothing left to support.'

Dina paused.

'I have a parcel,' she said. She put her right hand on the brown paper square and slid it forward two inches across the table. 'I would like to show you what is in it.'

'Yes,' Elena said.

Dina untied the kitchen string with the unhurried fingers of a woman who had practiced untying the same knot many times. She folded the string into a small loop and placed it beside the parcel.

She unfolded the brown paper. Inside the paper was a cardboard box. Inside the cardboard box, layered between two pieces of tissue paper, was a single black-and-white photograph, eight inches by ten, printed on matte fiber paper.

She placed the photograph on the table between them.

Elena looked.

The photograph showed a man on a sidewalk in a city Elena recognized as Tel Aviv from the angle of the light and the particular pale stone of the building behind him. He was wearing a charcoal suit. His face was not at the camera—he was looking slightly to his left, at something out of frame. His left hand held a folded newspaper. His right hand was at his side, the fingers slightly curled, and on the little finger of the right hand was a gold signet ring.

The ring was the ring.

Elena recognized it the way she'd recognized it on a marble table in a Viennese coffee house in October 1985 and on a folding table in the basement of a building on Pettenkoferstraße in June 1987. The same gold. The same heft. The same small worn flatness on the inner curve where the ring had touched the next finger for so many years that the gold had developed a faint memory of the finger beside it.

The face was one Elena did not remember. She had seen it twice and her memory had refused to retain it. The unseeing was not her failure—it was a property of the face itself, the result of training or endowment that operated on anyone who looked at it directly and that could not operate on fiber paper exposed through a camera shutter at one one-thousandth of a second.

The photograph was the face. The face her memory had been unable to retain.

She had it.

'Where,' she said. Her voice was quiet.

'Tel Aviv. October. Three days before I last had coffee with you.

'He was at a reception at the Spanish embassy. I had been told by an analyst friend who works on cache disposition that a man would be present whose name was not on any guest list and whose identity nobody at the reception was supposed to acknowledge.

'I was at the reception because I had asked to be added to the guest list. I had asked through a channel I had been keeping clear for exactly this kind of opportunity for nine years.'

She paused. Her hand was on the table.

'I brought a camera in a brooch. Fourteen photographs. Twelve normal. Two of them are this man.

'I have brought you the better of the two.'

A breath.

'The other one is in a safe deposit box in Lucerne. In a box that opens with a key only I have. The key is in a place no one will find before I am dead, and after I am dead the existence of the box does not matter, because the box has an instruction inside it directing whoever opens it to send the contents to the *Guardian*, the *New York Times*, *Le Monde*, and the BBC simultaneously.'

Dina paused. She tapped the photograph with her index finger.

'I am telling you about the box,' she said, 'because I want you to know that the photograph in front of you exists in two copies and that the second copy is beyond the network's reach, regardless of what happens to either of us in the next thirty days. I am telling you about the box because the telling is the only form of insurance the two of us have against the kind of operation the network ran against you in Brixton in March 1986.'

Elena did not move her eyes from the photograph.

Late fifties. Clean-shaven. The hairline receding evenly. The nose was average. The mouth was a mouth. The eyes—the photograph showed only the profile—were the eyes of a person whose attention was on something more important than the person photographing him.

She had been looking at this face without seeing it for thirteen years. In Vienna. In Friedrichshain. The architecture of unseeing had kept it shapeless in her memory. Now the shape was an eight-by-ten on her kitchen table, and the shape was ordinary, and the ordinariness was its last defense.

The photograph was the only photograph of the network's *administrator* that existed outside the network's own records. Dina had taken it through a brooch at a Spanish embassy reception on a night when Elena had been in London making lamb she had not eaten and watching television.

'There is something else,' Dina said.

She reached into the leather shoulder bag on the chair beside her. She removed an envelope. The envelope was manila, business-sized, slightly bulged in the middle by something that was not a stack of paper but a single object of irregular shape. She placed the envelope beside the photograph.

'Tom Hatch,' she said. 'Has been missing for nine days.'

Elena looked up.

'Missing how.'

'Missing in the way that journalists go missing when journalists go missing in this profession. Missing without notice. His flat in Hackney is empty in a way a flat is not empty when its tenant has gone on holiday. His office at the *Guardian* has been entered. His files are gone.'

Elena did not move.

'His landlord has been told by a man with a Home Office identification that the tenant has had to leave the country on a personal matter and that the rent is being paid by an agency. The agency does not exist. The flat will be re-let in February to someone who does not know the previous tenant ever existed. The man with the Home Office identification was not Home Office. I had a colleague check.'

Elena did not breathe for a moment. Tom Hatch in the 2 AM kitchen in West Berlin in the autumn of 1976, cleaning his glasses. The four pages he had laid in front of her on a bistro table in Geneva in March of that same year. The Sacco document. The cadence she had been counting for thirteen years and the man whose face was on her kitchen table in front of her now and the missing journalist who had begun this entire chain in a kitchen at two in the morning by saying I didn't type them.

'Is he alive,' she said.

'I think yes,' Dina said. 'I think he went to ground before they came for him. He is somewhere none of us can find, in a place he prepared years ago. I do not have the location. I would not tell you if I did.'

'What is in the envelope.'

Dina picked up the envelope. She unfastened the clasp. She tipped it slightly and a single object slid onto the table beside the photograph.

The object was a small metal reel of recording tape.

It was quarter-inch tape, on the same size of metal reel that Elena's Nagra used. The reel was unlabeled. There was a small piece of tape across the center of the reel on which someone had written, in pencil, in handwriting that Elena recognized from across the years—from a 2 AM kitchen in West Berlin, from an *Observer* byline, from notes Tom Hatch had once written in the margins of a draft article and shown her without permission—three words.

For Elena. Now.

She did not touch the reel.

'When,' she said.

'Posted from a public box in Edinburgh on the second of November,' Dina said. 'Reached me through an Israeli press friend who Hatch trusted and who did not know what was on the reel and who handed it to me at a café in Jaffa nine days ago. I have not played it. It will not play on anything except a Nagra. I do not have one and I will not borrow one from anyone whose Nagra is connected to a service. I assume you have a Nagra.'

'I have one,' Elena said. 'It is failing. The spindle has had a nick for sixteen years and last time I checked it was ticking at approximately thirty per minute. I do not know if it will play this reel without damaging it.'

'Then you will need to play it carefully,' Dina said. 'Once. To memorize what is on it. I do not think we will have it twice.'

Elena nodded.

She looked at the photograph. She looked at the reel. She looked at the woman across her kitchen table who had carried both of these objects through Heathrow on a Saturday afternoon and who had waited three nights in a London hotel before coming to her door.

'Why now,' Elena said.

Dina looked at her for a long moment.

'Because of this,' she said.

She reached into the shoulder bag a third time and placed a photocopied directive on the table. Three typewritten lines instructing an unnamed Mossad asset to be present in a Bermondsey hotel lobby on January third at 16:00.

The rhythm of the directive was the tell Elena had been counting since 1976.

'Bermondsey,' she said.

'Bermondsey,' Dina said. 'Three weeks from Wednesday. A small hotel near the river the network has used before. January third is the first assembly since the Wall came down. They will decide what to do with the remaining warheads.'

Dina paused.

'I will be in the lobby at sixteen hundred,' she said. 'I need someone outside—across the street, photographing every face. Someone whose camera is not connected to the network. I cannot be outside because I will be inside.'

'You want me to be the photographer.'

'Yes.'

Elena thought about the F-21 Ajax in the Ronson lighter in the drawer beside the stove. One hundred and seventy-eight frames remaining. Third striker pawl twice. The lighter she had not carried operationally since 1977. The instrument she'd been keeping for a use she'd never been able to name—and the name was now spread across her kitchen table, two feet from the drawer that had been holding it.

'Yes,' she said.

Dina exhaled—a small audible release. The two of them sat across the kitchen table with the photograph and the tape reel and the photocopied directive and the drawer and the mark on the wall, and eleven years of separate and parallel investigations were becoming, in the space of seven minutes, a single architecture.

'There is one more thing,' Dina said.

Elena waited.

'I know about James Calder,' Dina said. 'I have known since 1981. I know you destroyed his marriage on instruction. I know the destruction was not yours. And I know you have not told him what you are. He should know what he is walking into, and he should know who is walking beside him.'

'Ask.'

'I want you to tell him,' Dina said. 'Calder.

'I want you to tell him everything. Before Bermondsey. Before the third of January.

'I want him to know who you are. What you have done to him. What you have been doing alongside what you have done to him.

'I want him to make the choice—fully informed—to join us at Bermondsey or to walk away.'

She looked at Elena across the kitchen table.

'I am asking you to do this not because I think he will join us. Although I think he will.

'I am asking because the operation we are about to run requires the kind of trust that cannot be built on a lie. And the lie you have been operating under with him is the lie that, if it survives Bermondsey, will destroy all three of us afterward.

'The lie has to die before the operation.

'Otherwise the operation will die because of the lie.'

Elena did not say anything.

Calder. The diazepam from Boots. The shake in his hand. The wine glass. The night in 1985 when he'd said I don't know what's happening to me into the dark and she'd said *you're going to be all right* and the lie had been the worst of her career. The silver key on Margaret's bracelet. The FEUERWERK page she'd read at 4 AM. The forty percent of his professional standing she'd destroyed through the campaign, and the kind of woman she'd been to do that.

She thought about the conversation she'd been not-having.

The conversation that was, she now understood, the conversation she had been preparing to have since the moment she'd opened the door for Dina Sharabi on a Tuesday evening in early December.

'Yes,' she said. 'I will tell him.'

'When.'

'Before the third. I will find the courage because the alternative has just become operationally unacceptable for the first time in sixteen years.'

Dina nodded.

The two of them sat across the table for another moment. The tea had gone cold. The lamb on the counter had been cold for an hour. The television in the next room was still murmuring about Eastern Europe.

Elena reached for the photograph. She picked it up. She

turned it over and looked at the man with the gold ring once more.

She placed the photograph on the table.

She rose from her chair. She went to the drawer beside the stove. She opened it. One by one, she set the contents on the table beside the things Dina had brought—diary, recipe book, candle, pen, the cards, the reel, the knife, the photographs, the drawing of the yellow-sun house. The two archives lay alongside each other. She did not need to count.

The drawer's contents were now spread on the table. The drawer was empty. The kitchen table held sixteen years of two parallel archives that had begun in Geneva in March 1976 and Tel Aviv in March 1978 and that had been running, separately and together, in two notebooks and across one rhythm, since.

'This is what I have,' Elena said.

Dina looked at the table.

'And this is what I have,' she said.

She took her own notebook out of her shoulder bag. It was a plain black hardback notebook, slightly larger than Elena's red one, three-quarters full. She placed it beside Anneliese's drawing.

'We will have to copy them,' Dina said. 'Yours and mine. Two complete copies. One for the safe deposit box in Lucerne. One for a place I have not yet selected. We do this tonight. Before either of us leaves this flat. The copying is the next thing.'

'Yes,' Elena said.

Dina looked at her for one more long moment across the kitchen table in the Kensington flat where Margaret had once made rosemary chicken on Wednesdays and Calder had once cooked lamb and Elena had once thrown a glass at the wall in 1985 because three words on a piece of paper had told her that Margaret's marriage was over. The mark from the glass was still on the wall behind Dina's chair.

Dina reached across the table.

She put her hand on Elena's hand.

Elena let her.

Neither of them said anything for almost a minute.

Then Elena rose to find paper and pens.

They worked until 2 AM.

They copied each other's notebooks longhand onto loose sheets of paper at the kitchen table. Elena copied the entries in Dina's black hardback into a fresh stack of A4 from the desk in the spare room. Dina copied the entries in Elena's small red cloth-bound into a second stack. They worked across the table from each other in silence, with the kettle going every forty minutes for fresh tea. The lamb was finally eaten cold around midnight—both of them remembered they had not eaten, and the not-eating was not a thing the operation could afford to maintain. The eating took eight minutes. They returned to the copying.

Dina's notebook contained eleven years of observations about Mossad tells, suspect operatives, and missing colleagues. Elena's contained thirteen years of KGB cadences, the Geneva document, and the network's fingerprint across four services. Together the two notebooks were the only case that existed.

On one page of Elena's notebook, the line she'd written the morning after Friedrichshain, which Dina copied without comment: *The Wall is not a border. It is a blast radius.*

By 2 AM the two stacks of copies were complete. Dina folded her copy of Elena's notebook and placed it in a manila envelope and put the envelope into the inside pocket of the charcoal coat that was hanging on the hook beside Alice Marsh's camel coat. Elena folded her copy of Dina's notebook and placed it at the bottom of the drawer beside the stove, beneath the orchid photograph and the reel and the diary and the knife. The drawer had grown again. The drawer was the only reader either of them trusted to keep what they had just shown each other, and the drawer could only keep one of the two copies.

'I will go now,' Dina said. 'Bermondsey. January third. Sixteen hundred. Each of us now has the other's archive.'

'Yes,' Elena said.

'Tell him,' Dina said. 'Before the third.'

'Yes,' Elena said.

Dina rose. She put on the charcoal coat. She stood in the kitchen door for a moment and looked at the room one more time—the table, the cabinet above the sink, the small Flemish print, the mark on the wall. She nodded once to the mark, the small private acknowledgment of one woman to another woman's evidence.

She let herself out.

Elena stood in the kitchen and listened to her footsteps go down the stairs. She heard the front door of the building open and close. She heard the sound of a London December night through the kitchen window—the low constant hum of a city that did not know it had become the place where two women had decided, in a kitchen at the end of an empire, to stop carrying their archives alone.

The filing she had deferred while the parcel was on the table was waiting for her in the kitchen. She chose not to open it. The not-opening was the only courtesy she and Dina had left.

She returned to the table.

The drawer was open. The drawer's contents were laid out on the kitchen table the way the drawer's contents would be laid out on the table at Bermondsey in three weeks when she sat down across from James Calder in a room she had not yet found and told him sixteen years of truth in whatever language the telling required.

She picked up the photograph of the man with the gold ring.

She looked at the face. Her breathing changed.

The face did not refuse her this time.

A photograph was the right instrument. The mechanism that had operated in the rooms with him was the mechanism of his presence—the trained averageness of a live body performing its own concealment, the calibration Bruhn had once described. The photograph could not perform. The photograph simply was. What had refused her in Vienna and Friedrichshain was a live architecture; what lay on her kitchen table was a piece of paper, and paper had no architecture to deploy.

Outside, Dina walked east toward Russell Square with the envelope inside her coat. She did not look back.

The first part of the operation was complete. It had taken eleven years.

27
SIXTY TICKS

London—early December 1989, the morning after

The morning after Dina, Elena did not sweep the kitchen.

The flat was cold. The heating had been off since she pulled the curtains the evening before, and the December night had entered through the single-glazed windows the way December nights entered all London flats of a certain age—gradually, without permission, settling into the plaster and the floorboards. The kitchen light was the same dishwater gray it had been on the Saturday morning she wrote the letter to Margaret, nearly six years ago. The same angle. London winter light did not change. It endured.

The drawer's contents were still on the table where she and Dina had laid them out at 2 AM. The diary. The recipe book. The candle and the pen. The cards. The reel. The knife. The prints of the *rothschildianum*. Anneliese's drawing. And, beside them, the new objects Dina had brought: the photograph of the man with the gold ring. The photocopied directive about Bermondsey. The small metal reel with three words written on a piece of tape across its center.

For Elena. Now.

Elena made coffee. She did not drink it sitting at the table—the table was no longer a kitchen table. It was a surface holding two converged archives. The table was the operational planning floor of an operation that had three weeks to run.

She drank the coffee standing at the sink. The street was doing what Kensington streets did on a December morning—a milk float, a man walking a poodle, a woman collecting post from the brass slot opposite. The ordinariness was the same ordinariness that had been outside her window every morning for sixteen years. The ordinariness had not changed. Everything else had.

She made the decision about the reel while she drank the coffee.

She would play it that evening. After the gallery. Alone. With the door locked and the lights low and the Nagra placed on the kitchen table and the reel threaded with the careful slow attention an operator gave to a precision instrument she'd been carrying for sixteen years and that was now, by every measurement Elena had been making since 1973, on the edge of complete mechanical failure.

She would play it once.

She would memorize what she heard.

She would unload the reel and place it back in the metal case Dina had brought it in.

And then she would do whatever the reel told her to do.

She finished the coffee. She went to the bedroom to dress for Alice Marsh's day at the gallery.

The gallery was busy. December was always busy. Elena spent the morning cataloging watercolors with the precision she brought to everything Alice Marsh did—the precision was the surface, and the surface was what stood between Elena and the men who would come for her if they ever realized she existed.

At lunchtime she walked to the small Italian café on the high street and ordered a sandwich she did not eat. She sat at a window table and watched the street.

The reel was in her handbag, in the inner pocket beside the notebook. It had been there since 2 AM. She carried it through the morning the way a woman might carry a piece of jewelry she could not put down, except the reel was not jewelry and the not-putting-down was not sentimental. The reel was evidence. The reel was Tom Hatch's voice from a place in the country he'd prepared in 1985 and not told anyone about. The reel was, possibly, the last operational message Tom Hatch was ever going to send.

She had known him for thirteen years. The first eight months had been the campaign. The remaining years had been something else—an acquaintance maintained through dead drops and brief encounters, sustained by a respect neither had acknowledged and that had deepened without either of them noticing. They had not seen each other often. The last time had been a coffee shop in Bloomsbury in October 1988, fourteen months ago, when he had said good-bye in the absent way old friends said good-bye when every meeting had become both ordinary and not ordinary.

She had not known, in October 1988, that it had been the last time.

The coffee shop had been on Russell Square. He had ordered too much—two coffees and a Danish, which he split into halves and gave her the larger. He had been thinner than the previous time. He had spoken about Claire's allotment, and a piece he was writing on Iran-Contra. He had not spoken about FEUERWERK. They had agreed in 1985 not to. When they parted on the pavement, he had held her hand a second longer than usual. She had not, at the time, given the second a meaning. She gave it one later. He had already been, in October 1988, the man Elena would see fourteen months later in the country-house recording, completing a list. He had simply not yet started recording it.

She returned to the gallery at 14:30. She finished cataloging the watercolors and wrote the descriptions for the exhibition catalog. She spoke to Gerald about the Christmas closing schedule. She performed Alice Marsh's afternoon with the precision of a woman who understood that the precision was the only thing that made the evening possible.

At 17:45 she put on her camel coat, said good night to Gerald, and walked home through the early December darkness, past the Christmas lights in the Kensington shop windows, past the brick and stone and lit windows of a city preparing itself for the end of the decade with the same patient unhurried British sense of occasion it brought to all the things it considered worth marking.

She reached the flat at 18:13 and let herself in. The door closed. Curtains drawn across the front windows. Deadbolt locked. The coat went on the hook beside the place where Dina's charcoal coat had hung the night before.

She was ready.

The Nagra lived in a fitted leather case on the top shelf of the wardrobe in the bedroom. The case was the original Kudelski—black leather with brass corners and the maker's embossed monogram on the lid. Built to protect a precision instrument through a working life. In the sixteen years Elena had owned it, the case had absorbed more punishment than its designers anticipated.

She brought the case down. She placed it on the kitchen table beside the photograph of the man with the gold ring. She opened it.

The Nagra was the same Nagra. Black anodized aluminum body the size of a paperback novel, small precise dials, the spindle, the recording head, the small VU meter that had been measuring the voices of other people's conversations since 1966. The case had a small scratch at the lower left corner from an incident in East Berlin in 1977. The spindle still had its nick. The nick had been getting worse since 1982. The machine was failing. The machine was too old to repair and too precious to replace. The machine was hers.

Elena turned it on.

The mechanism hummed. The hum was the same hum it had always made—the soft electrical activation of a device that had been built to operate quietly. Elena listened for the tick.

The tick came within a second.

She counted the way a doctor counted a pulse. The defect rate was about one per second now. Sixty per minute. She had thought: thirty. For seven years she had been carrying thirty, assuming that was still the worst of it. The nick had been deepening on its own timetable, in the wardrobe on the top shelf, while she was doing everything else. It had been failing the whole time. She had assumed the last number was still the true number.

She had done the same thing to herself.

Elena knew the mechanism was at the end the way she knew everything she knew operationally—by frequency, by the change in the small ambient sounds that constituted an instrument's working voice. The tick was no longer a defect that interfered with recording. The tick was now scratching Hatch's tape as it played—a small physical wound at every beat, delivered to the testimony of a dying man whose voice the tape would not survive a second playthrough of. The tick was also a metronome of the instrument's failure, and the metronome was now running at a tempo that meant the next failure would not be a tick but a stop.

She had told herself, in December 1982, that the Nagra would not last another year. The assessment had been wrong. The Nagra had outlived it by seven years, because Swiss precision instruments did not fail catastrophically. They failed by attrition, by the gradual accumulation of small accommodations, by the operator's patient willingness to nurse a dying mechanism through every operation it had left.

The slowness had nearly run out.

Elena threaded the reel.

The Hatch reel went onto the right reel post. The empty take-up reel was already in place. She threaded the tape through the heads with the slow careful attention she'd brought to threading reels for sixteen years. The threading took ninety seconds. She did not hurry. Hurrying with a dying mechanism was the operator's last mistake.

Every other reel she had ever threaded she had made—she knew what was on it before the first second of audio came through the heads. This one she had not made. This reel carried the voice of a man who might be dead by the time she heard it, recorded on a machine in a cottage she would never find. If the failing spindle let the speed drift before it found its tension—if the heads scraped the magnetic coating from the tape in the first thirty seconds—whatever Hatch had said in those thirty seconds was gone. Not damaged. Gone. The particles that held his voice would be abraded from the tape and his voice would be gone with them. She would never know what she had not heard.

She set the Nagra to PLAY.

She did not press the play key yet.

She sat down at the kitchen table across from the photograph of the man with the gold ring. She placed her right hand on the kitchen table beside the Nagra. She placed her left hand on her thigh under the table. She breathed once.

She pressed PLAY.

The reel turned.

◆◆◆

For four seconds there was nothing. The leader tape, white and silent, ran through the heads at the standard speed of three and three-quarter inches per second. Elena counted the seconds.

At the fifth second, the recording began.

It was Tom Hatch's voice.

It was the same voice she heard in a Geneva bistro in March 1976 when he'd said I didn't type them. It was the same voice she had heard in his 2 AM kitchen in West Berlin in the autumn of 1976 when he cleaned his glasses three times in two minutes and told her about the Italian magistrates. It was the same voice she heard at a conference reception in Amsterdam in 1979 when he'd introduced her to a colleague as *the most thorough researcher he had ever met*. It was the same voice she had heard for the last time in a coffee shop in Bloomsbury in October 1988 when he'd said good-bye.

The voice on the reel was thinner than the voice Elena remembered. The thinning was not the recording. The thinning was the voice itself—the voice of a man speaking from a body that was no longer fully working.

'Elena.'

The voice paused. Elena heard him swallow.

'Elena, if you are listening to this, then Dina has reached you and the reel has reached you, and I am either dead or beyond the use of my own voice. I am recording this from a cottage on the west coast of Scotland that I have been keeping since 1985 for exactly this kind of week. I do not have much time, for two reasons. First, because the men looking for me are competent. Second, because I believe I have been poisoned.'

A breath. The breath had a small wet rattle in it Elena had never heard in his breathing before. Beneath it, the Nagra ticked.

'The poison was in a glass of water at a hotel bar in Glasgow on the twenty-ninth of October. I was meeting a source. The source was good. The source did not know that the man at the next table had switched my glass during a moment when I was distracted by the source's story.'

The breath rattled again. Elena realized she was holding her own breath. She released it quietly.

'I noticed the switch four hours later when I felt ill. I do not know what I was given. I have approximately the symptoms of a man who has been administered a slow heavy metal—thallium, perhaps. Perhaps polonium. I am not certain. I am not going to a hospital because going to a hospital would identify me. I am recording this instead.'

Another breath. Elena did not move. Her right hand on the table was still. Her left hand on her thigh was still. The Nagra was running. The tick was running. The tick had become, since the recording began, the quiet percussion beneath Hatch's voice—the small relentless beat of a mechanism that was carrying the recording across whatever remained of its useful life and that was also, with each beat, measuring the distance from the start of the playback to the end, and leaving a small scratch at every beat.

'I need to tell you several things,' Hatch said. 'I am going to tell them in the order of importance. The first three are operational. The fourth is personal. I would prefer to tell you the personal one face to face, in a coffee shop in London with both of us forty years older than we were in 1976. That is not the kind of telling that is going to be available to either of us. The reel will have to do.'

A pause. He cleared his throat.

'First. The meeting on the third of January in Bermondsey is real. Dina is reading her own intelligence correctly. The hotel is the hotel where the network has met three times since 1981. I have the dates and the names of two of the people who attended on each occasion. I have written them on the inside of this reel's metal case in pencil. You will find them when you open the case.'

The Nagra ticked faster. Elena could hear her own pulse. She did not move.

'The meeting on the third of January is the network's first consolidation since the Wall came down. It is not going to be about the warheads in the way you and Dina think it is going to be. It is going to be about who keeps them. The network is dividing.

'There are two factions.

'The first wants to keep the warheads operational. To sell their existence to the new governments forming in eastern Europe—the position of leverage. Operational means: the new government in Warsaw signs what it is told to sign, or a block off Marszałkowska becomes the next Fanano.

'The second wants to disappear them. Recover quietly. Melt down. Erase all traces. Continue operating without the physical evidence that has been the network's only material vulnerability for twenty-five years.'

She heard him exhale—a long, controlled release, the breath of a man rationing his air.

'The two factions are going to meet in Bermondsey on the third of January. One of them is going to win. The winning will determine what the next decade of European politics is going to look like.

'You and Dina will be photographing the meeting. The photographs will be evidence the existence of which neither faction can afford.

'Whichever faction wins on the third will spend February

and March looking for both of you.

'Plan accordingly.'

The voice paused again. Elena heard him shift his position, somewhere far away, in a cottage or a flat or a single room in a part of the country he had been keeping for four years.

'Second. The man with the ring. I have his name.'

Elena did not breathe.

'I am not going to say his name on this tape. His name is in a file. The file is in a metal box buried below the third paving stone at the disused lavatory in Highgate Cemetery—the western half, Swain's Lane gate. I dug it in the spring of 1986. The third stone is loose. The moss on it is younger than the moss beside it. Open the box. Read the file. Then decide what to do with the name.'

He coughed. A small, wet sound. Then silence.

'I will say only this about the name.

'You have seen this man twice. Vienna, October 1985. Friedrichshain, June 1987. Both times you were under conditions that made faces hard to keep—the compound the first time, fatigue and dim light the second. His face was built to be the one you'd lose first.

'Ordinary. Unmemorable. The opposite of distinctive.

'A face the way a passport photograph is a face.'

A breath. The wet rattle was nearer the surface now. Beneath it, the Nagra ticked.

'The file contains the face. And the name the face was born with. On the second page, a list of the four institutions that have known the name and have agreed, across forty years, not to use it.

'Knowing the name will not, by itself, end the network. The

network is bigger than one man.

'But the name is the corner of the curtain.'

A pause. Elena did not move.

'Pulled at the right moment by the right people, it will produce the kind of public exposure the network has spent twenty-five years preventing.

'Pull the curtain at Bermondsey or after. You will know the moment.'

Elena did not move.

The Nagra ticked. The tick was, by her count, slightly faster than it had been at the start of the playback. Sixty-five per minute. Seventy. The mechanism was warming and the warming was accelerating the failure Elena had been tracking for seven years. The Nagra was dying faster now than it had ever died before. The dying was, like everything tonight, a conclusion. The machine had outlived its usefulness. It had outlived the era that had made it necessary. It was running out the last of its runtime in a Kensington flat while the voice of a dying journalist described the operation that had killed him.

'Third,' Hatch said. 'James Calder.'

The Nagra ticked.

'I am telling you about Calder because I think you need to know it before you do anything else. James Calder has been protecting you for at least nine years. He has known about you—about the second identity, the Tel Aviv channel, possibly the Lillehammer night—since at least 1980. He has not told MI6. He has not told anyone. He has built a private file on you that he keeps in a place his colleagues do not know about. The file does not contain the evidence that would expose you. The file contains what prevents that evidence from being assembled by anyone else. He has been keeping his colleagues away from you for nine years by feeding them other directions to look in.

The Nagra ticked. Elena had not moved since the word Calder. Her tea, which had been half a cup when Hatch named the first operation, was still half a cup.

'I know this because a source inside MI6 described, in 1985, an operation run by a single officer whose entire purpose was keeping his colleagues from looking at a particular London art historian. The source did not know who the officer was. The source knew only that the operation existed and that the officer had never filed a single piece of paper documenting its existence. I worked out that it was Calder in 1986, after I cross-referenced the dates of three internal MI6 inquiries into your cover that had been opened and then closed without conclusion. Each inquiry had been closed by the same officer. The officer was Calder. The closures were the operation. The operation was the protection.

'I did not tell you in 1986 because my source was alive. The source is dead now. So I am telling you. The man whose marriage you destroyed under instruction from the cadence has been, throughout the entire destruction, the man keeping you alive inside his own service's files. Both facts are true at the same time. I am not going to tell you what that means. You have always been the only person I've known who could carry two truths without dropping either one. Carry these two.'

The voice stopped.

Elena's right hand on the kitchen table had begun, very slightly, to shake. She noticed the shaking without judgment. Without reaction. She made no attempt to stop it.

Hatch's voice resumed.

'One more item before the fourth. This one is practical.

'Claire left me in eighty-six. She is teaching at a village school in Shropshire now. She still wears the green hill on the chain—she told me when she left that the hill was from before me and would be from after me, and she was right. She does not know I am dying. She should not. She never knew what I was looking at for any of the thirteen years she was with me, and the not-knowing was the work of keeping her outside it. If the network ever pulls on the thread that leads to her, I am asking you to cut it. Do not go to her. Do not send anyone. Let her read in the paper that I am gone. It is the last protection I have left to offer to anyone who is not you, and I am asking you to extend it for me.'

'Fourth.

'I have been wrong about you for the entire thirteen years I have known you.

'I assumed you were KGB. I assumed the cover was a cover. I assumed you were running an operation against me from our first meeting in Geneva.'

His breathing had changed. The rattle was closer now—not beneath the voice but inside it.

'I do not know the full truth of who you have been. But I have come, over the years, to recognize that whatever you have been, you have also been the only person besides myself who was looking at the thing the four pages I gave you in March 1976 were pointing at.

'We have been looking at the same thing from different sides of the same room for thirteen years.'

A pause.

'I am sorry I never said this to you in person.

'I would have said it on the third of January in Bermondsey if the third of January had not become a moment I am not going to be present for.

'This recording is the closest I can come.'

'That is the personal one. I do not have anything more to say about it, because anything more I tried to say would be the kind of thing the body produces when the body knows it is leaving and that the people listening to the body are going to remember the last thing the body said. I do not want to leave you with the wrong last thing. I want to leave you with the operational facts and the practical one and the personal one and the silence after. Take the silence. The silence is where the work is.

'That is all the operational content of the tape. The remainder of the reel is the names and the dates and the document references that go with the things I have just told you. There are six pages' worth. Listen carefully. The reel has approximately seventeen more minutes. I do not know if your equipment will hold up that long. I am told it has been failing for some years. Please play the reel only once. Memorize what you hear. Do not transcribe what you hear onto any paper that could be found by anyone other than yourself.

'Goodbye, Elena.' He used her real name the way a man sets down something fragile. 'I hope you are well. I hope this reaches you in time.'

The voice stopped.

For three seconds there was only the tick. Then a different voice—flat, bureaucratic, the voice Hatch had used in his recordings when he was reading source material into a tape rather than speaking from himself—read names.

The names came for sixteen minutes.

Elena did not write any of them down. The names entered her memory the way names had always entered in the moments when entry mattered—as patterns, each slotted into retrievable position. Three names from the 1981 Bermondsey meeting. Three from 1984. Three from 1986. Two men attended all three: a German banker and a French aerospace executive. She had heard of one. She kept both.

Then the dates. Seven dates between 1962 and 1989 corresponding to seven cache placements that were not in any inventory either of the official services maintained. The dates were tied to specific NATO logistical exercises that had provided cover for the placements. Elena recognized two of the exercises. The other five had been compartmentalized at a level her own research had not reached.

Then the document references. Folder numbers, archive codes, the small precise indexing that intelligence services produced to know where things were and that journalists who had been investigating intelligence services for seventeen years also produced for the same reason. Hatch had been keeping his own catalog. The catalog was now hers.

The Nagra ticked all the way through.

The tick rate continued to rise. By the eighth minute it was eighty per minute. By the twelfth minute it was a hundred. By the fifteenth minute the tick had become almost continuous—a small fast clicking that ran underneath Hatch's voice like the second hand of a watch the watchmaker had made for a man who needed to know exactly how much time was left. Beneath it, Hatch's voice was thinning. Each scratch took a fraction of his clarity, and Elena leaned in to catch what remained.

At the sixteenth minute, the voice stopped.

There were perhaps thirty seconds of trailing tape after the last name. Elena let the reel run. She let the silence run. *The silence is where the work is,* Hatch had told her. She listened to the silence and to the tick beneath it—the small percussion of a mechanism finishing its work in a Kensington kitchen with the curtains drawn and the lights low.

The trailing tape ran out.

The reel turned in the air on the right reel post, empty. The Nagra clicked into the end-of-reel position automatically. Elena pressed STOP.

The mechanism stopped.

It did not start again.

The Nagra was dead.

The kitchen was so quiet she could hear the clock in the bedroom.

The tick had stopped. The mechanism had been failing since November 1973, and now it had finished. The silence was the silence of a Swiss precision instrument that had carried its defect through sixteen years and every operation it had been asked to perform—and that had held together until the final word of Hatch's catalog crossed the playback head, and the work was done.

Elena placed her hand on the top of the Nagra's case. The metal was warm. The warmth was the last warmth the mechanism would produce. The mechanism would not be warm again, because there was no longer a mechanism.

She held her hand on the case for a long moment.

Then she said, quietly, in Russian: 'Thank you.'

The flat was quieter than it had been in twenty-eight minutes. The tick had been so small she had not consciously heard it. Now that it was gone, its absence was enormous—the silence of a machine that had carried a voice across time and had used the last of its mechanical life to do it. The Nagra had been built in a workshop in Lausanne. It had recorded Elena's first conversation with Calder in a Fitzrovia gallery in October 1973. It had just played its last recording. Between those two moments, the machine had been more reliable than any institution Elena had ever worked for.

She did not know whether she was thanking the Nagra or Tom Hatch or the Lausanne workshop or the Soviet officer in Bern who had purchased the unit through the channel in 1973 or the woman in Leningrad who had taught a girl named Elena, in 1965, that the proper response to a long service from any instrument was a quiet word at the moment of the instrument's retirement. She thanked all of them. The thanking was the only ritual the moment permitted.

She unloaded the reel from the right reel post. She placed it back in the metal case Dina had brought it in. She inverted the case and looked at the inside of the lid.

Hatch's pencil writing was there. Six rows of names and dates, written in the small precise hand of a journalist who had been compressing intelligence into margins for seventeen years. Elena read the writing twice, slowly. She matched it against the names she'd memorized from the audio. The two matched. The reel and the case were redundant copies. Hatch had built the redundancy in 1986 because Hatch had been the kind of journalist who built redundancy into everything that mattered.

She retrieved the 1973 reel from the drawer and placed it in the case beside the Hatch reel. The two recordings—the first audio she had ever kept and the last one she would ever need to hear—had found the same housing. The Nagra had died while one was playing. Now both were silent in the same dark. She closed the metal case. She placed it in the drawer beside the stove, beneath the diary, in the false-bottom compartment she'd built in 1979 and that now held the second copy of Dina's notebook and the metal case with Hatch's catalog in it.

She closed the drawer.

She returned to the table. She sat down across from the photograph of the man with the gold ring. She looked at the photograph for perhaps a minute. The man's face—the unremarkable late-fifties face with the receding hairline and the eyes looking left at something out of frame—was not the same kind of object now as it had been an hour ago. An hour ago the face had been the face her memory had been unable to retain. Now the face had a name. The name was buried in a metal box under a paving stone in Highgate.

She thought about Calder.

She thought about Calder for a long time. Perhaps an hour. The entire interval after the Nagra's death.

Nine years.

She did not move. The kitchen had become very quiet, the way kitchens become quiet when a body inside them has stopped breathing for a count and has not noticed it has stopped.

She breathed.

She subtracted. 1989 minus 9 was 1980. In 1980 Elena had been in Tel Aviv as Sara Lerner. The table with Doron and Yael had happened in June. The Yael passport line had happened in June. The third withholding—the one that had begun the pattern of softening rather than reporting—had been Yael's sleepy passport reference. And somewhere in that same summer of 1980, without her knowing it, Calder had begun protecting her from his own service. Calder had learned something about Alice Marsh in 1980 that should have ended her career as an illegal and had chosen, at Century House, to file the knowledge in a drawer nobody would open. He had been protecting her then. He was still protecting her now.

In the year of the table, while Elena had been beginning the four-year cultivation of Doron and Yael that would produce the first hard intelligence on the European caches, Calder had been beginning the operation of preventing his colleagues at Century House from looking at her.

He had begun in 1980.

She'd begun, in a different sense, also in 1980. Both of them had begun in the same year. Each had started the off-books work the institution would not have authorized. Each had begun it because the institution had stopped producing answers and the absence of answers had become more dangerous than the asking of unauthorized questions. Each had carried it for nine years in private interior spaces the institution had not built and could not see.

The mirror was complete.

Elena had known the mirror was incomplete in 1983, when she'd searched Calder's desk at 4 AM and found the FEUERWERK page and had recognized he was pulling the same thread she was. She'd thought the recognition was the completion. She had been wrong. The invisible half of the mirror was the operation Calder had been running to keep his service from looking at her—an operation that had begun three years before her 1983 recognition and that had been running silently underneath every dinner at his house, every night in his bed, every day of the campaign against him.

He'd been protecting her while she'd been destroying him.

She had been the only person in the world who had been doing what she had been doing.

He'd been the only person in the world who had been doing what he had been doing.

The two solitudes had been running side by side for twelve years, and the running side by side had been the marriage neither of them had known they were in.

Elena put her hand flat on the kitchen table.

She thought: *I am going to tell him. I am going to tell him before the third of January. I am going to tell him.* In the way Dina said. For the reason Hatch said. And for the third reason Hatch did not say but that I now understand, which is that the telling completes the mirror, and the mirror has to be completed before the operation, because the mirror is the operation—nine years running on each side of the same wall, and the wall is now ready to come down.

She thought: *I will tell him at Bermondsey. Before the operation. Because the telling and the operation are the same architecture now, and the architecture is Bermondsey.*

She rose from the table.

She reached into the open drawer beside the stove and removed the F-21 Ajax from beside the Mercator knife and the brass key, where it had been living since Yuri had placed it in her hand in Bloomsbury in November 1973—the Ronson lighter that was not a lighter, the third striker pawl that was not a striker pawl, the one hundred and seventy-eight frames of fine-grain archival Soviet film that had been waiting sixteen years for an operational use Elena hadn't been able to name. She placed it on the table beside the photograph of the man with the gold ring and the dead Nagra and the emptied contents of the drawer that had kept it.

The lighter was the operational instrument for Bermondsey.

The photograph was the target.

The drawer was the dossier.

The Nagra was the closed circuit. The Nagra had ended the way circuits ended, by passing the last current through to the receiver and then ceasing.

Elena sat down at the table again. Her hand moved to pick up Margaret's charm bracelet. The bracelet was not on the table. It had never been on the table. It had been in Margaret's pocket when she walked out of the Chiswick house in June 1984. Elena did not have the charm bracelet. Elena had only the memory of the charm bracelet and the memory of *the silver key* she had not been able to identify and the memory of the unfilled gap in her mental inventory of Calder's wife where *the silver key*'s meaning had refused to settle for twelve years.

She would ask Calder about *the silver key* at Bermondsey.

She would ask him at Bermondsey because Bermondsey was the place where she would ask him everything.

Elena closed her eyes.

The kitchen was quiet. The Nagra was quiet. The street outside was quiet. The mark on the wall behind her chair was quiet. The drawer was open. Soon she would go to Highgate. The day after that, she would find Calder. Before the third of January, she would arrange the room where the telling would happen.

The room would be in Bermondsey.

A week had passed since Thornley had left her flat. Bermondsey was day twenty-eight by his count. The man with the gold ring had given her a number, and the network was not in the habit of changing numbers it had given.

The Wall was over.

The mechanism was over.

The work was beginning.

She opened her eyes and looked at the photograph of the man whose face her memory could not keep, and the face looked back at her from a piece of fiber paper that did not require a memory to hold it, and Elena understood that the next twenty-eight days were going to contain everything the previous sixteen years had been preparation for.

She did not move from the table for another hour.

The Nagra stayed on the kitchen table. She did not move it. There was nowhere left to take it that was worth taking it to.

There was nothing more it could do for her, and there was no point in putting it away.

She left the flat at three in the morning.

Not to Highgate—that was later. This was the hours before later, the hours when the machinery continued but the operator could not, and Elena had always walked when a thing was too large to carry in stillness.

She walked south through Kensington and entered Hyde Park through the Albert Gate. The park was dark in the way London was never dark in daylight—a complete, settled dark, the lamps along the Ring Road tracing their amber ellipse through the blackness of the grass, and everything between them belonging to a city that had agreed, temporarily, to pretend it was something wilder.

She walked to the Serpentine.

The water was black. Perfectly black, perfectly still—the winter surface sealed against a sky that was beginning, at its furthest eastern edge, to separate from the night by one degree of gray. No wind. No movement. The water held the few stars the London sky permitted like evidence: small cold points, suspended in something that absorbed.

Elena stood at the edge.

She had stood at the edge of water many times with many things in her hands. The Makarov PB going into the Mjøsa before morning—sixteen years ago, a continent away, the first killing's instrument surrendered to a Norwegian lake that received it without comment. Water received everything without comment. That was the thing about water. It asked no questions about what you brought to it. It simply took.

Tonight she brought it nothing. The knife in her coat pocket still had a use in it that the Makarov had spent, and the water did not receive instruments that were not yet spent. She stood at the edge for another minute. Then she turned and walked back.

28

THE THIRD PAVING STONE

London—mid-December 1989—2 January 1990

Elena took the Northern Line to Archway.

She did not take a taxi. Taxis kept records—a driver who remembered a woman who asked to be dropped at Swain's Lane on a Monday morning in December would be, if asked later by a man with a warrant card, a witness. The Tube kept no records.

Elena dressed carefully. The coat was the darker heavier garment with the deep pockets she had used for the Brixton operation in 1986 and that had lived in the wardrobe since then, kept for the night she might need a coat that did not advertise which version of herself was inside it. The shoes were flat. The hair was pinned. The face was the face she had been using for surveillance work for fifteen years—unmemorable at thirty meters, forgettable at ten.

She carried the gardening gloves and the trowel because Hatch had told her the metal box was twelve inches below the third paving stone left of the entrance to the disused public lavatory at the eastern end of Highgate West Cemetery.

She reached Archway before nine. She walked south down Highgate Hill. Christmas lights hung in the windows of the small shops on the high street. A woman was walking a terrier. A postman was doing his rounds.

She reached Swain's Lane.

The gate into the western half of the cemetery was chained. Elena walked past it for another two hundred meters until she reached a particular section of the cemetery wall where the wall was low enough to climb and where the climbing was shielded from the lane by a stand of yew trees. Hatch had mentioned the section on the reel.

The third yew north of the lower gate. The wall is forty-six inches there. I climbed it in 1986 and I never left through the gate.

Elena climbed the wall.

She landed in soft ground on the cemetery side. She crouched, listening. The cemetery was silent in the way only old cemeteries in early December were silent—the damp quiet of a place that had been built for silence and that had been performing silence for a hundred and fifty years. No birds. No footsteps. No voices.

She stood up.

The cemetery smelled of damp stone and decaying leaves. She walked east through the cemetery on the path Hatch had described.

A man in a faded green Barbour was walking a terrier on the path beyond the wall, fifty meters away. She tracked him for four minutes before concluding he was a local exercising a dog he had clearly been exercising along this path for years.

The disused public lavatory was at the end of the path. A small brick structure with a corrugated iron roof, condemned since 1979, the entrance boarded up.

She was not going inside. The third paving stone left of the entrance was what she was going to.

The paving stones were the original Victorian flagstones—rectangular, approximately two feet by three, weathered to the color of old bone, half-covered with moss. Elena knelt and counted the stones to her left. One. Two. Three.

The third stone was the stone Hatch had described. The moss on it was visibly younger than the moss on the stones beside it. There was a small chip at one corner and a hairline crack running diagonally across the upper surface. The crack was the kind of mark that made a particular stone identifiable to the person who had buried a box beneath it.

She inserted the blade of the trowel into the seam between the third stone and the fourth. She worked the blade in and levered. The stone was heavy—perhaps thirty kilos—but it was loose. She lifted the stone and set it on the bed of wet moss beside the path.

The soil beneath was dark and cold. Elena dug. Twelve inches took her perhaps six minutes. At the ten-inch mark, her trowel struck metal.

It was a metal box. Approximately twenty centimeters long, fifteen wide, ten deep. Galvanized steel. The seams sealed with the waterproof compound British plumbers used to seal underground pipe joints. The seals were intact.

Elena lifted the box out of the ground. She placed it on the stone beside the hole. She looked at it.

She did not open the box yet.

She sat on the stone beside it. The December cold came through her coat. Somewhere above her the terrier barked once at something it had decided was not worth barking at twice.

She had known Hatch for thirteen years.

After the *Zersetzung* campaign ended they had continued meeting. Not often. Coffees in Bloomsbury. A pub in Clerkenwell. Once, a Thursday afternoon on the Albert Embankment in 1982, when Hatch had spent an hour describing, without seeming to describe, the structure of an investigation he was running and that had Elena's profession in its shape. He had cleaned his glasses when he was thinking. He had laughed at his own jokes one beat before the other person.

He had been, in a way Elena had never quite named for herself, a friend.

The word arrived in her throat without warning.

Friend.

Tonight, wherever Hatch was, he was no longer available to continue the arrangement. The arrangement was what it had been: a friendship neither of them had been permitted, under the terms of the lives they had chosen, to conduct as one.

Her hand was on the lid of the box. She had not noticed she had placed it there.

She removed the hand. The back of the glove came up and passed across her cheek. The dirt on the glove left a small smear. She did not wipe it off.

She opened the box.

The box was the box Hatch had buried in the spring of 1986, at the beginning of a chain of preparations for exactly this moment. The box had been waiting for three and a half years. Elena had been the person the box was waiting for.

They had been brought to the same Geneva café in 1976. They had spent fourteen years being what the network had needed them to become—Hatch the journalist who would carry the document, Elena the operative who would prevent it from being published. Tonight the box in Highgate was Hatch's instrument speaking to Elena's instrument across the years they had spent unable to speak as themselves.

She unwrapped the manila envelope from her handbag. She placed the box inside the envelope. She folded the envelope over the box and tucked it under her arm. She shoveled the loose soil back into the hole. She replaced the paving stone and pressed the moss back into place. She scattered dead leaves over the top. The stone looked untouched.

Elena walked back through the cemetery the way she'd come.

She climbed the wall at the same place. She dropped down into Swain's Lane. She had been in the cemetery for twenty-three minutes. Elena left no trace. She had the box.

She opened the box in the reading room of the London Library in St James's Square.

The London Library was the oldest private lending library in London and the place Elena had used for cover research since 1978. She had a membership under the Alice Marsh name. The reading rooms were quiet in the particular way libraries were quiet—not the institutional quiet of public buildings but the self-selecting quiet of a space whose members had agreed, tacitly, that silence was the library's primary product.

Elena took a desk in the back of the stack room. The desk was between two rows of shelves containing the nineteenth-century German theological section, which was a part of the library that Elena chose because no other member of the library had any reason to walk through it on a Monday morning in December. The desk had a small reading lamp. It was on.

She placed the manila envelope on the desk. She removed the metal box from the envelope. She took her penknife from her pocket and worked it carefully along the seals until the waterproof compound separated from the metal. The compound came away in small brittle strips. The box opened.

Inside the box were two pages and a photograph.

The photograph was first—lying face-up on top of the two pages, as if Hatch had wanted the face to be the first thing

Elena saw. Elena looked at it.

The photograph was a different photograph from the one Dina had brought her. This photograph was older—perhaps a decade older, maybe fifteen years—and was printed on the glossy paper that British passport photography studios had used in the seventies. It was a studio portrait. The man was wearing a charcoal suit and a dark tie. His hair was fuller than it had been in Dina's photograph, and darker, and the face was more clearly visible because the subject was looking directly at the camera.

The face was the face.

Elena looked at it for a long moment. The photograph did not refuse her. She committed the face to memory. Then she turned the photograph over. On the back, in Hatch's pencil handwriting, were three lines:

Laurence Henry Thornley. Born Vienna, 14 March 1931, to an English father and an Austrian mother. Died officially in a motor accident in Kent, 11 September 1974. Not actually dead.

Elena read the lines three times.

Laurence Henry Thornley.

She had been looking for this name for thirteen years. In Geneva bistros and Vienna hotel rooms and a basement in Friedrichshain, the name had been a face her memory refused to hold, a ring on a finger, a rhythm in prose that was not Yuri's. Now the name was a few syllables on the back of a photograph in a cemetery, and the syllables were ordinary, and the ordinariness was the point. The network had always been ordinary. That was how it survived.

The name did not match anyone in her mental file of British intelligence officers or European financiers or NATO counter-proliferation staff. She had never seen the name before. The name was the kind of name that would pass unremarked in every room in which its owner would later operate.

She turned to the pages.

The first page was a summary. Handwritten, in the small precise hand Hatch had used for his private notes—the same hand Elena saw on the inside of the metal reel case. The summary was one side of one sheet of A4. Elena read it.

Thornley, Laurence Henry. MI6, 1953—1967. Four postings: Vienna, Beirut, Nicosia, Geneva. Transferred to NATO counter-proliferation at the request of an officer whose name appears in no personnel file. Reported dead in a single-car accident on the A21, autumn 1974. Death certificate signed by a coroner who retired six weeks later. Body cremated on the instruction of a cousin who does not appear in British civil records. The motor accident did not happen. Thornley was not in the car. The car was empty. The car was driven off the road at the requested time by a man who died of a heart attack four months later.

The second page was the list.

The list was titled, in pencil, at the top, with three letters and a number: *4-SVC P.* Below the title, in four columns, were the names of four intelligence services: CIA, MI6, BND, SDECE. Two columns were intact. A third had water damage from the box's years underground; half its names were illegible. The SDECE column was in a different ink, added later in a hand that did not match the original three. Below each heading, three names and dates. Twelve names total. Twelve men who had agreed, in writing, to protect a secret that had outlived most of them. Twelve senior officers, across four services, who had signed documents agreeing to treat Laurence Henry Thornley as a classified asset whose existence would not be acknowledged and whose operational activity would be protected from inquiry by any of the four services individually or jointly.

Twelve signatures. Four services. Forty years of institutional silence.

Elena read the twelve names. She did not recognize all of them. She recognized six. The six she recognized were senior officers whose names had appeared in the intelligence histories she'd studied and whose careers had been, in the official record, unremarkable in the specific way that senior intelligence careers became unremarkable when the careers were being managed so that the unremarkableness was the point. Two of the six were still alive. Four were dead. The two who were still alive would, if they ever read the page in front of her, recognize immediately that the page was the end of both of them.

Elena read the list twice. She memorized it. She closed her eyes and ran through the twelve names and the twelve dates and the four service columns and the overall architecture, and she confirmed to herself that the memorization was complete.

She opened her eyes.

She put the photograph back on top of the pages. She closed the box. She placed the box in the envelope. She placed the envelope in her handbag.

She sat at the London Library desk for another three minutes without moving, because the three minutes were the time her body required to absorb that she now had, in her handbag, the name of a man who had been operating invisibly across four major intelligence services for forty years and whose existence had never been written down in any document that any of the four services had been willing to retain.

Laurence Henry Thornley.

The man in Vienna. The man in Friedrichshain. The man in the photograph Dina had taken at the Spanish embassy reception in Tel Aviv in October. The man with the gold ring on the little finger of his right hand. The man whose face her memory had refused to retain twice, and whose face she now had in two photographs and in her memory and in the knowing that the refusing had not been her failure but his training.

The name was the beginning of the end of the network.

The name would not be the end of the network by itself. Hatch had said so on the reel. *Knowing the name will not by itself end the network.* But the name was the corner of the curtain. The name was the thing that, at Bermondsey, if the photographs were taken correctly and if the faces were captured and if the names could be matched against the face through the right channels, would produce the kind of public exposure the network had spent forty years preventing.

Elena rose from the desk. She replaced the two books she took from the shelf as cover—a volume of nineteenth-century German theological commentary she had not opened and a biography of Schleiermacher she had no intention of reading—and she left the London Library at 11:32.

She walked out into St James's Square and turned left.

Then she noticed the tail.

The tail was a man in a navy overcoat and a charcoal scarf. He was walking approximately forty meters behind her on the south side of the square. He was not looking at her. He was looking at the middle distance—the specific non-looking of a surveillance officer who had been trained to keep his target in peripheral vision without making the looking itself visible.

Elena registered him in three seconds.

She did not react.

She continued walking at the unhurried pace of a woman leaving a library—brisk but not hurried, her handbag over her shoulder, her eyes on the pavement in front of her with the mild preoccupation of someone thinking about errands. She turned right onto King Street. She turned left onto St James's Street. She walked south toward Pall Mall.

The tail followed.

Forty meters back. Professional pace. The network, then. A single watcher to see what she did next.

The network wanted to know where she'd come from.

The network wanted to know where she was going next.

The network would not know about the box unless she led them to it. The stone had been replaced with enough care that nobody not specifically looking would notice it had been lifted. The network might suspect the box existed. It would not know where. And it could not follow her backward—the library-to-cemetery trip was already complete, and there was no backward to follow.

She would have to lose him without him knowing he had been seen. Escalation was the one thing she could not afford with two weeks until Bermondsey.

She turned toward Waterloo. Waterloo at noon was the geometry of dispersal—several thousand people moving in every direction, and a service corridor she had mapped in 1982 and never used.

The tail was still with her. She could see him reflected in the glass of a photographer's kiosk she passed at a specific angle —the kind of angle she'd been using for reflection surveillance since her second year at the Red Banner Institute. He was thirty-five meters back. He was maintaining the gap.

She walked onto the Hungerford Bridge footbridge.

Halfway across the bridge, she looked over the railing at the

Thames.

She looked at the water the way tourists looked at the water. She paused. She pretended to be admiring the view—the Palace of Westminster upriver to the west, the dome of St Paul's downriver to the east, the gray December sky over the gray December water, the whole small municipal picture of central London from the height of an old iron footbridge. The pause lasted twelve seconds. It was the kind of pause any tourist might make.

The tail had to choose.

He could stop on the bridge with her, which would place him too close and would compromise his cover. He could continue past her, which would put him ahead of her and out of the tail position. Or he could slow down imperceptibly and match her pace, which was the professional's choice and which Elena had been waiting for him to make because the slowing would commit him to a particular rhythm she could then use against him.

He slowed.

Elena resumed walking. She did not look at him. She walked off the footbridge onto the South Bank and turned left toward Waterloo. She increased her pace by perhaps ten percent—not enough to announce that she was hurrying, but enough to require the tail to adjust his own pace upward to match hers. The match was the kind of small unconscious calibration a tail made without thinking, and the calibration was the commitment.

She crossed the concourse to the men's toilet at the east end.

She walked into the men's toilet through the concourse entrance.

A man in a business suit was at the sink. He saw her enter and his eyes widened with the specific surprised expression of an English man who had just seen a woman walk into a men's toilet and who was trying to decide whether to say something. Elena did not give him time to decide. She walked directly through the room to the second door on the opposite side—the door to the service corridor—and pushed it open and stepped through.

The service corridor was empty. The corridor smelled of industrial disinfectant and the metal cold of a back-of-house space in a railway station. Elena walked down the corridor to the back of platform 17 and emerged onto the platform behind a stationary train.

She moved along the platform at a pace that was neither running nor walking. She walked past three carriages and stepped onto the train through the door of the fourth carriage. The train was a South Western service to Portsmouth Harbour. The train was half-full. Elena walked through the carriage into the next carriage and the next, moving away from the door she'd entered through, until she reached a carriage toward the front of the train where she sat down in a window seat on the far side from the platform.

The train departed three minutes later.

Elena ran the standard counter-surveillance route—eight legs, two hours and forty minutes, nobody following her past the third.

She walked home from South Kensington station through the December afternoon. Reflections in shop windows. The geometry of pedestrians behind her. Parked cars and the traffic lights and the small details of a street she'd walked a thousand times. She saw no tail. She saw no repetition. The man in the navy overcoat was gone—had been gone, she was reasonably certain, since the moment she'd stepped into the men's toilet on the Waterloo concourse and emerged thirty seconds later on the back of platform 17 through a door the tail had not known existed.

She reached her flat by mid-afternoon. She let herself in. She locked the deadbolt. She placed the manila envelope with the metal box on the kitchen table beside the dead Nagra and the photograph of the man with the gold ring and the open drawer with its contents.

She made tea.

She stood at the kitchen window drinking the tea. She watched the street. The street was empty in the way Kensington streets were empty at 3 PM on a December Monday—a woman pushing a pram, a cat sleeping on a front step, the slow flat December light fading toward the early winter dusk that would arrive in another hour.

No one was watching her building.

She was reasonably certain.

She went to the study and took a plain white card from the drawer of the desk. The card was the size of a gallery invitation card—the exact size Calder had used for the invitations he'd left for Alice Marsh in October and November of 1973 when they'd been arranging to meet at galleries they had not formally arranged to meet at. Elena had kept a small supply of plain cards in the desk drawer for years for the occasional social correspondence Alice Marsh was required to send.

She took her fountain pen. She wrote four lines on the card, in English, in the careful even handwriting Alice Marsh used for personal correspondence.

The Mayflower Hotel, Bermondsey Wall East. Room 14. The evening of the second of January. Twenty hundred hours. Please come.—A.

She looked at the card. She read it once. Her hand was steady. It had been steady for the four lines. It would not be steady for a fifth.

The card was the invitation. The kind Calder had left for Alice Marsh in the autumn of 1973, when every small piece of paper passed between them had been a question the other was being asked to answer. She was asking him one more. The card was the question made small enough to carry.

She placed the card in an envelope. She did not address the envelope. She sealed it.

She would deliver it herself. Not by post—post created records, and post was too slow. She would walk to Chiswick and she would put the card through the letterbox of the house Calder had lived in alone since June 1984, and he would find it when he came home, and he would decide whether to come.

She picked up her coat.

She left the flat for the second time that day. The afternoon was cold. The Christmas lights in the shop windows on Kensington High Street were on now, because the December light was almost gone. Elena walked to South Kensington station and took the District Line to Turnham Green.

The house in Chiswick was dark.

Elena walked past it once on the opposite pavement to confirm its darkness and to scan the street for observers. The street had the same early-evening quiet it had always had. The houses on both sides had lights on—dinner was being made in several of them, a television was audible from one—but the Calder house was dark except for the small outside light above the front porch that Margaret had installed in 1981 and that Calder had never bothered to turn off in the five and a half years since she left.

Elena crossed the street. She walked up the short path to the front door. She opened the brass flap of the letterbox. She pushed the envelope through.

The envelope fell onto the hallway floor on the other side of the door with the soft papery sound an envelope made when it landed on a wooden hallway floor in an empty house.

Elena closed the letterbox flap. She turned and walked back down the path to the pavement. She walked back along the street toward the Tube station with the unhurried pace of a woman who had completed an errand and was going home.

She did not look back because looking back was the kind of thing that would have made her a woman who had just delivered something rather than a woman who was walking through Chiswick on a December evening. She was a woman walking through Chiswick on a December evening. The envelope on the hallway floor of the house behind her was no longer her responsibility. The envelope was now Calder's problem—whether to open it, whether to read it, whether to understand it, whether to come to Bermondsey on the second of January at twenty hundred hours.

She took the District Line back to South Kensington. She walked home from the station in the December dark. She reached the flat at 18:47.

She did not eat. She did not drink. She sat at the kitchen table with the metal box and the photograph of the man with the gold ring and the dead Nagra and the open drawer, and she looked at the objects on the table, and she waited.

The waiting would last just over two weeks.

Just over two weeks to the second of January, when she would take the train to Bermondsey and let herself into room 14 at the Mayflower Hotel and open the bag containing the objects from the drawer and lay them out on a table that was not this table, and then open the door at twenty hundred hours and see whether James Calder was standing on the other side of it.

The waiting was the work now.

Hatch had said the silence was where the work was.

The silence had begun.

The days between the delivery of the card and the second of January passed in a quiet Elena did not try to describe to herself.

The gallery. Meals. Sleep. She walked in the late afternoons in Hyde Park through the cold December and early January light that was the light of a year ending and another beginning. She read the newspapers without retaining the headlines. The Wall was gone. Czechoslovakia had happened. Ceaușescu had been shot on Christmas Day. The world had decided, between 9 November and the new year, that it was done with the arrangement it had maintained for forty-five years, and the decision was arriving, day by day, as the news of particular governments that had stopped existing in particular ways.

In the hours she did not permit herself to think about Calder, she thought about the network's methodology.

Twenty-five years of surviving partial exposures across four services. She had been reading the pattern in her private ledger for a decade. When a piece of the architecture came close to visibility, the network did not defend the piece; it spent it. A controlled demolition—one building ended to prevent a block from going up. The building was always one the network had decided, in advance, it could lose. In every instance she had tracked, the machinery had continued beneath. The exposure had been the dust the building threw up as it came down; the machinery had simply shifted a street over and resumed.

She did not hold the principle up against Bermondsey. The not-holding was an operational discipline. She had maintained it, without effort, for sixteen years. It was maintaining her now.

She did not hear from Calder.

She hadn't expected to hear from him. The card had not asked for a reply, only for a presence. He would come or he would not come. She would know at twenty hundred hours on the second of January.

Christmas passed. Helen came on the Sunday after Christmas for biscuits. She brought a tin of shortbread she had made herself, the tin tied with a bow, and sat in Elena's kitchen for forty minutes talking about her niece in Salisbury. Elena listened with the full attention she always gave Helen.

Years of Sunday shortbread. Years of Helen's company in a kitchen Helen believed belonged to Alice Marsh. Elena had never told Helen what either of them had meant. She did not tell her today either. The not-telling was the oldest discipline she had. She understood, this afternoon, that it had also been a kind of theft.

Helen left without noticing that the drawer beside the stove was empty and that the dead Nagra was still on the kitchen table where it had been since the night of the reel.

Helen did not notice because Helen had never been the kind of woman who noticed drawers, and because the Alice Marsh Elena presented to Helen on Sunday afternoons had, for all those years, been the kind of woman whose drawers were not worth noticing. Elena was grateful for the non-noticing in a way she'd never been grateful for anything Helen had given her before.

New Year's Eve passed. Elena sat at the kitchen table at midnight with Earl Grey and watched the year change on television. Berlin again. The crowd on the Wall, cheering for a new decade nobody had named yet. She thought about the boy in the death strip. About Anneliese in 2B. About women in both cities who had hung curtains next to death strips and made the small adjustments that had been their lives. She wondered whether any of them were also drinking tea at midnight with the kind of silence Hatch had taught her to honor.

At 00:14 on the first of January 1990, Elena rose from the table, washed the cup, and went to bed.

She slept five hours.

She woke on the morning of the first. She spent the day at the flat, reviewing the mental map of the Mayflower Hotel, room 14, the sightline from the window, the rooftop access through the service door, the approach routes to the other hotel whose lobby Dina would enter at 16:00 the next afternoon. She reviewed the operational plan she'd assembled in her head across two weeks of silence and she confirmed to herself that the plan was sound.

She ate a small meal in the evening. She slept six hours.

On the morning of the second she packed a small canvas bag.

She'd spent an hour the previous evening at the kitchen table with a reversed fifty-millimeter lens, a light stage she'd built from a desk lamp and a sheet of glass, and the small red notebook she'd been carrying since 1976. The lens and the film stock had been at the back of the cupboard since the basement in Normannenstraße in 1975, kept against a contingency she had not been ready to name. Thirteen years of investigation compressed into eleven microdots—each one the size of a printed period, each one containing a full page of the notebook's contents, each one mounted with a needle and a drop of adhesive onto the inside cover of a paperback novel she would carry in her coat pocket.

The paperback was a used copy of Le Carré's *A Perfect Spy*, bought from a stall in Charing Cross three days earlier for seventy pence. The dots were on pages 34, 55, 89, and 144. She'd chosen the pages from the Fibonacci sequence—each one the sum of the two before it. If the novel was scanned and the dots found, a cataloger might see the pattern. Most would not.

If the operation went wrong and the notebook was lost, the novel would survive. If the novel was searched, the dots would look like printing imperfections. She had learned the technique in a red-lit basement beneath the Normannenstraße nearly fifteen years ago from a woman with amphibian glasses who had told her that her hands were still.

Her hands were still steady. She thought of the woman in the Stasi basement who had said the hands were always the problem. Elena's hands had never been the problem. She was beginning to wonder if that was the problem.

The bag contained the drawer's full contents—every object she'd been assembling on the kitchen table since Dina's visit in December, and every object Dina had brought her—along with the two pages and the photograph from the Highgate box. In the inside pocket of her coat, she carried the F-21 Ajax in the Ronson lighter, with one hundred and seventy-eight frames remaining.

The dead Nagra stayed on the kitchen table. There was no point in taking it. It would not come with her to Bermondsey. It had done its work in this kitchen and its work was over, and taking a dead instrument to the end of an operation was the kind of sentimental gesture Elena had been trained out of and that she had not, even now, allowed herself to make.

The drawer beside the stove she left open. She had closed it every day by a discipline so complete she had stopped noticing it was discipline. She did not close it today. Closing the drawer had been part of Alice Marsh. Alice Marsh was over.

She put on her coat.

She left the flat at 16:30. The light was already beginning to fade. She took the District Line east. She changed at Monument. She took the bus over Tower Bridge. She walked the last mile through Bermondsey in the cold January dusk, past the old warehouses and the small pubs and the quiet riverside terraces of a district that had not yet been discovered by property developers and that still held, in its narrow streets and its smell of the Thames, the quality of a London neighborhood that had been working for three hundred years and that had accepted the working as its life.

She reached the Mayflower Hotel at 18:47.

The Mayflower Hotel was a small three-story Victorian building on Bermondsey Wall East with a pub on the ground floor and ten rooms on the two upper floors. The pub was full. The rooms were mostly empty—the Mayflower was the kind of hotel that took walk-in custom and did not require reservations, and the second of January was not a night on which many people walked in. Elena took room 14 under the name Alice Marsh and paid for it in cash for two nights. The woman at the reception desk asked no questions.

Elena walked up the narrow stairs to the second floor. She unlocked room 14 with the iron key the woman at the desk had given her. She entered the room.

The room was small. A single bed. A wooden table and two wooden chairs. A small wardrobe. A washbasin in the corner. A single window overlooking the river. The window was the reason Elena chose room 14—the window faced east, toward the bend of the Thames where the warehouses of the old Surrey Docks stood, and the small hotel whose lobby Dina would enter at 16:00 tomorrow was visible from this window, two hundred meters east along Bermondsey Wall, across a narrow street and a low wall and a cobbled yard. Elena had scouted the location in the third week of December. The sightline from room 14 to the lobby entrance was clear. The rooftop of this building was accessible through a service door at the end of the second-floor corridor. The rooftop was where the F-21 Ajax would be used tomorrow at 15:00.

But that was tomorrow.

Tonight was the night before.

Tonight was the confession.

Elena placed the canvas bag on the wooden table. She opened it. She arranged the archive on the table the way she'd arranged it in Kensington three weeks ago when Dina had sat across from her—every object in its accustomed place, sixteen years of withholdings laid out between the chair she was sitting in and the chair she was waiting for Calder to sit in.

She did not place the F-21 Ajax on the table. The F-21 stayed in the inner pocket of her coat, because the F-21 was tomorrow's instrument and tomorrow was not yet.

The table was laid.

The dossier was ready.

Elena sat in the wooden chair facing the door. She looked at her watch. 19:42.

Eighteen minutes.

She placed her hands on her lap. She waited.

The waiting was the last waiting.

29
THE ENVELOPE

Chiswick, London—2 January 1990

Calder had not picked up the envelope.

The envelope had been on the hallway floor for sixteen days.

Calder had stepped over it every morning on his way to make coffee. He had stepped over it every evening on his way back from work. He had stepped over it on Christmas Day, which he spent alone in the Chiswick house with a tin of biscuits and the radio, because Margaret had the children—her sister's children, technically, but Margaret treated them as her own—and the invitation to her sister's house in Hampshire had not included him. It hadn't for five Christmases—not since the letter arrived, not since the marriage ended.

He stepped over the envelope on Boxing Day. He stepped over it on New Year's Eve, when he drank a bottle of Chablis in the kitchen and listened to the fireworks in the garden two doors down and thought about 1973 and did not think about the envelope.

The envelope was cream-colored. It was lying face-down on the wood. He had not turned it over because he did not need to. He had seen the handwriting when it came through the slot on the evening of 17 December, and the handwriting had been enough.

He knew whose hand had written on the envelope because he had been reading that hand for sixteen years. On gallery invitation cards left in his mailbox. On the small notes she left on his pillow when she went home early. On the inscription in a book about Flemish painters she gave him for Christmas 1981, which was the last Christmas they had spent in this house together—the three of them, Alice and James and Margaret and the real tree Margaret had insisted on.

The book was still on the shelf in the study. The inscription read: *For James. Who sees the curtain and the window. A.*

He had not opened the envelope. He had read the outside—the handwriting he recognized, the address he would go to or not go to, the date and time that were either a summons or an invitation and that he had not yet decided which. The Mayflower Hotel. Bermondsey. Room 14. 20:00. 2 January.

Today.

Calder made coffee. He made it the way he had been making it for five and a half years of mornings alone in this kitchen—kettle, cafetière, the same blend from the same shop on the Chiswick High Road, because changing it would have been an admission he was not yet prepared to make.

The kitchen still had Margaret's geraniums on the windowsill. They were alive. He watered them. He had never been interested in plants—except once, in a gallery in Fitzrovia, when a woman told him that the real subject of a photograph was that someone was still growing things next to it. The watering was a thing his hands did on Tuesday and Saturday mornings, the way the central heating timer still ran on Margaret's schedule and the radio was still preset to Radio 4. The military face of his watch sat above the civilian strap, the way it had sat for sixteen years. The house was full of Margaret's habits running on his body.

He drank the coffee standing at the window. The garden was January-bare. A blackbird was sitting on the wall—the same blackbird that had been sitting on that wall at this hour for three winters.

He looked at the garden and thought about Alice Marsh.

He had been thinking about Alice Marsh for sixteen years. For twelve of those years the thinking had included the knowledge that she was not Alice Marsh. The knowledge had arrived on a Tuesday evening in November 1977 at the Special Forces Club—a hotel register from Lillehammer with her name in it, six blocks from the Hamidi shooting. The copy had sat in a filing cabinet at Century House for four years. Nobody had noticed the name. Nobody had been looking for it. Calder had been sleeping with it for four years.

Calder had noticed the name because Calder had been sleeping with the name for four years.

He had sat in the club with four whiskies and a hotel register and the glass warm in his hand, and he had thought: she was there. Not: *she is a spy.* Not: *she is the enemy.* The first thought, the thought that the whisky let through before the professional apparatus could intervene, was simply: *she was in Lillehammer and she didn't tell me.*

The not-telling was the thing. The lying was professional—he lied professionally every day. The not-telling was the betrayal. She had been in Norway on the night a man was shot and a defector was killed, and she had come home and lain beside him and said nothing. She had made tea in the morning and touched his face with the hand that had done whatever it had done in Lillehammer, and the hand had been warm and steady, and the warmth and steadiness had been professional.

The professional assessment took forty-eight hours. He ran it in his head while driving to work, while eating lunch alone with the door closed. The accent. The gaps. The precision of a life that had been built rather than lived.

KGB illegal. Deep cover. Long-term.

Calder did not file the assessment.

He did not file it because the filing would have put her in a cell or on a plane. It would have ended his career. Both of these were true and neither was the reason.

The reason was a doorway in East Berlin in 1968. A woman named Natalia who let a stranger sleep on her sofa without asking who he was. The belief—irrational, unprofessional—that kindness existed inside the machinery. That somewhere inside Alice Marsh was a woman who had chosen him because something in the choosing was real.

He could not prove it. The hypothesis was unfalsifiable—any evidence of genuine feeling could also be evidence of a well-executed operation. But the thing he read in Alice Marsh on certain nights, in the half-second between the performance and the recovery, was something the training could not produce. The training could produce warmth. It could not produce the way she looked at his face when she thought he was asleep—not surveillance but study. The look of a woman trying to memorize something she expected to lose.

He had never told her he was awake. He closed his eyes and let her look.

This was his version of the filing system. Not a drawer beside a stove. His filing system was the decision, renewed every morning for twelve years, not to know what he knew. Kenyan coffee and Radio 4 and the watering of geraniums—the careful maintenance of a life that was, from the outside, the life of a man managing. From the inside it was the life of a man who knew the woman he loved was carrying something she could not put down, and that his silence was the only thing protecting her from the consequences of what she carried.

He had been protecting her since January 1978.

The choosing was the morning, every morning, for twelve years.

The FEUERWERK investigation had nearly ended the silence three times.

The first time was 1979—a margin notation in a NATO inventory that belonged to no institution Calder could name. The second was 1983, when a journalist named Hatch described a pattern in weapons decommissioning records that mirrored the pattern Calder had been tracking alone. Hatch was pulling the same thread from the other side.

The third time was when everything broke. The anonymous letters. Margaret reading one in the staffroom at school and folding it into her bag and going home and not speaking about it for three days before she told him she was moving to Salisbury. Margaret moving to Salisbury. The divorce filed in August. The diazepam that was working less well than it had been. The symptoms he had attributed to overwork and unhappiness and the stress of a marriage ending, and that he had, in one specific hour in March 1985 at his kitchen table after Elena had left for the morning, considered attributing to Elena. He'd considered it for forty minutes. He had then dismissed it as paranoia, because the alternative explanation was that the woman he loved was poisoning him, and he was not prepared to hold that explanation.

The knowledge should have destroyed him. Instead it destroyed the last wall between his professional life and his private life. In the rubble he found something unexpected: Elena—he had started thinking of her as Elena, although he did not know her name—was trapped inside the same machinery he was. The machinery was using her to destroy him. She knew it. She hated it. She was doing it anyway because the machine did not offer refusal.

He took the diazepam. He let his professional performance decline. He let the campaign work. Ending her was the one thing the FEUERWERK investigation and the twelve years of not-filing and the slow destruction of his own career had been designed to prevent.

Margaret left in June 1984. She took the small green suitcase and the photograph albums and the charm bracelet with the five charms—the book, the cat, the heart, the M, and the small silver key that had appeared on her bracelet in November 1977 without explanation and that she had never asked him about. Calder had never told her what it opened. She wore it anyway.

Calder knew this because Margaret still called, twice a month, on Sunday evenings. She told him about the school. He told her about the blackbird. Neither of them mentioned Alice Marsh. The not-mentioning was the last piece of the marriage that still functioned.

At noon Calder walked to the high street. He bought the newspaper. He bought a ham-and-mustard sandwich—the same one he had bought every Tuesday for five years, the only routine that survived Margaret. He bought a half-bottle of Jameson from the off-license and then put it back on the shelf and bought a bottle of sparkling water instead, because tonight required sobriety. Whatever was waiting in room 14 at the Mayflower Hotel required him to be the man he had been before the diazepam, before the campaign, before the four whiskies at the Special Forces Club. The man who could read a file and hold a silence and walk into a room without knowing what was in it.

He had not been that man for a long time. He would have to be that man tonight.

He walked back to the house. He ate the sandwich at the kitchen table. He read the newspaper. The newspaper was full of Eastern Europe. Romania was in chaos. Ceaușescu was dead. The Wall was rubble. The entire edifice of the Cold War was collapsing. Calder read about it the way a man reads about a weather event taking place somewhere he no longer lives.

At two o'clock he went upstairs. He opened the wardrobe. He looked at his suits. He chose the charcoal—the suit he wore to briefings, the suit Margaret had helped him choose at a shop on Jermyn Street in 1976, the suit that still fit because Calder had not gained weight since 1976, which was not discipline but the metabolic consequence of a man who forgot to eat most days and who drank his calories instead.

He laid the suit on the bed. He showered. He shaved. He dressed with the attention of a man preparing for something important—the first time he had dressed with that attention since the gallery in November.

He checked his watch. 16:30. Three and a half hours.

He went down to the darkroom under the stairs. He spent forty minutes there. The prints went into a second manila envelope. He left the envelope on the worktable. He came back into the hall with nothing in his hands, and the smell of fixer on the back of his wrist that he noticed only when he buttoned his coat.

He went downstairs.

The envelope was on the hallway floor.

He stood over it for a long time. The cream-colored paper on the dark wood. Her handwriting on the front—the address of the hotel, the room number, the date. The handwriting was Alice Marsh's. It had been Alice Marsh's for sixteen years. He knew Alice Marsh's handwriting the way he knew his mother's. He had received cards and notes and shopping lists in that handwriting for a decade and a half. The handwriting on the envelope was Alice Marsh's, and the name on the envelope was his, and the request inside was a request to come to a hotel in Bermondsey on the evening of the second of January, 1990, and stay with her.

He had gone back and checked, after the hotel register, pulling every gallery invitation card from the drawer where he kept them. The third card was where the Cyrillic was clearest. He had not told anyone. He had placed the observation in the file he kept in his head—the file that had no number and no classification and no distribution list and that was, after twelve years, the most comprehensive unauthorized investigation in the history of the British intelligence service.

The Geneva and Berlin entries had come from a Nordic liaison exchange he'd requested on a different pretext in 1977. He had never been certain it was his idea. The investigation would never be filed. The investigation existed only inside him. If he died tomorrow, the investigation would die with him, and the only evidence it had ever existed would be a slight statistical anomaly in the number of times Calder had checked out the Lillehammer archive file from Century House records—four times, which was three times more than his operational responsibilities required and which nobody had flagged because nobody was looking.

He bent down. He picked up the envelope. He held it. The paper was cold from sixteen days on the hallway floor. It was light—a single card inside, by the weight of it. Nothing operational. No photographs. No documents. No evidence. Just a card.

He turned it over. The flap was sealed. He did not open it.

He did not open it because the envelope was the last sealed thing between them, and the unsealing was something he wanted her to see. The unsealing would happen in the room or it would not happen at all. He would carry it sealed to Bermondsey and he would place it on whatever table she had prepared and the sealed envelope would say what he could not yet say with his mouth: *I came without reading it. I came because you asked. The asking was enough.*

He put the envelope in the inside pocket of his overcoat.

He checked his watch. 17:15.

He had two hours and forty-five minutes. He would arrive early. He wanted to arrive early. He wanted to walk the streets around the hotel before going in, the way he had been trained to walk the streets around any location before entering it, because the training was the thing that still worked when everything else had stopped working and because the walking would give him time.

He put on his shoes. Good shoes—the brown leather pair, clean-soled, the pair he kept for occasions that required him to look like a man who was in control of his approach. He put on his overcoat. He checked the pocket. The envelope was there.

He walked to the front door. He stopped. He turned back.

He walked into the kitchen. He watered the geraniums. A Tuesday's worth. Then, after a moment, a Saturday's worth too.

He stood at the sink with the watering can in his hand.

Margaret had bought the geraniums in June 1978 at a market stall in Chiswick, carrying them home in the string bag she kept folded in the bottom of her handbag for the chance arrivals of small portable living things. She had unwrapped them at this sink. She had trimmed two yellowing leaves. She had said, without looking at him, that the plants would live longer than most things in this house. He had registered the sentence at the time as the kind of thing Margaret said when she meant something she was not going to name, and he had filed it as a sentence to return to, and had not returned to it until now.

She had been right. The geraniums were on their twelfth year. The marriage had ended in their sixth.

He set the watering can on the draining board. The kitchen was cold—cold in the specific way rooms were cold when the warmth had been a function of a person and the person was no longer in the room.

He thought about the register Margaret had kept at school. Year Six. Present, absent, late. And, in the private column she had added to the bottom of the page when the staff room was empty, 'somewhere else.' She had told him about the fourth column once, on a Sunday in 1978, in bed, in the gray morning light, in the specific admission-tone she used when she was telling him something she had been carrying long enough to decide it was worth carrying less. He had laughed. He had said something affectionate. He had not told her that he had recognized, in the admission, his own condition in their marriage—that he had been in her fourth column for most of the time they had been under the same roof, and that she had known, and that the knowing had been the thing that made the marriage, for her, livable.

Margaret had loved him anyway. Margaret had loved him while knowing.

He was going to Bermondsey tonight to sit across from the woman who had lived in that column.

He did not know what he would say to her.

He knew that Margaret, somewhere in Salisbury at this hour, was probably grading exercise books on a Tuesday evening with a mug of tea at her elbow, and that the silver cat charm on the bracelet she had worn every day for twenty-one years was catching the lamplight, and that the key beside it was a silence neither of them had broken, and that the silence was the marriage, and the marriage had lasted, in its truest form, since the fourth column had been added, and had never, even now, ended.

He picked up the watering can. He rinsed it. He set it upside-down to drain.

Then he left.

The Tube was quiet. 2 January, the dead space between the holidays and the return to work. A few passengers in each carriage. A woman reading a paperback. A man asleep against the window.

Calder sat with the envelope in his pocket and thought about the word investigation.

He had been conducting an investigation for twelve years. Not the FEUERWERK investigation—that was, by now, institutional, authorized, filed in the proper channels, progressing at the institutional pace. The other investigation. The private one. The investigation into the woman he loved.

The investigation had no name. It had no file number. It had no methodology beyond the oldest methodology in the intelligence profession: watch, and wait, and try to understand what you are seeing. He had watched Alice Marsh for twelve years the way a birdwatcher watched a species he had never seen before—with patience, with attention, with the understanding that the watching itself changed neither the watcher nor the watched and that the only product of the watching was knowledge, and that knowledge, once acquired, could not be returned.

He knew things about her that she did not know he knew. He knew she carried a small red notebook in the inner pocket of her handbag and that she wrote in it in a handwriting that was not the handwriting she used for gallery correspondence. He knew the language of the notebook was not English. He knew the drawer beside her stove contained a reel of tape he had watched her not listen to for twelve years. He knew she had kept his first card—the one about the Wall being better from the Eastern side—in the same drawer since November 1973. The drawer was sixteen years of evidence a man did not gather by accident.

He did not know what she carried in the drawer beside the stove. He had never opened it. The not-opening was his version of the not-filing—a deliberate act of restraint that cost him something every day and that was, after twelve years, the most expensive thing he had ever purchased.

The train passed through Earl's Court. He changed. The platform was cold. A busker was playing guitar at the far end, something by Leonard Cohen, and the sound of it carried through the tiled corridor with the specific melancholy of a man singing about love in an underground station on the second of January.

He got on the eastbound train. Monument. Change for the East London Line.

He thought about the gallery in Fitzrovia in October 1973. The photograph of the Wall. The curtains in the window. The woman who had said: I think that's the photograph's real subject. Not the Wall. That someone is still growing things next to it.

He had known, in that moment, that she was something. Not what she was. Something. The quality of attention. The way she tracked the room in small economical glances and then gave him her full focus as if the room had been cleared and they were the only two people in it. He had known, and the knowing had not stopped him, and the not-stopping was the act from which everything else had followed—the sixteen years, the geraniums, the envelope.

The train surfaced at Wapping. River light. Gray January sky. The Thames outside the window, wide and flat, the color of old silver. He could see Bermondsey on the south bank.

The train pulled into Bermondsey station. He stood. He buttoned his coat. He checked the pocket.

The envelope was there. Still sealed. Still carrying whatever she had written on the card inside it. He would never read it. He would carry it sealed into room 14. The sealing was the only honest thing he had left to offer. He would place it on the table and she would see that it was sealed and she would understand what the sealing meant, and the understanding would be the first true thing that passed between them since October 1973.

He stepped onto the platform. The air was cold. January cold, river cold, the cold of a London evening that had committed to darkness at four o'clock and had not looked back.

He walked south toward the water.

30

THE MAYFLOWER

Bermondsey—2 January 1990

At 19:58, Elena heard footsteps in the corridor—the specific weight and rhythm of a man walking on old wooden floorboards, the gait of a man who had been carrying something for many years and was not sure, even now, whether the thing was a weight or a gift.

The footsteps stopped outside the door.

There was a long pause.

Then the knock came—three taps, conventional—and Elena rose from the chair and crossed the room and placed her hand on the knob and turned it and opened the door.

James Calder was standing on the other side.

He had the envelope in his left hand.

He had not opened it.

The Mayflower Hotel smelled of the river—the old smell, damp stone and tidal mud, the mineral patience of water that had been rising against this stretch of bank for a thousand years. The corridor was narrow. The carpet was the color of dried blood, though this was coincidence. The light came from a single fixture at the far end that buzzed at a frequency Elena could feel in her back teeth. January cold pressed against the window at the end of the hall like an animal waiting to be let in.

He was wearing a dark overcoat over a charcoal suit. His hair was grayer than it had been the last time Elena saw him in person—at a gallery opening in Mayfair in mid-November, six weeks ago, the kind of chance encounter they had long since perfected into the unhurried mutual pretense that each was surprised to see the other and that the evening did not require either of them to account for the surprise. His face was the face Elena had been seeing for sixteen years. The face she first looked at in a Fitzrovia gallery in October 1973.

She did not know what he saw when he looked back. She knew what was there—the dark hair cut close now, the jaw-line that had once softened a recruitment poster and had stopped softening anything. The mouth that had spent the years deciding had decided. The eyes that had never changed. She was forty-one years old and she looked like what she was: a woman who had been carved by the work until the work was the shape. The face that had been in her bed more nights than she could count. The face she'd woken up beside and left behind and returned to and lied to, the face she'd mapped the load-bearing walls of and then demolished along with the walls.

The face was older.

The eyes were the same.

The eyes were looking at her the way they had looked at her every time something significant had passed between them —the quiet total attention that was both their professional baseline, the medium through which they had communicated since the first gallery, when the words they used aloud were covers for the words they were not saying.

Elena stepped back from the door to let him in.

He entered the room. He did not hand her the envelope. He carried it past her into the room and stood in the small space between the door and the wooden table, and he looked at the dossier laid out on the table.

He looked at the objects for a long moment.

The diary. The recipe book with Margaret's inscription on the flyleaf. The candle and the pen. The Yuri card. The fountain-pen card. The Mercator knife Elena had taken from Voss in October 1977. The brass key dropped into her pocket on Yefet Street in December 1982. The two prints of Kessler's *rothschildianum*. Anneliese's drawing of a yellow-sun house signed *Anneliese, 2B*. The metal reel case with Hatch's pencil catalog inside the lid. Two photographs of the same man—a black-and-white eight-by-ten taken in Tel Aviv in October 1989 and a glossy studio portrait from fifteen years earlier. The two handwritten pages from the Highgate box. The red cloth-bound notebook from the inner pocket of her handbag, open to a middle page she had not chosen deliberately.

The object in Calder's left hand—the sealed unopened envelope with her four-line card inside it—was the fourteenth object.

Then he looked at Elena.

The room smelled of old carpet and radiator heat. A window looked onto the river. The January dark was absolute.

'Hello,' she said. In English. The word was the word Alice Marsh would have used. It was also the word the woman she was would have used, because the distinction between Alice Marsh and the woman she was had narrowed in the three weeks since Dina had sat at her kitchen table to the point where the distinction was no longer available to her. She said 'hello' the way one person said 'hello' to another in a room where something enormous was about to happen.

'Hello,' Calder said.

He was still standing. She was still standing. Neither of them had moved toward the chairs.

'I did not open the card,' he said.

'I know.'

'I recognized your handwriting.'

'I thought you might.'

'Alice.' He said the name the way he had said it for sixteen years. Except now the name was a door he was holding open, and what was behind it was not Alice.

'I came because I recognized the handwriting. I came because the card said Bermondsey, and I have been expecting Bermondsey for two weeks.' He paused. 'I came because the envelope was on my floor for sixteen days and I stepped over it every morning and I could not step over it one more time.'

Elena nodded.

'Please,' she said. 'Sit.'

Calder placed the envelope on the table beside the dossier. He placed it very precisely, at the edge of the table, equidistant from the nearer corners, with the small careful motion of a man who understood that the envelope was now part of the arrangement on the table and that its placement mattered. He did not open it. He took off his overcoat and hung it on the back of the second wooden chair. He sat in the chair facing Elena across the table.

Elena sat.

Between them, on the wooden table of room 14 at the Mayflower Hotel on Bermondsey Wall East, sixteen years of her professional life were laid out under the small yellow light of a bedside lamp.

She looked at the objects. Then she looked at him.

'My name is Elena Vasilieva,' she said. 'I was born in Leningrad in 1948. I have been an illegal in London for nineteen years. I have never said my real name aloud in any of them. You are the first person I have said it to since 1970.'

She paused.

Calder was looking at her. His face had not changed. His hands were on the edge of the table, palms down. He was breathing normally.

He said: 'I know.'

His voice did not break. His hands on the table had not moved.

Elena looked at him.

'I know about Lillehammer,' Calder said. 'Since November 1977. A hotel register with Alice Marsh's name six blocks from the Hamidi shooting. I know about Petrov—the caliber, the timing. I know about East Berlin. I know about Tel Aviv.' He paused. 'I never tried to learn the operational details. I needed to keep loving you more than I needed to know what you'd done.'

'I also know,' he said, 'that the Zersetzung was yours. The letters. The drinking narrative at Century House. The small things moved in my flat on the nights you were there.' He looked at her. 'I knew by the spring of 1984. I have never been angry at you for it. I knew what you were doing and I knew why, and the why was a why I—'

He did not finish. After a moment he said, in the register he had used for the rest, 'I recognized it.'

The room was quiet.

Elena had placed her hands flat on the table when Calder had begun speaking. She had not moved them since. She was breathing in the slow measured way she'd learned to breathe at the Red Banner Institute in 1968 when the training had taught her that the body's breathing was the body's first and last tell and that the breathing had to be managed under every circumstance, especially the circumstances in which managing the breathing was the hardest.

She breathed.

She looked at the man across the table.

'Before the operational things,' she said, 'I am going to tell you a thing that was not operational. The operational things came out of it. I will not let you hear them first.'

Calder did not move.

'The first night,' Elena said. 'Your flat in Chiswick. December 1973. Margaret was in Salisbury. You had been carrying the invitation card in your jacket since November.'

'I remember.'

'For three seconds, in that bed, the filing system went dark. The machinery the Red Banner Institute had spent three years installing in me went quiet. For three seconds I was not Alice Marsh and I was not a KGB officer and I was not the woman who had been in Lillehammer five months earlier. I was a woman in a room with a man. The three seconds were the first time in my adult life I had been that. They were a catastrophe. They were a training failure. They were the thing that was supposed to be impossible and that happened anyway.'

She paused.

'I filed them the next morning. Not to Moscow. To the place in me where I was starting to keep the things I could not file to Moscow. The place was small that morning. It has grown for sixteen years. Most of what has grown in it has had you in it somewhere. The three seconds were the first entry in the second ledger. Everything that came after—Berlin, Tel Aviv, the withholdings, the drawer beside my stove, the notebook I am about to put on the table between us—all of it began the night the three seconds happened.'

Calder was looking at her with the stillness he used when he was absorbing information that changed the shape of what he already knew.

'I did not have the word for them,' he said. 'I knew something happened in the bed that night that was not in any category either of us had been trained to recognize. I have thought about it every week for sixteen years. It has been the thing I have been checking against.'

'Checking for what.'

'For whether the woman in the bed the first night was the same woman who came back from Berlin and went to Tel Aviv and sat across from me in this light for sixteen years. I did not know if there had been a woman in the bed that first night or if I had imagined one. The ambiguity was the working condition.'

'There was a woman,' Elena said. 'She is the woman sitting across from you tonight. She is the same woman.'

Calder closed his eyes for a second. When he opened them, something in his face had shifted by one degree. The one degree was the part of him that had been waiting for the sentence Elena had just said.

'And now,' she said, 'the operational things.'

'Yes.'

'The letter to Margaret,' she said. 'I typed it on a machine I bought for the one letter and dismantled afterward. I posted it from Paddington on a Tuesday so it would reach her school on the Wednesday, in the staffroom, when her colleagues would be there as she opened it.'

Calder did not look away. 'I know,' he said. 'I have known since the Wednesday it arrived.'

'How long have you been protecting me,' she said.

'Since January 1978.'

Elena closed her eyes for a moment.

January 1978. The month she returned from the East Berlin secondment with the Mercator knife and the *rothschildianum* photograph and the newly visible shape of a thing she had not yet named. The month she had not seen Calder for three weeks after coming back and had then seen him at a gallery in Hampstead where he had appeared unexpectedly and had looked at her with the expression of a man who had been waiting longer than the three weeks had accounted for. She thought the look had been about the absence. She'd thought the look had been about the eighteen months in Berlin and the not-knowing what she'd been doing in them. She had thought wrong.

The look had been about November 1977.

The look had been the look of a man who had found a hotel register two months earlier and had been carrying it since. The woman it named had been in East Berlin learning Zersetzung from a Stasi major. He had been deciding whether to confront her or bury the register in a drawer and build a second file whose only purpose was preventing the first from being found.

He decided to bury it.

He decided in January 1978.

'Tell me,' Elena said.

Calder did.

'Petrov,' Calder said. 'The defector who died in his flat the same night as Hamidi. Two rounds. Small caliber. The Norwegian police called it a burglary. I never believed them. The timing was the signature—Moscow waiting for a night when every officer in town was running south. That's not a local station decision. That's an illegal.

'I had been looking, on and off for four years, for the illegal.

'In November 1977 I was in a records archive, reading a file that had been declassified to the level of my clearance that week. A routine cross-reference from Scandinavian liaison—a list of hotel registrations for persons of interest who had been in Lillehammer during the week of the Hamidi incident. Compiled by the Norwegian police in August 1973. Forwarded to Oslo station as a courtesy. Filed and forgotten. One of forty-one files I was reading that afternoon.'

'The register listed seventeen names. Sixteen of them were unremarkable. The seventeenth was Alice Marsh, New Zealand passport, checked in 20 July, checked out 22 July. The name did not mean anything to the Norwegian police who had compiled the list. The name did not mean anything to the Oslo station that had filed the report. The name meant something to me because I had been sleeping with a woman named Alice Marsh for four years, and Alice Marsh had never told me she'd been in Norway in July 1973, and I had, in the seconds after I read the name, the specific physical sensation that people describe as the floor falling out from under them.

Elena did not move. She was looking at her hands on the table. Both hands were flat.

'I read the seventeenth line four times. The archive was cold. I remember the cold.

'I checked the dates. I checked the dates. I checked the passport number. I committed the page to memory. I closed the file. I replaced it in the archive. I walked out of the building. I walked for two hours through a London afternoon whose specific details I do not remember because the walking was the kind of walking a body does when the mind has stopped routing sensory data to the parts of itself that form memory. I ended the walk at the Special Forces Club. I went inside. I ordered a whisky.

'That was the beginning of the file. The hotel register. Then everything I'd been choosing not to notice—the phrasing, the patience, the way you listened to me when I talked about work.' His voice was quiet. 'I added the East Berlin secondment in 1982. The Sara Lerner receipt in 1983. The FEUERWERK file—because the papers on my desk had been disturbed in the night, and I understood what you'd been looking at.'

'But the file was not designed to expose you. It was designed to keep you from being exposed by anyone else.

Elena's breathing broke its pattern once. One breath, fractionally too long. She recovered it before the next sentence.

'I realized this in January 1978, two months after the hotel register. I realized it in the Special Forces Club, over my fourth whisky, on a different night from the November night.'

She did not interrupt.

'I was not going to report you. I was going to build the kind of file that would, if any of my colleagues ever started looking in your direction, produce enough noise to redirect them. I was going to be, professionally and privately and without ever telling you, the single mid-level MI6 officer who ensured that the KGB illegal I was in love with continued to operate in London without the institution I served ever catching up to her.

'I started the operation in January 1978. I have been running it for twelve years. I have been running it while sleeping beside you and waking beside you and cooking for you in a kitchen you were searching while I was downstairs. I left the FEUERWERK file on my desk because I wanted you to find it. I did not investigate the anonymous letters because I recognized the architecture. I knew by the spring of 1984 that they were yours. I did not ask where you went on the evenings you would not account for because I knew where you went. Every question I did not ask was a door I closed to prevent someone else from opening it.'

'Three times in twelve years, an inquiry into Alice Marsh was nearly begun. Each time I was the officer asked for input on whether the pattern warranted further investigation. Each time I said it did not. And I gave my colleagues three alternative directions they could look in that I had arranged to be more interesting than Alice Marsh.'

He paused.

'The first time was 1980.

'The second was 1983.

'The third was 1986, after the Brixton fire.

'Each time the redirection worked. Each time nobody looked at you again.'

He stopped. He picked up his glass of water from the table and held it without drinking. His hand was steady. Elena watched the hand the way she had watched it for sixteen years—for information, for pattern, for the thing between the lines. The hand was steady and the steadiness was not performance. The steadiness was the man.

He set the glass down.

'Hatch figured this out in 1986. A mutual contact—someone inside the service—mentioned in 1987 that Hatch had been asking questions about an MI6 officer who appeared to be protecting a London art historian. I understood immediately that Hatch was writing the story of my operation to protect you. That the story was going to be written whether I cooperated. The best thing I could do was to say nothing and trust that Hatch would handle it the way he handled everything.

'I never met Hatch.

'I hope Hatch is alive.'

Elena said nothing. She was hearing the reel. The wet rattle in the breathing. The tick accelerating beneath his voice. The goodbye said to a woman in a room he knew she would reach in time.

She had been listening to Calder for several minutes without interrupting. Her hands on the table had not moved. Her breathing had stayed in the slow measured pattern she'd been maintaining since the confession began. Underneath the pattern, her internal machinery had been doing the work it did when asked to absorb information that changed the shape of sixteen years of experience retroactively.

Calder had begun his operation in January 1978. Elena had begun her own private investigation in March 1976, twenty-two months earlier. They had both been running parallel off-books operations—his to protect her, hers to pull the thread on FEUERWERK—for most of the years they had been together, while sharing meals and beds and conversations about galleries and restaurants and the operational failures of other services, never discussing the intelligence service operation being run by the one person across the table.

Each of them had been the other's operation.

Each of them had been the subject and the object simultaneously.

Elena opened her mouth to speak and then did not speak.

Calder waited.

Then he said: 'There is one more thing. In October, ten weeks ago, a report arrived on my desk at Century House through the FEUERWERK channel. A single page. It described the emergency relocation of a warhead from a cache site in Vienna to a secondary site in southern Germany. It contained a railway routing number. Südbahnhof. 14 November.'

Elena's hands, which had been flat on the table, went still.

'You received the same report,' Calder said.

'Through a different channel,' Elena said. 'Three weeks before the Wall came down. The dead drop on Hampstead Heath.'

'The same report. The same details. The same routing number. Fed through two channels that should never have intersected.' He paused. 'Unless someone was watching both channels simultaneously. Unless someone fed the same bait into both streams and waited to see if the bait surfaced in a pattern that indicated the two streams were connected. Connected through us.'

The room was quiet.

Elena's left hand, still flat on the table, did not move. She stopped breathing for the count of two. Then she breathed.

Calder did not reach across the table for her hand. The not-reaching was its own sentence. There was no gesture he could make that would not also be one door acknowledging the other—each of them, for sixteen years, the door the hand had been reaching through to the other.

'I mentioned the Vienna report to Dina,' Elena said. The sentence arrived in the room like a stone dropped into still water.

'And I mentioned it to a contact at Century House,' Calder said. 'A man I trusted. A man I now understand was reporting to the same desk that fed me the report in the first place.'

'The silver key,' Elena said, eventually. 'On Margaret's bracelet.'

Calder nodded slowly.

'I put it there in November 1977,' he said. 'A week after the hotel register. I added it to her bracelet while she was making tea. She found it the next morning. She looked at me. Neither of us spoke about it again.

'The charm points to a box in Zurich. Everything I found that pointed toward you—I put it in the box. If I die, Margaret opens it.' He paused. 'She doesn't know the box exists. She's been wearing the key to it on her wrist for twelve years without knowing what it opens.

'I gave it to her because I needed her to carry something she didn't understand. She took the bracelet when she left. She's that kind of woman—she doesn't leave her things behind.

'Margaret is alive. She lives in a flat in Ealing she has rented since the autumn of 1984 and that she has kept uneventfully for five and a half years. She teaches at a primary school in Acton. She sees her sister in Salisbury for holidays. She is not married, and as far as I am aware has not been in another serious relationship since she left me.'

Elena said nothing. She had not seen Margaret since March 1983.

'I do not know why. I have a theory but the theory is a thing I made up to be able to bear it, and the theory does not deserve to stand in for whatever the actual reason is, which is hers, and which I have not earned the right to know.

'Margaret has the key.

'Margaret is the insurance. Margaret has been the insurance since 1977. If tomorrow goes badly in the specific way that tomorrow could go badly, Margaret will be informed about the box by means of a letter I am going to write tonight and place in the inside pocket of the coat I am wearing tomorrow. The letter will be found on my body if my body is found. The letter will explain the box to the people who find it and direct them to Margaret. Margaret will do the rest.

'Margaret has not been an operative in the sense we are operatives, but she has lived with the fact of one for over a decade, and she has been carrying a silver key whose meaning she has not asked about for twelve years, and she will understand what the key opens when someone explains it to her.'

Elena exhaled.

The exhalation was the first time her breathing had broken the slow measured pattern since the beginning of Calder's monologue. She did not try to recover the pattern immediately. She let the exhalation be what it was—a small involuntary release. It acknowledged that the silver key she had wondered about for twelve years had been the physical sign of the protection she had not known she had. She had first caught sight of the key on Margaret's wrist at a chance crossing in Kensington, a few months after the Berlin secondment ended. The woman who had been wearing the charm had been the woman whose marriage Elena had ended.

Margaret.

Margaret with the silver key.

Margaret who had taken the bracelet when she left. Who had walked out of the Chiswick house on a Saturday in June 1984 carrying a key she was not permitted to understand. Who was at this moment asleep or reading in Ealing, entirely unaware that the key's use was being decided in room 14 by her former husband and the woman who had ended her marriage.

The three of them.

The three of them had been tied by the key for twelve years and had not known they were tied.

Elena held the tying in the place where the noticings went.

There was a question she did not ask. She could feel it forming—the question of what Margaret had made of the key across the years of wearing it. What she had decided the silence meant. Whether the not-asking had felt like patience or acceptance or the kind of knowledge a woman acquired by living beside a man who kept things.

She set the question aside. Not because she didn't want the answer. Because the answer belonged to after, and she intended to come back for it.

'Tell me about the woman in the doorway in 1968,' she said.

Calder looked at her.

'You know about that too,' he said.

'I have known since 1983. I saw the shape of it in your face one night when you did not know you had produced a shape.'

'Yes. I had crossed at Checkpoint Charlie on what my service would have called an assessment visit and what was actually a night of poor judgment in a divided city. Her name was not Natalia. Natalia was the name she gave a stranger in a city that made the giving of names more important than the keeping of them. I do not know her real name. I do not know whether she is alive. I do not know whether she was in the doorway by accident or by design.

'What I remember of her is not the story.

'The story is the story. It is well-worn in my own head by now, and telling it to you would be telling you the version I have told myself so many times that I no longer trust it.

'What I remember is smaller.'

He paused. His hands had not moved on the table.

'She had mended her cardigan at the elbow with thread of a slightly different color.

'I noticed this because I was sitting on her sofa and her arm was across the back of the sofa, reaching for a cup of tea on a small shelf, and the mended elbow was perhaps fourteen inches from my face.

'The thread was slightly darker than the wool. She had mended the sleeve with care but she had not had the exact right thread.

'I noticed the slightly wrong thread, and I put the noticing in the place where I have been keeping everything about that night ever since.'

Elena's left hand moved to the edge of the red notebook on the table. She did not open it. She touched the cloth binding with one fingertip and left it there.

'What I remember of her is that she made me tea, and that the tea was not very good, and that she did not speak more than six sentences in the four hours I was in her flat, and that when I left at six in the morning she did not say goodbye. She opened the door for me and she stood in the doorway and she watched me walk down the stairs without saying anything. I turned at the bottom of the stairs and I looked back up at her. She was still in the doorway. She nodded once. Then she closed the door.'

Elena exhaled. The exhale was quiet enough that Calder would not have heard it if the room had contained any other sound.

'I never reported her. I never wrote her name—which was not her name—in any document. I never told anyone she'd existed. She is in the file I have never written and that has been running underneath my official service for twenty-two years.'

He looked at his hands. They were on the table. He did not move them.

'She is the first thing I ever withheld from my institution. I withheld her because to name her would have been to betray the specific small act of shelter that had kept me alive on a night when I had no other protection available, and I had been trained to convert every event into institutional knowledge and this had been the first event I had refused to convert.

'The refusal was the beginning of the part of me that was able, nine years later, to decide not to expose you.

'I have thought about this a lot. I have thought about whether the protection I have been giving you for twelve years is a debt I have been paying to the woman in the doorway, or whether I was going to protect you anyway and the woman in the doorway was just an early rehearsal for the protection. I do not know.'

The river moved outside the window. Something large passed on it—a barge, from the sound.

'I do not think it matters. I think the two things are the same thing. I think the doorway and the protection are made of the same material. The institution I work for does not have a name for it.

'Nine years later I did the same thing for you.

'The doorway is who I am.'

He said it the way you say something you have been carrying for twenty-two years and have never said aloud.

A pipe knocked once in the wall. The room held its quiet.

Elena looked at him for a long moment.

'Mine is the rope,' she said.

Calder waited.

'East Berlin, February 1975. A boy of nineteen came into the death strip with a rope coiled on his shoulder because the rope meant he had a plan for the Wall itself. The SM-70 took his left leg. The guards took the rest. The rope slid off his shoulder and lay beside him in the sand in a coil that looked, in the flat white light of the guard tower, like something a sailor had dropped on a dock.

'I was in a car behind a stand of trees, with binoculars and a notepad. I watched all of it. I wrote nothing.

'That was the night the archive became a weight I have carried since.

'My doorway is a strip of raked sand.'

She had been listening with her hands on the table and her breathing in the measured pattern. Her training had never contemplated the possibility that the person across the table would be simultaneously telling her the worst thing she had done and the best thing that had been done to her.

She said, in Russian, very quietly:

'Лучшая ложь—это правда. Так всегда было.'

The best lies are true. They always are.

Calder did not move. His face did not change. He had, Elena understood in the silence after she spoke, heard her. He heard the Russian. He had heard the sentence. He'd been waiting, possibly for years, for the moment when she would speak Russian in his presence. The moment had arrived. The sentence was one she'd been carrying since the Red Banner Institute and had spoken only three times in sixteen years—each time to him, each time in English, each time as a private signal that the line between the cover and the truth had shifted by one millimeter.

The fourth deployment was in Russian.

The fourth deployment was to him, as the first three had been, but it was no longer a signal to herself. It was a sentence spoken aloud in the language it had first been taught in, to a man who had been doing the equivalent of the sentence in his own way, in English, from inside his own service, for twelve years, without ever having heard the sentence spoken in Russian and without ever having needed to.

He understood the sentence. She had been right about his Russian.

'Yes,' he said. In English. 'I know.'

He looked at her across the dossier on the table.

'I would do it again,' he said.

Elena closed her eyes.

The room held the sentence.

'The protection,' he said.

'The file. The twelve years of redirections. The silver key. The Zurich box.

'The letting you into my flat knowing you were putting things in my drawers I would later attribute to my own confusion.

'The not-asking where you had been when you had been in Tel Aviv. The not-looking at the edges of the cover when the edges showed.

'All of it.

'I would do it again.'

A pause. He looked at her across the dossier on the table.

'I would do it from 1977 again. Starting with the hotel register in the archive. Walking for two hours through London afterward. Deciding at the Special Forces Club that night that I was going to build the file that would keep you from being exposed.

'I would do it the same way and for the same reason. And the reason is the reason I am not going to say aloud, because the saying would be a kind of reduction, and the reason does not want to be reduced.'

'I know you would do it again too. Even the parts that were me.' He looked at the dossier on the table between them. 'The far side is this room. We are on the far side.'

Elena opened her eyes.

She was crying. She had not noticed she'd started crying. The tears were small—a few at the corner of each eye, the physical kind of crying the body produced when the containment had become, for a brief moment, permeable. The crying was not the crying she'd done in Vienna in October 1985 with Katya on the hotel bed. The crying in Vienna had been the collapse of her defenses under a chemical assault. The crying now was the architecture holding but becoming, for a moment, a little less watertight than it had been.

She did not wipe the tears.

She said, in English: 'James.'

It was the first time she'd ever called him by his first name aloud in the sixteen years she'd known him. Alice Marsh had called him James in public settings where the name had been operational. Elena Vasilieva had never called him anything. Tonight Elena Vasilieva said the name, and the saying was the small completion of a thing that had been incomplete since October 1973.

'Elena,' Calder said.

The saying of her name to her—not by Yuri, not by Bruhn, not by Mikhail in the Lada in Friedrichshain, not by Dina in the kitchen in Kensington, but by the man who had never said her name before and who had been in love with her for sixteen years without having been able to say it—produced the kind of small physical completion she had not known she'd been waiting for.

She reached across the table.

He reached across the table.

Their hands met above the dossier—above the photographs and the knife and the *rothschildianum* prints and the red notebook and the metal box from Highgate—and neither of them said anything for a long time.

Her eye went to the small faded scar at the corner of his left eyebrow—the one she had cataloged without filing in a Fitzrovia gallery in October 1973, wondering whether she would ever be close enough to ask. She did not ask. She was close enough now. The closeness was the answer.

When they finally moved again, it was because the small clock on the bedside table had become the loudest thing in the room.

21:47. Elena read the clock. She looked back at Calder.

'Tomorrow,' she said.

The radiator ticked. Outside, the river moved.

'Tomorrow,' Calder said.

She walked him through the plan in the concise operational language they had each been trained to use and had never used with the other before. The lobby of the other hotel. 16:00. Dina inside. Two factions meeting. The meeting room on the second floor. The F-21 Ajax in the inner pocket of her coat—one hundred and seventy-eight frames. The Mayflower rooftop, accessible through the service door fifteen minutes before the meeting began. The sightline to the other hotel's lobby entrance: clear, approximately forty-five meters, six meters elevation. The shooting window: 15:45 to 16:30.

Calder listened. When she finished he asked two questions. What was the extraction route if the rooftop position was compromised? And did she have a plan for the film itself after she'd exposed it?

She answered both. Extraction route: back through the service door, down the corridor to the stair, into room 14, out the first-floor window onto the pub roof below, down the back alley to Bermondsey Wall, east to Fountain Dock, across a footbridge she had scouted in December. The film would go to a photographer in Southwark—a man Hatch had named in his reel—who would develop the F-21's frames within four hours and produce two sets of prints. One set to Dina, for Mossad-internal handling. The other to Calder, for the route into Century House: walk the photographs into the Chief's office the morning after the operation and resign the moment he had laid them on the desk.

Calder nodded.

He named one last detail of the plan.

'Greenwich. A flat I have kept since 1984, above a bookseller's on the river side. The key is with the bookseller's widow. Nobody at the service has ever used it or knows I have it. Ruskin will bring the second set of prints there tonight. I will walk there from Century House the morning after the resignation. You will come when your extraction is clean.'

Elena nodded.

'The resignation is the only thing that will make the photographs stick,' he said. 'A serving officer walks in with an evidence package like that and the package goes into a review that takes months and that can be intercepted by any of the people whose names you will by then have matched to the faces in your photographs. A resigning officer walks in with the same package and the resignation is the kind of event that forces the package into a different category of institutional response. The resignation is the weight that keeps the package on the table. I have been thinking about the resignation since Hatch started asking about me in 1987. I have been ready since Hatch went missing.'

'You are going to lose your career.'

'I lost my career the week Margaret left. The career has been a shape I have been wearing since. I am returning the shape to the cupboard it belongs in.'

Elena nodded.

'The disappearance is not for me,' she said. 'I will not go. I will stay in London until you are through the debriefing. I will change flats. I will change the name. I will become a woman neither of us used to know, and I will wait for you to decide, at your own pace, with the time and the institutional space you will need, whether you want to find me again. If you do not want to find me, you will not find me. I will not contact you first. The contact will be yours to make or not to make. I owe you the not-finding if you choose it.'

'I know,' Calder said. 'I knew when I wrote the disappearance plan in my head two weeks ago that the plan was the plan I was going to offer you and that you were going to refuse, and that the refusing would be the answer. I am telling you the refusing is the answer.'

'Yes.'

'Yes.'

The clock said 22:14.

The planning was finished. The revelations were finished. The dossier was still on the table. The envelope with the card inside it was still on the edge of the table, still unopened, its single function having been fulfilled by Calder's having recognized the handwriting and come.

Calder rose from the chair.

The room was different now. The dossier on the table was the same dossier but the room that held it had changed, the way a room changes when the last lie leaves it.

'I need to sleep for a few hours,' he said. 'So do you. Tomorrow starts at 14:30, which is when you will need to be on the rooftop making final checks on the F-21. I will take the sofa in the corner of this room, if you will permit it. I am not going to sleep in a separate room tonight. We have been sleeping in separate rooms for sixteen years. Not tonight.'

'Yes,' Elena said.

Calder moved to the small sofa in the corner of room 14. It was not large enough for a tall man to sleep on comfortably. He removed his shoes and his jacket and lay down on the sofa with his overcoat spread over him as a blanket and his face turned toward the table where the dossier was laid out and where Elena was sitting.

Elena did not move to the bed. She sat in the wooden chair facing the sofa. She did not need sleep. Sleep would come or it would not come. The hours until 14:30 were the hours.

Calder closed his eyes.

After perhaps two minutes he said, without opening them: 'Did you ever love me.'

'Yes,' Elena said. 'I have loved you since the geranium in the photograph in the gallery in October 1973. I did not know it then. I knew by the third dinner. I have been trying not to love you ever since, and the trying has been the most unsuccessful operation of my career. I have loved you without interruption for sixteen years. The campaign against you was the love, not the contradiction of it. I am not going to explain that because I cannot.'

Calder did not open his eyes.

'Thank you,' he said. His voice had changed. The operational surface was gone. What was underneath was not smaller. It was larger. Elena looked at his face and saw it for the first time without the cover between them. The face was the same face. The face had always been this face. She had been looking at it for sixteen years and she was seeing it now.

'You are welcome.'

'Elena.'

'Yes.'

'The woman in the doorway. In 1968. I want you to know that I have sometimes thought, in the last sixteen years, that you were the same woman.'

'I was not.'

'I know. I have always known. I mean that the part of me that loved her was the same part of me that loves you, and that the not-knowing her name and the not-knowing your name in the specific way I have not known your name for sixteen years are the same not-knowing, and that tonight you have told me the name and the telling is the kind of completion that doorways produce when the doorways are finally closed.'

'Yes,' Elena said.

Calder fell asleep.

Elena watched him sleep. She watched him for approximately an hour. The clock on the bedside table ticked through the hour with the quiet percussion of a mechanism that was still running—not a dying mechanism, not the Nagra on the kitchen table in Kensington, just an ordinary bedside clock in a small hotel room in Bermondsey on the night before the operation. The dossier on the table was silent. The objects in the dossier were silent. The photographs of the man with the gold ring were silent. The unopened envelope was silent.

At 23:47 Elena rose from the chair. She crossed the room to

the sofa where Calder was sleeping. She leaned down and placed a kiss on his forehead—the quiet kiss that people gave each other in moments that were not about desire but about the completion of a piece of recognition that had been incomplete for a long time. He did not wake.

She returned to the chair.

She sat.

She watched the room.

At some point in the night she slept—in the wooden chair, with her head on the table next to the red notebook, with the F-21 Ajax still in the inner pocket of her coat because she had not remembered to take the coat off before sleeping. She slept for perhaps three hours. When she woke, the window had begun to show the first gray suggestion of the January dawn.

Calder was sitting up on the sofa watching her, and his face in the thin dawn light had the specific expression of a man who had been awake for an hour and who had been watching her sleep and who hadn't wanted to wake her because this was the first time she'd slept in the same room as him without lying about the room.

He did not say anything.

She did not say anything.

Outside, beyond the small window of room 14, the city was beginning the slow movement of a January Wednesday morning. Milk floats. Early buses. Commuters walking to the Tube through the cold dawn. None of them knew what was about to happen in Bermondsey.

The day had begun.

The operation was now.

Elena reached for the F-21 Ajax in the inner pocket of her coat.

She took it out.

She placed it on the table beside the red notebook, the two photographs, the two pages from Highgate, and the dossier she'd been carrying toward this room in Bermondsey for sixteen years.

The F-21 was the fifteenth object on the table.

31

TWO SHOTS

Bermondsey—3 January 1990

At 06:47 on the third of January 1990, Elena Vasilieva was sitting in a wooden chair in room 14 of the Mayflower Hotel on Bermondsey Wall East, watching James Calder tie his shoes.

He was sitting on the edge of the sofa. Jacket on. Tie knotted —the precise neutral knot of a man who had tied one every morning for thirty years and was not going to stop because this morning was different.

The knot was a small Windsor. The tie was dark gray with a thin maroon stripe. Elena had given it to him for his birthday in 1981.

She watched him tie his shoes. The double knot. The pat of his palms on the knees as he straightened. She placed her left hand flat on the table. The Omega on her wrist—the one he'd given her in 1974 for a birthday she'd invented—had been covering the compass rose for sixteen years. She had never taken it off. She had never asked herself why.

The kitchen table in Kensington. The drawer beside the stove. The notebook. Calder's face when he carried the classified files home in his overcoat pockets—a man equidistant between two lives. She understood him now.

The watch sat exactly over the compass rose. The compass rose sat exactly under the watch. The arrangement had held for sixteen years. The watch was a gift from a man who had not known what was under it. Two lives meeting at a single point of skin on her left wrist that no one had ever seen except a Leningrad tattooist dead since 1972 and one Mossad officer in Tel Aviv.

Elena adjusted her cuff. The watch slid back into place over the tattoo. She did not look at the tattoo. She had not looked at the tattoo in years.

Calder finished with the shoes. He rose. He stood in the center of the small room and looked at the dossier one more time.

'I'll walk the area first,' he said. 'Two buses. Different routes. I'll be across from the hotel by 16:00. No camera. Eyes and memory.'

'You are the second eye.'

'I am the second eye.'

He reviewed the photographer's address—47 Webber Street, the side door, two flights, ALLEN PHOTOGRAPHIC—and the meet time of 18:00. He stood in the center of the room.

'Elena.'

'Yes.'

'If something happens to me—deliver the film to Allen. Go to Dina. Disappear.'

'I will come looking for you.'

'I know.' He paused. 'That's why I'm saying it now, while you can still promise not to.'

'I'm not promising.'

'No.' He almost smiled. 'You're not.'

He crossed the room. He placed his hand on her cheek. The hand was warm. The hand was the hand that had been touching her face for sixteen years. He leaned down and kissed her forehead. He picked up his overcoat and his hat. He looked at her one more time.

'Until 18:00,' he said.

'Until 18:00.'

He was at the door when she said: 'James.'

He stopped. He did not turn around.

'The tie is crooked.' She reached across and straightened it. Her fingers on the knot. His throat beneath her fingers. Neither of them mentioned that her hands were shaking.

He adjusted it without looking. 'Thank you.'

He turned and let himself out of the room. She listened to his footsteps go down the corridor and the narrow stairs. She heard the front door of the building open and close. The silence of room 14 returned.

She did not move from the chair for a long time.

She spent the morning preparing.

She cleaned the F-21 Ajax. She unscrewed the small brass fittings of the Ronson lighter with the flat of her thumbnail, lifted the baseplate, examined the clockwork. She pressed the third striker pawl twice—the small test firing the instrument permitted without burning a frame—and listened to the clean click. The mechanism was operational. She reassembled the lighter and placed it back in the inner pocket of her coat.

The rooftop route reviewed three times in her head. The extraction route. The twelve things that could go wrong. She reviewed the photographer at 47 Webber Street.

At 09:00 she wrote three short notes. One to Helen, thanking her for the years of shortbread. One to Gerald at the gallery, apologizing for the resignation she would post next week. One to Anneliese in East Berlin, at the address that was still the family's address, telling her that the drawing of the yellow-sun house had lived in a London kitchen for nearly three years and had been looked at every day by a woman who owed the drawing more than the drawing would ever know. She sealed the three notes in three envelopes. She did not address two of them. She left them on the kitchen table.

She checked her watch. 10:14. Beneath the Omega the compass rose continued to point in the four directions it had been pointing in for twenty-four years.

At 12:00 she sat at the table with the dossier and thought, for seven minutes, about the boy in the death strip. The rope coiled in the sand beside him. The parallel lines of the raking. The young guard raising his rifle. Today the image was the weight keeping her grounded.

At 12:30 she ate a tomato and cheese sandwich the Mayflower's kitchen had prepared for her at her request.

At 13:45 she put on her coat. The F-21 was in the inner pocket. The Mercator knife from Voss was in her handbag. She had decided to carry the knife—not because she expected to use it but because the working chain of objects she was carrying into the day included the knife the way it included the photograph and the notebook, and the inclusion was the only way her hands could hold sixteen years in the small transport a coat and a handbag permitted.

She checked the watch one more time. 14:09.

Twenty-one minutes.

She left room 14.

◆◆◆

The roof was empty.

Flat tar-and-gravel, the standard construction of Victorian

commercial rooftops in this part of London. A square brick chimney at the north end. A maintenance access grille in the center. A low brick parapet along the street edge. The rooftop was approximately eight meters wide and twelve meters long. The building to the north—47 Webber Street, the small printer's shop she had been surveilling for four hours—was accessible by crossing the pub's shared west wall and dropping two meters onto the printer's slightly lower roof. The printer's roof had a skylight and a roof hatch.

She knelt at the east parapet. She removed the Ronson lighter from the inner pocket of her coat and placed it on the top of the parapet, braced against a small irregularity in the brick that would hold the lighter steady without requiring her hand to be in the image.

She checked the watch. 14:34.

She took her 7x50 Zeiss binoculars from her handbag and raised them to her eyes.

The lobby of the other hotel was visible at magnification. The woman at the reception desk. A porter moving a small luggage trolley. A guest reading a newspaper in one of the lobby chairs. The small quiet of a Bermondsey hotel at 14:35 on a January Wednesday afternoon before an operational meeting at 16:00 that most of the staff did not know was happening.

She lowered the binoculars.

She waited.

The cold was the cold. The wind across the tar and gravel. The small burning in her cheeks that came from London winter air at six meters above an exposed street. Her gloves were thin enough to operate the F-21 and thick enough to keep her fingers functional for the ninety minutes the operation would require. She blew on her fingertips through the wool.

At 14:58 a man in a blue overcoat walked into the lobby. Not a face on her list. She did not photograph him.

At 15:12 Dina walked into the lobby.

Elena did not photograph Dina. Dina was wearing the charcoal coat Elena had last seen on the hook in her Kensington hallway three weeks ago. Her shoulder bag was tucked against her hip the way operational Dina tucked it. She walked to the reception desk, spoke with the woman at the desk, was handed a key, and crossed the lobby to the staircase at the back. She disappeared up the stairs.

At 15:23 the first network attendee arrived.

Heavy-set, late sixties, dark wool coat, fur hat. The face matched the French aerospace executive Elena had memorized from Hatch's pencil writing inside the metal reel case. She pressed the third striker pawl twice. Two frames. The small clockwork advanced. 176 frames remaining.

At 15:27 two men arrived together. Neither on the list. She did not photograph them.

At 15:31 the German banker arrived. Two frames. 174 remaining.

At 15:44 four men arrived within ninety seconds of each other. She photographed three. Six frames. 168 remaining.

At 15:52 a woman arrived. Elena had not expected a woman. She photographed her—four frames, multiple angles, the long coverage operatives used when an unexpected subject appeared. 164 remaining.

At 15:58 two more men. Four frames. 160 remaining.

At 16:00 a dark green Jaguar XJ pulled up to the curb outside the hotel.

Elena raised the binoculars.

The driver got out and walked around to open the rear passenger door. A man got out of the back of the car.

The man was Laurence Henry Thornley.

Elena knew him the way she knew every face she'd been studying. Late fifties. Clean shaven. Receding hairline. The face from Dina's photograph and from the Highgate studio portrait and from the two nights in Vienna and Friedrichshain in which her memory had refused to retain him. One face, not two. The *administrator* had been Thornley all along, and the ring was his ring.

Her memory was retaining him now.

He stepped onto the curb. He straightened his overcoat with a small unhurried gesture. He looked around—left, right, the casual scan of a man arriving at a meeting. His gaze passed across the buildings on the far side of the street. The gaze passed across the rooftop of the Mayflower. The gaze did not stop.

Or it stopped for a fraction of a second and continued. Elena could not tell. The binoculars were excellent but the angle was wrong for that kind of micro-observation, and the moment was a moment, and Thornley was already turning toward the hotel's front doors.

She pressed the third striker pawl twice. Two frames. She pressed it again. Two frames. She pressed it a third time. Two frames.

Six frames of Laurence Henry Thornley on the curb outside a Bermondsey hotel, his face clearly visible, his right hand at his side, the gold signet ring on the little finger of the right hand captured in the small clockwork aperture of a Soviet camera that had been waiting in a Ronson lighter for sixteen years for this specific sequence of shutter actuations.

He turned and walked into the hotel.

Elena lowered the binoculars.

She continued shooting through the arrivals window. At 16:04 the last of the expected attendees arrived. Two more frames. 152 remaining. She waited. At 16:47 the first departure—a man she'd photographed at 15:23 walking back to his car. She did not waste a frame. At 16:58 two more departures. She photographed one of them—the body language of a man leaving a meeting he was unhappy about, the signature of a faction that had lost. Two frames. 150 remaining.

At 17:04 Thornley left.

She photographed him on departure. Four frames. 146 remaining. He did not look up.

At 17:12 Dina walked out of the hotel. The shoulder bag against her hip appeared, to the binocular assessment, to be slightly fuller than it had been when she entered. Dina walked east along Bermondsey Wall and turned the corner at the end of the block and disappeared from Elena's sightline.

The operation was complete.

Elena unbraced the F-21 from the parapet and returned it to the inner pocket of her coat and turned to descend.

Then she heard the door.

Not the roof hatch. A different door. The door in the maintenance shaft below her, opening from the corridor side.

Elena froze.

Footsteps on the iron ladder. Two sets. Moving up.

She had perhaps fifteen seconds.

The rooftop had no other exit. The fire escape on the north face terminated at the second-floor level and did not connect to the roof. The brick parapet on three sides overlooked a three-story drop. There was no way off the roof except through the maintenance shaft she had come up through.

Unless.

She ran to the north end of the roof.

Beyond the north edge of the Mayflower roof was the pub's roof—a lower structure, perhaps two meters below, separated by a gap of approximately one meter. The pub roof had an access hatch near the west edge that would drop her into the pub's back kitchen. Beyond the kitchen was the alley. Beyond the alley was the rest of Bermondsey.

Between the edge of the Mayflower roof and the edge of the pub roof was a single vertical line of old iron railing —a leftover structural element from a previous renovation that had been left in place because removing it would have been a nuisance. Around the top of the railing, someone had wrapped barbed wire approximately twenty years ago—rusted, weathered, a cheap deterrent to a thief who had never come.

Elena opened her handbag and removed the Mercator knife.

The knife had been in a drawer beside her stove in Kensington since January 1978. It had traveled to Bermondsey on the second of January in her handbag as part of the dossier. It had not been used operationally since the night she took it from Voss at Checkpoint Charlie in October 1977. The blade was nine centimeters of German carbon steel. The mechanism was the original lock, well-oiled.

She opened the blade. The lock engaged with the clean click it had made for twelve years.

She stepped onto the iron railing and reached up to the barbed wire with the knife. The wire was rusted; the knife was sharp. The blade did its work the way it had been designed to—not a sawing motion but a single clean draw across the axis. The first strand parted. The second. The third. She worked methodically, with the speed of necessity and the precision of a woman who had been carrying a knife she had not allowed herself to use for twelve years and that had been waiting for exactly this moment.

Footsteps in the maintenance shaft, getting louder.

Six strands. Seven. Eight.

The last strand parted.

Twelve years in a drawer for eight strands of wire.

She heard the roof hatch open behind her—the soft metallic click of the latch releasing—and she did not turn around. She put the knife back in her handbag with the blade still open, because there was no time to fold it, and she stepped onto the top of the iron railing with both feet, and she jumped.

She landed on the pub roof two meters below with the impact-and-roll she had been taught at the Red Banner Institute in 1969. Her left knee took most of the impact. The roll absorbed the rest. She came up to a crouch, looked back once at the Mayflower roof—saw a man in a dark coat standing at the open hatch, looking across the gap at her with the specific surprise of a man who hadn't expected a woman to be jumping off a roof he had been sent to intercept—and she turned and ran to the access hatch at the west edge of the pub roof.

The hatch was unlocked. She opened it and dropped through onto the small wooden platform at the top of the pub's back stairs. She closed the hatch behind her. She descended at a controlled pace. She reached the back of the pub's kitchen. The kitchen was busy with the early evening service. Nobody looked at her. She walked through with the unhurried efficient gait of a woman who worked there, pushed through the back door into the alley, and emerged into the Bermondsey evening.

The alley was empty. The cold was the cold.

She folded the Mercator knife with her thumb on the spine. The lock engaged with a small metallic click. She dropped the knife into her handbag. She walked east along the alley to Bermondsey Wall. She turned south. She walked through the warren of streets she'd rehearsed in December.

At 17:34 she reached the footbridge at Fountain Dock.

At 17:47 she reached the photographer's shop at 47 Webber Street.

She checked her watch one final time before climbing the stairs. 17:48. Twelve minutes early. The Omega's second hand was sweeping the cream face the way it had been sweeping the cream face for sixteen years. Beneath it, the compass rose pointed in the four directions it had been pointing in for twenty-four.

She did not look at the tattoo.

She climbed the two flights.

The side door at the bottom of the stairs was unlocked. The sign above it read ALLEN PHOTOGRAPHIC. The narrow staircase was lit by a single bare bulb. The wallpaper was an old beige floral that had been fashionable in the 1950s. A small framed print of Brunel's rotunda hung on the landing.

The door at the top of the stairs was open.

Elena stepped through.

The workroom was a single large room with a darkroom at the back and a worktable at the front. The worktable held a chipped tea mug, a stack of unused photographic paper, a small enameled tray with developing chemicals, and a pair of bifocal spectacles folded on top of a closed ledger.

Mr. Allen was not at the worktable.

Dina was.

She was sitting in the chair Mr. Allen would have been sitting in. Her charcoal coat was draped on the chair beside her. Her shoulder bag was on the table. Her hands were folded on the table in front of her.

She looked up when Elena came in.

'Hello, Elena,' she said.

Elena did not move.

She stood in the doorway of the workroom on the second floor of 47 Webber Street and she looked across at the woman she'd been having coffee with on alternate Tuesdays since 1978. She looked at Dina's face. She looked at Dina's hands. She looked at the worktable and at the small enameled tray and at the bifocal spectacles folded on top of the closed ledger and at the absence of Mr. Allen.

She ran the assessment.

The assessment took less than two seconds.

Elena said, in Russian, very quietly: 'How long.'

'Since 1981,' Dina said. In Russian. 'March. I am going to be brief.

'The cadences I caught were real. I caught them honestly. The catching brought me to their attention. They gave me a choice—my sister and her three children in Haifa, or my co-operation. A hotel bar called the Cinema. Three years after our first coffee.

'Everything since has been theirs.' She paused. The pause was Dina's way of letting a sentence land before adding weight to it. 'The coffees. The kitchen in December. Your tattoo—I was told to find it. I was told to file the location. I was not told why. I am telling you why now.

'The photograph was real. The reel was real. Hatch is dying, though it is taking longer than they expected. Bermondsey was real. Thornley was real. Your photographs will reach the Chief's desk tomorrow morning and do exactly what they were designed to do.' She paused. 'Calder will resign. He will go to the Greenwich flat expecting to find you. He will find two men instead. They are already in the building.'

Dina's voice did not change.

'There are no other layers.'

Elena did not move.

She thought, for one second, about the Mercator knife in her handbag. The knife that had cut barbed wire on a rooftop forty minutes ago—the cutting Dina had wanted her to do. Producing it now would be the same kind of operationally meaningless gesture as the F-21 frames she'd pressed and the rooftop she'd escaped from and the entire sixteen years of her professional life, all of which had been moves on a board the woman across the table had been playing.

She did not reach into her handbag.

The room was very quiet. She could hear Dina breathing.

'Where is Mr. Allen,' she said.

'Asleep. In the back. He'll wake around ten with no memory of the evening. His glasses are where he left them.'

'The photographs.'

'I had my own camera inside the meeting. A Minox, in the shoulder bag. You were never going to be the only photographer today. I developed them while you were on the rooftop. The workroom was prepared before you went up. The chemistry was waiting. Allen was under by seventeen hundred. There are two sets of prints. One is in the envelope on the chair beside me. Andrew Ruskin will collect that envelope at 18:30 from this room and take it to Calder at the Greenwich flat. The second set is in a manila envelope inside my shoulder bag. I will deliver the second set to Thornley personally at a location I will not name. Both deliveries will happen this evening.'

'Ruskin.'

'Ruskin is straight. He'll deliver the prints to Calder tonight believing everything he's been told. The photographs will reach the Chief's desk by 09:30. Nobody in that chain knows what I am.'

'The photographs were never about Thornley.'

'No.'

'About removing Calder.'

'Yes. Twelve years of him closing inquiries into Alice Marsh. He was useful while the closing was all that was visible. When the closings became a pattern visible to the desks above him, he stopped being useful. His resignation ends the closings. By then Thornley has his own set.'

'And Hatch's reel.'

'The network wanted you at Bermondsey today. I was there as the network's own observer; the Mossad directive that put me in the room was written by the same desk that wrote yours. My Minox produced both sets—the set on the chair for Ruskin, the set in my bag for Thornley. The Chief will see the first through Calder tomorrow. Thornley will hold the second tonight. Both sets are the network's. The reel was the prompt that made the carrying look like yours.'

'Calder will know I am gone.'

'Ruskin will tell Calder you've been delayed. Calder will wait. He'll fall asleep on the sofa. He'll wake at three and spend the rest of the night writing his resignation. In the morning he'll walk into Century House and lay the photographs on the Chief's desk and walk out. Then he'll go back to Greenwich.' Dina paused. 'The men will be quick. He won't suffer.'

Elena absorbed this in the small interior space the assessment had been keeping open.

The space her training had built for absorbing information that changed the shape of an operation in real time. Tonight she understood it was the only thing about her that had ever been hers.

The plan she had explained to Calder at the Mayflower had been the network's plan for her to believe she had. The F-21 in her coat pocket had been waiting for a darkroom that was never going to exist.

She filed the information.

The filing took perhaps four seconds.

When the filing was done, she said: 'And me.'

'And you,' Dina said.

'The dossier in your drawer is the only complete account of the network ever built from inside it. The network does not let such accounts survive.'

She unfolded her hands and reached into the shoulder bag on the table beside her. From the bag she removed a suppressed pistol and placed it on the worktable between them.

The pistol was a Makarov PB. Black. Soviet. KGB-issue for close-range work. The same model Elena had fired twice into Grigor Petrov on the kitchen floor of an apartment on Storgata in Lillehammer.

Elena looked at the pistol.

Elena understood the choice immediately. The choice was not Dina's. The choice was Thornley's. Thornley had read her file, had read the Lillehammer entry, had seen the Makarov designation, and had selected the weapon for tonight with the specific patient attention the network brought to the small circular closures of its operations. The network was a network that liked its work to rhyme.

'That is an elegant touch,' Elena said.

'It was not my idea,' Dina said. 'It was requested. I agreed to it because the request made a specific kind of sense to me that I am not going to explain. I am telling you it was requested because you deserve to know it was requested. I am not asking you to admire it.'

'I am not admiring it.'

'I know.'

A silence. Dina's hand was resting on the worktable three inches from the pistol. She had not yet picked it up.

'The body,' Elena said. 'Where does it go.'

Dina leaned forward. Her voice dropped.

'Two men. Tonight. A container at the Royal Albert Dock. A farm in Iowa.' She stopped. 'You don't need the details of the farm.'

The building settled around them. Somewhere below, a pipe ticked in the wall.

Dina's fingers moved a quarter-inch closer to the pistol.

'We've been owing each other for eleven years.'

Elena watched her fingers. She did not look at Dina's face.

'Calder will join you in the container on the afternoon of the fourth.'

Elena looked at her for a long moment.

She did not see anger in Dina's face. She did not see triumph. She did not see regret in any form she could read. She saw the specific neutrality of a person who had decided, nine years ago, to do this thing and who had been arranging her life around the doing ever since, and who had reached the moment of the doing with the kind of inward composure that came from long preparation.

Elena understood the composure.

She carried her own version of it for sixteen years.

She recognized what the composure was built over. Not the operational decision—that had been made in a hotel bar in 1981. What it was built over was the same thing Elena's composure had always been built over: the conversion of something personal into something functional, carried so long that the two had become indistinguishable. The alternate Tuesdays. The kitchen in December. The hands that had been steady throughout and were steady now.

The two of them were, in this small workroom on the second floor of 47 Webber Street in Southwark on the third of January 1990, two operatives of the same kind of preparation, completing a transaction that the eleven years had been arranging.

'I would like to say one thing before I do this,' Dina said. 'It is not an apology. It is not a justification.'

She did not look away from Elena.

'It is the only true sentence I have ever said to you in eleven years that has not been routed through a service.'

A small pause. A breath. Not longer.

'The sentence is this: I have loved you.'

Elena did not move. She watched Dina's face the way she had watched so many faces—reading, calibrating. There was no calibration left to run.

'The loving was not the work. The loving was something the work did not consume.'

'Bermondsey was always going to happen regardless of what you told him. I wanted you to have the room.'

'I am sorry the loving did not produce a different ending. I do not have any other ending to offer you.'

Elena opened her mouth. She closed it. What she had been

about to say was the last thing in her life that would join the category of things she could only carry.

Dina's right hand moved the final inch. Her fingers touched the grip of the pistol.

'I am going to do this now.'

Elena said: 'Yes.' The word arrived without performance.

The chair was hard beneath her. She could hear Dina breathing. She could hear the building settling around them. She could feel the last of the January light through the window on her neck.

She thought about Anneliese in 2B in Friedrichshain.

She thought about the boy in the death strip in February 1975. She thought about the boy on the fishing boat to Malmö.

She thought about James Calder in a small flat above a bookseller's shop in Greenwich, waiting for her.

She thought about the silver key on Margaret's bracelet, and about her not being the one to find out whether Margaret ever learned what the key opened.

Her mother in Leningrad in 1953. *Lena, dochenka, posmotri na menya. Little daughter, look at me.* A small kitchen table. A bowl of buckwheat her mother had warmed for her on a Tuesday morning that Elena could no longer locate in any specific season but that was, in this final accounting, the room she had been carrying inside herself for thirty-seven years without knowing it had been the room.

The filing system had failed her. It had failed as a filing system and succeeded as the only proof she had ever been alive.

The best lies are true. They always were.

Dina picked up the Makarov PB.

The suppressor reduced the two shots to something between

a book being dropped and a heavy door closing—a concussive thud that would not carry through the walls of the small workroom on the second floor of 47 Webber Street in Southwark on the third of January 1990. The first round entered through the upper sternum slightly left of midline and went forward into the heart. The second followed a quarter-second later, higher, because her body was already beginning to fold forward and her head had shifted; it took her at the base of the throat—the same geometry Elena herself had produced in Grigor Petrov's kitchen on the night of the twenty-first of July 1973, now performed on the reverse side of the transaction, with the same model of pistol, at the same distance, by an operative of the same species of preparation. Her body moved against the back of the wooden chair, then forward against the worktable, then to a final rest at the half-position the chair permitted. The cuff of her left sleeve had ridden up in the small involuntary movement; the Omega had slipped a quarter-inch on the wrist beneath; and the compass rose she had carried for twenty-four years showed at the inside of the wrist with the small dot at the center where the four directions met.

Elena Vasilieva, born in Leningrad in 1948 to a woman named Lyudmila and a man who had died of a chest wound from Stalingrad before she could remember him, who had inked a compass rose on the inside of her left wrist in the spring of 1966 as the only personal gesture of disobedience her training had ever permitted, who had spent nineteen years in London as Alice Marsh while loving a man named James Calder she'd been instructed to destroy and who had loved her in return without telling her, who had counted six cadences across thirteen years and built a notebook nobody had ever read and a dossier nobody would ever see, who had been the sole occupant of an interior space she spent her life trying to convert into something operational and who had failed at the conversion in the only way the failure had ever mattered, was dead in a wooden chair at 18:14 on the third of January 1990. The filing system, in the last second of its operation, produced a single image. Not operational. Not useful. The way James Calder had looked at her in a gallery in October 1973, when neither of them knew what the other one was.

The body that had refused to feel had stopped.

32

THE MACHINERY

London—Iowa—January 1990

Dina lowered the pistol.

She sat for perhaps ten seconds without moving.

Then she rose.

She crossed to where Elena had slumped forward against the worktable. She placed two fingers against the side of Elena's throat. The pulse was absent. She held the fingers there for five full seconds anyway, because an operative owed the work that confirmation, and because she had been touching Elena across tables in Tel Aviv for eleven years and wanted the last touch to be honest.

Then she lifted Elena's left arm gently from where it had fallen across the worktable.

She unbuckled the small leather strap of the Omega that Elena had worn every day since 1974. She slid the watch off the wrist.

The compass rose was underneath.

It was small. Two centimeters. The ink had faded over twenty-four years but the four points were still clear—north, south, east, west—with the small dot at the center where the directions met.

Dina looked at the mark.

She first saw it in the summer of 1982, across a café table on Sheinkin Street in Tel Aviv, when Elena had reached for a sugar bowl and her sleeve had ridden up for a half-second. Dina had noted the mark, filed its location, and never mentioned it aloud, because the noting and the filing had been the instruction she'd been given in the spring of 1981. The instruction had been quiet and specific. Find the mark. Record the mark. Do not speak of the mark. Wait.

She waited for almost eight years.

She placed her two fingers lightly at the center of the compass rose, where the four directions met, where the Leningrad tattooist had placed his most careful mark because the center had been the part that mattered most. The skin under her fingertips was still warm. It would cool over the next several hours, in the back of a van, in a refrigerated container, across an Atlantic crossing and a continent and a small rail spur in Iowa, until the warmth that remained was only the temperature of the room the body was in, and then only the temperature of the chamber beneath the second hog barn, and then not even that.

She took her fingers away.

She placed the Omega in the inner pocket of her own coat. She folded Elena's sleeve back down over the wrist. She adjusted the cuff. The compass rose was once again covered, though now the covering was the sleeve and not the watch, and the distinction would not matter because the men who would arrive at 23:47 were not being paid to examine anything.

She left the Ronson lighter where it was in the inner pocket of Elena's coat. The hundred and forty-six frames on the film inside it would not be developed in any darkroom that existed.

She picked up the Makarov PB from the worktable and returned it to her shoulder bag. She picked up the envelope of prints intended for Ruskin and placed it on the chair beside the door. She picked up her own bag with the second envelope inside it. She crossed to the workroom's back kitchen and confirmed that Mr. Allen was breathing slowly and evenly on the small cot beside the sink where she'd laid him at 17:30. She returned to the workroom.

She did not look at Elena's body a second time. She looked at her own hands.

She crossed to the door, switched off the workroom light, and let herself out.

The stairs were quiet.

The Bermondsey evening, when she emerged onto Webber Street, was the cold blue of a January night in London at 18:23 with the streetlamps just lit and the small foot traffic of office workers moving toward the Tube stations.

She walked east toward Blackfriars Road and did not look back.

Andrew Ruskin arrived at 47 Webber Street at 18:33. He climbed the two flights and let himself into the workroom through the unlocked door. The workroom was dim—the worktable lamp was still on—and he saw, immediately, two things.

The first was a manila envelope on the chair beside the door, with his name in pencil on the front in a hand he did not recognize.

The second was a woman slumped forward in the wooden chair facing the worktable, her left arm lying across the table and her right side darkened in two places across the front of her coat where the fabric had been punctured and where the blood had not yet fully dried.

Ruskin crossed to her. He placed two fingers against the side of her throat. There was no pulse. The skin was cool but not cold. He estimated, with the small medical training MI6 had given its mid-level officers in 1979, that she'd been dead for between fifteen and forty-five minutes. He noted the two entry wounds on the front of the coat and the absence of exit wounds on the back and held the geometry for later: close range, small caliber, suppressed weapon, professional shooter. One shooter, not two. Someone who had been waiting for her in this chair.

He stood still.

He understood, in the four seconds of standing, several things at once. The woman in the chair was the operative Calder had described. The operation had gone wrong. The manila envelope was his. It was the only piece of the operation still in motion, and his job was to deliver it.

He picked up the envelope.

He placed it inside his jacket.

He looked at the woman in the chair one more time. He did not know her name. He did not know how she'd died. He did not know whether the killing had been done by someone who was still in the building or by someone who had already left. He did not investigate. His job was the envelope.

He left the workroom.

He locked the door behind him with a small set of picks he carried in his coat for exactly this kind of field improvisation, because the door had no inside lock and he wanted to make sure no member of the public would walk in and find what was in the chair before he'd done what he needed to do.

He descended the stairs and walked out into Webber Street and turned south toward the river.

He delivered the envelope to James Calder at the Greenwich

safe flat at 19:47.

The message he delivered with it had been specified by his handler that afternoon. Operational discipline meant he delivered it unmodified.

He told Calder that the woman had not been at the workroom when he arrived but that the envelope had been there with his name on it and that she'd instructed Mr. Allen, before her own departure, that she would meet Calder at the flat by 22:00 tonight.

Calder accepted this.

Calder waited until 03:00.

At 03:00 he rose from the small sofa in the front room and went to the desk and wrote the resignation letter he had been planning to write for two weeks. The letter was four paragraphs. He addressed it to the Chief and dated it 4 January 1990. He folded it into an envelope and placed the envelope in the inside pocket of his overcoat alongside the two manila envelopes of photographs and the second sealed letter he'd written on the second of January in the small hours, the letter that explained the Zurich box to the person who would find his body if his body were to be found, the letter that named Margaret.

At 09:00 on the morning of the fourth he walked into Century House.

At 09:30 he laid the photographs on the Chief's desk.

At 09:32 he laid the resignation letter on top of them.

At 11:47 he walked out of the building and across Westminster Bridge in the cold January light with his hands in the pockets of his overcoat and his face set in the specific neutral composition of a man who had just finished the only thing he had ever needed to finish.

While he was crossing the bridge, two men let themselves

into the Greenwich flat with a key that had been cut for the purpose. They confirmed the layout, identified the exit routes, and took their positions in the armchairs by the gas fire to wait.

He returned to the Greenwich flat at 12:34. He had taken the long way.

He let himself in with the key the bookseller's widow had given him years ago. The widow had been in Devon since the second of January, as she had been every first week of January for three years.

The hall smelled of cigarettes. He had never smoked. He had never permitted smoking in any flat he kept. He registered the smell and understood it in the same second. His face did not change. His hands did not move. He had been trained out of involuntary recognition in 1968, and the training had held.

In the second after that, he opened the door to the front room.

The two men were in the armchairs by the gas fire. Their coats were folded across the arms. Their hands were not.

He understood, in the half-second between the seeing and the next thing, that the photographs at Century House were going to do their work. That the woman he'd been waiting for since 22:00 was not going to arrive. That the absence of her arrival meant exactly one thing—the meaning he had been preparing for since the morning of the second when he picked up the envelope from his Chiswick floor.

The half-second was the half-second. It had always been the half-second. Since October 1973, in a gallery, when a man and a woman looked at each other across a room full of photographs of a divided city.

He smiled. The second man saw it and did not understand

what he was seeing. He had been trained in many things; he had not been trained to read a smile delivered at gunpoint.

The photographs were on the Chief's desk. That part had worked.

The first man's shot was clean. The second man did not fire. The first man fired a second time, in a different direction. The second man had not been told why.

Calder had been thinking about the tie. For the half-second his consciousness remained, that was what remained in it. The way she had straightened it. The way her hands had shaken.

A body was on the floor of the front room of the small flat above the bookseller's shop in Greenwich at 12:34:08 on the afternoon of the fourth of January 1990.

The two men who had killed him were efficient. They wrapped the body in plastic sheeting they had brought. They carried him down the back stairs and out into the small alley behind the bookseller's shop and loaded him into the back of a black panel van that had been parked there since 11:30.

The van pulled away at 12:51.

It drove east toward the Royal Docks.

Elena's body had been removed from 47 Webber Street at 23:47 on the night of the third by two different men in a different van. They wrapped the body in plastic sheeting and cleared the table into a canvas bag without examining what it contained. The handover at the docks happened at 02:00 on the morning of the fourth.

Calder's body joined Elena's in the same container at the Royal Albert Dock at 14:20 that afternoon. The container had been logged into the manifest of a freighter departing that evening for Norfolk, Virginia, described as agricultural processing equipment bound for a co-operative buyer in the American Midwest.

The photographs, Ruskin would later learn from a colleague with a clearance higher than his own, had produced a forty-eight-hour institutional crisis at Century House before someone with the right clearance had the right conversation with the right desk and the crisis became a committee. The committee was still sitting when the spring came. In June it produced a classified finding distributed to seven recipients at a level that prevented any of them from discussing it with the others. The committee dissolved. Ruskin never learned what the finding said.

The freighter was the *Atlantic Compass*. It departed at 17:42 on the fourth of January 1990. Eleven days later it unloaded at Norfolk. The body identified as Calder's weighed eleven stone. Calder's own weight, per the service personnel record Andrew Ruskin would consult the following March, was thirteen. A refrigerated rail car carried the container west to Iowa.

The bodies arrived at the Holman farm on the night of the twentieth of January, in the back of a refrigerated truck that pulled up to the second hog barn at 02:14. The driver had been not thinking about what the truck contained for eighteen years.

He helped the two men carry the bodies down the concrete steps into the rendering room beneath the barn. A room built in 1956. A room that did not appear in any inventory. A room that had been rendering bodies on an irregular schedule for thirty-four years, operated by men rotated through the same channels the bodies arrived through.

The room had two fluorescent tubes and a drain set into the concrete. The room smelled of bleach and something underneath the bleach that the bleach had been chosen specifically to mask but did not. The two men wore rubber aprons over coveralls. Their hands did not shake.

Thirty-four years was longer than it had taken Kessler to grow a *rothschildianum*. Thirty-four years was the length of a patient operation. The network did not grow only orchids. It grew rooms. It grew farms. It grew rendering schedules and drivers who had learned, in 1972, not to think. The growing was the same growing. Slow. Deliberate. Across decades. The network waited for the bloom, and when the bloom arrived—the flower, or the body, or the fizzle in a water-treatment facility outside Trier—the network absorbed it, and the waiting began again.

The room had been used approximately forty times. The number was not exact because nobody had ever counted. The not-counting was the room's other purpose.

The processing took six hours.

The output was a fine bone-and-tissue meal packaged in ordinary feed bags and added, in measured proportions, to the standard hog feed the Holman farm produced for its own animals and for sale to two neighboring farms.

The feed was eaten by the hogs.

The hogs were processed at a slaughterhouse in Council Bluffs.

The slaughterhouse's product entered the American food supply through ordinary commercial channels—institutional kitchens, supermarket chains, school district contracts in three Midwestern states.

There was no record of any of this.

Earl Holman, sleeping in the farmhouse, did not wake when the truck pulled up. He did not wake at 04:00 when the rendering machinery began. He did not wake at 08:14 when the truck pulled away empty. He woke at 06:30, made coffee, listened to the agricultural report on the AM radio, and went out to feed the hogs, and the hogs were the hogs, and the morning was the morning.

The Holman farm continued. Twenty-four hundred acres of flat Iowa nothing, and a horizon that looked like someone had drawn it with a ruler.

The machinery continued.

Nobody thought about the farm.

That was the point.

In Kensington, the drawer beside the stove was still open.

In Ealing, a woman wore a silver key on her bracelet. She had worn it for twelve years. She would wear it for the rest of her life without ever learning what it opened.

...

On the west coast of Scotland, a journalist with three months to live wrote a sentence in pencil that nobody would ever read.

Somewhere in Europe, a man with a gold ring on his right little finger ordered filet mignon for breakfast.

In a small port on the Atlantic coast, a man whose body had supposedly been processed on a farm in Iowa opened the FEUERWERK file, and began the list.

A NOTE ON SOURCES

This is a work of fiction set inside a real history. The central story is entirely invented. The apparatus described in the book—the four-service protocol, the cached warheads, the forty years of institutional silence—does not exist. But the history it is built on does, and I used real names where the use mattered.

LILLEHAMMER

The events in Chapter 1—a Mossad team killing the wrong man on the night of 21 July 1973 in a small Norwegian town—happened. The man they killed was Ahmed Bouchiki, a Moroccan waiter. His pregnant wife survived. The names in this novel—Rachid Hamidi, Marit—are inventions; the wrong-man killing is not. Six members of the Mossad team were arrested by Norwegian police within days. The Israeli government has never apologized for the killing.

FRANK OLSON

Frank Olson was a biochemist at Fort Detrick, dosed without his knowledge with LSD by the CIA's MKULTRA program in November 1953. Nine days later, he went through a window at the Statler Hotel in New York and fell to his death. The CIA called it a suicide. His son Eric spent decades arguing otherwise.

ANNA AKHMATOVA

The line on Elena's ribcage—*I taught myself to live simply and wisely*—is the opening of a poem by Anna Akhmatova, written in 1912 and published in her collection *Чётки* (*Rosary*), 1914. The Russian reads *Я научилась просто, мудро жить.*

The tattoo is an invention. The line is not.

OPERATIONS

The operations referenced in the book—Wrath of God, Gladio, Zersetzung, COINTELPRO—are historical and described in the Field Manual. Their use as the real ground beneath a fictional apparatus is my construction.

SOURCES

Aaron Klein, *Striking Back* (2005). Ronen Bergman, *Rise and Kill First* (2018). Anna Funder, *Stasiland* (2003). Timothy Garton Ash, *The File* (1997). Ben Macintyre, *The Spy and the Traitor* (2018). Christopher Andrew, *The Sword and the Shield* (1999). Thomas Rid, *Active Measures* (2020). Daniele Ganser, *NATO's Secret Armies* (2005). Simon Reeve, *One Day in September* (2000). Seth Rosenfeld, *Subversives* (2012). Betty Medsger, *The Burglary* (2014). H. P. Albarelli Jr., *A Terrible Mistake* (2009). Senate Church Committee Final Report, Book III (1976).

This book was not written from classified material. All operational details were assembled from open sources, declassified archives, and the scholarship that has accumulated in the decades since the Cold War officially ended. The story is invented; the world it is set in is not.

ABOUT THE AUTHOR

STEN SVEHN was born in Oslo and has lived and worked across Northern Europe, the United Kingdom, and the United States. He spent two decades in roles that required him to understand how institutions communicate, how information moves, and what makes it into the official record.

His nonfiction book, *Survival Over Service*, examined the documented history of institutional self-preservation across the major intelligence agencies.

The Line Between Lies, The List, The New Fire, and *Auspex* are his first novels.

www.ingramcontent.com/pod-product-compliance
Lightning Source LLC
LaVergne TN
LVHW091248110826
845146LV00002BA/454

* 9 7 9 8 9 9 5 1 6 6 7 7 1 *